Promises to Keep

By Rachel Moore

Days to Remember
Summer of Love
Promises to Keep

Promises to Keep

RACHEL MOORE

First published in Great Britain in 2011 by
Allison & Busby Limited
13 Charlotte Mews
London W1T 4EJ
www.allisonandbusby.com

A CIP catalogue record for this book is available from
the British Library.

10 9 8 7 6 5 4 3 2 1

13-ISBN 978-0-7490-0988-5

Typeset in 11/16 pt Sabon by
Allison & Busby Ltd.

Paper used in this publication is from sustainably managed sources.
All of the wood used is procured from legal sources and is fully traceable.
The producing mill uses schemes such as ISO 14001
to monitor environmental impact.

Printed and bound in the UK by
CPI Mackays, Chatham ME5 8TD

Promises to Keep

CHAPTER ONE

First nights were always fraught with nerves for the performers, however small the theatre – and Columbine village hall could hardly be called anything so grand. The portents didn't look promising, in any case. Kerry Penfold put the finishing touches to her stage make-up, sure that the show by Mrs Holliday's dancing troupe to welcome the arrival of yet more GIs in Falmouth and surrounding areas was going to be a disaster, since the dress rehearsal had already ended in panic, with one of the girls slipping and breaking her ankle. The performance had to be rearranged at the last minute – to say nothing of the poor girl wailing like a banshee, certain that the accident would ruin her chance to bag a handsome Yank for herself. The whole area was bursting with these good-looking blokes now, with vehicles rumbling back and forth, day and night, in preparation for something big. Everyone knew it. The only thing they didn't know was what, and when . . .

'Just listen to her,' Kerry's friend Claire said as the other girl had been whisked off in the ambulance to have her leg set in plaster. 'You'd think this was a West End production, instead of a potty little village show out in the sticks. Who'd give porky Pam a second glance, anyway? You're the one most likely to get off with one of them, Kerry.'

By now Kerry was trying to tame her wayward brown hair into submission and glaring at herself in the cracked mirror of the crowded back room that passed for a dressing room. 'Well, for the tenth time, Claire, I'm not interested, so stop going on about it.'

'Do you really think your Tom's never given a second glance to another girl when he gets the chance? I bet there's not many young chaps going abroad for the first time, even in the middle of a war, who don't take advantage of what's on offer, and he's been away for months now. You should live a bit, kid, instead of writing those endless lovey-dovey letters to him.'

Kerry's patience snapped. 'And you should give it a rest! Tom and I have got an understanding, and I promised to write to him every day. Besides, I'm not interested in Yanks. They're not all straight out of Hollywood, as you seem to think. Some of them probably live in backwaters just like this one, or worse.'

Claire snorted. 'And some of them may not. Well, I'm glad I didn't get myself half tied to some boy who was going off to war, but if that's what you want to do it gives the rest of us more of a chance with the GI Joes.'

She preened herself, putting on another dollop of lipstick and swirling around in her wide-skirted dress with the frilly petticoats, then crossing her eyes at her image and making Kerry laugh. She couldn't stay mad with her for long, even though they had very different ideas from one another. Maybe that was how they had remained friends since schooldays, despite the many arguments they had, which never lasted long, thank goodness.

'Oh, come on, you look lovely, so stop titivating, or Mrs Holliday will have a blue fit if we're not all ready for the opening number,' Kerry added as she heard the small group of hired musicians tuning up.

Ancient relics, most of them, she thought with a silent chuckle, since all the able young men in the area had either enlisted voluntarily or been called up long ago. But the old boys were still capable of playing a cracking good tune, she added to herself loyally. The Yanks wouldn't get any jitterbug music from them, and would probably find it all far too tame, she thought, with sudden nerves!

She smoothed down her own matching dress with the neckline that was far lower than she would normally wear, and felt her heart give a jump. Seeing herself in the cracked mirror, it was like looking at somebody else tonight. That was what performing did for you, even in such a small way. It took you out of yourself for a few hours, and gave a touch of glamour to everyday life. And, Lord knew, everyday life had changed so much over the last few years that it did people good to enjoy themselves without worrying over when the telegram boy would come knocking at the door with the news that everyone dreaded.

Down here in the far west of Cornwall, they might not get the amount of air raids and bombing that the poor devils did in London and other big cities, but they'd had their share, and their boys had gone off to fight, just the same. They already knew the effect of the dreaded arrival of the telegram boy, even here in sleepy Columbine, and no one could predict who might or might not be coming home at the end of it all.

Kerry shivered, willing away the gloomy thoughts. After nearly five years of war, everyone said it had to end soon, and here in Cornwall at the start of a soft and mellow summer, it was good for morale to forget the dangers and tragedies, even for a little while. And there was a show to go on.

It was also probably true what Claire said. She did spend far too much time writing long letters to Tom, and she never got back the screeds she wrote. She could hardly expect it, since he was fighting the Jerries somewhere in France. He couldn't sit down every night the way she did, and pour out his heart to her, much as she would have liked him to do. Even when he did, half the letters he wrote were censored, the same as hers were, she guessed, with some of the words crossed through with a thick black pencil or even cut out.

Just as if they were all spies, she'd thought indignantly when she'd first seen it – or that the letters would be intercepted and strategic positions given to the Germans. It had made the letters she wrote – and especially those she got back from Tom – more cautious than necessary, since who would want some unknown official reading the things that sweethearts said to one another? They were for their eyes only, not for some cynical third party. Such an unwelcome intrusion into private feelings would add to the insular feelings of any girl who lived in a small Cornish village where nothing very much went on.

But tonight, she was going to be somebody other than herself. She was one of Mrs Holliday's dancing troupe, and she wore one of the amazing costumes that Mrs Holliday somehow always managed to fashion out of scraps for her 'poppets', as she called them, which made them all feel different and special.

'Don't go letting one night onstage give you any ideas about getting above yourself, my girl,' her aunt Lil had commented with mock severity as Kerry twisted and twirled to show off her costumes beforehand.

'I'm not likely to do that,' Kerry had retorted airily. 'This will be my last time with the troupe, so if Hollywood hasn't discovered me by now, I doubt that it ever will!'

Her aunt had laughed, thankful for the girl's common sense. She had toyed with the idea of becoming a land girl in due course, but Lil had persuaded her against it, having known what farm life was like from her one brief stint with it years ago. Lil Penfold had never fancied having to do all those messy jobs with cows and the like. And since her middle-aged bones were becoming too stiff with the arthritis now to sit still for a couple of hours in a draughty village hall, not even to see her only niece performing, she was content to have a private showing in their own small cottage, tapping out her steps on the lino floor in the kitchen.

Lil had the dubious delight of having her cousin from Bristol coming to live with them in a week or so, finally taking fright from all the air raids when a whole street near her had been demolished by the bombing, so she'd hardly have been lonely while Kerry was off tending to the cows or pulling turnips, but she was glad her niece had decided to stay.

Kerry's big regret that evening was that Mrs Holliday hadn't managed to find any red tap shoes like the ones you saw at the pictures, since they were so hard to obtain nowadays. But at least they all wore matching silver ones, and she could clatter her way across the stage with the best of them. She had a solo spot too, which she was privately calling her swansong.

It had caused a bit of friction between her and Claire at first, and Claire was never going to let her forget that Kerry had got the plum part, as she called it. You'd think that now both of them were nearing eighteen, she could put such small pettiness behind her, Kerry thought, but that was Claire.

Anyway, there was no time now to think about anything but the show. The village hall would be packed to capacity that evening, with the newly arrived GIs from the neighbouring base and as many locals as could fit into the remaining seats. Most of the locals were more agog to see the latest arrivals of these fast-talking, gum-chewing strangers in the smartly cut uniforms and with their lovely manners – according to some of the girls who'd already had the pleasure – rather than the show.

At the end of it, when all the chairs were pushed back to one side, there was to be general dancing, and that was something else to make any red-blooded girl's heart flutter, including Kerry's. Despite the way so many GIs had infiltrated into their lives now, she had never danced with a Yank before, and that was a first in anybody's diary!

Until recent months most of them had been based in different parts of the country, but it was common knowledge now that something big was in the offing, and that the big natural harbour at Falmouth was part of whatever hush-hush planning was going on, just as it had been when the troops were evacuated from Dunkirk, when ships, large and small, had taken the hazardous shipping route to France to bring their boys home. This was different, though.

There had been endless activity for weeks, especially around the US advanced amphibious training bases, now well established in the area, and far from getting a minority of GIs based here to arouse curiosity, they had certainly got their share of them now, Claire had commented gleefully. And this show was to welcome the latest intake. It was also Kerry and Claire's last performance, since Mrs Holliday had an age limit for her poppets, and they had reached it.

And all right, Kerry acknowledged the small thrill inside her whenever she thought about the Yanks, even though her heart belonged to Tom Trevellyan and always would. It didn't mean she had to turn into a nun, did it?

'They're here, Kerry!' Claire's voice almost cracked with excitement, interrupting her thoughts. 'Take a look through the curtain.'

With some of the other girls, they crept to the middle of the small stage and parted the curtain a fraction to peep through. Mrs Holliday had informed her poppets proudly that she believed this was the origin of the expression 'break a leg', since the curtains were known as 'legs', Kerry thought, with a burst of apprehension as she saw their audience for the first time. As always, the Americans all looked large and smart and sophisticated. What on earth would they see in a little village production like this one? It was madness to think they'd be impressed. Bored, more likely.

'At least we'll get first chance for a dance afterwards,' Claire was rattling on. 'They'll know we're not clodhoppers after they've seen us onstage.'

'No, but they might be,' Kerry said, forcing her nerves to settle.

What was it Aunt Lil always said? Once you strip away the fancy outer trappings, everybody's the same under the skin, so just imagine them that way. Modestly, of course . . .

At that moment Kerry's eyes met those of a russet-haired, dark-eyed young man in the second row, with a look on his face that could almost be interpreted as nervousness. How weird, when she had assumed they would all be full of brash self-confidence like the stars of the Hollywood movies.

But why shouldn't they be nervous? They were all as young as Tom, and they were thousands of miles away from home too, not knowing what the future held for any of them. They were already overseas, and going heaven knew where in the next days or weeks. As such thoughts whirled through her head, the soldier smiled at her, and she dropped the edge of the curtain as if it was red-hot.

'Well, that one's definitely yours,' Claire whispered, not missing a thing as usual. Several of the other girls were clamouring behind them now, trying to get a good look before Mrs Holliday hissed at them to come away and line up in the wings for their opening number and stop showing themselves up.

And after all, they might all be amateurs, but they had

always presented themselves as professionally as possible in their shows. Lately, of course, it was always to raise money for their troops overseas, and since there was no one amongst them who didn't have a brother or a father or an uncle, sweetheart or husband serving for their country, it always gave them an added incentive to do nothing but their best.

For some reason the thought triggered the memory of the Promise they had chanted when Kerry and Tom were in their junior school branch of the Brownies and Cub Scouts respectively. It ran through her head now . . . even though the words were muddled after all this time, but the sentiments still counted.

I promise to do my best . . . to serve God and the king and my country . . . to help other people . . .

'Right, my poppets, let's put on a good show for our visitors tonight!'

As the music started up, the strident voice of Mrs Holliday put all other thoughts out of their minds, and as the opening chorus began, the curtains were drawn back to reveal the troupe of a dozen well-rehearsed girls tapping their way across the stage to much applause.

After that, there was no time to think of anything else but changing costumes and getting in the right mood for whatever piece they were performing. Most of it involved energetic tap dancing, but Kerry's solo was a more balletic piece, with the rest of the girls swaying in the background, and as she flitted across the stage she was very aware that all eyes were on her, especially one pair of dark eyes in the second row.

'Did you see how loudly he clapped you?' Claire

whispered when she took her solo bow at the end of the show. 'Tom's definitely got a rival there.'

'Don't be so daft, Claire, and stop trying to make something out of nothing,' Kerry said, flushed with relief at how well it had all gone.

But, of course, she had seen it, and registered it, and when the girls had changed back into their normal clothes, still in a flurry of excitement at Mrs Holliday's praise over the performance, the many helping hands pushed all the chairs in the hall around the sides of the room, and the general dancing began.

The hall was crowded, and Claire had gone off to find her parents and to get their approval, while Kerry took a breather and was talking to one of her aunt's friends in the audience, when she suddenly became aware of a shadow in front of her, and that her companion's chatter had died away.

It was one of those moments that was almost surreal, when you didn't need to know who was there, or what was about to happen. It didn't only happen to Cornish girls who believed in omens or signs, and it took no account of emotions or loyalty. It was fate taking over whatever else you might have planned for yourself, and there was nothing you could do to stop it, whether you wanted to or not. It was like an express train rushing towards you . . .

'Pardon me for interrupting, ma'am, and I wonder if I might introduce myself? Lieutenant Marvin Mcleod of the United States military. May I have the pleasure of the next dance with you? It would be a real honour,' came the oh-so-polite words from the soldier who Kerry knew instinctively was going to be the owner of that voice, as rich as honey.

Beside her, she heard the older lady giggle slightly at such charming formality. She would approve, though, Kerry thought, feeling a slight sense of panic as she finally looked up into the face she had known to expect. He held out his hand and gave her that smile again and she was lost. She squashed such ridiculous feelings. He was only asking her for a dance, for goodness' sake.

'I'd be happy to,' she murmured, remembering that they were supposed to be welcoming their new visitors. The next moment she had put her hand in his as he led her into the middle of the room where others were already moving to the serene music of the waltz.

Why couldn't it have been a hokey-cokey or a progressive barn dance? Anything that didn't involve them dancing so close to one another, with one hand holding hers, and the other one in the small of her back where she could feel its warm pressure as he guided her past other couples.

'I'm Kerry Penfold,' she said primly, 'and it's good to welcome our American cousins to our shores, even in such uncertain times.'

Good grief, where did all that come from? She cringed inwardly, knowing she had never said anything so pompous in her life . . .

'It's good to be here, even in such uncertain times,' Marvin Mcleod said, just as primly, and then he laughed. 'So now we've got the preliminaries over, maybe we can just relax and enjoy the dance. What do you say, Kerry?'

She found herself laughing back. 'I think that's a very good idea.'

'I guess I shouldn't monopolise you for the rest of the

evening, much as I'd like to,' he went on, 'but while I've got the chance, tell me a bit about yourself. Do you live around here? In Falmouth, maybe?'

He pronounced it 'Fal Mouth', which she decided to find charming . . . and she wished she could have said that she did and that she had some glamorous job, but she wasn't about to start inventing things for somebody she would probably never see again after tonight . . .

'I live here in Columbine, and I work in a village shop that sells a bit of everything – when we can get it, that is. There's a war on, you know!'

She bit her lip, knowing what a stupid remark that was. Didn't he know there was a war on? Why would he be here otherwise, miles from home?

But his eyes shone, seeming to find everything she said amusing. Was he laughing *at* her or *with* her, she wondered?

'I love your accent. It's so soft and gentle.'

Kerry blinked. 'I don't have an accent. Not like yours!'

They both laughed now. His hand pressed even tighter in the small of her back as he steered her out of the way of other dancers. He was no expert, but he knew his way around a dance floor, Kerry registered.

'Let's say we both have one, and that's what makes us interesting to one another – or am I being presumptuous? You certainly interest me, Kerry Penfold, and when you were on that stage I couldn't take my eyes off you, but you're even more beautiful in the flesh.'

She felt a spark of alarm. He flattered her, and he still spoke in that oh-so-smooth way that could turn any girl's head – if she let it. This wasn't the way Tom Trevellyan had ever spoken to her, but Tom had known her all her life, and there was no need for flowery talk like this.

'Well, thank you. My boyfriend would be glad to know I'm not letting myself become dowdy because of all the restrictions in this old war,' she said, as clumsily as if she was a child.

Out of the corner of her eye she could see Claire talking enthusiastically to the soldier in whose arms she was firmly held. Kerry was every bit as articulate as Claire, but tonight she felt almost tongue-tied.

'I'd say you could never be dowdy in a million years, and your boyfriend's a lucky guy,' she heard Marvin Mcleod say, and then the music ended, and he escorted her back to the seat with his hand lightly beneath her elbow, and saying he hoped he might have another dance before the evening ended.

He was lost in the crowd before she could think of a reply, and then Claire was sitting down beside her, full of excitement over her dance with someone called Glenn, and how he had invited her to the night they were permitted to ask outsiders to the base to see a movie.

'It didn't take you long, did it?' Kerry said, still trying to get her tumbling thoughts together.

'Nor you! I told you that one fancied you, didn't I?'

'Yes, you did, but I don't fancy him, so don't get any ideas about it,' Kerry said almost crossly.

'Oh, don't be so stuffy, Kerry. It was only a dance, wasn't it? Glenn thinks our old-fashioned dances are cute. I bet yours asks you again. Tom wouldn't object, and besides, what he doesn't know won't hurt him, and I'm sure you don't tell him everything in your nightly letter.'

'Yes I do. It's our special link and it keeps him in touch with home.'

'You're nuts,' Claire said bluntly. 'He's seeing something of the big wide world, and you're reminding him of what's not going on in boring old Columbine!'

'You're the nutty one. He might be seeing something of the "big wide world", as you call it, but it's at the expense of losing his liberty. He didn't ask to be caught up in a war, any more than these GIs did.'

Claire's face altered at her friend's words. 'You're right, as usual, and we shouldn't be bickering like this. My fault, of course,' she added generously. 'Let's go and get some lemonade and request a ladies' excuse-me, and then see who else we can find.'

There was no stopping her, Kerry thought with a wry grin, but it was pointless for them to be arguing over things that couldn't be changed, and to spoil what had been a successful evening so far. And ten minutes later, after a brief interval for refreshments, a ladies' excuse-me dance was announced.

Claire sped off at once to find a suitable partner, and when Kerry subconsciously looked around for Marvin Mcleod, it was to find him already claimed by one of the other girls in the dancing troupe. Her flutter of annoyance was completely irrational, but she couldn't deny it. And when the music stopped, and ladies were invited to break in and choose their partners, it was as if her feet moved of their own accord until she was tapping the other girl on the shoulder.

'Excuse me, June. My partner, I think,' she said steadily.

'Thank the Lord,' Marvin said as she slid into his arms

again. 'Your friend never stops talking, and I couldn't follow half the things she said.'

'Really?' Kerry felt a wild urge to giggle. 'I thought we were the slow talkers, not you!'

He didn't rap out the words like the movie stars did, though. He spoke in a slow, modulated way that you wouldn't normally associate with big cities – as far as she knew.

'Where do you come from, Marvin?' she asked, in the small awkward pause that followed. 'No, let me guess.' She rattled out the few American cities she had heard of. 'New York? Or Boston, where the famous Tea Party happened? Or New England, where the Pilgrim Fathers landed?'

He laughed. 'I see you know your history.'

She spoke airily. 'We had to learn those things, if only to remind us that we were first to cross the Atlantic. Oh, flip, that sounds very patronising, doesn't it?' she added, hot with embarrassment.

'Not at all. Americans are a mixture of many nationalities. My folks came from Scotland a couple of generations ago, hence the name Mcleod. I was hoping to be posted somewhere near enough so I could go and look up some family history, but it wasn't to be.'

'And instead you were landed down here in the sticks,' Kerry said.

The music ended, and before she could quiz him further, someone else had claimed him, and she had to wait for the next break before she grabbed him again. It was merely to continue the unfinished conversation, she told herself.

'So where do you come from?' she prompted.

'It's a little town in Montana in the Midwest. My folks

are farmers, and we grow wheat and other crops. You might think this quaint little place is out in the sticks, but you ain't seen nothin' – pardon my grammar – until you've seen a one-horse town called Jefferson with nearly two hundred miles between it and the nearest city!'

Kerry found that hard to believe, but she assumed it must be true. Maybe they didn't do much jitterbugging in Jefferson either, she thought inanely. Then the music ended again, and the last waltz was announced. Before she knew it, panic set in. The last waltz was something special, and she didn't want to float around the room to the strains of the emotive music in Marvin Mcleod's arms.

Twisting free of him, she almost gasped that she had to leave to get home to her aunt and help her to bed, even though it was a downright lie, and the last thing her stalwart Aunt Lil would want was for a sprightly young whippersnapper to be helping her into bed. But Marvin Mcleod didn't know that. All he saw was concern for an imaginary elderly relative, and the respect in his eyes almost made her blurt out the truth. Almost.

'Can I see you again sometime?' he said, still holding her arm.

'I don't know. I may be starting a new job soon, so probably not.'

Even as she said it, she didn't know why she'd invented such a thing. She didn't normally lie, but there had been no need to tell him anything at all. Why would he care? They were ships that passed in the night, and nothing more.

But she couldn't stop him waiting for her after she had fetched her coat and bag, to a chorus of 'mind the blackout' as he opened the door for her. She fumbled for her bicycle from the rack outside the hall and thrust her tap shoes and bag into the basket, and he was still there.

'I'd like to see you home, if it's not too much of an imposition,' he said.

'Honestly, it's not that far, and I know the way blindfold. I'm sure you've got transport waiting to take you back to the base, so I'll say goodnight, Marvin – and it was nice meeting you,' she said pointedly.

'Goodnight, Kerry, and I hope we'll meet again.'

She got on her bike and pedalled away with his voice echoing behind her, wondering why she felt such a darned fool, and why she couldn't just behave naturally. But she knew why. It was the first time any young man, apart from Tom, had shown the slightest interest in her, and she didn't need to be psychic to know that he had definitely been interested. And it scared her to know that she had been attracted to him too. Far more than an almost-engaged girl ought to be.

It might just have been because he was different, of course. The way he looked, and spoke, and behaved. It was all so different from the boys she had known since childhood. It was like getting a glimpse into another world from the one she had always known, and that was pretty damn stupid as well. From what he said, his world was as insular as hers. A little one-horse town in the wilds of Montana, wherever that was. And she was letting it all get out of perspective, and she honestly doubted that she would ever see him again.

'Did you have a good time, dear, and how did the show go?' Aunt Lil said, the minute she got indoors, the way she always did from her fireside chair. 'Make us both a cup of

23

cocoa before bedtime, there's a love, and then you can tell me all about it.'

The ritual was always the same. Lil would wallow in Kerry's description of the evening, sure that her girl had been the best performer, and Kerry would give her choice anecdotes of who was there and what they wore and what was said. And then they would each go to their beds, and Kerry would write the highlights in her diary, and finish the evening by writing her lengthy letter to Tom, the way she did every night, bringing him near with titbits of home.

Except that tonight, instead of being exhilarated that the show had gone well, she felt extraordinarily tired and the words that she wanted to say to him wouldn't come. It would be best left until tomorrow morning before church, when her brain wasn't so muddled. And when she didn't have other words intruding inside her head, telling her that she looked beautiful in a voice that oozed with something she couldn't quite explain, but which made her heart leap with something between anxiety and pleasure every time she remembered it.

CHAPTER TWO

'I never thought I'd say it but I'll be glad when your Aunt Maud arrives now,' Lil said to Kerry a few days later, when the newspapers were giving graphic details of the bombing in various towns in England, and the news on the wireless was as cagey over details as the starchy announcer knew how.

'Why wouldn't you say it?' Kerry asked. 'Don't you get on with her?'

Lil snorted. 'Well, she was always a bossyboots, and you know what they say about two women sharing the same kitchen. She got a bit above herself when she married that Jim of hers too, just because he ran his own little shoe-repairing business. Fat lot of good his so-called empire did him when some baker's van lost its brakes on a hill and ran him down.'

'Crumbs, Aunt Lil, that must have been horrible for them both.'

'I daresay, but she was always mutton dressed as lamb, and she never found it hard to find other company, and that's all I'm saying about that, so you can get that nosy look off your face.'

Kerry grinned. 'Quite a girl in her youth, then, was she?'

'Shouldn't you be getting ready to go to work? The shop won't open by itself, and Mrs Polby won't thank you for being late.'

Kerry had to be content with that. She had never met Aunt Lil's only cousin, whom she only knew as Aunt Maud, but the snippets she had heard about her were always intriguing. They were a pretty sparse family, she sometimes thought. Her mother had died from polio when she was little more than a baby, and she had been whisked away to her Aunt Lil's cottage for fear that she could catch it, and had lived there ever since her father died from a farm machinery accident a short while later. Aunt Lil was Kerry's dad's older sister, and had brought her up in a stoic and dutiful way, saying that it had still been something of a miracle that the child hadn't succumbed to the polio as well. Somehow she had survived, which Lil always said was partly due to luck, and mostly due to the girl's inborn stubborn nature. Sometimes, Kerry couldn't help wondering guiltily how different life would have been if she'd had the normal two parents and brothers and sisters of her own, the way Claire did.

But there was no point in wishing for something that could never be changed. If you couldn't have what you wanted, the only way to survive was to switch your wishes to something else. It was something she strongly believed in, especially when Tom had declared his intention of enlisting as soon as he was old enough, which had almost broken her heart. It was a surprise that he had chosen the army too, when he was a ferryman through and through, like his dad.

He might be two years older than her, but he was still her boy, and at the time she had bitterly resented his boy's eagerness to go away and fight, just like Claire's older brother. But now she was proud of him, and she gave him all the news from home as cheerfully as she could, never letting him guess how much she was counting the days until it was all over and they could be together again.

She had forgotten such inhibitions when she wrote to him on that Sunday morning after the show, pouring out all her feelings and uncaring whether it was censored. Let the military snoopers snigger if they must. Tom was her sweetheart, and she wanted him to know how much she was missing him.

She cycled to the shop that morning, still wondering what Aunt Maud was going to be like, and if there was going to be real friction between her and Aunt Lil, imagining two middle-aged women squabbling over who was cooking the sprouts! Mrs Polby was already in the shop, which sold everything from scrubbing brushes and blue bags to shirt collars and knitting needles and everything in between. And as the acknowledged fount of all village gossip, Mrs Polby had plenty to say and to find out as usual.

'Enjoyed seeing you in the show on Sat'day night, Kerry

love. You looked very pretty, and I reckon that young GI thought so too. Me and Polby both said he had his eye on you from the start. Young Tom would have summat to say if he'd been there to see it,' she added with a chuckle, hardly pausing for breath. 'Did you hear there'd been another scuffle in Falmouth between some local lads and the Yanks a couple of nights later?'

Kerry sighed. Yes, she'd heard it from Claire, and she hadn't thought much about it. But she might have known Mrs Polby would have all the details.

'What happened?' she asked, wishing she didn't feel compelled to know.

'The usual bit of resentment over the Yanks and the girls, but you can't blame any of them for wanting a bit of fun, can you?' she said. 'The girls need cheering up, and I daresay those GI boys are getting nervous, wondering where they'll be sent to next. Polby says there's more of 'em arriving by the minute. We'll soon be turning into another Yankee state if we're not careful.'

'What does he think it's all about, then?' Kerry asked, sure that he'd have an opinion, if not inside knowledge!

'A big onslaught on the Jerries, of course, so they need more troops than they can drop by parachute onto the French coast, which is why there's so many ships in the harbour now, as well as our own airbases being so busy all the time. Besides,' she added sagely, 'what's the point of having allies, if they're not here to do their bit? That's what Polby says, anyway.'

It must be right if Polby says it, Kerry thought dryly. But he was more often right than wrong, and as he spent so much time at the riverside pubs and hobnobbing with the Yanks, to say nothing of his Home Guard duties, he got to hear plenty. It was hard to say who was the biggest gossip, him or his wife. But at least it produced results, and everything was so hush-hush and full of wild speculation these days, it was good to know something. Much of it might be guesswork, but it was an open secret that an invasion was on the cards soon.

'I hear that young Pam Wyatt was going to work as a land girl before she broke her leg,' Mrs Polby suddenly said, with more acquired knowledge. 'You had a fancy for it too, didn't you, dearie?'

'I did once. I wanted to do something useful for the war effort as well, Mrs Polby, and you don't really need me here, do you?'

She couldn't argue with that. Everything was in such short supply, and the village shop could hardly support one person, let alone two. Mrs Polby could manage perfectly well on her own, and she always had the customers to gossip with. But she didn't see it that way.

'People always need goods to buy, and your Aunt Lil needs you more than those old cows on Gillagy's Farm,' the woman went on, 'and it would be a shame to go spoiling that pretty complexion by tramping in muck in all weathers.'

Kerry laughed. 'Well, I reckon Pam will have to do what Farmer Gillagy tells her, if she ever gets there. He's got two land girls already, and she struck lucky in being allocated somewhere close to home.'

'How is your auntie? I haven't seen her for a few days. Looking forward to having Maud Jenkins moving in?' she said with a sniff.

Was there anything the Polbys didn't know!

'She's well enough. What do you know about Aunt Maud, then?'

'Only what I've heard from your auntie at Friendship Club, dearie, though I vaguely remember her from years back. I don't think it'll be a marriage made in heaven, if you get my meaning. I daresay she's more than glad you'll still be around to act as peacemaker.'

As one of Mrs Polby's cronies came into the shop, the conversation came to an end, but curious as she was at Mrs Polby's somewhat cryptic remark, Kerry didn't like the thought of acting as any kind of peacemaker. She wondered again at the wisdom of Aunt Maud coming down to Cornwall, but she couldn't blame her, even though there wasn't much heard about any Bristol bombings lately. Their terrible blitz was in 1941, when so much of the city had been destroyed. But Kerry was intrigued to meet her. She was younger than Aunt Lil, and she sounded as if she had had quite an eventful life after her Jim had had his fatal accident – to put it kindly!

'Well, I don't envy you, living with two old dears,' Claire remarked that evening after work, sitting on one of the benches alongside the meandering river that led down to the sea at Falmouth. 'How old is this Maud, anyway?'

'I'm not sure. Mid fifties, I would imagine.'

'Like I said, two stuffy old dears,' Claire said, dismissing them easily. 'They'll be getting you to join the knitting circle at their perishing Friendship Club before you know it.'

'Not likely! Besides, Aunt Lil's not a stuffy old dear. She can't help her joints giving her trouble.'

'She's still getting on a bit. What will you do when she pops her clogs?'

Kerry leapt up from the bench, her nerves unexpectedly going haywire.

'I don't want to think about that! Why must you always be so negative about everything?'

'I'm not! It happens, that's all. People get born, they live their lives and then they die. You can't change that, and for pity's sake, sit down again. You look like an avenging angel, standing there with your arms crossed.'

They were so busy arguing they hadn't noticed the group ambling towards them along the towpath, but at the sound of their low chuckles, they noticed them now.

'Now, what are you two lovely gals doing here all alone? You look as if you could do with a bit of company,' one of them said with a lazy twang in his voice. 'Is there a local pub around here where we could buy you a drink?'

Kerry and Claire both started at the sight of the three American soldiers grinning at them now. One of them was oh-so familiar, making Kerry feel about ten years old as she stuttered out what had to be said.

'We don't go into pubs,' she croaked.

'Say, that's a shame, but it's no matter. How about if me and my buddies just join you and admire the sunset, all in the name of establishing Anglo-American relations, of course?'

So far, Marvin Mcleod hadn't said anything, leaving it to his buddies to break the ice. Claire was giggling by now, and making room on the bench for the GIs to join them. One of them was Glenn, whom Claire had danced with, and the other was called Chuck, and Kerry was still standing with her arms crossed like an idiot and hardly knowing what to do next when Marvin finally spoke.

'There's not much room on the bench for five, so how about if Miss Kerry Penfold takes a walk along the towpath with me while you three get acquainted?'

She could hardly do otherwise now that he had made it obvious that he knew her name, but this wasn't how this evening was meant to be. She had wanted a heart-to-heart with Claire, talking over things the way they always did, from Aunt Maud's imminent arrival, to her own uncertainties at not hearing from Tom very much lately, to what the many ships in the harbour and the large influx of Yanks really meant, to the now burning question over whether or not her Aunt Lil could really be on her last legs . . .

Instead of which, she was walking awkwardly beside this man she had met for the first time a few nights ago, looking every bit as if they were a couple to anyone else who was also out and about before the enforced blackout shut out the night for good. It wasn't what she wanted, and even less than that, she hoped she didn't meet anyone who knew her.

'Is something bothering you?' Marvin said.

'No. Sorry. I was just thinking.'

'Don't you know that too much thinking can be bad for your health?' he said, so seriously that she jerked her head up to look at him, cricking her neck in the process, to see the laughter in his eyes.

She stopped walking, forcing him to do the same. 'Look, I was just out for a while with my friend, and I'd like to go back there, if it's all the same to you. We've got a lot to discuss.'

In the still of early evening, Claire's burst of laughter could clearly be heard, and Kerry bit her lip. Trust her to take everything in her stride. Why couldn't she do the same? It was only a walk, for God's sake!

'There's another seat along there, so can we sit down for a moment? I'd like to show you something,' Marvin said abruptly.

It would be churlish and infantile to refuse, so she simply nodded and joined him on the bench as he brought his wallet out of his pocket. Not knowing what to expect, she felt her heart beat much too fast. Maybe she was being totally idiotic, but he was a stranger, and she didn't want any kind of relationship with him, Anglo-American or otherwise. She averted her eyes until she heard him speak again.

'This is my girl. She's quite a looker, isn't she?'

Kerry looked down at the photo he was holding out to her. The girl looked like a film star, with tumbling blonde hair and a wide smile with the miles of white teeth all Americans seemed to have.

'Her name's Shirl, and if my attentions were bothering you, they needn't, since I'm planning to ask her to marry me when all this is over,' Marvin went on.

'She's very pretty,' Kerry mumbled, feeling stupid.

'She was Miss Montana last year,' Marvin went on proudly, 'and a cheerleader for the local college football team before that.'

Kerry had no idea what a cheerleader was, but she wasn't about to admit as much. The fact that his glamorous Shirl had been Miss Montana last year seemed to put her streets apart from any normal girl, anyway, and in turn, that put Lieutenant Marvin Mcleod a world apart from her.

'So tell me about your guy,' he said, putting the photo back in his wallet. 'Is he in the service?'

For a moment her mind went blank. They truly did speak a different language. *In the service* could mean anything – in the church, in catering, in hotel management – but of course, he meant none of that, she thought, her senses clicking into place again.

'He's somewhere in France,' she said, trotting out the phrase that was commonplace nowadays. 'He joined up two years ago. That would be before you became our allies, wouldn't it?'

She hated herself for coming out with such an unintentionally bitchy remark. It was hardly his fault that the Americans didn't come into the war until the Japanese had bombed Pearl Harbour! Nobody in Columbine, nor anywhere else, Kerry suspected, had even known where that was before the terrible Japanese raid that had destroyed so many valuable ships of the neutral American navy. And killed so many unsuspecting men too . . .

'As a matter of fact, I was stationed at Pearl Harbour at that time.'

He said the words in such a monotone that she knew instinctively it hid far too many unsaid things that were too horrific to mention.

'Oh God, I'm sorry.'

'Yeah. I lost a good few buddies. In hours, Pearl Harbour changed from being a little bit of paradise on earth to an unbelievable scene of bloody carnage, and that's all I'm going to say about it.'

34

That he didn't even apologise to her for his language told her that he was caught up in the memory. She hardly knew how they had become so serious. They could hear Claire's chatter drifting along the towpath, followed by laughter between her and the two other GIs. She swallowed hard. Her annoyance at not hearing regularly from Tom was suddenly as nothing to what this man had seen.

'Look, I really do have to go. We're expecting my auntie's cousin to come and stay with us for the duration, and I have to help get her room ready.'

Futile as it sounded, she wanted to get away from him before she could get any more involved in a life that had nothing to do with her, but which she already felt she knew far too much about. She knew of his glamorous girlfriend Shirl, who he was intending to marry; about his time at Pearl Harbour, where he would have seen as many horrific things as any Cornish boys who were fighting in France. She felt mildly ashamed of the way that she and Tom, and many like them, had felt scathing of the Yanks for waiting too long before entering the war. She didn't feel like that now.

'I hope we can meet again sometime,' he said, standing up and not attempting to detain her.

'Perhaps we will,' Kerry muttered.

Without waiting for him to follow, she almost ran back to the bench where Claire was in full flow with the other Yanks now, and told her quickly that she was getting off home and would see her tomorrow. She turned and sped along the darkening towpath, where the moon was already turning the river into a sheen of silver ribbon. Moonlit nights were welcome, since it made the sky bright enough for enemy planes to be picked out by searchlights; it was mainly on the darkest nights that they heard the drone of enemy aircraft, near or far.

It wasn't what moonlight was for, Kerry found herself thinking, almost hysterically. Moonlight was for sweethearts, not for planes to be shot out of the sky in a burning mass of twisted metal, with the poor devils inside them seared to a crisp . . . One of Claire's brothers was a gunner in the RAF, and she didn't want to think about that either.

She was almost sobbing by the time she reached home. She fell inside the door to lean against it, with her imagination taking her to places she didn't want to go. Marvin Mcleod had somehow brought the impact of war home to her in a way not even the Jerry planes had done, despite the raids they had suffered recently, an onslaught in which many bombs had been dropped indiscriminately in isolated outlying areas and harmed no one. Such short-sightedness by the German pilots had made them complacent, even scornful, sure of their insularity, their invincibility. But nobody was invincible. Pearl Harbour had proved that.

'What's the matter, Kerry?' she heard Aunt Lil say anxiously. 'You look as if you've seen a ghost.'

Maybe she had. The ghost of the future . . .

'I'm all right, Aunt Lil,' she said quickly. 'I ran home and I've got a stitch in my side, that's all.'

'Have you and Claire been squabbling again?'

Kerry forced a laugh at the natural assumption.

'Something like that. I'll be all right in a minute.'

'You'll be even better when you see what's arrived for you,' Lil said with a small smile.

She handed over the letter with the familiar handwriting on the envelope, and Kerry's world turned the right way up again. She knew that Tom loved her, but she needed to see the words, to sense what he couldn't say without feeling his arms around her, holding her close. But this was the best they could hope for in the circumstances.

'I'll take it upstairs to read, and then I'll come down and help you get the front room ready for Aunt Maud,' she said quickly.

'Mr Coombes from the Friendship Club has already had the bed delivered,' Lil called, but by then Kerry had sped upstairs with the precious letter in her hand. Once in her room she opened the envelope, her heart thudding.

Ten minutes later she was bursting with rage. Oh, all the usual sentiments were there, about how much he missed her and longed for the day when this ruddy war was over and he'd be back home again. But although the words were guarded as always, it was pretty clear that he, too, knew that something big was in the offing. And maybe she was feeling extra-intuitive that evening, but underneath it all she could read his boyish eagerness to get stuck into the fight, to be a comic-book hero, no matter what the cost. His barely hidden excitement totally deflated her. So much so that she screwed up the letter and flung it across the room, to rescue it a moment later, smoothing it out and weeping over it.

What in God's name was wrong with her? This was her boy, her sweetheart, and all she could do was to pinpoint the thrill he was undoubtedly feeling, and hate him for it. It was a man thing . . . but he wasn't a man. He was still a boy, *her* boy . . . but even as she thought it, she knew he was far more than that. All those young boys, little more than schoolkids, who had gone away so eagerly in the cause of king and country would come back as men. She should be proud, and she *was* proud.

She just wanted him home, the same as before, but for the first time she wondered if that was going to happen. He would be changed, the same as she was changed. Or was she? She felt the same, if a few years older. But none of them could remain the same for ever. It didn't happen, and they were no longer children, any of them. *You were born, you grew older, you died.* She gave a sudden shudder, remembering Claire's blunt words.

'Are you coming, Kerry?' she heard Aunt Lil call out. 'I've made some nice rabbit stew for our supper.'

'I'm coming, Aunt Lil,' she said quickly, smothering such depressing thoughts, and putting on a forced smile as she ran downstairs again.

'You've been through all this before, haven't you, Aunt Lil?' she said later when she had given her a few details from Tom's letter.

By now, replete with the succulent rabbit stew, they were making up the single bed in the front room for Aunt Maud's use, and Lil paused.

'There's not many folk of my age, and older, who don't know what it means to be worrying over a loved one caught up in a war, my love. They said the last one was the war to end all wars, but there's always some madman somewhere ready to start another one, and to whip up his followers to do likewise. It's a weird thing that this one started twenty-one years after the last one ended, though.'

'What's weird about it?'

'The timing, girl. There's always babies being born after the end of a war when the troops come home again and I don't need to spell out what I mean by that. So those that were born a couple of years after 1918 are just ripe for serving in this one, aren't they? It's almost like God decided to produce fighting fodder, just in case, and I feel blasphemous even saying such a thing, but I can't say I've never thought it, and I'm sure he'll forgive me for it.'

Kerry was a bit stunned at her sudden passion, and even more at such a confession from her church-loving auntie.

'Cripes, Aunt Lil, I've never heard you talk like this before!'

Lil whipped the final cover over the single bed and straightened up cautiously to ease her back. 'Well, you don't know everything about me, my love, so you go on writing your letters to your young man, no matter if you get as many back or not, because he needs to know that you're still waiting for him when he comes home.'

'He knows that already,' Kerry mumbled, embarrassed to be sharing such intimate details. But it was a curious thing to say, and she said as much to Claire when she popped in at the small lending library where Claire worked.

'Maybe she didn't always write to your uncle as much as she should, and this is her roundabout way of telling you,' Claire offered. 'Wasn't he killed in the Great War?'

'Yes, but she never talks about that, and I don't want to talk about it now, thanks very much.'

'I've got some news, anyway. You know those two Yanks I was talking to the other night on the towpath?

Well, Glenn came into the library earlier today and we're definitely invited to go to their base to see a movie on Saturday night, which will be far better than having to take the bus to the picture house in Falmouth. What do you say, Kerry? Are you game?'

'Are you sure they included me?'

'Well, Glenn said it was a message from that other one as well, Marvin or something, and it was for both of us. You'd better say yes, because I know my dad won't be too keen on me going there on my own!'

Kerry wasn't keen on going at all. The thought of it conjured up too many sweet memories of sitting in the back row of a darkened cinema in Falmouth and snuggling up to Tom.

'I don't want to go,' she said abruptly.

'Kerry, you've got to!' Claire wailed. 'Oh, don't spoil it for me just because you think Tom would object. You're not married to him yet, and he doesn't *own* you!'

'I don't think that at all. I can think for myself, and if I don't want to go, it has nothing to do with Tom and me.'

But of course it did, and Claire knew darned well that it did. Just as Kerry knew she would back down, if only so that Claire wouldn't think her a total wimp. She also had the backing of her Aunt Lil, and also from Aunt Maud, who arrived with due ceremony and far too much luggage on Friday afternoon, indicating a lengthy stay.

Aunt Maud was a younger and more garish version of Aunt Lil, thought Kerry, without the soft Cornish voice or much refinement. Maud was loud, both in voice and dress, and her response to Kerry's comment that she was going to the

US base unwillingly on Saturday night was a raucous and approving laugh.

'You go and enjoy yourself, my girl, and never mind what folk say.'

'I wasn't minding any such thing,' Kerry said crossly, annoyed that she had put the suggestion in her mind. 'It's a nice gesture from the Americans to do this and to invite some of the locals, and it's not just for Claire and me. It's more likely a thank you for the show we put on for them when they arrived.'

'Oh well, you can think that, but two good-looking girls like you and your friend should make the most of it,' Maud said with a grin. 'You're only young once. What do you say, Lil?'

'I say that Kerry knows how to look after herself, and to remember her young man somewhere in France.'

'There's no danger of me forgetting where he is, Aunt Lil. Nor that the GIs will probably be over there with him pretty soon, from what Mr Polby says.'

'Well, then. That's what I mean, Kerry,' Maud went on. 'You've got to snatch a bit of pleasure where you can when there's a war on. People learnt that in the last lot, didn't they, Lil?'

To Kerry's horror, her Aunt Lil's face went a sickly white, and she turned abruptly and went out of the room, saying she was going to make some tea.

'Aunt Lil, are you all right?' she called out, but the door had closed behind her, and Maud snorted.

'She was always one for shutting her eyes to what went on right under her nose, but you can't stop human nature, whether you're a prince or a beggar.'

'Am I supposed to know what that means, Aunt Maud?'

As if realising she was being too free and easy with her chatter, Maud clamped her lips together before muttering that it was nothing, and when Lil came back she looked and acted so normally that Kerry began to wonder if she had imagined it all. But she was too intuitive for that. There was something here that she didn't know, and neither of these two was going to tell her.

'Well, what do you think it could be?' Claire asked when they were cycling over to the American base on Saturday evening. 'If it was something that happened in the last war, your Aunt Lil might have been having a fling with somebody while your uncle was away at the front. Can you imagine it?' she added, giggling.

'Of course not,' Kerry snapped. 'Aunt Lil's always been a bit strait-laced, and it was more likely to be Aunt Maud than her. Maybe she went a bit off colour because she didn't want Aunt Maud to be indiscreet and start telling me any wild tales of her youth.'

'That'll be it, so can we forget the old dears, and enjoy the flicks?' Claire said as they arrived at the base and were escorted to the newly erected cinema.

The Americans certainly knew how to do things in style and to enjoy themselves, even in the middle of a war, Kerry found herself thinking resentfully. She doubted if Tom had any such luxuries wherever he was stationed.

'I'm glad you came,' she heard Marvin Mcleod say. 'We can't do much to repay the hospitality of our hosts, but at least we can do this.'

Kerry soon saw that she and Claire were not the only invited ones. In fact, it seemed as if half the village were here, and she had been foolish to read anything into the invitation other than the well-documented Anglo-American relationship that the GIs were keen to foster.

'I'm glad I came too,' she replied, relaxing with a smile.

CHAPTER THREE

Maud Jenkins was more sprightly than Lil, whom she privately thought of as her country cousin. She dressed more smartly, was more modern in her ways, and was very loath to join in any of Columbine's activities. She had left Cornwall many moons ago, and wasn't ready to be dragged down by any insular society, thank you very much. It was a bit of a safe haven for her now, although she wasn't slow in criticising everything, and Kerry sighed as she heard her aunts wrangling even before they went to church on the following Sunday morning.

'If you're going to be here for any length of time, you may as well see what we have to offer, Maud,' Lil said in annoyance at her flat refusal to go to 'any old Friendship Club', as she called it.

'Well, first off, I shall go to this dance the Yanks are hoping to arrange as a thank you to the locals,' she said.

'At least they know how to enjoy themselves, and if you moved around a bit more, it would do wonders for your hips, old girl. Me and a gentleman friend had a go at doing the jitterbug at some dances in Bristol, and you never used to be so slow in coming forward, if I remember rightly.'

'I don't want to hear any more of that talk. What's past is past.'

Kerry heard Maud give a laugh that was decidedly taunting.

'I bet you want to keep it that way too. It wouldn't do for the young 'uns to know what went on in the last lot, would it?'

Kerry caught her breath. There was something here that she didn't understand. Whatever it was, these two definitely shared secrets. When you were seventeen, it was weird, and a bit creepy, to think that two rather dumpy, middle-aged women could have done anything scandalous in their past. But why not? They weren't born middle-aged . . . but she suddenly felt sorry for Aunt Lil, who had cared for her all her life. Nobody could deny that she was a bit strait-laced, even reserved, and if this so-called woman of the world was going to start spilling secrets that were nobody else's business but Aunt Lil's own, she for one didn't want to hear them. She ran down the stairs with more clatter than usual.

'Well, I'm ready,' she announced. 'Are we going to church today or not?'

'Of course we are, love,' Lil said at once.

Having overheard what went on before, Kerry couldn't deny that she said the words with obvious relief. And if it wasn't a wicked thing to do in the small village church that morning, as they listened to the interminably long sermon by the vicar, she would have wished with all her heart that Aunt Maud would hurry up and go back where she came from. She suspected that she had only come here for a change, and not from any fear of air raids. She might fancy herself as a bit more sophisticated than her Cornish kin, but her roots were still here, for all that. But hopefully she would soon tire of the simple life. Good riddance too, Kerry thought uncharitably. For the life of her, she couldn't take to the woman, and there was no law that said you had to like your relatives, was there!

'How long are you planning to stay, Aunt Maud?' Kerry said casually as they ate their Sunday dinner later.

'That's not a very polite thing to say, Kerry,' Lil chided her.

'I'm only asking. I should think you'd find it pretty dull and boring after Bristol, and I bet you'll be missing your friends, too,' she commented to Maud innocently.

Maud laughed, her eyes sparkling, and Kerry got a glimpse of the girl she had once been, vivacious and lively.

'Well, I'm hoping one of them might be coming down to see me in a few weeks' time if we can find some suitable lodgings for him. Respectable, of course,' she added with a grin, as if there was any hint of anything more.

'Every time she opens her mouth I'm beginning to dislike her more and more, even if it's totally unreasonable,' Kerry complained to Claire that evening. 'Now it looks as if she's got a gentleman friend who's going to come and visit her.'

'Blimey, Kerry, what's your Aunt Lil going to say about

that? She won't put up with any goings-on in her front room, will she?'

'Don't be daft. The idea is to see if we can get him some lodgings for a few days.'

'Gillagy's Farm sometimes does bed and breakfast,' Claire said. She gave a snigger. 'I can just imagine your Aunt Maud tripping over there in her high heels and done up to the nines, and falling in some cow muck. Why don't you suggest the farm to her as a likely place for her bloke? I bet he's some kind of gigolo, but I wouldn't worry. He'll probably take her back to Bristol with him and then all your troubles will be over.'

By now they were both laughing hysterically at the image of Maud falling in cow muck, and being helped up by some ageing Lothario.

'He might be a young bloke, out for what he can get from a dozy woman with a bit of money behind her,' Kerry said choking. 'I don't know what her Jim left her from his shoe-mending business, but she's not short of cash from the look of her. And by the way, she's heard about some dance the GIs are thinking of arranging at their base, and if it happens she says she'll be going to it.'

Claire stopped laughing and grabbed Kerry's arm so hard that it hurt. 'She *what*? You are joking, aren't you?'

'I'm not! She says she knows how to do the jitterbug. I daresay she'll show me if I ask her.'

She started to laugh again, but Claire was patently angry now.

'Heaven forbid! She's too old, and too lumpy, and she'll put us off our stroke if she's there. You've got to stop her, Kerry.'

'I can't say I want her there, but what can I do about it? It's not definite yet, anyway, and you're not getting in too deep with these Yanks, are you? They won't be here for ever.'

'I might. Me and Glenn got on really well at the movie show.'

'I noticed.'

'Oh well, I didn't expect Miss Goody Two-Shoes to do anything more than sit up straight beside *Lootenant* Marvin!'

'I never intended doing anything else. It wasn't a date!' Kerry snapped. 'And don't call me Goody Two-Shoes.'

As the belittling phrase surged into her mind, she felt her face go hot, caught up in the memories of the last time Tom was home on leave, when they had spent a few precious hours together up on the moors. It was months ago now, and the weather had really been too cold for being outdoors, but snuggled together in one of the secluded hollows in the shelter of an old tin mine chimney, the cold had been the last thing on their minds. In fact, the atmosphere between them had become so intense that Kerry had felt a sense of panic at how feelings and emotions could run away so easily if they didn't hold them in check.

But it wasn't the time for being sensible. It was the time for showing someone you loved how desperately you were going to miss them, especially when the love of your life was persuading you so tenderly to go all the way. Nice girls didn't do it, but girls in love often forgot such caution . . .

'I would never ask you to do anything you don't want to do, sweetheart, but no matter where I'm sent or what happens to me, I need to have something I will always remember,' Tom was saying huskily as his hands slid all over her body, bringing her shivering senses to life.

'Like a talisman,' the romantic side of Kerry breathed.

'Like a talisman,' he echoed softy. 'You'll always be that, my love, and having you to come home to is what will keep me going, no matter how rough it gets, but I don't want to think about any of that. I just want to think about us, here and now, and to know that you belong to me.'

'You know that I do, Tom. I always have.'

Was it so wicked to have given in to what he wanted and needed? What they both wanted and needed? She hadn't thought so then, and she didn't think so now . . . only sometimes, when she realised what the outcome of that one brief love-making could have been, and sometimes the shame of it rushed over her. But nothing bad had happened because of it, and it was a secret only the two of them shared. Not even Claire had been privy to that sweet wonderful time of belonging that was hers and Tom's alone . . .

'What the hell's up with you, Kerry?' she heard Claire say crossly. 'That's the second time I've asked you how long your perishing Auntie Maud is staying.'

'I don't know,' Kerry said jerkily. 'For the duration, she said, but I doubt that she'll last out that long.'

And remembering the conversation she had heard between her aunts that morning, she knew she didn't want to hear any more. Secrets were meant to be just that, and if either of the old girls had any secrets of their own, they were private and not meant for sharing. She certainly wouldn't want to know.

'It's a nice evening, so why don't we cycle over to Gillagy's Farm and ask about bed and breakfast?' she said hurriedly. 'I told Aunt Maud I'd enquire, and if her chap turns up, at least we'll know where to send him.'

'Good idea,' said Claire. 'And we'll be passing the GI camp on the way.'

Kerry didn't answer that. With the memory of that last night with Tom still fresh in her mind, the last thing she wanted was to encounter any of the sociable Yanks and have to get into conversation with them.

They cycled through the leafy lanes, fragrant with the wild blossoms of early May, clover and wild yarrow and yellow gorse; past the tents and buildings that made up the nearest American base to Columbine, until they saw the sprawling outline of Gillagy's Farm ahead. The fields that weren't ploughed up under ministry instructions to plant crops were dotted with lazy sheep and grazing cows. And away from the coastline that was heavy with the intrusion of barbed wire now, and the constant rumble of military machinery and planes overhead, Kerry thought ruefully that you could almost imagine it was any blissfully normal Cornish day in early summer.

'I wonder when it will all end,' she said involuntarily. 'We can't even have proper lights on our bikes anymore, for fear we'll alert enemy aircraft. Did you know that just before Christmas one of Mr Polby's Home Guards was killed because of that, when he rode straight into a swollen ditch that he couldn't see?'

'Blimey, you're gloomy tonight, aren't you?'

'It's the Maud effect,' Kerry said solemnly, and then they were both laughing, and wobbling on their bikes as they neared the farmyard.

*   *   *

The Gillagys were a comfortably rounded couple who welcomed the girls with a cup of tea and a slice of home-made cake, saying it was a pity they had missed meeting their land girls, who had gone into Falmouth for the evening.

'Not that they'll find much to do there on a Sunday, but the Services Social Club is always open, and they miss the bright lights, coming from London,' Mrs Gillagy said with a sniff, and then burst out laughing at her own joke. 'Not that there's many bright lights in London or anywhere else now, is there, my lambs? So to what do we owe the pleasure?'

Kerry explained their query, saying that it was just on the off chance. Mrs Gillagy's eyes gleamed as she finished her tale.

'So you've got Maud Jenkins staying with you, have you? Well, it don't surprise me none that she's got a gentleman friend. A bit of a flighty one was our Maud, and a scatterbrain too, forever changing her mind about things. She was always keen to get away, though, and we were never good enough for her. Still, I daresay she's settled down a bit now. We heard that her husband had died a few years ago and presumably left her well set up.'

Kerry tried not to look too interested, while digesting everything. She didn't know what Aunt Maud had been like in her youth, but if this was settling down, anticipating doing the jitterbug with the Yanks at her age, then she was the queen of England!

'So if her friend does arrive, can you put him up for bed and breakfast?' Kerry said at last.

'Oh yes, we can do that,' the farmer's wife said amiably.

'You just let us know when, and we'll see to the rest.'

Before they left, they had been shown what was grandly called the guest bedroom with its chintz curtains and eiderdown and heavy rose-patterned wallpaper, and told that the gentleman would get a hearty breakfast, but that they would need his ration book if he intended staying more than a few days.

'I bet they don't go short,' Claire said, as they cycled back to Columbine. 'They get as many eggs as they want from their hens, and plenty of bacon too. They don't look exactly underfed, do they?' she sniggered.

'Perhaps Aunt Maud should stay there too.'

'What, with only one guest room? Or would that bother the two old codgers, do you think?'

'Oh, *don't*,' Kerry groaned, willing the image away.

They were nearing the base now, and a group of GIs were coming out, forcing them to stop and let them pass.

'There's Glenn,' Claire said eagerly. 'He's coming over. Now don't get all shirty, Kerry. He only wants to talk.'

'I'm not getting shirty!'

But even as she said it, she couldn't miss the way Glenn spoke quickly to his buddies and then walked towards them, his expression more serious than usual. She assumed he was going to talk to Claire, but to her surprise he was looking straight at her. A sixth sense sent her heart plummeting.

'What is it?' she said, before she could stop herself.

'This is awkward, Kerry, but I know you and Marvin had a bit of an understanding,' he began clumsily.

'We had no such thing,' she said, her voice shriller than she intended. 'We just talked, that's all.'

53

'Gee, I didn't mean anything by it, honey. I know he liked you and found you easy to talk to, that's all.'

'For pity's sake, Glenn, stop messing about and tell us what's happened,' Claire said in a rush.

'He's gone AWOL,' he said flatly.

Kerry looked at him stupidly. 'What do you mean?'

'I mean he's gone off God knows where. We're due to ship out in a few weeks, and he'll be in for a bunch of trouble if he's not back at the base pdq.'

'I know what AWOL means,' Kerry said, her voice shaky. 'But why has he done it?'

'He got a Dear John letter and it's sent him haywire.'

Both girls looked blank, and Glenn sighed, hearing his buddies call out to him to get a move on if they were going into town.

'It's a letter from his girl, saying she's met someone else. It happens in a war, and it's brutal. A lot of guys get them, but not many take it as hard as Marvin did. Now, sorry, dolls, but I gotta go.'

He turned and walked away quickly, leaving Kerry and Claire hardly knowing what to say, never having heard of a Dear John letter before – not that name for it, anyway.

'What an awful thing to do to somebody fighting a war and thousands of miles away from home,' Kerry finally burst out.

'Don't take it to heart, kid. Like Glenn said, these things happen,' Claire said uneasily.

'Well, it would never happen to Tom and me,' she went on passionately. 'I can't imagine anything worse than not having the guts to say it face-to-face.'

'It would be a bit difficult with an ocean between them,'

Claire said dryly. 'Come on, you've only just met the bloke, and no doubt he'll get it out of his system and be back at the base before you know it.'

'I've seen her photo, and she looks like a film star. He was so proud of her having been Miss Montana and a cheerleader for a college football team.'

'Crikey, you got to know him a bit better than I thought. Have you been holding out on me? You haven't been meeting him on the sly, have you?'

'Of course not. I'm just sorry for him that this has happened, that's all.'

They got back on their bikes and began the ride back to the village, and as they parted at Kerry's cottage, Claire spoke more sharply.

'Just don't be too sorry for him when he returns, will you? He may want a shoulder to cry on, if that's what Yanks do, but you don't want to get into a situation you can't get out of, Kerry.'

'I'm not likely to, but if he wants somebody to talk to, I won't turn my back on him either. Shirl's already done that.'

She put her bike in the shed and went indoors, more upset than she had expected. All she could think about was the look on Marvin Mcleod's face when he'd shown her his girl's photo. That was love if ever she saw it. And now she had done this to him, sending him over the edge if what Glenn said was true, and who knew what effect it could have on a serving soldier?

They weren't actually fighting here in Cornwall, although they were constantly out on manoeuvres somewhere or other, but very soon now, if what Glenn said was true, they would be shipping out. And everybody knew what that meant. The big push to get the Germans out of France would be under way.

As she went indoors her aunts stopped whatever they were saying, unable to miss the distress on her face.

'Has something happened, Kerry?' Lil said at once. 'You and Claire haven't had a falling-out again, have you?'

'Did you speak to the farmer?' Maud put in.

The incongruity of her remark after the concern in her Aunt Lil's eyes made Kerry's temper spill over.

'There are more important things in this world than talking to a farmer about your blessed gentleman friend, Aunt Maud, and no, me and Claire haven't had a falling-out!'

She flew out of the room and up the stairs to her room, slamming the door behind her. On her dressing table was the last photo she and Tom had had taken together, both laughing into the camera, carefree and full of plans for the future. She sat down heavily on her bed, gazing at the photo and into Tom's warm, so confident eyes. What did that future hold for any of them now, she wondered, with a dire sense of foreboding?

What did it hold for poor Marvin Mcleod, who had clearly taken his sweetheart's betrayal so much to heart and been devastated by it? How reckless would it make him when and if he encountered the enemy? Her all-too-vivid imagination leapt forward, almost as if she could see the bleakness of those coming days in a different country, those bloody, harrowing, terrifying days . . .

'Kerry, I'm coming in,' she heard Aunt Lil say sternly after a brief knock on her bedroom door. She couldn't speak, and she remained where she was, knowing this was something she couldn't avoid.

'Whatever's happened, girl, there was no need to be so rude to Maud,' her aunt began, but when Kerry still didn't reply she saw the photo held tightly in her hand now, and her face altered.

'Have you heard something about Tom?' Her hand went to her throat. 'He's not . . . his mother hasn't had bad news, has she?'

Kerry shook her head. 'No. It's not Tom. It's one of the Americans I met, and it's just *awful*.'

A guilty sliver of relief flashed across Lil's face that at least something bad hadn't happened to Tom Trevellyan. But her expression was quickly replaced by concern at Kerry's flushed face.

'Well, I know their manoeuvres can be quite dangerous at times, so has he been in an accident or something because of it?'

Kerry shook her head, feeling foolish now. Compared to being blown up by a bomb or a grenade, or being shot out of the sky in a plane, she supposed having your girlfriend send you a Dear John letter wasn't a great disaster. Except for the person concerned, of course. Unexpectedly, her eyes blurred with tears.

'I talked to him several times, and I really liked him, Aunt Lil. Not in the way I feel about Tom, of course. It was never like that, and never would be. But he was a long way from home, and he just wanted to talk. He showed me a photo of his girlfriend, and she's really beautiful. He was so proud of her and he was going to ask her to marry him after the war. And now she's written to him to say she's met someone else, and he's gone AWOL.'

She was almost gasping by the time she finished, and she hardly noticed how her aunt's arms were around her, hugging her while she cried herself out. It was crazy to feel so intense about someone else's problems, but everything in this damn war made people feel more intense, waiting for news they were desperate to hear, or fearing the worst when they heard nothing at all, and knowing that things like this could happen to them, to anyone, to *her*. Knowing that far worse things could happen than a Dear John letter.

'Now you listen to me, Kerry, because I'm going to tell you something that will put it all in perspective,' Aunt Lil was saying close to her head, her voice strangely tight. 'Things like this happen when people are parted for a long time. Not to everybody, of course, but to some people. And they get over it, just as this young man will get over it.'

'Will he? What if it makes him uncaring about what happens to him from now on? I could tell that he really loved her, Aunt Lil.'

'Of course he did. But loving somebody doesn't blind you to being a friend to someone else. You've already found that out, by being able to talk to this young man so easily. It doesn't affect your feelings for Tom, does it?'

'Of course not,' Kerry said, embarrassed at such unexpectedly frank talk from her aunt.

'It didn't affect my feelings for your uncle when something of the sort happened to me at the end of the last war.'

Kerry's attention was caught now. Was she about to hear the great secret that Maud had been taunting Lil about so snidely? If so, she suddenly knew that whatever it was, she didn't want to hear it. She'd heard enough already.

'Don't tell me, Aunt Lil,' she choked.

Lil gave a heavy sigh. 'I think I must, my love, if only because the longer Maud stays here, the more likely it is you'll hear a garbled version of it from her. If she and her so-called gentleman friend go out for the evening, she can get very reckless with her speech after a few drinks, not to say spiteful, so I'd rather you heard the truth from me.'

'All right,' Kerry muttered, hating everything about the way this evening had turned out now. If only they could turn back the clock to an hour ago . . . to five years ago before the world had been turned upside down by a power-hungry madman . . . but you could never go back, not in time, anyway.

'The man in question was Polish, and he was interned in a camp near here. Some of the more trusted men were sent to work in the area, under strict supervision, of course. He was very pleasant, blond-haired and blue-eyed, a real charmer, and the complete opposite in temperament from my Freddie.'

Kerry could tell that her aunt was almost lost in the memory now, and she hardly dared to breathe, wondering what was going to come next.

'He was also a tease, and he made me laugh, saying he was going to take me away from all this after the war ended. It was all harmless nonsense, but for a very little while I even started to wonder what life would be like in another country. I wasn't young and foolish, Kerry, and I was already a married woman. Maud was still living here then, and she'd always had a fancy for my Freddie herself. But she'd seen me and Pieter talking together a lot, and she threatened to write and tell Freddie if I didn't come to my senses.'

'She wouldn't have done that, would she? *Did* she?'

'No. There was no need, because I got the news that Freddie had been killed in France,' Lil said, her voice brittle now, the sorrow evident on her face. 'I was so shocked and distraught, wondering if I'd brought it all on myself by my brief attraction to another man, even though it meant nothing compared to the way I loved Freddie. It was a wretched time for me, and I couldn't bear to go anywhere near Pieter after that. Then the war ended, and the POWs were all repatriated, and I never heard from Pieter again.'

Kerry was sitting rigidly now. It was bizarre to listen to a woman nearing sixty years old talk about her attraction for another man when she was already married; a woman who had always seemed strait-laced to Kerry. It was a shock, to put it mildly, and far too much a mirror image of what was happening, or could be happening, between herself and Marvin Mcleod. It also made her wonder if you really knew anybody. Everybody had secrets, even Aunt Lil . . .

She didn't know what to say, aware of a fierce mixture of love and loyalty for the woman who had brought her up. Lil Penfold didn't normally find it easy to talk about her innermost feelings, and now she had found herself obliged to do it for fear her mean-spirited cousin might do so in an unguarded moment. Involuntarily, Kerry put her arms around her aunt and hugged her tight.

'I've never heard you say a bad thing about Uncle Freddie. I never knew him, but I always knew that you loved him, and I'm sure he must have loved you too. Maud would never have stood a chance,' she added clumsily, trying to take the heat out of the situation.

She felt the touch of Lil's cool lips on her forehead.

'You're a sweet girl, Kerry, and you have a loving nature. I'm sure this young man will return to his comrades very soon and realise that there's still a job to do. And if you see him again, you must be strong and not let your soft heart be swayed by his problems. They're *his* problems, not yours. You understand me, don't you?'

'Of course I do. Claire's already warned me of that. And Aunt Lil – about all the rest – this conversation never happened.'

'Good. Then I shall go downstairs now before Maud thinks I've taken to my bed. Come down for some cocoa when you're ready, love.'

Kerry sat on her bed for a while longer after hearing the heavy steps going back down the stairs. It was true what she had thought previously. People weren't born old . . . but just as she had imagined Maud's girlish face earlier, for a few moments that evening she could imagine the vibrant young woman Lil had been too, with all the promise of a long life ahead with her Freddie, and the prospect of a family of their own, until another power-crazy madman had ruined all her hopes and dreams.

She picked up the photo of her and Tom again, holding it close to her heart before she kissed his smiling face, and breathing a silent prayer that someday in the not-too-distant future, the whole topsy-turvy world would come to rights, and they would be together again.

CHAPTER FOUR

With the influx of so many American and Commonwealth troops in channel ports and other strategic places, the constant roar of machinery and large-scale military operations had become an everyday occurrence. The certainty that an Allied invasion of France was imminent was on everybody's lips now, combined with a renewed optimism that the war must surely be coming to an end at last.

In the American army base near Falmouth Lieutenant Marvin Mcleod had returned very quickly and given himself up, over what was being seen as a bit of a breakdown. According to Claire, who had heard it from Glenn, he had been severely reprimanded for going AWOL for three days, but his reasons had been dealt with sympathetically.

Because of his excellent military record and the

importance of the coming operations, he was merely relieved of a number of privileges, including being allowed to leave the barracks. But as the momentum of the expected invasion gathered strength, all outside activities were already being curtailed, so it wouldn't affect him unduly.

Claire had wasted no time in reporting the news to her friend.

'Glenn managed to send me a note telling me what's happened, and asking me to pass on the news to you that Marvin's OK. He has to have some sort of counselling, whatever that is, but they wouldn't want to waste a hunk of manpower like him by putting him in the glasshouse, would they? Anyway, Glenn says he can't wait to get the hell over there now, and kick something or other out of the Jerries.'

Kerry looked at her in exasperation. 'Where do you learn all this stuff?'

'Never mind all that. They were Glenn's words, not mine. Aren't you pleased to hear that Marvin's all right?'

'Of course I am, but whatever they say, he'll still be feeling bad over what Shirl's done to him, and I hope he won't get too gung-ho. That *is* the right term for it, isn't it, Miss pseudo-Hollywood actress?' she added sarcastically.

Claire grinned. 'I suppose. But I reckon he's got his head screwed on the right way. Is there any news of Maud's fancy man yet?'

'Oh God, don't call him that! He's coming on Friday, and he's planning to stay for a week or so. Apparently he hurt his back lifting crates at work in the docks at somewhere called Avonmouth, so that's his excuse. And she's so twittery and girlish about it she makes me feel queasy.'

'There must be life in the old dog yet, then. What's his name? Rudolph Valentino?'

'Bert Figgins,' Kerry said solemnly, which started them off again.

But she was already sending up a silent prayer of thanks to God that Marvin seemed to have come out of his troubles unscathed. At least he had returned to his base and given himself up, which had to be a good sign for his peace of mind, and she would never have labelled him as unstable, anyway. Shirl may have done the dirty on him, but he was such a good-looking and likeable chap, he certainly wouldn't go without female company for long.

Bert Figgins arrived as arranged and whatever Kerry had expected, it was nothing like the small wiry man who appeared at the door of the cottage, his sparse grey hair heavily greased with Brylcreem. Maud was clearly delighted to see him, and immediately took over the cottage by insisting on making him tea and toast after the long train journey west. And anybody showing fewer signs of a bad back, Kerry couldn't imagine, she thought suspiciously.

'It's a well-known fact that anybody can get a sick note from the doctor saying they've got a bad back,' Claire snorted the next time they met.

'Is that so, Miss Know-All? Since when did you swallow a medical dictionary? Anyway, he seemed healthy enough to walk over to Gillagy's Farm with Aunt Maud a while ago, so I daresay she'll be spending less time at home while he's here.'

'That's a bit of a silver lining, then.'

Kerry couldn't argue with that.

'Ever since she knew Bert was coming, Maud has been dithering about like a teenager, dabbing herself with scent until the place smells like a chemist's shop. Aunt Lil told her to stop it or the place will need fumigating.'

'Blimey, the Gillagys won't like it if she goes over there smelling like a you-know-what, either. She'll put the cows off their milk.'

They began laughing hysterically at the thought, but nothing could dampen Kerry's spirits right now, because she'd had another letter from Tom, and this one was far more the kind of letter she wanted from him, telling her he was missing her badly too, dreaming about her constantly, and looking forward to the time when they would soon be together again. If it was meant to be a guarded message that the troops in France were well aware of the imminent plans to send the Germans packing, it sent her hopes rising as well.

In fact, she decided that considering the circumstances that everybody found themselves in these days, everything was more or less all right in her world. There had only been spasmodic air raids in the area lately, and they hadn't done any real harm; she was sure her new friend Marvin was going to get over his horrible Dear John letter in time; and she and Tom were going to be together again soon.

She crossed her fingers as she thought it, though, remembering how Aunt Lil always said that any kind of blissful complacency was in danger of being shattered when you least expected it.

On Monday afternoon Kerry was walking back to work in the late May sunshine when a small figure came tearing along the road like a whirlwind. She stepped in front of him, and caught the flailing arms of Claire's ten-year-old brother Jed.

'Hey, kiddo, not so fast, or you'll fall over yourself. Where's the fire?' she said, laughing. And then her expression changed as she saw his frightened, tear-stained, young face. 'What's happened, Jed?'

'Our Michael's plane has been shot down in flames and they say he's dead and drowned in the sea, and Claire can't stop our mum screeching and pulling her hair out, and I've been sent to get the doctor for her,' he shrieked, and then he had twisted away from Kerry, running down the road as fast as he could towards the doctor's house.

Kerry was frozen to the spot. She couldn't move and she couldn't breathe. In a moment all the air seemed to have gone from her body. There was a pain in her chest where her heart should be, and then all her breath came back in huge gasping sobs. Not *Michael*. Not Claire's handsome, daredevil, older brother *Michael*.

She suddenly found herself running too. Not towards the shop where Mrs Polby would be ready to open up again for the afternoon, but towards the house near the river, big enough to accommodate a large family, where they would be in a state of total shock, trying to take in the enormity of what had happened.

It never occurred to her not to go there, not for an instant. She had known these people all her life. Claire was like a sister to her, and they had shared all their childish hopes and dreams and secrets. Once, long ago, Claire had even wished that it could be Kerry and Michael walking down the aisle of the church, and then they would be sisters for real. And now Michael was dead, and she couldn't bear not to be with her sister and friend at such a terrible time.

She could hear the wailing before she reached the house where the Roddys lived. For the first time she baulked and her footsteps faltered. Was it right to intrude on a family's grief? But how much worse would it be, knowing, and doing nothing?

By now her heart was hammering as she pushed open the door without bothering to knock, her throat choking up as soon as she walked inside. Claire's mother sat rocking in her chair, with her younger children weeping and clinging to her, and Claire trying to calm them down. There was no sign of their father.

As soon as she saw her friend, Claire burst into noisy tears.

'I don't know what to do for her,' she wept. 'She keeps calling for Michael and Dad said she should see the doctor.'

'I know. I saw Jed. He did the right thing,' Kerry said jerkily. 'Where's your dad now?'

'He's gone to fetch the vicar, though I don't know what good he can do,' Claire said, her voice savage and bitter in an instant. 'Where was his precious God when he blew Michael's plane out of the sky?'

'It wasn't God who did it, Claire,' Kerry whispered clumsily. 'It was the enemy. You know that.'

'But God let it happen, didn't he? He didn't stop it. He didn't save our Michael!' She was becoming more shrill now, and Kerry wondered which of them was going over the top first, Claire or her mother.

She had never felt so helpless. What could anybody do to

help? What would Aunt Lil do if she was here? Her aunt's practical solution entered her scrambled thoughts. It would be the English thing. The panacea for all ills.

'Shall I put the kettle on and make some tea?' she said, and without waiting for an answer she rushed into the small kitchen and put the water in the kettle with shaking hands.

There had been casualties of war in the village before. This wasn't the first family to hear that a loved one had been wounded or missing or killed. But it was the first time it had been someone so close, someone close to her best friend, someone Kerry had gone to school with, and whom Tom had called one of his closest friends too. Oh, dear God, *Tom*! How was she ever going to tell him? And how could she not?

The front door banged again as she was still putting cups and saucers on a tray and searching in the pantry for milk and sugar. Mrs Roddy needed strong sweet tea for shock. There wasn't much sugar in the bowl. Nobody had much sugar these days, just a meagre ration that was supposed to last a week. That was the fault of the bloody Germans too, Kerry raged, almost out of control as she failed to find the drawer where the spoons were kept.

'I'll help you, Kerry,' came the small, sweet voice of Claire's five-year-old sister Molly, probably not understanding everything yet, but knowing that something terrible had happened, all the same.

In answer, Kerry bent down and gathered the child up in her arms, letting the tears flow over her head before she swallowed down her own grief and smiled tremulously down at her.

'That will be lovely, sweetheart,' she said, as steadily as her wobbling voice would allow. 'You put the spoons in the saucers and I'll pour the tea when it's ready, and we'll take it in for your mum and show her what a grown-up little girl you are.'

Instead of which, this bright-eyed tot, who was little more than an infant, was about to learn what being grown-up really meant.

Toby, her eight-year-old brother, poked his head into the kitchen. 'Dad's come back, and the vicar's with him,' he said, his voice scratchy, his eyes full as he tried not to cry.

'Then we'll make them some tea as well, won't we, Molly? You can help us, Toby. With all these people in the house, we'll have to keep busy.'

She didn't know where the words kept coming from. She just knew she had to do something, and to take the stark, frightened look out of these children's eyes for a little while, at least. She could still hear Mrs Roddy wailing, and she didn't think the old vicar was going to do a great deal to calm her down, and if he started solemnly quoting one of his blessed Bible verses, he'd be just as likely to get a tongue-lashing from Mrs Roddy. It needed the doctor and one of his magic potions to do the right thing for her. So where the hell was Jed?

Claire appeared behind her next, squeezing her hand and mouthing a silent thank you. 'Doctor Graham's just arrived, and I know you'll want to get to work, so I'll take over now.'

'It's all right, Claire.'

'No. I have to do this, and if you really want to help, you can let people know what's happened.' Her voice faltered but she took the teapot out of Kerry's hand and began pouring it into the cups on the tray. 'Me and Molly and Toby can manage here, and Jed can hand the cups round. It will be a bit like a little tea party, won't it, kids?'

As she saw the despairing, almost pleading look in Claire's eyes, Kerry realised what she was trying to do. It wasn't pushing her out. It was gathering the family all around, like the close-knit clan that they were. Needing each other, helping each other, and keeping one another strong, even the little ones.

She swallowed hard, saying she'd come back later if that was all right. Maybe this evening, and she was sure her Aunt Lil would want to come to see her mother too. Claire nodded vaguely, and Kerry wasn't even sure if she heard her, but for now, it had to be enough. She got out of the house, with the lasting image in her mind of the younger ones looking gratefully to their big sister, their leader. And the agonising sight of Claire's parents hugging one another in silent grief now, while the doctor and vicar stood by, talking quietly to one another.

So this was what it was like to have a real family, the irrational thought spun round in Kerry's mind, as the fresh air outside cooled her anguished face. This coming together, needing one another, and somehow finding the strength to cope with it all, no matter what. At least, she hoped they would cope, and she was sure that they would, however long it took. It was just that Michael, their so handsome son in his RAF uniform, of whom they had been rightly proud, would never again be there to get them through it.

Kerry suddenly found herself overcome by a torrent of tears, and she sank down on the soft tender grass alongside the towpath and wept for the loss of someone she had known all her life. It wasn't right that some unknown assailant had done this, killing a young man and ruining a family. It wasn't *fair*. Whoever it was who said that all's fair in love and war was just some crass, unfeeling, insensitive fool!

How long she lay there she couldn't have said, but eventually she knew there was something she had to do. She had to tell people. She had promised Claire. The news would soon get around the village, but first of all it would come from someone who cared. She dried her eyes and went to the shop. Mrs Polby deserved to know why she hadn't arrived back for work that afternoon. The woman looked up from serving a customer as Kerry walked inside and started to give her a mock dressing-down.

'Well, this is a fine time to turn up, my girl. Has your Aunt Maud been keeping you amused with some of her wild tales?'

Kerry found it difficult to speak for a minute, but as it dawned on the two women that something was very wrong, she finally blurted it out.

'I've been at Claire Roddy's house. They've just heard that their Michael has been killed when his plane was shot down.'

'Oh, my dear Lord, that lovely young man and that poor family,' Mrs Polby said at once. 'What does your Aunt Lil have to say about it, her being so pally with Claire's mother?'

'I haven't told her yet. I came straight here,' Kerry said woodenly.

'Then you go straight on home and don't worry about

working today, Kerry, love. There are more important things than selling a few oddments.'

She didn't wait to hear anything more. In any case, she knew she could leave any more telling to these two, and she needed the comfort of being at home herself now. The news had somehow taken all her confidence. This was something else that war did. No matter who you were, it stripped you of everything you held dear, and it could happen to anyone. It could happen to Tom.

She was almost sobbing by the time she reached home, where Aunt Lil was in the kitchen baking bread. The glorious fresh smell of it was so homely and welcoming, so *ordinary* and normal, that she could have wept anew. As Lil looked up in surprise to see her back home, Kerry wanted to hold this moment just a fraction longer, yet knew that she couldn't. Because however long she held off the telling, it could never be changed. It was a moment of growing up, a revelation, almost like a rite of passage, to realise it.

'Aunt Lil, something terrible's happened,' she choked out, just about managing to gasp out the rest of it.

Lil's arms went around Kerry at once. It was a good thing they did, because by now Kerry felt as if she could no longer hold herself up. Her moment of revelation had come and gone, leaving her more vulnerable than she had ever felt in her life.

Her legs seemed to have turned to jelly from the dash home from the shop, praying that she wouldn't meet anybody who would stop her and ask what was wrong; praying, praying, as she had never prayed before, that it was all a mistake, and the Air Ministry had got it all wrong, and it wasn't Michael Roddy's plane that had been shot down at all. And knowing all the time that officials didn't make such cruel mistakes, and that it had to be horribly true.

'You just hold yourself together now, my lamb,' she heard her aunt's voice say. 'Your friend Claire will want to know she can depend on you for support and friendship.'

'Well, of course she can,' Kerry almost sobbed. 'But what can anybody do, Aunt Lil? Whatever I say it will come out all wrong, and whatever I do, it won't change anything. Michael will still be dead.'

She shivered as another thought struck her. From Jed's garbled words it would seem that Michael's plane had been shot down over the sea, presumably the Channel, so that could only mean one thing.

'They won't even be able to have a funeral for him, will they?' she said shrilly. 'I mean, if the plane was shot down in flames and blown to bits and he's drowned in the sea, they won't ever find him, will they?'

Oh God, she wished she had never thought of such a gruesome thing, let alone put it into words. But it must be what Claire and her parents were thinking as well, and how much worse would it be for them?

Lil was speaking more firmly now. 'You can be sure that even if they can't have a proper funeral for him, the vicar will suggest a special service to commemorate Michael's life. It will be a comfort to the family and to the village to know that he's not forgotten. We always take care of our own.'

Kerry wondered if she was thinking about her own husband then, although she was one of the lucky ones, with a grave in the churchyard to visit every Sunday, even after all these years. And how bloody, bloody *awful* to think of such a visit making somebody one of the lucky ones. Aunt

Lil wouldn't approve of the way the curses crept into her head so often lately, but somehow it seemed the only words that were harsh enough in the circumstances.

She took a deep breath and extricated herself from Lil's arms where she seemed to have been clinging for ever.

'I'll go and wash my face and try to calm down,' she muttered.

'Good girl,' Lil said. 'And after tea we'll go and see Michael's family together. You're good with the little ones, and it will be good for them to see a cheerful face, so keep your pecker up, Kerry.'

She gave a wan smile as she made for the stairs, and then Lil's next words made her hand go rigid on the banister.

'You'll need to let Tom know, of course, and it will be a sad day for him. Have you told his parents yet?'

Even as Kerry heard the words she knew it was something she had been subconsciously putting off. Tom and Michael had been the greatest of friends and it would be devastating for him, in the middle of a war zone, to read the difficult letter she knew she had to write.

Her thoughts chuntered on. It was far worse than having to write or receive a Dear John letter. In a crazy way it brought it into a weird kind of perspective. Miss Montana Shirl wasn't dead. Michael was. Marvin Mcleod would get over it in time and find someone else. Michael's family never would. Michael would never marry and have a family of his own. She gripped the banister more firmly, suddenly faint and wondering how anybody ever got through it.

'I'll go and see the Trevellyans soon, I promise,' she croaked.

*   *   *

75

Tom lived a short distance away from the rambling lane where the Penfolds lived, and once Kerry had splashed cold water on her face and tried to soothe her swollen and reddened eyes, it took no more than a few minutes to walk there. As always, Tom's mother opened the door with a pleased smile on her face as soon as she saw Kerry.

'Well, this is a nice surprise in the middle of the afternoon on a weekday. But you're not unwell, are you, love?'

The sudden concern in her voice made Kerry's eyes sting anew, and she shook her head quickly as she was ushered inside the cottage. She caught hold of Mrs Trevellyan's hands and held them tight.

'Something awful's happened,' she whispered, wondering how many more times she would be repeating similar words.

Mrs Trevellyan would know nothing had happened to Tom, because, being his mother, she would get any news first. Before Kerry, who loved him with all her heart, but was only his sweetheart, not his family. The brief selfish thought was swept away as she saw the look in the older woman's eyes.

'It's not your Aunt Lil, is it, darling? I'll come at once.'

'No, it's not Aunt Lil.'

It should be, of course. It should be any one of the older generation. They should go first, not strong young men on the brink of life. It was the wrong way round. It wasn't meant to be like this. Mothers shouldn't be left without sons to care for them. The sons should care for the mothers in their old age. She tried desperately to ignore the ghastly, selfish thoughts that darted around in her head.

'Then you had better tell me what's wrong before I start

imagining it for myself,' Mrs Trevellyan said more calmly, guiding her to a chair and sitting down beside her.

They could always do that. Take the initiative. Be strong when you wanted them to be. Most of them, anyway, and most of the time. Not Mrs Roddy, right now. But she would be, in time. The older generation, who had seen it all.

'Michael Roddy's been killed.' She almost whispered the words, as if saying it quietly would have less of an impact. 'His plane was shot down over the sea and apparently there's no trace of him or his crew.'

She hadn't actually been told as much, but it was blindingly obvious by what wasn't being said. Once a plane was on fire and shot down into the sea, there wasn't likely to be much left of the crew. She heard Tom's mother give a sharp intake of breath, and then, as she moved away, oh dear God, was she the one who was going to be offered *tea* now, as if she was the bereaved one?

'From the look of you, you need a tot of brandy, Kerry, and so do I. And then you and I will decide together how we're going to break the news to Tom.'

The gratitude Kerry felt at that moment couldn't be measured in words. Someone else was taking over the task she had dreaded so much. She wasn't alone, as she had felt so alone from the moment she had heard Jed Roddy's shrieking voice. This was something Tom's mother would share with her, both of them wanting to ease the shock and pain Tom would undoubtedly feel.

'I've never tasted brandy,' she mumbled, for want of something to say.

'Then now's the time for it, my dear. We keep it in the

house for medicinal purposes – and for times like these when we all need a little propping up.'

Kerry sat perfectly still while Tom's mother bustled about, still talking, though Kerry couldn't have said what she was talking about. She must be in shock herself, having had Michael in this house so many times with Tom in their growing-up years. In such a small intimate village as Columbine where everybody knew everybody else's business, all their lives were inextricably interwoven. It was alternately an irritation and a comfort.

Even without the propping up of any brandy, Kerry's brain seemed to go from sharp to muzzy and back again without warning. Her eyes were drawn instinctively to the framed photo on the mantelpiece, one of the last photos before Tom joined up. She remembered taking it herself on her old Brownie camera. As always, Tom was laughing confidently into the camera, and his arm was loosely around his great pal, Michael Roddy, already so smart in his RAF uniform.

'I remember taking that photo,' she said inanely, as Mrs Trevellyan thrust a small glass into her hand. 'I remember Michael saying he was going to come back a hero or bust.'

She bit her lip, and Tom's mother touched her hand gently as she told her to drink the brandy quickly. She did so, wincing as the fiery, unfamiliar liquid trickled down her throat.

'He'll always be a hero,' she was told. 'They all are. So when you're feeling a little better, let's get down to it, Kerry, and see about writing that letter to Tom.'

She nodded, knowing it was going to be one of the

hardest things she ever had to do, but seeing the resolve in the other woman's eyes, it had to be done, and here in Tom's house, almost able to imagine that he would come running down the stairs at any minute, it seemed the right and proper place to do it.

Unaware of the tragedy behind her, Maud had gone over to Gillagy's Farm to suggest to Bert that they went into Falmouth to the local pictures that evening. There was no point in him coming all this way for them to sit indoors in a poky little cottage with her cousin, or alternatively to listen to the Gillagys telling their interminable stories of life on the farm. They could go for a drink afterwards as well. Lil might be disapproving of such evenings out, and of Maud having a gentleman friend at her age, but she wasn't Lil, thank God.

'How long are you planning to rusticate down here, then, old girl?' Bert said when Mrs Gillagy had finally gone to feed the chickens and left them alone in what she grandly called the 'parlour'.

'Not too long, I reckon. Why? You're not bored with it already, are you? You've only been here a coupla days!'

Bert sniffed. 'I only came to see you, Maud, but it's not my idea of living, bogged down here in the back of beyond. If I stick it out for the week, I'll be surprised, and I never took you for much of a milkmaid, either. You ain't even dressing as smartly as the way you always did in town.'

'I could hardly come tramping over here in my dancing shoes, could I?' she snapped.

Bert chuckled. 'All right, don't get on your high horse. I'm only kidding. You'll always be a smart bit of goods to me, girl, though with a shortage of men nowadays, there's plenty of fancy pieces on the loose in Bristol, war or no war.'

Maud heard warning bells in her head. 'I'd better not stop here too long, then, had I, or you'll be finding somebody else to play happy families with of a Saturday night.'

His cheeky reply to that was enough to put a healthy glow in her cheeks. Lil might be happy to stagnate down here among the hayseeds, but there was plenty of life in old Maud yet! By the time he went back to Bristol, she was confident she would soon have him by the short and curlies, so to speak.

Bert decided that they might as well go straight into town and have a bite to eat in a caff before they went to the flicks, if she fancied it. Maud did.

'I don't have to report back to Lil for my movements, so let's do it,' she said, which brought another saucy comment from Bert and sent her screaming with laughter.

Oh yes, thought Maud confidently as she linked arms with him as they struck out for the bus that would take them into Falmouth for the rest of the day. In not too many months from now, she had every intention of becoming Mrs Bert Figgins, sharing his house and his pension when the time came.

Completely ignorant of the trauma that was happening in her cousin's cottage right now, she was already planning the big day, with a nice little singalong with their friends at one of the local pubs, after as much of a slap-up do as rations would allow.

CHAPTER FIVE

Maud came home late on Monday evening, slightly the worse for wear, and knowing she'd better creep into the cottage as quietly as she could, for fear of not outraging her more strait-laced cousin. It had been a good day with Bert, she decided satisfactorily. She had been at her most girlish, and was almost sure she had nearly hooked him. Whispering goodbye to him at the cottage door with a couple of boozy kisses, she giggled like a schoolgirl as she bade him to be careful on the narrow lanes or he'd find himself walking on cowpats and other unmentionables and smelling like a shitehouse before he reached the farm.

'Don't you worry about me, old girl,' he chuckled, with a sly slap on her ample backside. 'You take care of yourself and don't upset the sainted one!'

The words made Maud giggle again as she blew him a last kiss and sent him on his blundering way. God help him if he fell into a ditch. Still, providing he managed to clamber out it might help to sober him up, she thought, with barely concealed mirth again at the comical image.

She fumbled to open the door, shushing herself at the thought of Lil snoozing peacefully in her bed. Her cousin might be a saint now, but she hadn't always been so damned prissy, but presumably having to take care of Kerry from an early age would have added to all that. She was sure that if Lil was still awake and didn't have blackout curtains up at her bedroom window, the old witch would have been glaring down at her and Bert as they wove their way home, and praying for their ungodly souls! It was a pity Lil didn't have a man in her life too, thought Maud cheerfully as she pushed aside the heavy chenille curtain that blocked out any chink of light from the front door, and went inside.

Then her heart thumped. Far from being in total darkness, the gaslight was still burning low, and Lil was sitting stiffly in her chair by the fireside – so rigidly, in fact, that for one horrible moment Maud thought she must have had a stroke or popped it. And then her cousin turned her head.

'Good God, you gave me a hell of a fright,' Maud hissed. 'What are you doing, sitting there like a statue? I thought you were dead!'

Lil's answering breath was laboured, and as she got nearer, Maud still couldn't be sure that she hadn't indeed had a stroke or something. She looked weird and grey-faced. Then she reverted to normal and snapped at Maud.

'You reek of drink. It's disgusting at your age. And why couldn't you have left a note to say you were going to be out all day and practically all night? Your meals were ruined, and it's disgraceful to have to waste good food these days.'

Maud almost reeled at such a venomous attack, which to her more tolerant way of life was completely unfounded.

'Well, I'm sorry! I didn't know this was some kind of concentration camp. What's got your knickers in such a twist, anyway? You're not jealous of me and Bert having a bit of fun, are you?' she said, lashing back.

'You say the most ludicrous things, Maud. I certainly am not jealous of you and Mr Figgins, and there are more important things going on in this world than just enjoying yourself, or have you forgotten that there's a war on?'

'Hardly, ducks. Not with all these lovely Yanks about, I haven't!'

But she said it with an uneasy snigger now. Something was wrong, and she didn't yet know what it was. She got nearer to Lil and couldn't miss the raw emotion etched on her face. Without thinking, she dropped to her knees beside Lil's chair and took her lifeless hand in hers.

'What's happened, old girl? I know something has. Oh God, you haven't had bad news about Kerry's young man, have you?'

Lil bowed her head. Now that the moment was here, she didn't want to say the words. Not to this woman, who seemed to have no concept of village life anymore, nor how they all drew together in good times and in bad. But how could she know? She had left Cornwall many years ago. She was no longer one of them and never could be again. But there was no disguising the anxious look in her eyes now, and the grip around her hand tightened as Lil finally spoke.

'You've met Kerry's friend Claire,' she said.

'Course I have. Lovely girl, and bright as a button.'

'Her brother Michael was killed when his plane was shot down over the sea. No survivors, by all accounts,' Lil said, her voice taut, and to her surprise she felt Maud's arms go around her.

'God, that's bloody rough luck.' She paused, clearly trying to think of something to say. 'Brings it all back, don't it? Nothing you can do about it, though, Lil, except to be a friend and be there when you're needed.'

She took her arms away from Lil, both of them embarrassed at such an unexpected embrace.

'Me and Kerry have been at their house all evening,' Lil went on. 'There's nothing you can say to help, but making tea and helping to put the little ones to bed while Mr Roddy sorted out the business details was something, I suppose.'

'What business details? You can't have a funeral without a body.'

It probably wasn't the best thing to say, but despite knowing that she should be sympathetic, and she truly was, Maud was desperate now to go to bed and sleep it off before she threw up and disgraced herself.

'They're going to have a special church service for Michael very soon,' Lil said more sharply, 'and now that you know why I waited up for you in case you'd had an accident or something, I'll get to my bed, and I think you should do the same.'

'All right, and I'm sorry I never let you know where I was going today,' Maud said more humbly. 'You go on up and I'll turn off the gas. I've got my little torch to find my way upstairs.'

It was a good thing they'd had the torch earlier to avoid tripping one another up and falling into the river on the way back, she thought wildly, but now wasn't the time to think about the hilarious moments when they'd clung to one another in mock terror, fearing that every cow cough was a monster coming at them out of the dark. She watched her cousin's awkward gait up the stairs, turned off the gaslight and then set about following her.

The last thing Maud thought, as she fell across her bed without bothering to take off her clothes, was that if only Lil had had a man to comfort her tonight, she wouldn't have had to sit in the near dark all alone, waiting for an errant cousin to come home. Two middle-aged women without a man between them. It made her all the more determined to see that such a thing didn't happen to her.

She awoke late the next morning, with the mother and father of a headache. Groping her way downstairs to find some aspirin, she found the house empty. There was a note from Lil on the table.

Gone to the Roddys to see what I can do. Kerry's gone to work. See to yourself and I'll be back later. Lil.

It was short and to the point. It suited Maud. She didn't fancy meeting the accusing eyes of her cousin after her entrance last night, and nor could she cope with seeing Kerry all red-eyed and upset over her friend's brother. She guessed they would have grown up together, and of course, everybody knew everybody else in a small place like this, so it must have made the girl worry even more about her own boy being somewhere in France or God knew where, Maud thought suddenly. Poor young devils, all of them.

It didn't do to waste a minute of your life, since you

never knew how long you'd got. She found a packet of aspirin and a glass of water and swallowed several of the tablets, and decided that would do for breakfast. The very thought of food made the bile rise again. Then she had a quick sloosh and got ready to go out, scribbled an answering note to Lil and left the cottage.

She needed some fresh air. Mostly she needed to see Bert so that he could jolly her up before she started to get too depressed over something that didn't really concern her, but in which she seemed somehow to have got entangled.

If she was entirely honest about her feelings, which Maud didn't often choose to be, it had shaken her a bit. She had come down to Cornwall to get away from the devastation the Blitz had left in Bristol, the bombed-out houses and streets and churches, and the loss of neighbours she had known for years. She had never expected the war to follow her down here, which was how it seemed to her now. You couldn't escape it. Which was why she was going to suggest to Bert that when he went back home, she'd be going with him, even if she had to put on the little woman act.

Kerry hadn't wanted to go to work that morning, and had hinted that she too should go to the Roddys, but Lil had told her severely that there was no point in both of them crowding in on the family. Besides, she was sure that Claire would be taking the little ones to school as usual and going to her own job.

'Life has to go on, love,' Lil said for the umpteenth time, when Kerry burst out at her angrily for being so insensitive.

'Well, I can't imagine that Claire will be at work!'

'It's the best thing for everybody, to carry on as normally as possible.'

'How can things be normal at a time like this?'

She turned away blindly. Having had a terrible night, when horrific images she didn't want kept intruding into what little sleep she had, she didn't know how anything could ever be normal again. But Lil would have seen it all before, of course, just like so many older people in the village and everywhere else in the country. The many war memorials from the Great War in towns and villages were testimony to that.

'Isn't there something else you said you had to complete this morning?' Lil was reminding her now.

Kerry nodded, biting her lip. The letter that she and Tom's mother had cobbled together yesterday with many crossings-out and tears, had still to be rewritten with her own private messages, and then posted, in the hope that Tom would receive it soon. She couldn't do it last night. She had put it aside until she felt more able to cope, knowing that she never would. She almost wished the letter would get lost in transit and that Tom would never have to receive it at all. Never have to know that one of his best friends had died so horribly. But that would be just as cruel, because of course Tom needed to know.

'I'll do it now,' she said.

Later, with the most difficult letter she had ever had to write in her hand, she walked through the village to the little post office. She was stopped every few yards by people wanting to know if it was true, and offering their own words of shock and comfort in equal measure, knowing how close she was to Claire. It was an ordeal, and if it was so bad for her, then she couldn't imagine how much worse it would be for Claire and her family.

She lifted her chin and gave what information she felt able, without betraying too many confidences. Death should be a private matter, even in such sickening circumstances as these, and not aired among an entire community, even though it was obvious they made their enquiries out of friendship and love.

But once the letter was posted, it was out of her hands. She had to pass the little lending library on the way to Polby's shop, and she saw that the door was ajar. Claire was inside, stacking a few books tidily on a shelf. For a moment it all looked so much like any other day, when Kerry would have breezed inside for a quick chat and plan what they would do that evening. She couldn't face doing that today, but then Claire turned and saw her. Her friend's eyes were still swollen in the pallor of her face, but as she lifted her hand in a small wave, Kerry had no option but to go inside.

'I didn't think you'd be here today,' she said inanely.

'Mum insisted, saying she wanted to be on her own for a while, and you know what they say – life has to go on . . . for the rest of us, anyway.'

'That's what Aunt Lil keeps saying. It's driving me nuts.'

She felt so awkward with her best friend, so helpless, and so desperate to get away from her. She had never felt like that before. It was as though they had suddenly become strangers. She didn't ever want to feel like it again, and she forced herself to get over it.

'Have the kids gone to school, then?'

'All except Jed. He was so grown-up this morning, and he insisted on going to see the vicar with Dad, to talk things over about the service for Michael. We couldn't make any real sense of what we wanted yesterday.'

'And you do now?'

'A bit. Oh, and while you were putting the kids to bed last night your Aunt Lil said she was sure the Friendship Club would want to do something, maybe to make a tapestry hassock for the church in Michael's name. She's going to suggest it to them the next time they meet. I keep forgetting what was said, and then things come back to me.'

Kerry could understand that. Her own head seemed to resemble a whirlpool. She swallowed. 'Aunt Lil always thinks of practical ways to help.'

Claire suddenly spoke more fiercely. 'I know we always thought their Friendship Club was a bit daft, Kerry, all the old codgers in the village getting their heads together over some scheme or other. But doing something practical is what Mum needs to hear right now. None of us want people wallowing over us. We can do that in private. But if people want to show that they remember Michael, well, that's good, isn't it?'

'Of course it is. Look, I have to go now. I'll see you again later.'

She felt momentarily stifled. The whole world was going crazy. The fact that the mention of creating a tapestry hassock for the church in her brother's name could put a small light of pleasure in Claire's eyes was heartbreaking and bizarre, when until yesterday he had still been so dynamic, so alive.

She walked into someone without even noticing where

she was going, and then she felt someone grip her arm as if she had been in danger of falling down. As she probably had.

'Hey, watch out, honey,' said a low voice she recognised at once. 'Me and my buddies were in the pub last night and we heard what happened to Claire's brother. Is she OK?'

She looked up into Glenn's concerned eyes, and felt a brief stab of anger that he looked so well, so bloody healthy and handsome, and hadn't had the merest taste of fighting the Jerries yet, the way Michael had. The way Tom Trevellyan was doing right now. And then her anger subsided, knowing that all that was still to come for them. And that, like Marvin Mcleod, he had undoubtedly lost some good buddies at Pearl Harbour too.

'I doubt that she'll ever be as OK as she was before,' she said.

'I called at her house and her mom told me she'd gone to work, so I'm going to see her for a few minutes.'

'I don't know if that's a good idea,' Kerry began, trying to imagine how Claire would feel, seeing him in his smart uniform. But that was crazy too. She couldn't avoid seeing servicemen in uniform for the rest of her life, could she?

Glenn pressed her hand. 'Trust me, Kerry. And by the way, Marvin's doing OK too, and he said to say hi if I saw you.'

He was gone before she could think of anything to say to that. She watched as he strode towards the library, went inside and closed the door behind him, and she hurried on to Polby's shop, still in turmoil.

By now, the news was all around the village. You couldn't keep much quiet in a small place like Columbine, and time and again Kerry was struck by the sheer compassion of the villagers. The same concern came from the GIs who were off duty, and called in for something or other and wanted to pass on their respects any way that they could.

'They're decent folk,' Mrs Polby said at last when they were closing up for dinnertime. 'They may speak in that funny way, but their hearts are in the right place. Mind you, not everybody thought so during the last lot, when they left behind a few unwanted packages, so to speak.'

'What's that supposed to mean?' Kerry said, feeling an urge to laugh for the first time in that dismal day at her arch turn of phrase. She was obviously in a talkative mood and more outspoken than usual.

'*Babbies*, Kerry. There were quite a few unexpected surprises when some of our chaps came home on leave and had to start counting back over the months, and I'm saying no more. But premature babies don't normally look like bouncing full-time ones!'

Kerry's attention was caught at once. 'Cripes, Mrs Polby. *Who?*'

The woman laughed. 'Oh, I'm saying no more, and nothing like that happened in the village, anyway. In other places where there were more good-time girls it was a different matter. But it just shows how you shouldn't let your feelings get carried away by these fast-talking charmers so far from home.'

Was that a dig at how she and Claire had been enjoying their brief chats with the Yanks? But they certainly weren't the only ones, and it would have been impolite to ignore them completely. Maybe Aunt Lil had said something about Marvin's Dear John letter at the Friendship Club,

Kerry thought suspiciously, and then dismissed the thought at once, knowing her aunt would never have been so indiscreet.

But it had taken her mind off Michael Roddy for those brief moments and given her something else to think about. She walked home for dinner feeling more thoughtful than when she had left.

'Maud's left a note to say she's gone to see Bert,' her Aunt Lil greeted her. 'After the sorry state she was in last night, I'd say she's not too keen on facing me yet today.'

Were they both avoiding the topic that was in everybody's mind?

'I saw Claire at the library,' she said abruptly. 'She doesn't look too bad, so how was Mrs Roddy?'

'As you would expect, my love, but carrying on in the only way she can. The children are a comfort, of course. While you have young children to care for, you can't let yourself break down in front of them, and young Jed seems to have grown up overnight, poor little dab.'

For a moment, Kerry realised how lonely it must have been for Lil herself when her husband was killed, having no children of their own, and nothing left of him but memories.

'I hope me and Tom have lots of children,' she said without thinking.

Lil stiffened immediately, and to Kerry her response was so predictable she could have written it herself.

'There'll be plenty of time to think about that when this war is over and you've both had the time to get to know one another again. That will be the time to think about getting engaged and married and settling down, before you harbour any ideas about having children. Everything in its proper order, Kerry.'

'Yes, ma'am,' she murmured beneath her breath, wondering what she would say if she knew they had already taken that one glorious step that should come after marriage, in Lil's rigid opinion – and in the church's opinion, and every other solid citizen's opinion too, Kerry thought guiltily.

But she didn't feel guilt about it. Nor regret. How could she, especially now? She didn't want the thought to enter her head, but remembering how Michael's life had been cut short without him ever knowing the joy of marriage and children, how could she ever regret what she and Tom had done?

At the time, she had been so thankful that the outcome hadn't been a baby, which would have been so scandalous and made her the bad girl of the village. But now, she could see so clearly how those bereaved women left behind because of the war would have clung to those babies, whether conceived in wedlock or not, if only as the lasting proof that they had been loved, and that there was still a part of their beloved left behind for them to cherish.

'Are you going to eat that dinner, or just toy with it, Kerry?' Aunt Lil said sharply, as she pushed the fried potatoes and Spam around her plate.

'I'm eating it,' she said quickly. 'And I want you to know that I love you, Aunt Lil, and I love your dinners too.'

Why she said it, she never knew. But the look of astonishment on her aunt's face had them both bursting out in awkward laughter a minute later.

'Claire tells me the Friendship Club might be making

a tapestry hassock in memory of Michael,' Kerry went on hurriedly.

'It's still to be decided, but I hope it will go ahead.'

'Well, so do I,' Kerry said, lest she should think any different. 'It's practical and long-lasting, if you can think of a suitable design.'

'I've spoken to a few of our members this morning, and we thought we might ask the Roddy children to do some drawings that we could incorporate. Jed's quite the little artist, I've heard.'

'That's a lovely idea, Aunt Lil. It will bring them into it, and I know Claire's parents would be pleased.'

She was choked by the thought, but since Michael had been far too young to die, what better than to have his younger siblings contributing in their own way to such a memorial?

That afternoon, excusing herself from the shop for a few minutes, she sped along to the library again, and was relieved to see that Claire was in a totally different mood from the morning. She didn't know whether she should mention her aunt's idea so soon, but she couldn't resist it. To her relief, Claire was immediately caught by it.

'The kids will love that,' she said. 'They're forever drawing pictures, and your aunt's right about Jed. He's got quite a talent.'

'Well, don't say anything yet,' Kerry warned her. 'Aunt Lil's hoping to get agreement from the rest of the Friendship Club tonight, and then she's going to suggest it to your parents. She doesn't want to do it too soon, for fear of upsetting them more, but obviously it will take time, so they need some idea of what the finished design will be.'

'I always knew your Aunt Lil was born to be an organiser,' Claire said with a grin.

'And what she wants, she usually gets. So what did Glenn have to say this morning?' Kerry asked, unable to resist the question a minute longer.

'He was lovely,' Claire said softly. 'He wasn't mushy about how I'd be feeling about Michael, but he made me feel so much better. I do like him, Kerry, a lot, and I'm going to ask Mum if he can come to tea one Sunday.'

Kerry's heart jolted. 'Are you *mad*? The last thing your mum will want is a chap in uniform sitting round the table right now!'

'I think it's exactly what she would want. He said she offered him a cup of tea when he called in this morning, so it didn't upset her to see him then. The kids would love it too, since they're so excited about the Yanks being here. We have to start believing that the world doesn't stop because our Michael's not here anymore,' she went on, her voice breaking as she said it. 'I think Glenn will help Mum to see that. Dad too,' she added, though with less certainty now.

'I think your dad will have a blue fit if you even suggest it.'

'Well, obviously I'm going to sound them out about it first, but whatever happens, I'm not going to stop seeing him.'

Kerry suddenly remembered the conversations she'd had with her aunt and Mrs Polby, and she had to say what was in her mind, however much it might annoy her friend.

'Claire, be careful,' she pleaded. 'You're vulnerable right now, and Glenn's a lovely person, I agree, but don't do anything you'll regret, will you?'

'You don't regret anything you ever did with Tom, do you?' Claire said, looking at her unblinkingly.

To her horror, Kerry felt her face colouring up. *She knows*, she found herself thinking. *How the hell she knows, I don't know, but she does . . .*

Claire gave a short laugh. 'Oh, Kerry, you couldn't hide a thing like that from me. I could tell straight away what you and Tom had done. You had such a glow about you at the time, and I was so envious, and desperately wanted you to tell me, but you never did. I can see why now. It was too private, too special.'

'Oh God, so you think that you and Glenn should have those private and special moments too, do you? This is wartime, and he'll be going away in a few weeks. He might never come back.' She hastily rushed on, realising the tactlessness of her words. 'What I mean is, when he does, he'll go home to America and you'll never see him again.'

'Unless I go with him. I could be a GI bride.'

'Or you could end up as an unmarried mother and have to face the shame of your parents and the village,' Kerry said bluntly.

As they heard people talking in the street and glancing towards the open door of the library, Claire turned away quickly, blinking her eyes.

'Claire, I'm sorry,' Kerry said quietly. 'We shouldn't be arguing like this when you and your family have got so much else to think about. Look, can I come round to the house tonight? I'll help with the kids again, if you like.'

'Of course you can come round. I'll see you later, then.'

What else was there to offer? She seemed to have done too much harm already, trying to crush Claire's fantasies of becoming a GI bride. But she didn't believe it was a serious hope. She hardly knew Glenn, however instant the attraction between them had been. There was something else too. Something so selfish she didn't want to think about it. But she couldn't help it. If it ever actually happened, Claire would leave Cornwall for good, and she would be losing her best friend for ever.

The hollow feeling in her stomach whenever she thought about it just wouldn't go away. Everything was changing. You couldn't ever go back to the way things used to be, and only a fool would think that you could. But things sometimes moved too quickly, taking your breath away before you could get used to the new order.

Going home for tea that night, and wondering if she was being totally mean-spirited in wishing that nothing would ever take Claire away from her, she was faced with another change, but one that wasn't altogether unpleasing.

'Well, kid, you'll be losing your lodger soon,' Aunt Maud greeted her.

'You're not moving to Gillagy's Farm as well, are you?' Kerry said without thinking, and saw a dull flush rise to her aunt's parchment-dry cheeks.

'Of course not. Whatever put such an idea into your head? Young girls these days! That's Hollywood for you, I reckon,' Maud said with false indignation. 'No, I've decided to go back to Bristol when my gentleman friend does, so we can travel back together. He says it's safer for a woman these days to have a man as protection with all these young servicemen about.'

Kerry had a job not to laugh out loud. For one thing, she couldn't imagine Maud getting accosted by any virile young chap, on a train or anywhere else. And for another, it was all too obvious that she had Mr Bert Figgins very firmly in her sights as a likely suitor.

'We'll miss you when you leave, won't we, Aunt Lil?' she said, barely able to keep a straight face.

'That we will, Miss,' Lil said, just as carefully. 'Maud certainly livens up the place, but she must do as she thinks fit.'

They were both aware that Maud was looking at them oddly now, and Kerry hurried to the kitchen to start setting the table for tea. Only then did she indulge in a barely suppressed chuckle at the thought of Aunt Maud reeling in the unsuspecting Bert Figgins like a mackerel on a hook. He never stood a chance.

Her hands paused over the tea plates. Again, for those few brief moments she had forgotten the momentous thing that had happened to her friend's brother and desolated a family. It had been possible to smile and share an unspoken joke with Aunt Lil at Aunt Maud's expense. It was true what everybody said. Life did go on, and you had no option but to go on with it.

CHAPTER SIX

A week later Maud was preparing to leave, and Bert had arrived with his small suitcase, having grandly ordered a taxi to take them to the railway station at Falmouth. It would be a rare event to see a taxi turn up in a small road in Columbine, and sure to cause some comment, Lil had told her smartly. But Maud, being Maud, had merely tossed her head, and said it was what posh people did, so why shouldn't she and Bert do the same?

But now that the last few minutes were dragging by with nothing much to say, there was an awkwardness between them all, the way it happened when people were about to part. It was a relief when Kerry turned up to say goodbye, having felt obliged to beg a few minutes away from work to do so. She prayed there would be no effusive hugs and kisses, but she was startled when her arrival gave Maud something to say that she hadn't expected.

'A letter arrived here for you this morning, Kerry. Have you got a new admirer that you've been keeping from us?' she twittered.

Kerry's heart jumped as she saw the letter on the sideboard. A letter from Tom . . . but he couldn't have received the one she and his mother had worked on so carefully yet, let alone have had the time to reply. But one look at the unstamped envelope and she knew it wasn't from him. Nor did she recognise the handwriting.

'Aren't you going to open it, Kerry?' Maud was still going on, her eyes alive at the thought of intrigue.

'Later,' Kerry said, inventing quickly. 'It's only from Pam Wyatt, one of the girls at our dancing class, so it won't be anything important.'

She avoided Aunt Lil's eyes as she said it, for why on earth would any of the girls write to her, when they only had to call at the shop or the cottage to talk to her? Especially Pam Wyatt, who had never been a close friend. Thankfully, Maud wasn't bright enough to question that, and as they all heard the sound of a taxi coming to a halt outside the cottage, she breathed a sigh of relief in the flurries of goodbyes as they waved off the visitors.

Lil cleared her throat in the small silence that followed.

'Well, I won't say I'm sorry to see the back of Maud, irritating as she always was, but the place will be a lot quieter without her, my love.'

'It certainly will. I'll help you get the front room back to normal this evening, Aunt Lil. And unless you want me to do anything else now, I'd better get back to work.'

'Not so fast, young lady. Haven't you got something else to tell me?'

100

'I don't think so.'

'Really? Then how about that little white lie for a start? Why would Pam Wyatt be writing to you?' she asked, predictably.

Kerry sighed. 'I'm sorry about that, but you know how Aunt Maud likes a bit of gossip, and it seemed the easiest way to put her off.'

'So who is the letter from?'

'I don't know!'

'Well, there's only one way to find out,' Lil said dryly.

Since there was no reason to think there was anything sinister in the letter or that she needed to open it in secret, Kerry ripped open the envelope. There was only a short note inside, but as she glanced at the signature, she felt her face go hot – and Aunt Lil was still waiting for an answer.

'It's from Marvin Mcleod, the American who got the Dear John letter I told you about,' she murmured, scanning it quickly.

Her aunt said nothing, but as if Kerry was clairvoyant, her silence said far more than if she'd been outwardly condemning. It said that since Kerry was so devoted to her young man who was away fighting for his country, she had no right to be receiving letters from someone else, especially a handsome GI who was close at hand . . .

'Read it, Aunt Lil,' she said, handing it over.

'Not if it's private.'

'It's not. Otherwise I wouldn't be asking you to read it. Go on, please.'

The words were already fastened in her brain as she watched her aunt read the brief note.

Since we'll be moving out real soon now, I want to thank you for your friendship, Kerry. It means a lot to us guys. I also want to let you know that I'm going to move heaven and earth to try to get Shirl back. I don't believe it's all over for us, and I think she's just got cold feet.

Wish me luck. Marvin.

'Not quite what you were expecting, is it, Aunt Lil?'

'It's not,' Lil said slowly. 'He sounds a very nice young man.'

'He is, and I just hope his Shirl realises it. Now I'd better go, or Mrs Polby will think I've deserted her for the day.'

She wished she hadn't used that particular word. *Deserted* sounded so final, so awful. But Marvin hadn't deserted for good. He'd gone back to his unit and now it seemed as though he'd recovered his senses. She hoped so, anyway. And she prayed that the unknown Shirl would want him back.

She went to Claire's house after work that afternoon, needing to show her the letter and get her thoughts. She was close enough to the family to know that her visit wouldn't be unwelcome. The Roddys were still immersed in grief, though not quite in the way Kerry had somehow expected.

She had been too young to experience grief when her own parents died, but she had expected a house full of hushed silence, interspersed with tears, yet the Roddy house wasn't like that. There was a sense that they all had to keep things going, not just for outward appearances, but for their combined sanity. They all bolstered one another's spirits in a way that Kerry found touching and somehow wonderful.

The parents were as stoical as the older generation always managed to be, even if Mrs Roddy's eyes were often redder than usual from her private crying. Jed was a little star, Claire told Kerry in admiration, and even though he was only ten years old, it was almost as if he had subconsciously taken on the big brother's role in the household. The younger ones didn't really appreciate the half of what was going on, and their childish laughter, and even their usual squabbles, brought a strange sense of continuity to the home.

The girls went up to Claire's bedroom to look at the letter in private.

'Well, I think it shows a lot of guts,' she said at last. 'God knows what Shirl's been up to while he's been away, but from what you've told me, he seems like a real treasure. I hope he gets her back, but I know he liked you, Kerry. It shows he did, if he felt able to write to you like this. And just think. If you didn't have Tom, and he didn't have Shirl, maybe we could both have been GI brides!'

'Yes, well, I do have Tom, and nothing's going to change that.'

'I was only kidding. I know nothing's going to change the way you two feel about each other. You're the lucky ones, Kerry. When the war's over, it'll be happy ever after for you, won't it?'

'I hope it will be for most people.'

'Well, not for our Michael.'

'Oh God, I'm sorry,' Kerry said, horrified at her thoughtlessness.

In an instant they seemed to have gone from Claire teasing her about the unlikelihood of Kerry being a GI bride, to being miserable. Claire shrugged.

'It's something we've all got to get used to. So what are you going to do about Marvin? Will you write back to him?'

'I don't think so. I hadn't even thought about it. I shouldn't imagine he wants me to. I expect he just wrote it to reassure me that he was all right. When you see Glenn you can pass on the message that I'm glad he's coping.'

Claire was smiling again. 'How do you know I'll be seeing Glenn again?'

'Call it second sight,' Kerry retorted.

She really hoped it would all turn out the way her friend clearly wanted it to. She had stars in her eyes every time she mentioned Glenn's name, and that was so often it was a sure sign that she couldn't stop thinking of him, even after the dreadful news about her brother. But maybe that was a good thing too. It just added one more aspect to the awful cliché that life went on, even if Kerry wished to God she could stop thinking that way. But if she never learnt anything else from families like Claire's, it was that it was the only way to survive.

'So the lovely Maud's finally gone back to Bristol,' Claire said next. 'I bet your Aunt Lil will miss her.'

'I suppose she will in a funny way. At least it gave her someone to disapprove of besides me.'

'You don't get the chance to do much for her to disapprove of without Tom around,' Claire said teasingly.

'Would she have anything to do so as far as you're concerned?'

As Claire turned away slightly, Kerry knew without telling that she had something on her mind. She sat up quickly.

'Oh, don't tell me you've done anything stupid, Claire. It would just about kill your mum right now.'

'I'm not telling you anything of the sort,' Claire said crossly. 'If you must know, me and Glenn have made a pact.'

'What kind of pact? Good Lord, Claire, you hardly know him, and that sounds really serious.'

Claire's face was scarlet now. 'It is serious. We've made a pact *not* to do anything stupid, as you put it. And I don't need to have known him since we were infants to know that he's the one I want. He's written to his mother about me, and he's given me his home address and asked me to write to her too.'

It was all happening so quickly it almost took Kerry's breath away, but before either of them could say more, they were interrupted by the sound of small footsteps tearing up stairs, and Molly's voice shrieking at them that tea was ready and that her mum said that Kerry could stay and have it with them.

She laughed as she caught the small girl in her arms, her feet still running, the reality of what Claire had told her still spinning in her mind.

'That would be lovely, Molly, but it will have to be another day. Aunt Lil will be all by herself, so I have to go home and keep her company.'

It was suddenly essential that she did so, Kerry thought.

Claire was right. Despite the antagonism between Lil and Maud, and the way they differed so dramatically, Lil was going to miss having her cousin around. Tomorrow it would be different, but today she needed to have someone still in the house.

All the way home, she kept thinking about what Claire had said. Making a pact with Glenn sounded so solemn and yet so sweet. It said more than words what a long way they had come in so short a time. But she was right. Love at first sight took no account of whether or not you had known one another since you were infants. It was just as intense, and just as wonderful. As the drone of aircraft returning to their home bases made her glance up at the sky, she prayed that it would all turn out the way Claire wanted it to.

She was glad she'd had the sense to go home and not linger at Claire's. There was work to be done here, and Aunt Lil was stripping the single bed that Maud had used, and getting the bedding ready for washing. Their front room already looked like a room bereft of its former occupant, and it couldn't help having a lost feeling about it.

Even as she thought it, Kerry told herself not to be so daft. As if a room had feelings! Aunt Maud would have said it was the *Cornish* in her, as if it was something quaint and peculiar, but if it was, it made her who she was, and Kerry couldn't deny it.

'It looks a bit empty now, doesn't it?' she made herself say, when Aunt Lil seemed unusually silent. Was she actually sad that Maud had gone? After all their bickering there was undoubtedly a bond between them that was more than just being cousins. Like herself and Claire, she thought. Whether they were laughing or squabbling, it made no difference to the closeness they shared.

She was trying to find the right words to say to comfort Aunt Lil without making it sound slushy, when her aunt nodded firmly.

'I've been thinking that when this bed's taken away we might see about getting a piano in here. We can pick one up at the salerooms in Falmouth cheaply enough. I used to play a bit in my youth, and you always liked tinkering about on the ivories at school and at Mrs Holliday's house, didn't you?'

Kerry was stunned for a moment, and then her aunt laughed.

'Did you think I was going to wither and die because my sparring partner's gone back to Bristol, love?'

'Is that what you call her?' Kerry almost squeaked.

'Well, only sometimes. But even if she was only here for a short time, I think we'd both be better off without her, so what do you think?'

'I'm thinking I don't know you as well as I thought I did. You never told me you could play the piano.'

'Oh, it was years ago and I'm no expert, but I could teach you a few pieces. Come the long winter evenings it would be a nice way to relax, and when Tom comes home you can show him how clever you are.'

You mean as long as you can hear me bashing away on the piano keys, we couldn't be getting up to anything else!

She hadn't said the words aloud, but the thought of it was enough to make her blush. And she couldn't imagine that Tom would care whether she was clever at piano playing or not. Just as long as she was here for him to come home to.

'Well, it's up to you if you think it's a good idea,' she told Lil without much enthusiasm. It had never been high on her list of things to do to learn to play the piano.

Lil smiled. 'Oh well, it was only an idle thought, and I can see you're not too keen, but I'm going to Falmouth tomorrow with a couple of ladies from the Friendship Club to get some materials for Michael Roddy's memorial hassock, so I may have a look around.'

'You're definitely going to make the hassock, then?' Kerry said, glad to turn Lil's mind to other things.

'Mrs Roddy is all for it, and she's going to ask the children what they would like on it. I gather young Jed is going to adapt their ideas and finish designing it. It gives them all a purpose.'

She straightened up and handed the pile of bedding to Kerry.

'I lit the boiler earlier, and it's still early evening, so we can get these sheets done tonight, and once I can get someone to take the bed away I can give the room a good spring clean.'

Keeping busy was clearly to be the order of the day, but Kerry could tell there was also something else on Lil's mind, and when they had got the sheets and pillowcase bubbling away in the boiler in the scullery she finally came out with it as they sat down with cups of tea.

'What are you going to do about the American's letter?'

'Nothing,' Kerry replied. 'I don't think he's expecting a reply, and in any case Claire is in contact with one of his friends, so I've asked her to send back a good-luck message through him.'

'I see.' The lack of comment was eloquent, and Kerry sighed.

'Claire's got her head screwed on properly, Aunt Lil, and if she and Glenn have become fond of one another, I know it will be all right.'

She had no intention of saying anything more. It was Claire's business.

'I'm going to write to Tom again tonight, though, so I think I'll take my tea upstairs. Call me when the sheets are ready to come out of the boiler.'

Hauling the hefty weight of the wet sheets through the mangle and getting soaked in the process would be the next job, but hanging them out on the washing line overnight probably wasn't a good idea. Some overdiligent spark in the Home Guard would soon warn them that they could be sending a signal to German planes, Kerry thought, letting her imagination run away with her. But since they hadn't seen many German planes for a while now, it was easy to become complacent and scoff at such ideas. Besides, they had the weight of the American army and navy crowding every field and creek for miles, and who in their right minds would want to tangle with them!

But as the month drew towards its end, it was clear that something was going to happen very soon. There were very few troops visible outside their barracks any longer, so it was generally assumed that military silence had been ordered, and that the planned invasion was not weeks away, but more likely to be days. Just as in every other town along the south coast, preparations would be getting under way to move the thousands of men, ships and landing craft from the Falmouth area, and among the civilians there was a cautious air of buoyancy that once it happened, victory would be theirs.

'There will be a terrible cost to our allies before that happens,' the more pessimistic among them said. 'You can't fight a war without casualties, and we might not have seen the last of it down here either. All this Yankee military hardware makes them sitting targets, and us along with it!'

As if they were prophetic, they were soon rewarded by a terrible reminder that the enemy hadn't done with them yet. The German intelligence people would be certain the invasion was coming soon, even if they did not know precisely when, and as a warning, the English south coastal towns and cities received a massive aerial bombardment.

Kerry was woken up around midnight on 30th May by the sound of aircraft. Everyone was well attuned now to the different engine noises, and she knew at once that they were German. The sound was quickly followed by the sickening whine of air-raid sirens, and the next minute Aunt Lil had come into her bedroom, her dressing gown tied tightly around her waist, her hair a hedgehog of metal clips and pins. She was holding a small torch.

'We'd best get up, Kerry,' she said shortly. 'If the worst comes to the worst, you must get into the cupboard under the stairs.'

'A fat lot of protection that will be,' Kerry said. 'We should have had one of those Anderson shelters like other people have got.'

Lil shook her head, while hurrying her niece into her dressing gown.

'Nasty smelly things they are, half buried under the ground, and the damp wouldn't do my arthritis much good. They're not much better than those awful underground train stations where London folk go to sleep night after night, all crammed together. It's not hygienic, and if it's our time to go, I'd rather it was in our own home.'

'I'd rather it wasn't anywhere at all,' Kerry muttered, and then she gave a scream as an enormous explosion sounded far too close for comfort, rattling the windows, and shaking some of the crockery off the dresser downstairs.

The next minute she was running down the stairs as fast as she could, with Aunt Lil coming heavily behind her. There was smashed crockery and glass all over the floor and Lil wasted no time in getting a dustpan and brush to clear it up, grumbling loudly the whole time. It was clear that she wasn't going to let any Germans disrupt her way of life for very long, and the best way to deal with it was to remain angry.

Kerry admired her fortitude, but her own heart was beating frantically fast. They had thought themselves so safe now, and that the invasion was going to solve everything. They had been too complacent, secure in their own little insulated world. She seemed to be transfixed, and her throat had dried up totally, watching while her aunt stood up awkwardly, holding her hip.

'If you want to help, Kerry, let's have some cocoa and a biscuit,' Lil snapped. 'There's no need for us to be uncivilised just because a few bombs are falling.'

She was either completely insensitive to what was happening, or ruddy marvellous, Kerry couldn't help thinking. Yes, definitely ruddy marvellous, while she herself felt near to falling apart as the deafening explosions seemed to be all around them. If it was bad here in their little country village, how much worse must it be in Falmouth itself? She went to the kitchen to put the kettle on the stove with shaking hands, and then she took a peep through the heavy blackout curtains to see if she could see anything and almost recoiled in horror.

The noise was horrendous now, hurting her eardrums and vibrating in her chest. The sky was crisscrossed with searchlights, picking out the silver gleam of the darting German planes, followed by the deafening roar of gunfire. The sky itself was no longer the dark blue of midnight, but coloured dull red from burning buildings that were already on fire.

Her thoughts flew to her friends and neighbours, to everyone she knew: Claire and her family, Mrs Holliday, the Polbys, and the men who would be out doing their best to keep the fires at bay, to salvage what they could, and to help anyone who was injured. She thought of the many American troops cocooned in their barracks, most of whom, like Tom, were desperate to get to France and rout the Hun. What of their fate now? Were they all to be bombed out of existence, making their journey, so many miles from home, a complete mockery?

A sudden hammering on the door stopped her juddering thoughts. As Aunt Lil went to answer it, she tried to make her frantic heartbeats slow down. A fine example she was being, when people might be dying . . .

Claire's father came inside the house for a moment.

'Are you two all right? If you'd rather come over to our place we could squeeze you into the shelter. The Home

Guard and ARP are mustering, so I'm off to do my bit and help where I can.'

'We're all right where we are, Mr Roddy,' Lil said firmly. 'If you come across any casualties in need of a bit of indoor shelter, you're welcome to send them along to us.'

'Righto. Keep your heads down, then.'

He was gone again, and Kerry went back to making cocoa, amazed that he could be so stalwart in face of what had so recently happened to his son. Those planes bombing this lovely corner of Cornwall now could have been the very ones who shot Michael's plane out of the sky and sent him to his death. She took a few deep breaths and finished her task, putting a plate of biscuits on a tray to go with the cocoa, and prayed that this raid wouldn't go on for much longer.

As if to mock her thoughts, the bombardment got much worse, and without warning it was as though a volcano had suddenly erupted, spewing out tons of burning lava into the sky. As their bedroom windows were blown in by the blast, Kerry and her aunt rushed out into the garden to see what was happening. The eruption was to the west of the town, inland from Gyllingvase Beach, but to anyone with intimate knowledge of the area there was no doubting the location.

'Lord help us all. It must be over at Swanvale,' Lil gasped. 'They must have hit the petrol storage tanks.'

Even as she spoke, the sound of heavy lorries became evident, coupled with the sound of fire, police and ambulance sirens. In minutes, it seemed, the street was alive with people like themselves, horrified by what had happened, and not knowing what to do next. Columbine

113

was on the east of Falmouth and Swanvale to the west, but the stream of burning oil would almost certainly get into the river close to the village of Swanvale itself.

Lil grabbed at the arm of an ARP man as he came running by.

'What's happening?' she shouted above the din.

He shouted back, not mincing his words. 'It's like a bloody holocaust over there. I reckon Swanvale will have to be evacuated until we get this thing under control, so we're having to call out the bloody Yanks to help deal with it. This is no time for military silence, and the best thing for you to do is to get inside and stay there.'

'Not likely,' Aunt Lil said to Kerry. 'Not once we're dressed, anyway. Come on, girl, there might be folk who need shelter for the night, so we'd better be ready for them. Good thing we haven't got rid of Maud's bed yet.'

She almost dragged Kerry inside, her eyes alight now with determination. The Dunkirk spirit was clearly alive and well in Lil's mind at that moment. The kettle Kerry had put on the stove earlier was boiling now, and spluttering wildly.

She turned it off while she obeyed Lil's words. There'd be time for cocoa later once they were properly dressed and Lil had rid her hair of its menagerie. It might be the middle of the night, but when things had to be done Lil would be prepared, and heaven help anybody who didn't comply.

All the same, it was highly unlikely that anyone from Swanvale would seek refuge at Columbine. There were places far closer to them, and as always the churches would open their doors until people could return to their homes.

But at least it was better to be actually doing something, and a hot strong cup of cocoa wouldn't help to settle Kerry's nerves, even if she dared lace it with too much of their precious sugar ration.

'How long do you think it will last?' she said, her voice shaking.

By now they had turned off the lights in the house, and pulled back the blackout curtains so they could watch the ferocious display in the heavens through the window or the open door.

'There must have been an enormous amount of much needed petrol in those tanks, and the Jerries have struck lucky in destroying it,' Lil said savagely. 'That fire's not going to be put out in an hour or two, that's for sure, so let's just pray there are no casualties in the process.'

They were constantly given bits of information as people came rushing back with whatever news they could. When it seemed as though the main raid on Falmouth was over and the all-clear had sounded, people came out of their shelters and attention was centred on the water and foam now trying to put out the burning oil tanks, sending whirlpools of smoke and flames high into the air.

'I hope a second attack wasn't planned, or the Jerries would have no problem in seeing us now,' Kerry said, her voice rising in panic as the hours passed and there seemed little hope of quelling the fires easily.

As dawn was beginning to send a pale sheen of pink and gold over the horizon, they saw Claire's father and several others in the Home Guard coming their way, their faces grimed and weary.

'Too many of us are getting in the way now, so we're

leaving it to the firemen and the rest of them. The Yanks have come out of hibernation too,' one of the men told them. 'They're sending a couple of bulldozers over to dam the river and divert it away from Swanvale village. It'll take the buggers the rest of the day, I reckon, and if it works, they'll deserve a medal for their efforts.'

Kerry would dearly have liked to ask if Marvin or Glenn was among them but these men would hardly have known or cared, and anyway, they had already gone to see what they could do about bomb damage in the immediate vicinity. Columbine hadn't got off completely lightly, although they hardly expected refugees to turn up for the use of the Penfolds' front room.

The air raid was long over now, and folk in the area were starting to assess the extent of the bomb damage to property. The fires from the petrol storage tanks looked as though they would burn spectacularly all through the next day, and village shops were closed as the smoke and ash drifted in all directions. Kerry had already raced to the Trevellyan house to check that Tom's parents hadn't suffered any damage, and then to Claire's. They all seemed to be fine, and the Roddy children were simply excited at watching a giant firework display.

'I'm going back home,' Kerry said, once she was assured that they were all right. 'Aunt Lil's in an odd mood. She's working like mad in case we have to take in people. I know she likes to help, but this is ridiculous. Nobody's going to want to stay at our place!'

When she returned home she discovered she was wrong as she was met by the extraordinary sight of her prim Aunt Lil hugging the distraught figure of Mrs Holliday in her arms. Above the woman's head, Lil pointed to the kitchen and mouthed the words 'strong sweet tea'.

It was the panacea for everything as far as Lil was concerned, but Kerry was glad to do as she was bid, and she fled to the kitchen, more upset than she could say to see the normally robust and buxom Mrs Holliday like this.

A few minutes later Lil followed her into the kitchen, having now managed to quieten the woman.

'Her house was hit, Kerry, and it'll take quite a bit of repairing to get it straight, so she's staying here for a day or two until she can go to her sister and brother-in-law in Newquay. It's not the loss of furniture that's upset her, not even her precious piano or the damage to the house itself. It's all the mementoes of her husband that have gone up in smoke. You can't replace those.'

Lil turned away again, and Kerry knew at once what she meant, and why she was taking all this so much to heart. Her throat unexpectedly choked. Another war had taken away most of the mementoes of Lil's own husband too. She concentrated on making the tea, recklessly putting in as much sugar as Mrs Holliday needed, and then, feeling that her presence was intrusive, she left the two older ladies to share their memories.

CHAPTER SEVEN

The next chaotic days were taken up with clean-up operations everywhere. The Penfolds arranged for the windows to be replaced in their bedrooms, thankful that at least the weather was warm enough to manage with them being boarded up for the time being. The blackout curtains had contained much of the broken glass in one area rather than spreading it around.

Once the major fire at Swanvale had come under control, the Americans retreated to their bases and remained mostly out of sight and under orders once more. But not before Glenn managed a brief call on Claire, bringing a photo of himself in uniform for her, chocolates for the kids, and a couple of tins of Spam and corned beef for her mother.

'It's not much, honey,' he said, with a huge understatement considering their meagre rations, 'but I wanted you to have the photo to remember me by.'

'As if I need it,' she said, hugging it to herself all the same. 'I'll give you a photo of me as well, but just come back safe, that's all I ask.'

'I promise,' he said gravely. 'I'll never forget this cute little place, especially now I've got someone special to come back here for.'

She could hardly bear to say goodbye to him, but she knew he couldn't stay very long. She was also dying to show the photo to Kerry, but Kerry and her Aunt Lil were now busily helping to transport as many belongings as could be salvaged from Mrs Holliday's house to their front room. It began to resemble a small warehouse, for which Mrs Holliday was apologising all the time.

'What's going to happen about the dancing troupe while you're away at your sister's, Mrs Holliday?' Kerry asked suddenly. 'The younger ones will be missing it.'

'Well, we usually have a break in the summer, as you know. It will just have to be a rather longer break than usual this year, that's all,' she replied.

She continued tut-tutting as her belongings were stacked in the Penfolds' front room. 'I never realised I had so much, but I can't leave it in my house with half a wall hanging off, and it'll all be out of your way soon, Mrs Penfold.'

'That's all right,' Lil said stoically, her plans of doing a proper spring clean abandoned for the time being. 'If we can't help a neighbour in times of trouble, we're not worth much, are we?'

All the same, she couldn't quite hide her annoyance at the dust that drifted about the room from the rescued belongings, courtesy of the bomb blast.

'So when did you say your brother-in-law will be coming

to fetch you, Mrs Holliday?' she added delicately.

Kerry felt obliged to nip to the kitchen to make yet more tea for these two whose thirst seemed never-ending. If she hadn't done so, she'd have burst out laughing at her aunt's less than tactful question, to which the other lady seemed quite immune.

The brother-in-law owned a small garage in Newquay, and Mrs Holliday had been able to telephone him there to explain what had happened, and was assured that she was welcome to come and stay in their spare room for as long as she needed. He was coming to collect her on Saturday afternoon, and the Penfold household could hopefully return to normal again.

Kerry had spent last night writing a detailed letter to Tom about all the excitement and the spectacular display from Swanvale, and then torn it up, thinking that it would probably all get censored anyway. Imagine some German official getting hold of her letter and crowing over the descriptive details she had given him . . . Although, even as she thought it, it seemed pretty ludicrous that one letter from a Cornish girl to her boyfriend would fall into the hands of the Germans and give them vital information, but you were warned never to take chances these days.

After the last painful letter she had written to him about Michael, it also seemed a bit insensitive to imply that they had almost enjoyed the display. So she had started again, merely telling him that they had been raided, and about Mrs Holliday staying with them, which didn't go down all that well with Aunt Lil, but that she hadn't heard of many local casualties, so that was a blessing.

Then, rereading the second letter, it still seemed too cold

and impersonal, so she had torn that one up as well, and spent half the night trying to say what was really in her heart, that she missed him all the time and just wanted him home. She was tempted to mention Claire and how she had apparently found true love with her GI, but she decided that wouldn't be too clever either.

For one thing, she hadn't heard back from Tom about Michael yet, and it would be far too soon after he had got that sad letter to start writing about Claire and Glenn in such a way. And there was something else. If Tom thought that her best friend had got so cosy with a GI, what was to stop him wondering whether or not Kerry had got friendly with one of them too? How much torture would that bring to somebody fighting far from home? She only had to remember how Marvin had reacted when he'd got the Dear John letter from Shirl to know how devastating such news could be. It was common knowledge that the Yanks were here, with their smart uniforms and flashy ways, and Tom would know that too, so it was far wiser to say nothing about them at all. But frustration at being hampered in everything she so wanted to say was setting her nerves on edge.

So now, here she was, making tea for the two old dears, and thinking fervently that she'd be glad when she could go back to work tomorrow.

When she took the tray into them, it was to find their visitor starting to unpick a hideous green knitted jumper that Kerry remembered seeing covering her ample shape on numerous occasions. She looked up with a smile.

'Your auntie's going to help me skein this wool and wash it to get out the kinks, and then I'm going to use it to knit some cardigans for my sister's two girls while I'm there. I haven't seen them since they were infants, and they're ten years old now. There should be just about enough wool, I daresay, though I may have to add a few stripes of another colour.'

'Wouldn't they prefer you to teach them some dance steps?' Kerry said, avoiding her aunt's eyes as she imagined the young girls' horrified looks at the garish green colour.

'Oh, I shall do that too,' Mrs Holliday declared. 'I never believe in being idle and I like to earn my keep. I told your auntie I'll help her turn out the front room before I leave on Friday.'

'There's no need for that,' said Lil firmly. 'Me and Kerry know where everything goes, and you just concentrate on getting ready for moving.'

Kerry couldn't say she was sorry when Friday came. By then, the green wool from the jumper had been completely unpicked, skeined and tied loosely so that it didn't resemble a mishmash. It was then washed, and hung out to dry, dripping, while it unkinked, before being wound into balls with her Aunt Lil's help. It was what they all did nowadays.

In the words of the government, you had to make do and mend, and the ladies of the Friendship Club had become experts at it.

Mrs Holliday's pudding-faced brother-in-law turned up in a large van to take away Mrs Holliday and all her boxes, and with him were his two equally pudding-faced daughters, excited at the chance to visit a place that had been recently bombed, and at meeting their auntie again.

Seeing the dreary dresses they were wearing, Kerry knew they'd have no problem with their prospective green cardigans . . .

After some non-stop chattering, the van was finally loaded up with all Mrs Holliday's belongings, and after the flurry of goodbyes and an assurance that the long-suffering father would drive his clamouring daughters around the area to see some bomb damage, at last the cottage was their own again.

'Well, that's a relief,' Lil said finally. 'Not that she was any trouble, and it's good to help a neighbour, but there's nothing like being in your own home with your own four walls around you, is there? It's going to be some time before her own house is put back in order again, so let's hope she and her family will get on well together.'

Kerry laughed. 'My guess is that she'll soon be organising the lot of them, and those girls don't know what's in store for them. They don't look as if they get much exercise, and Mrs Holliday will soon get them tap-dancing and making them puff!'

She was glad to see Lil smile. These past few days had been more of a strain than her aunt would have admitted. Essentially she was a very private person, and Mrs Holliday was the complete opposite. They were like chalk and cheese, Kerry told Claire after work the next day, once the village shops and businesses began to get back to normal. But Claire obviously had something else on her mind.

'I've got something to show you,' she said excitedly, and produced the photo Glenn had given her. 'It's a keepsake. Isn't he gorgeous?'

Kerry stared at it. He was so tall and handsome in his

uniform, so full of life as he smiled confidently into the camera, as if nothing in the world could ever bother him. She felt a frisson of something she couldn't quite explain, almost a sense of premonition, a dread . . . and she brushed it quickly away, knowing that Claire was waiting for her to say something.

'If I say he is, you'll probably get jealous,' she said with a forced grin.

But nothing was going to dampen Claire's high spirits. 'No, I won't. I want everybody to think he's gorgeous and be jealous of *me*.'

'All right, then. He's gorgeous. Not as much as Tom, of course, but then, nobody is as far as I'm concerned. So you're really serious about him, are you?'

'Can't you tell?' Claire said softly. 'I can't wait for this war to be over and for us to be together for ever.'

'What will your parents have to say about you being a GI bride and going off to America to live, then?' Kerry said without thinking. 'After losing Michael, they'd be losing you too.'

She could have bitten out her tongue the minute she'd said it. Claire's family was still coming to terms with losing Michael in the best way that any of them could. And if Claire had found solace in falling in love, what right did she have to question it? But as she saw her friend's face crumple, she knew she had done exactly that.

'That's a cruel thing to say, Kerry.'

'I know, and I'm sorry. But it's true, and you have to face facts, Claire.'

Why the hell was she doing this, making it worse?

'Don't you think I've thought about that?' Claire went

on passionately. 'Don't you think I think about Michael every single day, and have a cry about him in private, the way we all do? But if we don't have something good to look forward to, what's the point of it all? We might as well all be dead!'

She turned and rushed away, leaving Kerry shocked at what had just happened. She hadn't meant to be cruel, but the weird sensation she had felt on looking at Glenn's photo had affected her in a way she hadn't expected. As if she was seeing a glimpse into an empty future for Claire, instead of the joyful one she was hoping for. And what had she done? She had brought up Michael's name to spoil her moment, and ruined their friendship into the bargain. A right Job's comforter she was turning out to be.

Kerry ran home to find it empty. Of course. Aunt Lil was still at her Friendship Club. The Roddy children had made their sketches for Michael's memorial hassock, and Jed had incorporated them into a final design for the ladies to work on their tapestry. They were all coping. Better than Kerry, when it wasn't even her problem. All she could do was imagine dire happenings in her head, when even the recent German bombings hadn't been able to quench the spirit of local people, and casualties hadn't been anything like they might have been. Property could be mended. People couldn't. She shuddered, wondering what on earth was wrong with her today.

At church on Sunday the prayers were all for the town and the people in the surrounding areas, and thanks to God for his mercy. Kerry didn't dare glance across the aisle at the Roddy family, so brave in coming to church at times like these, when one of their own certainly hadn't been delivered safely. But that was what God-fearing folk did. They believed, and they continued to believe, no matter what. Sometimes, deep inside her soul, Kerry questioned it all, but it was a private questioning that she never dared to voice.

Outside in the intermittent June sunshine, Claire walked over to her.

'Sorry,' was all she said.

'Me too,' Kerry said, knowing full well that she was the one who should be sorriest. She had dampened Claire's happiness when everyone was on a knife-edge. Who knew how many of these hundreds of GIs based in Cornwall, and every English coastal resort now, would ever come back safely from the mission they were due to embark on any day?

She tucked her arm in Claire's and said she thought she and her Aunt Lil might pop round that afternoon if her mum wouldn't mind visitors.

'I think she'd like it. She prefers to be surrounded by people these days. It stops her thinking too much.'

The younger Roddy children had caught up with them by then, and Molly was jumping up and down and tugging at Kerry's arm.

'Are you coming to our house, Kerry?' she shrieked in excitement. 'Will you play tiddlywinks with me, and read to me? Dad's taking our Jed and Toby fishing for tadpoles, and I've got nobody to play with.'

Apparently big sister Claire didn't count . . .

'All right,' Kerry said with a grin. 'If I must.'

When they parted, she had the constantly renewed feeling that theirs was a good family, despite it being depleted now.

They all pulled together, no matter what. They were like the pieces of a neatly fitting jigsaw, and although she and Aunt Lil were close, there was still something missing. The presence of Aunt Maud hadn't been the answer, and certainly not the boisterous Mrs Holliday. It was the sense of being part of a complete family that she didn't have and never could have. Not until she had one of her own.

The enticing fantasy of herself and Tom, bending over a cot in which there was a tiny replica of themselves, was almost heartbreakingly sweet at that moment, and she knew perfectly well that Aunt Lil would have thought it wicked for an unmarried girl to be imagining such things. It seemed perfectly natural to Kerry, but since it was Sunday, and you were supposed to put impure thoughts out of your head on the Lord's day, she hastily tried to think of something else.

She and Aunt Lil returned to the cottage to the welcome smell of Sunday dinner cooking, their meagre piece of meat being slow-roasted to prevent it shrinking even more, and boosted by plenty of vegetables, which the government assured them was beneficial to health. Kerry told her aunt they were welcome at the Roddys' that afternoon, knowing that she had already spoken to Claire's mother about it.

'She's a brave soul,' Lil remarked as Kerry set the table. 'It's hard to face people at such a time, and even their sympathy is hard to bear. But you have to go on. I know that for a fact.'

Since she so rarely spoke of her own experience when her husband had been killed, Kerry hesitated before asking the burning question.

'I don't know how I would cope with it if anything

happened to Tom. How does anybody do it, Aunt Lil? How did *you* do it?'

Was it too personal a question to someone who had always preferred to keep her feelings to herself? But it was too late now. She had put it into words, and the answer that came took her by surprise.

'I can't tell you that, my love, any more than I can tell you why night follows day. Everybody is different, and whatever troubles occur in a person's life, large or small, they find their own ways of dealing with it. There's one sure thing I can tell you. We all have to die sometime, and there's always somebody left to be sad and to weep and to remember. And the love that goes into the remembering proves that a person didn't die in vain. That's the best that I can say, so that's enough of that. Let's not waste a moment more of the day in depressing ourselves. Let's enjoy our Sunday dinner and thank God for it.'

It was an odd bit of conversation, Kerry reflected, and she had neatly skirted around her own feelings. But the reminder that everybody had to die sometime was an uncomfortable one. When you were young, you thought you were immortal and you expected to live for ever. It was always a rude awakening to discover that it wasn't so. She tried to put such dismal thoughts out of her mind and concentrated on helping her aunt dish up their dinner.

Even though the fires from Swanvale had long been put out now, the faint whiff of smoke still lingered in the air. But Molly Roddy was nothing if not persistent, so later that afternoon Kerry found herself sitting beside the child on one of their garden swings with one of Molly's school readers. It didn't look as though it was going to stay fine and warm for very long, and there were scudding clouds in the sky now. Claire had gone inside the house to fetch them some lemonade, while her mother and Aunt Lil were having a heart-to-heart.

But after a while, Molly's attention was waning, and she was more interested in a lone bee buzzing around a rose bush than listening to Kerry. She let the book close, and shut her eyes for a moment.

'Kerry, where's heaven?' she heard Molly say next. 'Our Jed says that Michael's gone to heaven and that God's taken him up to live with the angels, but if he was drownded in the sea, how did he get there?'

Kerry's heart jolted. Oh God, this wasn't a question for her. This was for Molly's mother to answer, or the vicar, or the Sunday school teacher – or *anybody* who was more qualified that her. But one look at the child's large trusting brown eyes, and she knew she had to think of something quickly.

'Well, darling, he was able to get there because God helped him. God can do anything, can't he? You learn that at Sunday school, don't you?'

'Yes, but where is it?' she went on. 'Jed says it's up in the sky but I can't see it. Do you think Michael likes it there, away from us?'

Her small, round face was suddenly anxious, needing answers that nobody could give, and Kerry knew she had to go carefully.

'Do you remember how Michael was always happy? He was always teasing you, wasn't he, and making you laugh?'

Molly nodded, her gaze still unwavering.

'Well, I reckon God needed somebody like Michael up there in heaven. I bet he's making the angels laugh now, so they're the lucky ones,' Kerry elaborated desperately. 'And just because you can't see heaven, that doesn't mean that it's not there. You couldn't see the seeds you planted in the spring, but they're growing into little plants now, aren't they?'

It was the best she could do, and she hoped it was enough. To her great relief, Molly's attention was quickly diverted.

'They're carrots, and I'm going to dig them up soon and Mum's going to cook them for us to eat,' she said importantly.

'That's good, so let's have some lemonade now, shall we?' Kerry said, mightily relieved to see Claire coming outside with a tray.

When they were alone, she told her what had happened, and how she had dealt with it. Claire nodded.

'She asked me about it too, but you had a better answer than I did. I guess I was too close to the reality of it all. It's hard for a five-year-old, but not so hard as for those who can picture it all too horribly.' She shivered. 'Anyway, let's go inside now the sun's gone in. It looks as if we might be in for a change in the weather if your Aunt Lil's to be believed. She says her joints are playing up and that's a sure sign of rain.'

'And she's never wrong,' Kerry said dryly, having heard it a thousand times. 'So if the GIs are confined to barracks now, Glenn never did come to Sunday tea after all, did he?'

'No, he didn't, so we've got that to look forward to some other time. Mum would have liked it, but you were right about Dad. It's too soon after Michael to be sort of entertaining. I don't count you and your Aunt Lil, of course. You're not proper visitors, are you?'

Kerry laughed. 'I'll take that as a compliment, shall I?'

'Of course! What else?'

'Have you heard back from Tom yet, about Michael, I mean?' Claire asked in a more subdued voice.

Kerry shook her head. She knew what she meant all right.

'It's too soon. I'm still sending him letters, but it's difficult to know what to say now. I can't be miserable all the time, since I'm supposed to keep up his morale, but I can't tell him everything's fine here either, can I?'

'You must have told him about the raid, though!'

'Oh yes, of course I did, and about Mrs Holliday moving in, and her ghastly green jumper that she unpicked. That'll make him smile.' She looked vacantly into the distance. 'It all seems so futile, though, doesn't it? Well, not that exactly. Just so *homely* and small-villagey, when he's somewhere in France, having to deal with God knows what.'

'Don't you think that's just what he'd want to read about? Homely and small-villagey things, I mean. Something to make him smile and forget for a few minutes what's going on all around him. It's what we've been told to do, isn't it? I'm going to write to Glenn as soon as he's on the move, and I shall fill my letters with homely things because I know he's missing them. They won't be American things, but I daresay every small town and village is much the same anywhere.'

'Sometimes, that noddle-head of yours can be quite bright, can't it?' Kerry said with a grin. 'So have you written to his mother yet?'

'Not yet. I don't know what the hell I can say to her!'

'You could tell her about the quaint little Cornish village we live in, and about Mrs Holliday's dancing troupe and her ghastly green jumper,' she said, poker-faced.

And then they were both giggling, and even if it was laced with a few tears, it was such a warm, refreshing sound in the middle of what had been a few terrible weeks, for the entire area and for this family in particular.

A sudden gust of wind accompanied by a sharp rain squall sent them scurrying indoors, to where Aunt Lil was still talking quietly to Mrs Roddy.

'It's raining,' Claire said unnecessarily, as if she wanted to break up the intense moments. 'Dad and the boys won't be out catching tadpoles much longer if it gets any worse.'

'They promised to bring some home for me,' Molly screeched.

'And I'm sure they will, my love,' her mother soothed her.

'I'm keeping them in a jar in my bedroom,' Molly told Kerry importantly.

'And just wait for the screaming to start when they turn into frogs and leap all over her,' Claire said in an aside.

'Well, I think we'd better get on home, Kerry,' Aunt Lil said, before Molly got wind of what Claire was saying. 'It's easing off a bit now, but we don't want to get soaked. Thank goodness Mr Coombes managed to get our windows replaced before the change in the weather.'

They said their goodbyes and hurried back to the

cottage, and though it was only drizzling intermittently now, the sky had really darkened and it looked as if the promise of a glorious early June was fading fast.

'It's so good to see them all pulling together and doing normal things, even though their hearts must be breaking,' Lil observed as they went inside. 'It's what keeps everybody sane in the bad times.'

'Claire said something of the same. I know you sometimes think she's scatterbrained, but it's why I write to Tom every day as well, to bring him a breath of home. She's promised to write to Glenn when he goes away too.'

She held her breath, wondering if she had said the wrong thing, knowing that Lil didn't hold with too much fraternising with the Americans. What she would say if she knew Claire was already dreaming of becoming a GI bride, Kerry didn't dare think.

To her relief, her aunt nodded thoughtfully.

'I think you're both growing up, my dear. Unfortunately, in times of war, young people have to grow up far too soon, but we can't change it and we have to make the best of it. All those poor boys need reminders of home, though I'm not sure the Americans think of Cornwall as home,' she added, Aunt Lil-wise.

It depended on whether or not you had a Cornish girl to come home to, thought Kerry, but she was also wise enough not to say so.

All next day the bad weather settled in, at least until evening, when it began to ease a bit. The air of expectancy that something big was in the offing that had hovered over everybody for so long now was fast fizzling out. The one thing they could hope for was that the Germans were

134

experiencing bad weather too, and wouldn't be inclined to make any bombing raids.

Soon after midnight Kerry woke with a jolt to the deafening sounds of heavy machinery, rumbling through the night. For a moment she lay there, unable to think what it was, and then she leapt out of bed and rushed to the window, pulling the blackout curtains back and staring out in shock. It didn't need the forbidden street lighting to gauge what was going on.

Their little village streets weren't made for the massive numbers of military vehicles making their way through them now as the ground and every building shook with the impact. With her heart beating rapidly, Kerry stood there transfixed, and within minutes Aunt Lil had opened her bedroom door and was standing beside her.

'So it's begun,' she said softly.

'The invasion?' Kerry said, even though she had already guessed.

'I see no other reason for so many of them to be on the move. They'll soon be on their way to France, and by tomorrow morning there'll be none of them left here, so let's pray to God to keep them all safe.'

'It will be really strange without them after all this time,' Kerry murmured.

Her thoughts flew to Claire, who must also be well aware of what was happening. Was she even now rushing out in the street, trying to catch a glimpse of Glenn . . . ? But not even Claire would be so foolish, and nor would her parents allow it. She gave a sudden shiver.

'We'll get no more sleep tonight until all the vehicles have passed, and probably not then,' Lil said briskly. 'Put

135

on your dressing gown and we'll go down and make a hot drink, and as soon as there's any news on the wireless, providing the accumulator keeps going, we'll be ready to hear it. And we'll say a prayer together for their safe deliverance.'

'And their safe return,' Kerry added.

CHAPTER EIGHT

Even if the night seemed interminably long, it was a sure bet that few people had gone back to their beds after the disturbance. There weren't normally any wireless transmissions during the night and early morning hours, but as Lil and Kerry Penfold dozed fitfully in armchairs, they switched their wireless on from time to time, hoping to catch the earliest announcement of the day they had all been waiting for. Even after numerous cups of cocoa and some biscuits to fortify themselves throughout their vigil, they were becoming chilled, and almost before it was properly light, they went back upstairs to get dressed before having an early breakfast. The weather improved and the air was calmer now, and the tension was becoming too unbearable for Kerry to stay indoors any longer.

'Aunt Lil, I'm going out to see if anybody's about,' she

said. 'Don't worry about me, and I'll report back if there's any news.'

Though what news could there be? It didn't need a clairvoyant to tell them that the Americans had moved out with their huge numbers of military and amphibious vehicles. Kerry guessed that the crowded harbour at Falmouth would have been stripped hours ago of the mass of vessels awaiting the embarkation. Now there was nothing but a great sense of anticipation, of breath holding, until they knew for sure what had happened.

Aunt Lil was prepared to stay sitting close to the wireless, eager to catch the first words of the day, but Kerry was too impatient to wait for an anonymous announcer to tell them the outcome of the most daring military operation in the war since Dunkirk.

And if it was the success they all hoped it would be ... then maybe it would signal the end at last, and Tom would be coming home. She prayed for all the men involved in this day, but however selfish it was, what Kerry wanted most of all was for Tom to come back home, safe and well, and for their lives to begin all over again. Sometimes she could imagine his voice in her head, telling her jokes, laughing with her, telling her he loved her, the timbre of it changing whenever the mood between them became intense ... and at other times she found it hard to imagine his voice at all, and those times really frightened her. She dreaded to think of it as some kind of an omen, but she was Cornish, so how could she think it was anything else?

She hardly knew where she was going that morning, but she was soon aware that she was far from being the only person outside so early in the day. In fact, as she left the cottage, she realised that the streets were full of people, all offering opinions on what could be happening now. There were men in Home Guard and ARP uniforms, trying to sound officious and knowledgeable with what little information they had, which wasn't much, if any, and women huddled together anxiously. The older ones among them were clearly remembering another war, and other perilous times.

Even small children raced about excitedly, not understanding what it was all about, but caught by the moment and the air of expectation everywhere.

Kerry caught sight of a familiar figure and ran towards her.

'Have you been up all night like we have?' she asked Claire.

'Yes, but the kids would have woken us up anyway. Molly was frightened by all the noise and wet the bed, so Mum and I had to change the bedclothes and get the washing on. Toby usually sleeps like a log, but not this time. Mum wouldn't let either of them go out yet, so she's stayed indoors to make sure they stay put, but Jed and Dad are somewhere in the crowd.'

She was shivering as she spoke, but Kerry guessed it wasn't only with the early morning chill, but rather with fear for Glenn.

'Shall we cycle over to Falmouth?' Kerry suggested.

'What for?' Claire said densely.

'I don't know. To find out if people there know anything. To see if there are still any ships in the harbour. To talk to people. I don't *know*!'

'I suppose it's better than doing nothing,' Claire

muttered. 'You go and get your bike and tell your Aunt Lil, and I'll tell Mum. It's nearly daylight now, anyway, so there's got to be some news soon.'

Predictably, Aunt Lil was against the idea.

'You never know who's out and about at this hour, Kerry.'

'What, like strange American soldiers?' she said sarcastically. 'I doubt if there are any more of them around now.'

'There's no need to be rude, my dear.'

'I'm sorry, but I just need to be doing something, and Claire's coming with me, so we'll report back later if we hear any news.'

She didn't wait to hear anything more, threw on a jacket and got her bike out of the shed, then raced around to Claire's house to find her already waiting.

'Did your mum object when you told her what we were doing?' she asked her as they began cycling towards the town.

'She's too busy with calming the kids down, and trying to keep them indoors, and she knows I'm old enough to look after myself.'

'I wish Aunt Lil thought the same about me. Sometimes I think she'd keep me wrapped up in cotton wool if she could,' Kerry complained.

'It's only because she loves you. She doesn't have to spread her love around the way Mum does, so you get the best and the worst of it.'

'Is that what your mum does? Spreads her love around?' Kerry said, for want of something to say as they cycled on.

'Well, it's a good thing if she does, because it gives her something to think about instead of brooding over Michael all the time,' she said, her voice brittle.

It was an odd thing to say, but Kerry supposed it made sense. It gave her a sudden shudder, all the same. Being part of a family was what gave you strength at such times, as she had thought many times before in these past weeks. If it happened to a family where there was only one son, it would be so much harder to bear, simply for the brutal fact that you had to spread your love around in a family. There were always others who needed it. It wasn't the way it would be if anything happened to someone like Tom, for instance . . .

She suddenly wobbled on her bike, nearly crashing into Claire as the hateful thought screamed through her head.

'What the hell are you doing?' Claire yelled.

'Sorry. My mind was miles away.'

'Well, keep your mind on the job before you have us both off,' Claire snapped back.

Kerry bit back any stinging retort. Claire was going to be edgy from now on, if not downright bitchy, until she got news that Glenn was safe. Didn't she know that this was how it had been for Kerry for months now? She was resentful at the thought, but it wasn't worth getting into a stew about because they were nearing the town now, and just like Columbine, there were hordes of people outside their houses, many of them around the harbour area, like themselves. As Kerry had surmised, the many ships that had been crowded there were gone, and there was a palpable air of excitement everywhere.

'It was a miracle the Jerries never bombed them out of

the water all this time,' Claire commented. 'Let's hope they weren't on to them during the night. That would have been too cruel.'

'Well, that's what enemies are, isn't it? Cruel, I mean. We're doing the same to them, aren't we?'

'Tell that to my brother! Oh, I forgot, you *can't*, can you!'

There were too many people about now for them to get into a blistering argument, or even to ride safely, so they got off their bikes and walked the rest of the way in frigid silence to the water's edge, breathing in the fresh, salty, morning air. Not really knowing what to do or to say to each other now, they simply stood and gazed up at the stark ancient walls of Pendennis Castle, the sentinel on the hill high above the town. The heightened buzz of conversation and speculation was all around them, and then they heard a voice they knew.

Pam Wyatt had obviously recovered enough from her broken leg to hobble towards them.

'How did you get here? You can't ride your bike yet, can you?' Kerry said without thinking.

'My dad brought me in his van. Do you think this is really it, then? The end of the war, I mean.'

'Doubt it,' Claire said with a shrug.

Pam looked at her. 'I heard about your brother. Sorry, Claire.'

Claire merely nodded. What reply was there? You couldn't say it was all right, because it wasn't. You couldn't say thanks, as if the other girl had done her a favour, and since there had never been any love lost between her and Pam Wyatt, she chose to say nothing.

Pam turned her attention on Kerry. 'Heard from Tom Trevellyan lately, Kerry? Or have you stopped writing to him now you've found a Yank?'

Kerry felt her heart stop for a moment at the spiteful note in Pam's voice.

'I don't know what the hell you're talking about, but I certainly haven't "found a Yank", as you put it,' she said furiously.

'Well, that's not what my gran heard at their daft Friendship Club. They hear all sorts of gossip there, and your Aunt Lil was the one who mentioned it. Or it may have been the other one.'

'She couldn't have!' Kerry snapped.

'Well, it was something about him getting a Dear John letter and you being all sympathetic and consoling him. You want to watch that sort of thing. That's how they take advantage of soppy girls like you.'

Before Kerry could rage at her again, the girl had turned around and was hobbling back as fast as she could the other way. Encumbered by their bikes and the crush of people all around them, neither she nor Claire could see her when she disappeared into the crowd.

'Take no ruddy notice of her, Kerry. She's just being her usual bitchy self,' Claire said, seeing Kerry's stricken face. 'She always had a bit of a fancy for Tom as well, not that it would ever have done her any good,' she added, making things worse.

'But did you hear what she said?' Kerry almost screeched, all else forgotten. 'I can't believe Aunt Lil was so indiscreet as to say anything about Marvin's Dear John letter at her Friendship Club, nor that I was consoling him.'

'I doubt that she said it to more than one person, and then it would have been in confidence. Pam Wyatt's gran was eavesdropping, that's the only way she could have got hold of it – and probably half a story at that. Forget it, Kerry.'

It was asking the impossible, of course, and they both knew it.

'What did she mean – "or it may have been the other one"?'

They said the same words together. *'Aunt Maud!'*

But where did she get it from?

'I'm going to have words with Aunt Lil when I get back home,' Kerry said furiously.

'Go easy on her, Kerry,' Claire said uneasily. 'Like you said, you didn't think she'd have been indiscreet, so don't go blaming her.'

'She must have said something to Aunt Maud, though, unless she just worked it out for herself.'

'She probably did. She could have heard gossip from anywhere. You know how people talk in a small village. Even kids can come out with stuff. Our Toby and Molly are so excited about Glenn and me, and have already been bragging about it at school.'

Kerry slid off her bike, forcing Claire to do the same.

'They wouldn't have said anything about me, would they? I mean, there's nothing to tell, is there?'

She felt chilled. Kids were so imaginative, and they had all been so thrilled at the GIs being here with their chewing gum and candies. The Yanks were especially fond of kids, and always stopped to chat to them and tell them stories of the magical land that was America, until they had become practically part of village life.

But she couldn't blame Pam Wyatt's spitefulness on a chance remark passed on and elaborated by a child. Could she?

'You're not going to blame our kids, I hope,' Claire snapped defensively, reading her thoughts. 'I bet your flashy Aunt Maud would have had a go at the Yanks herself if her precious Bert Figgins hadn't turned up.'

'She's not a tart!'

'Well, you could have fooled me,' Claire snapped again, and rode off furiously ahead of her.

Kerry got on her bike, angry and upset at the way the day was turning out, and it wasn't even time for everyday business to begin yet. This should have been such a good day, a marvellous, uplifting day, and suddenly it had all gone sour, and all because of something that catty bitch Pam Wyatt had said. Her eyes stung, hating the thought of her love for Tom being sullied like this. She had never had eyes for Marvin Mcleod, not in that way, anyway, and to think that things had been said about her behind her back was like a slap in the face.

What if the Trevellyans had heard the rumours, she thought suddenly, a cold shiver running through her again? What would they think of her, with Tom so far away and in whatever kind of danger he might be in? She could have wept with the injustice of it all.

She caught up with Claire and passed her without a word. What else was there to say? Right now they had reached a place of no return, and it would take a good while before feathers were unruffled enough for making up.

She wanted to go straight home and confront Aunt Lil,

but as she reached the village, shops were already opening, and she could see Mrs Polby outside hers, chatting to several neighbours. As she caught sight of Kerry, she waved her over, and Kerry had no option but to do as she was bid.

'We've got the wireless on,' the woman said excitedly. 'Polby's fiddling with it to get the best reception. Did you hear the announcement at eight o'clock that paratroopers had landed in France? We're waiting to hear more news now.'

'I didn't know about that. I've been to Falmouth to see what was happening there,' Kerry said woodenly. 'We've been up most of the night, and I couldn't stay indoors any longer.'

'Well, let's get inside, then, and we'll have a cup of tea and a bit of toast if you're hungry,' she said generously. 'Your auntie will know you've gone straight to work, I'm sure, unless you want to pop home and tell her.'

'No thanks,' Kerry said, her voice suddenly clipped.

From wanting to confront Aunt Lil, now she wanted to stave off the moment. In any case, she didn't want to repeat Pam Wyatt's poisonous words. As long as they remained unsaid, they didn't exist. It was a futile thought, but it was the only one in her head right now.

'You're looking a bit peaky, Kerry,' Mrs Polby went on as they went inside the shop. 'Start setting out some things on the counter and I'll fetch us that tea. Too much fresh air so early in the day isn't good for a body.'

She fussed about like a mother hen, and in the corner of the shop her husband was still fiddling about with the wireless, like so many other people were doing, Kerry suspected. Like Aunt Lil would be doing now. It was time for people to be together, to welcome the news they all expected, and to rejoice in it.

Aunt Lil would be all alone . . . but not for long, Kerry thought stubbornly. As soon as there was anything to know, she would be out of doors, chewing over any announcement with their neighbours, and Kerry would hardly be missed at all. And even if she didn't believe that for a minute, she wasn't in the mood to admit it.

At precisely 9.32 a.m. the steady resonant voice of the news announcer John Snagge came over the airwaves.

'This is the BBC Home Service, and here is a special bulletin read by John Snagge. D-Day has come. Early this morning the Allies began the assault on the north-western face of Hitler's European fortress. The first official news came just after half past nine, when Supreme Headquarters of the Allied Expeditionary Force issued Communiqué Number One. This said: "Under the command of General Eisenhower, Allied naval forces, supported by strong air forces, began landing Allied armies this morning on the northern coast of France".'

Whatever else he might have said was lost in a great roar of cheers from the Polbys and the people who had gathered inside the shop, who all seemed to be congratulating one another as if they had taken part in the successful mission themselves. It was like Christmas and New Year's Eve all rolled into one.

'Go home, Kerry,' she heard Mrs Polby shout in her ear. 'Your Aunt Lil will want to celebrate with you. We can manage for an hour or so.'

'All right. Thank you.'

What else could she say? And how right she was. It was a time for hugging friends and family and loved ones. It was a time of hope, that the long years of war could finally be coming to an end. Even though anybody with any sense knew that this was only the beginning, it was no time for being sensible.

She bumped straight into three of the Roddy children, the youngest ones hopping up and down like yo-yos, especially Molly.

'Why aren't you at school?' she said automatically.

'Our mum said we could stay home today, 'cos we didn't sleep much last night,' Molly screeched.

'That's not what I heard,' Kerry said dryly. 'So where are you going now?'

'Mum said she was glad to get us out from under her feet for a while, so we're going over to your cottage,' Jed said. 'We have to show your auntie the final design for Michael's hassock, 'cos the ladies want to get started on it soon.'

Kerry's heart gave a sick jolt. How could she have forgotten, for a single minute, that there wouldn't be the same kind of rejoicing in the Roddy house as there was everywhere else? For them, today's momentous announcement would only underline the fact that Michael Roddy would never be coming home.

She caught hold of Molly's small hand and hoisted her up on the saddle of her bike to give her a lift to the cottage. She was glad they were here. It would soften the awkward moment when she would face her aunt again, still not knowing what to say to her about Pam Wyatt's nasty little remarks, and in the end, deciding to say nothing.

'Let's see the design, then,' she said to Jed.

He unrolled the large piece of paper, and Kerry stared at it, her eyes smarting anew. It was true that Jed was turning into a fine little artist, and she hardly heard the excited screams of the younger two about their part in it.

There was a plane, as expected, zooming upwards towards the sun, and down below was the sea. She was glad Jed had had the foresight not to have the plane plunging downwards. The simple inscription that said 'Michael's hassock' was at the foot of the design. But it was the other part that caught her attention most, and made her eyes smart even more.

On the left of the design was a rose bush, and prominent on it was a bee. It was exactly the way it had been that day in the garden when she had caught Molly studying it so intently.

'I drew the bee,' she shrieked importantly now. 'Our Michael loved bees. He told me a story once about how you could tell the bees anything, and it would stay a secret for ever, so this is Michael's special bee.'

Kerry's heart jolted even more now, and a shiver ran through her. How weird. How creepy. Did this child study that bee in the garden and see something nobody else could see? Some said that the innocence of children could see things that were beyond the imagination of adults. Did she see *Michael* . . . ?

'I need a wee,' Molly shrieked next.

'We'd better hurry up and get to my house before I get a wet saddle on my bike, then,' Kerry said, thankfully pushing all thoughts of supernatural events out of her mind as Toby smothered a giggle.

They arrived as a small party, and Kerry quickly ushered Molly to the lavatory, while Jed unrolled his precious design for Aunt Lil to see, leaving Toby, who had no imagination at all, shouting out that he'd done the sun.

When they returned, with Molly having managed not to disgrace herself, there was lemonade and biscuits all round, and Aunt Lil was looking so cheerful at having the children over that whatever else was said this day, Kerry knew she was never going to divulge what Pam Wyatt had told her. It was probably all lies, anyway.

'You've heard the news, I take it?' she asked Kerry.

'We had the wireless on in the shop. It's wonderful, isn't it?'

'Wonderful, and dangerous. Nothing about war is pleasant, and let's pray to God that it doesn't result in too much carnage.'

'What's carnage?' Molly said at once.

'It means people being blown up and killed,' Jed put in before anyone could think of a way to soften it.

'What, like our Michael?'

'Nothing like that, my love,' Aunt Lil said hastily, clearly wishing she had said nothing. Little ears were too sharp for comfort, and they were all having to grow up far too soon. 'Now then, is that right that you've been growing vegetables in your garden, Molly?'

It was easy to divert her attention elsewhere, and she told Lil about her carrots and how her dad said she should stop pulling them up every five minutes to see what was growing under the soil, which made Toby hoot.

Half an hour later Claire turned up to collect her family, announcing that the library was closed for the day, since nobody seemed to want to borrow any books while more exciting news was going on, but she seemed to be brimming with something more than excitement.

'I've got something to show you,' she said directly to Kerry. Her tone told her it was something to be shown in private, so Kerry said they should go up to her bedroom. Clearly, the ruffles had been smoothed, and there were important matters to be discussed.

They sat on Kerry's bed, and Claire opened the neck of her dress to reveal a small gold cross and chain.

'Where did that come from?' Kerry exclaimed. 'It's not your birthday, is it?' she added, knowing very well that it wasn't.

Claire was almost overcome with emotion now.

'You know when Glenn came round to our house and left a few things for us, including his photo for me? Well, he gave this to Mum and said she had to give it to me once we knew that the Allies had landed in France and not before. She gave it to me when I got back from Falmouth and we heard the first news. It's to be our good-luck charm, Glenn said in a note, to ensure that he comes back safe.'

She suddenly burst into tears, and Kerry's arms were around her. It was the sweetest thing she had ever heard, and she could imagine so well how Claire was feeling. Hadn't she felt the same kind of worry and dread every day since Tom had gone away?

'Of course he'll come back,' she said unsteadily. 'He's got you to come back to now, hasn't he?'

'We thought that about Michael,' Claire choked.

Kerry didn't know how to answer that. All she could do was hold her mutely for a minute and then let her go in embarrassment as Molly's footsteps came thundering up the stairs.

'I want to go home now,' she yelled. 'Our mum said I can help her make some jelly for tea 'cos it's a special day, but I don't know why.'

'Come on, then,' Claire said breezily, recovering quickly, before she asked anything more. 'I'll race you.'

They were so lucky, Kerry thought, as she had thought a thousand times, to have each other.

It was a strange day. Nobody seemed able to settle to anything. Kerry went back to the shop, only to be told to take the rest of the day off, as nobody wanted to buy anything, just to chat and mull over what might be happening across the Channel, and be together, and the Polbys could manage that very well by themselves.

On the wireless there were brief items throughout the day by war correspondents, giving personal impressions and reports, and then at last the official nine o'clock news gave everybody the words they were waiting to hear.

'Here is the news, read by Joseph Macleod.'

Kerry's heartbeat quickened for a moment at hearing the name Macleod, but then she listened intently with Aunt Lil for what the announcer had to say.

'All still goes well on the coast of Normandy. Mr Churchill, in a second statement to the Commons this evening, reported that in some places we've driven several miles into France. Fighting is going on in the town of Caen between the Cherbourg Peninsula and Le Havre. Six hundred and forty guns of the Allied navies bombarded the German coast defences in support of our troops. Our

great airborne landings – the biggest in history – have been carried out with very little loss. About four thousand ships with thousands of smaller craft crossed the Channel this morning after the Allied assault had been postponed twenty-four hours through bad weather. On the beaches opposition was less than expected but heavy fighting still lies ahead. All through the night and today air support has been on a vast scale. Thirty-one thousand Allied airmen have been over France during today alone.

'The bulletin will end with the latest war report, including the voices of General Eisenhower, General Montgomery and General de Gaulle. It has also messages and recordings from correspondents in the field.'

Aunt Lil switched off the wireless to save the precious battery.

'I think we've heard enough for now, and God bless them all,' she said solemnly. 'I know we should be rejoicing, but the sheer scale of the operation shows how perilous it must have been for all those brave servicemen, risking their lives every minute.'

Kerry knew she had gone into serious mood now, and they would be praying together before very long. And suddenly, she couldn't bear it. After being up all night, and the various excitements of the day, she was now fit to drop. Lil must have been too, unless her stamina was more than Kerry's.

'I'm going to bed, Aunt Lil,' she said in a strangled voice. 'I'll see you in the morning.'

'Goodnight, dear,' Lil said absently, and Kerry knew that in spirit she was no longer with her, but in some other place with her memories.

Well, Kerry had memories too, and all she wanted to do was to be on her own and think of Tom. Where was he now, while all this fighting was going on? Was he somewhere in the middle of it, or far removed in some other part of that ravaged occupied country? She felt the sobs rising in her throat, knowing all too well that while she ached and prayed for all those thousands of Allies storming the Normandy coast now, she desperately yearned for news of Tom. And more than that. She wanted him home. She wanted him near, to hold and to love. She wanted to sleep and to dream of him, the way things used to be . . .

But, contrary to her wishes, she couldn't sleep. She had curled up in a ball in her bed, willing the elusive sleep to come, but her mind was now too active, too much in turmoil. In the end she got out of bed, put on her bedside light and fished out her old school atlas, studying it to find the Normandy beaches where the Allies had stormed so successfully. It had been a day of triumph, but only a fool could imagine that it wasn't also a day of death for so many. It could be hundreds. It could be thousands. Men killing each other, and for what?

There were many beaches along that coast. In happier days they must have been favourite holiday areas, where French families could relax with their children and be carefree in the sun. What were those beaches like now, running with blood . . . ?

God, how she wished her imagination would set her free right now!

There were French towns and villages, whose names had been heard on the news at various times because of intensive fighting. Was Tom somewhere in one of those? The not knowing was unbearable. Not even knowing if he was alive or dead . . . it was almost better to *know* than to live in this half knowledge, waiting for letters that sometimes came and sometimes didn't! Then the horror of what she was thinking made the sobs rise again, threatening to choke her, and she threw the atlas on the floor and buried her head beneath the bedclothes.

CHAPTER NINE

Nobody could live in a state of high tension for ever. Gradually the village of Columbine, and the rest of the country, settled down to normality – or at least, the new kind of normality that existed nowadays. The news from France continued to be positive, although the diehard older generation warned that much of the worst of it would be kept from public knowledge. Even so, every newspaper screamed with first-hand accounts of what was happening, as well as the official reporting, and some of the accounts made gruesome reading. If these were censored for public sensibilities, then what kind of hell must it really be like?

Kerry finally received the long-awaited letter from Tom. She knew now that her letter had followed him around as he had moved recently, but now he knew the sad news about Michael. As expected, it was a sombre letter, and much of it was necessarily about Michael and the shock of hearing about his old friend. It had been written before the Allies' invasion of the French coast, but after a guarded reference to that, it ended with the words she longed to hear.

'We're all expecting great things here very soon, sweetheart. You'll know what I mean, and I can't say anything more, except that we're all anxious to play our part in it. Then, maybe at last, this damn war will come to an end, and you and I can be together again. Till then, I send you my dearest love, as always.'

And as always, she had shed more than a few tears, holding the letter close to her heart, and wishing desperately that it was Tom himself that she was holding near. Did his guarded words imply that he was somewhere near the Normandy coast now where all the activity had gone on? And if so, didn't that put him in even more mortal danger than ever before?

Claire had had a letter too. Not from Glenn, which was hardly reasonable yet, but from his mother. She showed it to Kerry in a fever of excitement.

'I've still been dithering about what to write to her, and she's saved me the trouble, since Glenn had already given her my address and told her about me. She sounds so nice, Kerry, and she's sent me some photos of where they live, and the family. He must have told her a lot about me, don't you think? The kids are over the moon to think we've had a letter from America.'

She went pink as she said it, and it was clear that she was over the moon too, and obviously seeing the unknown Mrs Davison as a future mother-in-law. And she was so thrilled that Kerry didn't have the heart to dampen her spirits. At least it was something positive in that sad family.

'Let's see the photos, then,' she said instead.

Claire handed them over. The house was a large wooden structure with a sort of balcony, over which a family of four was leaning over the fence. They were presumably Glenn's parents, a photo of himself taken a while ago, and a small sister. There seemed to be a lot of trees surrounding the property.

'The sister's called Gloria. Sounds just like a film star, doesn't it?' Claire went on, already starry-eyed at the thought.

'Do they live out in the wilds?' Kerry asked.

Claire laughed. 'No. It's in Connecticut where they have lots of trees, and Mrs Davison says it's glorious in the fall – that's what they call the autumn in case you don't know! I've looked it up on the map. I'll show you, if you like.'

It was a bit different from Kerry's study of the atlas, trying to fathom out where Tom might be in relation to the D-Day landings, but she didn't comment about that, seeing that Claire was so happy. All she needed now was confirmation that Glenn was safe. And didn't she know that feeling herself!

Claire got the news she wanted a couple of weeks later, but relieved though she was, her face was guarded when she told Kerry.

'I don't think their letters are censored the way yours are from Tom,' she said. 'Glenn says that when they landed, after half of them being seasick on the rough seas, it was the worst hell they'd ever been through. The beaches were booby-trapped with landmines and . . .' she couldn't continue for a minute, her voice choked '. . . and almost as soon as Chuck stepped ashore – you remember him – he stepped on a mine, and that was that.'

She was clearly thinking that it could have been Glenn being blown to bits, and not his close buddy.

'What about Marvin?' Kerry heard herself say.

Claire didn't look at her, but kept her eyes on the letter in her hand.

'He says you couldn't see anything much for dust and grit and sand and you couldn't hear anything for the noise of shells and gunfire and mines blowing up all around them. It must have been horrific.'

'And Marvin?' Kerry persisted.

Claire looked up at last, her voice hoarse.

'There's been no news of Marvin at all since the day they landed. He hasn't shown up at his unit, and nobody's seen or heard of him. I'm sorry, Kerry, but he's had to be reported as missing, presumed dead.'

Kerry gasped. And yet, in the midst of the shock of hearing the words, she felt a burning anger. How *dare* they presume he was dead? He could be anywhere in that hellhole of a beach landing, trying to find his way back to his buddies. How *dare* they write him off like that, as if he had never existed? She didn't realise how much she was shaking until she felt Claire grabbing her arms.

'It's all right, Claire. I'm going home. I'm glad to know about Glenn.'

She twisted away from her, wanting to go home, to be alone, to curl up and think about those few hours she had spent with Marvin Mcleod, and his joy and pride in showing her the photo of his girl, his Shirl, the previous

Miss Montana. She thought about how he'd gone AWOL after his Dear John letter and then returned to his unit, stronger than before, and determined to try to win her back. And for what? To die in the muck of a foreign beach?

She was sobbing by the time she got home and into her bedroom, unwilling to acknowledge in her mind that her sorrow for Marvin was so mixed up with her fear for Tom. Somehow, as long as Marvin had been safe, so would Tom be. It was an irrational, illogical, crazy fear, but so was everything else about this bloody awful war. They all had such hopes about these D-Day landings, but people were dying for it, and that was the reality of it.

Lil Penfold came home from her Friendship Club that afternoon, having had a very satisfying meeting about organising the tapestry work for Michael Roddy's hassock. It had to be done as speedily as possible, now that the design had been stencilled and colour-coded on to the coarse material, with the work being passed from one to another, to save eyesight and fingers. As one of the Roddys' oldest friends, hers would be the first and last stitches, and she felt a quiet pride in that.

She became aware of a noise from upstairs, and assumed that Kerry had come home. Eager to show her the stencilled material, she went stiffly up to her bedroom and found her niece lying on top of her bed, curled up in a heap, her eyes swollen with tears.

'My dear girl, what's happened? You haven't had bad news of Tom, have you?' she exclaimed, although common sense should have told her the opposite, since Mrs Trevellyan had been at the Friendship Club that afternoon. But this was no time for common sense to be at the forefront of her mind.

Kerry shook her head. Her voice was thick with tears. 'It's not Tom. It's Marvin. I know I shouldn't take on like this, but I can't help it. It makes it all so real. And I know he was going to try to win Shirl back, and it's just so cruel.'

'What exactly has happened?' Lil said quietly, putting down the tapestry and sitting on the bed beside her. It wasn't hard to guess, but it was important to put such things into words. It was a hard lesson to learn, but she had learnt it herself from past experience.

'Missing, presumed dead,' Kerry said brutally. 'What else is there to say?'

'What it says is that he's *missing, presumed dead*, my love. It doesn't say he *is* dead. There's always hope. And no, you *shouldn't* take on so. It's not as if you even knew him very well. Did you?'

There was the tiniest hint of suspicion in her voice. After that encounter with Pam Wyatt in Falmouth, it was enough to make Kerry jerk upright.

'No, I didn't, but I'm grieving for him the way I would grieve for any friend, and no more than that. It's my Tom that I'm fearful for, and something in my head keeps tying them together.'

'Now you listen to me, Kerry,' Lil said, her voice harder. 'War is evil and it's obvious that many people are going to be killed. But many more of them will come home safely, and Tom has always been a lucky young man, hasn't he? Didn't his mother used to say he had the luck of the devil, with some of the scrapes he used to get into as a child, always knocking himself about and falling off his bike, and even falling into the river once or twice?'

'I suppose so,' Kerry said with a weak smile.

'You *know* so, so get off that bed and wash your face and go and make me a cup of tea. I'm parched after all that talking at the Friendship Club today.'

And right now, it seemed tactful not to start working on Michael's hassock tonight, until Kerry had come to terms with what had happened.

Less than two weeks after D-Day the Germans unleashed their most terrifying secret weapon, the pilotless jet-propelled aircraft carrying nearly a ton of high explosives. It was directed at the vulnerable south-east of England, and particularly London. Locals were already calling it the 'buzz bomb' because of its distinctive noise. The hell of it was that when it was ready to drop, all the engine noise stopped, and within seconds it had exploded over its target.

'The more derogatory name for it is the "doodlebug", as if giving it a comic name renders it less deadly,' Aunt Lil remarked, after reading out the first accounts in the newspaper.

But, dreadful though it was, it was more important to Kerry that she had had another letter from Tom, which had done much to relieve her mind after the shock of hearing about Marvin and Glenn's friend Chuck. Tom was now on the move yet again, so she wasn't to worry if she didn't hear for a week or two.

Or three . . . or four . . . Like everyone else, she lived for letters, and the fact that they seemed so sparse only made the waiting harder to bear. Even Claire had got one or two more from Glenn now, while she ached for more news of Tom.

Then, at the end of July, as if to lighten the gloom, came a long letter from Aunt Maud, written in so much more than her usual bubbling effervescent style that it made Lil laugh out loud.

'What does she say now?' Kerry said, unable to resist a smile at her aunt's obvious amusement.

'You'd better read it for yourself!'

She handed it over to Kerry, who grinned at the large, almost childish handwriting before she even began the letter.

'*Dear Lil and Kerry,*' she read aloud.

'*By the time you read this, I shall be Mrs Bert Figgins! Yes, the old boy has decided to make an honest woman of me at last, ha ha ha. Well, what with so much going on, and never knowing if we was going to last out the war or not, and with them awful doodlebugs dropping everywhere now, we decided to get wed before we was past it altogether, so we did the dirty deed a week ago. It was at the registry office, of course, both of us having been spliced before, but it was none the less legal, for all that.*'

Kerry paused for breath as she read on, her mouth in a permanent smile now, unable to avoid hearing Maud's cheery voice coming through the pages.

'*We had a grand old knees-up at the local after we'd tied the knot, with all the reg'lars there joining in the larks and the sing-song. If old Hitler had decided to drop any of his rockets that night, we'd never have heard 'em anyway! It's a pity you two couldn't have got here to celebrate with us, but we knew there was no point in asking you, being so far away, and it was all decided in a bit of a rush. Not that there was any hanky-panky going on, mind; well, there was plenty of hanky-panky, but no tiny footsteps as a result, not at my age, ha ha ha!*

'*I daresay I'm shocking Kerry now, but it's time you knew what's what, ducky, if you don't know already from your young man, and then having all them lovely GIs down your way. I bet all the local girls are missing them now that they've gone to fight the Jerries. But better late than never, like they were in the last lot, as we always say. And they were lovely boys too.*

'*Anyway, my dears, I'll love you and leave you, as they say, and think about getting my husband's tea. That's a turn-up, ain't it, after all these years without a man (ahem, in a manner of speaking!).*

'*From your cousin,*

'*Maud, alias Mrs Bert Figgins!!*'

Kerry was laughing out loud by the time she finished reading the letter, even though the arch comment about the local girls missing the GIs was a bit below the belt. But that was Maud, the new Mrs Bert Figgins, as wicked and as irrepressible as ever.

'She's very proud of her new status as a married lady, isn't she?' she giggled, though 'lady' wasn't the best word she'd have ascribed to Maud.

'And just as keen to get her hands on his pension in due course, I daresay,' Lil said tartly.

'Oh, that's not really fair, is it, Aunt Lil? I thought they seemed well matched when they were here.'

She had a vision of the small Bert Figgins with his smarmy Brylcreemed hair, and the brash overblown Aunt Maud, and wondered if she was smothering him to death in the bedroom by now . . . but since Aunt Lil would be thinking no such thing, she willed the unwelcome image out of her mind.

Lil sniffed. 'Oh, they were well matched all right, and well deserving of each other, I'd say. Still, I'd better write back sometime and give them my best.'

For one wild moment, Kerry wondered if Lil actually envied her cousin, having got herself a man after all these years of widowhood. But Lil had still been a young woman when her husband died, so she must have had her chances. It was more likely that she hadn't ever wanted anyone else.

'What do you think?' Kerry burst out the next time she saw Claire. They were sitting on the riverbank, so peaceful and silent now that the various craft that had been anchored there had gone. She went on in a fever of excitement, and not a little amazement.

'Aunt Maud and that slimy Bert Figgins have got married!'

'Crikey, there's hope for everybody, then,' Claire exclaimed. She giggled. 'I wonder what old fogies like them do on their honeymoon, if they had one.'

'Same as anybody else, I suppose.'

'And you'd know about that, wouldn't you?'

Kerry felt her face go red. She knew it was only teasing, but she didn't want to hear it.

'I hardly think what me and Tom did – which you don't really *know*, anyway – can be compared with Maud and Bert. And I don't want to think about them in that way, thanks very much!'

Claire giggled again. 'Why not? It's normal, isn't it? I can't imagine your frisky Aunt Maud getting married without knowing he could do the business.'

'I daresay,' Kerry said, as cool as you like. And then she giggled too.

'Oh, I'm sure you're right. I bet she had a right old time of it when the Yanks were here in the last war as well.'

'Well, everybody does it in wartime, don't they? With or without the Yanks. Or so they say.'

'*I* didn't.' She looked at her friend sharply. 'Is there something you want to tell me, Claire?'

It was Claire's turn to go red. 'Nothing to tell. I didn't get the chance, did I? That's not to say I wouldn't have, if Glenn hadn't had to go off to fight the Jerries. I *wanted* to, and I know he wanted to as well. It scared me to think just how much I *did* want to, as if something was taking over my life that I couldn't control. And that's all I'm going to say about it.'

'Do you think you're abnormal to want to make love with the one you love?' Kerry said. 'That *is* what we're talking about, isn't it?'

Claire kept her face averted, looking out across the still water, crystal clear and as blue as the sky now.

'Yes, that's what we're talking about. I never really

understood these girls who gave in to their blokes when they gave them that old chestnut that they might never come back again, but I can understand it now. You both need something special to remember each other by.'

'And a lot of girls got more than they bargained for,' Kerry said, her voice crisp. 'You wouldn't have wanted that, would you?'

'Of course not. But I wanted *him*!'

'I know. And I want Tom, but we can't do anything about it, can we? And when did this talk about dear frisky Aunt Maud become so serious?'

'I'd rather it wasn't serious! Let's imagine her in her flannelette nightie instead, and Bert in his striped winceyette pyjamas!'

'Better than imagining them in their birthday suits!'

The thought of which convulsed the pair of them.

Lil was working on the hassock when Kerry returned home, thankfully looking considerably brighter than on the day Claire had brought her the news about the American. Lil had worried for her niece then. It didn't need a clairvoyant to know that in Kerry's mind the fates of Marvin Mcleod and Michael Roddy and Tom Trevellyan were somehow bound up together. And there was that other one too, the friend of Claire's young man, Chuck someone or other. But Glenn was safe, and so was Tom.

'Claire and I have just had a hilarious chat about Aunt Maud and her new husband,' Kerry announced before she could stop herself.

'Oh yes. And what was all that about?'

Too late, Kerry knew she had to say something.

'Well, only to hope they had a good life together, and all that crackpot stuff,' she said awkwardly.

Lil put down the tapestry for a moment. 'For someone with a good vocabulary, Kerry, I always know that you're embarrassed about something when you resort to slang.'

'I didn't think that *stuff* was slang,' she muttered.

'It depends what you mean by it. If you and Claire were speculating whether Maud and Bert would have the same kind of marriage as lusty young whippersnappers, then I have no doubt about it.'

Who was using slang now! *Whippersnappers* indeed!

'We wouldn't be so rude, and I'm sure I don't know what you mean,' Kerry muttered, knowing that she certainly did, but desperate not to follow any more of this conversation before it got too personal for comfort.

'How's Michael's hassock coming along?' she said, changing the subject.

Lil spread it out. 'As you see. I'm doing the rose and the bee that young Molly drew so lovingly.'

Kerry's eyes blurred for a moment. 'Do you believe in the afterlife, and signs, Aunt Lil?'

She should have known it was a pointless question.

'You know the answer to that, but in what way, my love?'

There was no help for it now. She had to repeat that strange moment in the garden when Molly had been watching the bee so intently, and her words since, saying that Michael had told her stories about how you could tell the bees anything, and it would remain a secret for ever. And then she had drawn this bee in her childish fashion, calling it Michael's bee.

'I think there are more things in heaven and earth than we're privileged to know, Kerry,' Lil said. 'The tale of telling secrets to the bees is part of folklore. But if we see hidden meanings in things, that's our good fortune, and perhaps little children, untouched by life's miseries, are more privileged than most.'

'Well, Molly might be only five years old, but she was certainly touched by Michael's death, so she was hardly untouched by life's miseries, was she?' Kerry said more brutally.

'But if she found something to comfort her, that still makes her one of the lucky ones. Now, if you don't mind, I have to get on with this.'

'All right,' Kerry said, when she knew she was getting nothing more out of her. 'I think I'll go and write to Tom and tell him about Aunt Maud's description of her wedding. It'll give him something to smile about, anyway.'

She fled upstairs, disturbed over something she couldn't quite explain. She forced her thoughts back to Aunt Maud's letter and began to form the words in her mind as to how she would relate it all to Tom. She didn't want to appear too flippant, knowing he would still be grieving over Michael, but life did go on . . . and there hadn't been much to be cheerful about lately.

In the end, it was easy.

'You never met Aunt Maud, Tom, but I told you before that she was absolutely nothing like Aunt Lil. Far less refined, and that's putting it kindly! I didn't really think she'd marry her greasy Bert with a head so shiny with Brylcreem you could skate on

170

it, but that's just what she's done. She was very keen on him, though, so they must see something in each other. After the wedding, she said they had a right old knees-up in a pub, with a sing-song and a lot of leery jokes to go with it by the sound of it. She also said it was a pity we couldn't be there, but both me and Aunt Lil were pretty relieved about that!'

She always tried to write to him as if he was sitting right next to her and she was talking to him. She wanted him to hear her voice through her letters, the way she tried to hear his. Letters gave her comfort, whether writing them or receiving them, and right now, it was the only thing they had.

Her thoughts wandered. All this talk of weddings, however much she and Claire had scoffed and sniggered over Maud and Bert, had made her think about her own. *One day . . .* It wouldn't be a quick affair in a register office, as Maud had said. It would be in their own lovely little village church, and Claire would be her chief bridesmaid, with little Molly her flower girl. She wouldn't want anybody else. She felt a sudden pang, remembering that there was no one to give her away. Maybe she could ask Mr Polby, she knew he'd be honoured . . . but such matters were trivial, compared to the fact that it would be herself in a long white bridal gown, and that Tom, her dearest darling Tom, would be waiting for her at the altar where they would repeat the solemn vows that would bind them to each other for as long as they lived.

Her heart gave an uneasy jolt. *For as long as they lived* had such an ominous ring to it nowadays. The age-old wedding vows held such beautiful and emotional phrases in the sweet ordinary days that used to be, and *for as long as they lived* had held no fears in the days before war took Tom away from her.

She finished her letter quickly before her spirits plummeted again.

'Come home soon, my darling. And come home safe.'

She couldn't write any more without expressing all the fears that were normally hidden deep inside her. What if he didn't come home safe? What if he came home broken and wounded? What if he never came home . . . ?

She put the letter into an envelope and wrote his name and number and the field address on it. It always seemed so impersonal. Who knew how long these letters moved around from place to place, finding the right recipients? Wherever he was now, she prayed he would get this one soon, knowing her words about Aunt Maud would make him smile. It was a real relief to have something cheerful to write about, and she blessed Aunt Maud for giving her that chance.

She dreamt about her own wedding that night. She and Tom had promised one another so many years ago that one day they would be married. It was a promise that had never wavered. Childhood sweethearts did sometimes make their dreams come true.

The wedding dream wasn't one that came often, and Kerry always woke up half smiling at the wonder of it all, only to feel the dampness of tears on her face at the realisation that it had only been a dream after all. But it had been so vivid . . . so real . . .

In the dream she was wearing a floaty white dress that Aunt Lil had made for her, having been willingly given extra clothing coupons from the ladies at the Friendship Club to buy enough material for it. She wore Aunt Lil's own veil, and because it was springtime in her dream, she had worn fresh flowers in her hair, echoing the small posy that she carried. Not for her the extravagance of shop-bought flowers or a large trailing bouquet like the ones you saw in Hollywood pictures. All she and Tom wanted was a simple ceremony with families, friends and neighbours around them to wish them well.

The best man would have been Michael Roddy, of course, but in the dream there was no hint of sadness that he wasn't there, because this was a happy day, a glorious day. And young Jed Roddy, suddenly taller and more serious than usual, had performed the duty on his brother's behalf so splendidly.

It was all so happy, so dreamlike . . . well, it was a dream, after all, and it was always when Tom slipped the gold wedding ring on her finger that she woke up. Always before she had the chance to exchange her own vows with him. And that was when the tears came, on awakening. Because the wedding had never really happened, and perhaps it was a sign that it never would.

Claire was feeling exuberant now, and her mood undoubtedly helped to ease the gloom of the family. She couldn't remain in a constant state of sadness when she was now hearing from Glenn as often as he could manage to write, and his letters became ever more serious about a future for them together. She had finally hinted as much to her mother, and had the expected warnings that she hadn't known him long enough, and that she was far too young to think about marriage, and all the things that mothers said, she told Kerry.

'But I think she also recognises the fact that we really do love each other, and nothing's going to change that,' Claire said softly.

'Even if it means you'll be a GI bride and leave home?'

'Wouldn't you go anywhere in the world with Tom, if it meant you'd be together for always?'

'Of course I would.'

'Well then. And she approved of Glenn's mother writing to me too.'

She was in such a good mood that Kerry wouldn't dare say anything to change it. But the thought of Claire leaving Cornwall and going three thousand miles away to live in America was almost as bad as sending men away to war. Well, not exactly, she amended, but the result was the same.

'Anyway, we've got to sort out the Jerries first, haven't we?' Claire went on cheerfully. 'And it looks as if it won't be so long now.'

Ever the optimist, thought Kerry . . .

But her mood was starting to rub off on Kerry too, and if Claire could look forward to a possible future so positively, then so could she. Things had certainly settled down in the south-west of the country, even if the south-east was still getting their share of those terrible doodlebugs. According to the newspapers, the wireless reports and the Pathé newsreels the Germans were getting desperate now, being pushed back on all fronts, and by the end of August Paris had at last been liberated to great rejoicing and the feeling that the end was near at last.

Mr Polby was always expansive and hugely patriotic

174

about what 'our boys' were doing, helped by the Yanks and the Canadians and all the other Allies, he always added generously. It was clear in his mind that they were only the support group, despite the glowing praise that all the Allies received.

'He'll never believe that it's not just our Tommies who are doing all the fighting and winning the war,' Mrs Polby chuckled in an aside to Kerry one bright Monday morning when he was holding court as usual.

But she indulged him as always as he continued to expand all morning on the bravery of the British troops to everyone who came into the shop.

'Go and make us all a cup of tea, Kerry, there's a love,' Mrs Polby said when she could stand it no more. 'Perhaps he'll give it a rest when he's got something else to occupy his mouth.'

Smiling in agreement, Kerry went through the bead curtain into the back of the shop to what they grandly called the kitchenette, not too sorry to escape Polby's ramblings. She was still waiting for the kettle to boil on the small gas ring when Mrs Polby put her head around the curtain that divided the area from the shop.

'Kerry love, leave that for a minute,' she said oddly. 'There's somebody here to see you.'

She was about to go back to the shop, half amused at the woman's mysteriousness. And then her heart seemed to leap into her throat as Mrs Polby stood aside, and she saw who was coming through the bead curtain to the comparative seclusion of the kitchenette.

'Kerry, I've got some news,' Tom Trevellyan's mother said in a strangled voice, her arms automatically reaching out for her.

CHAPTER TEN

It was just as well Mrs Trevellyan's hands were gripping her, otherwise she was sure she would have passed out right there and then.

'What's happened?' she managed to croak. 'It's Tom, isn't it?'

But of course it had to be Tom. Why else would his mother be standing there, her face white and strained, forcing herself to say the words she never wanted to say, and which Kerry never wanted to hear?

'He's been wounded.'

She probably said a bit more, but there was such a roaring in Kerry's ears, it was all she took in at that moment. Wounded, not dead. *Wounded* . . . which could mean anything at all . . . but it was not the ultimate, thank God. He was alive . . . *Thank you, God, thank you, thank you, thank you . . .*

Then she realised that Mrs Trevellyan was shaking her, and she just about managed to hold herself together and to stop her legs from buckling beneath her. What kind of a simpleton was she being now, when everything was so much better than it might have been?

'Take her upstairs, dear,' she heard Mrs Polby say next. 'You can talk more privately there.'

She didn't want to go upstairs into the Polbys' old-fashioned sitting room with its antimacassars and the clutter of knick-knacks and Polby's piles of dusty old magazines and newspapers that she remembered from previous times. But she had no option as Tom's mother held her firmly beneath her elbow, and eventually she flopped down in one of the Polbys' chintz-covered armchairs. Seconds later Mrs Polby was bringing two cups of hot sweet tea for them.

'Extra sugar for shock, and Polby's gone for Mrs Penfold,' Kerry heard her whisper to the other woman before she left them alone.

She wasn't ill, and she didn't want tea. More alert now, she didn't want anything, only to know how bad it really was. How seriously wounded Tom was. She had to keep saying it to herself, to make herself believe it. She forced herself to drink a few sips of tea, hardly noticing how it scalded her tongue. Then she clutched Mrs Trevellyan's cold hand.

'Tell me the truth. How bad is he?'

'We had a telegram to say he's had several deep shrapnel wounds. This was followed almost at once by another telegram to say there's damage to his shoulder and leg, and possibly more bits of shrapnel for them to find. He's in a field hospital while they do the best they can to remove it all, but then he'll be sent home for further treatment.'

'He's coming *home*?'

Kerry hardly heard the rest. It was as if her brain would only let her pick out the bits of the information she most wanted to hear. She found herself smiling, and then laughing inanely. When she had first seen Mrs Trevellyan's face she had imagined the worst, and it was not the worst after all. It was far from the worst. Tom was coming *home*!

'Kerry, you do understand, don't you?' his mother went on anxiously. 'Tom's been seriously wounded, and we don't know how it will affect him yet, nor how long it will take for him to recover. I don't expect my boy will ever be the same as when he went away.'

Kerry stared at her as the words finally sank in. She saw the shine of tears in the woman's eyes, tears that she was trying so hard to hold back. But *her boy*? He was Kerry's boy, and always would be . . . Ever since she was five years old, Molly Roddy's age, she had adored the tall boy with the shock of unruly hair and the twinkly eyes who was two years older. She had even told him solemnly she was going to marry him one day, to which he had roared with laughter, but said that he couldn't think of any reason why not.

He had always been hers, and even as a child her Cornish intuition had told her she only had to wait until she grew up for Tom to know it too. But right now she smothered the selfish thought that he was only hers, and put her arms around Tom's mother. The roles had subtly reversed, and for the moment she knew she had to be the strong one for her.

'We'll cope, no matter what,' she said unsteadily. 'He'll always be our Tom, won't he?'

If that was being generous, she didn't register it. All she knew was that he was coming home. She didn't have a nurse's training to know what shrapnel wounds meant or entailed. She wasn't old enough to be conscripted, and in any case, she was sure she couldn't do the things that doctors and nurses had to do. It didn't make her a bad person, just a squeamish one. If it came to caring for Tom, though, she would do it and do it willingly. Girls a year older than herself could volunteer for such jobs, but she couldn't, she just couldn't deal with strangers in such a way, and she refused to be overcome with guilt because of it.

In the midst of Claire's delirium over Glenn's letters, she had mentioned that Pam Wyatt had already applied to be a nursing orderly, being a year older than the two of them, having finally abandoned her idea of being a land girl.

'I suppose she thinks that working in a hospital will be less messy than dealing with cows and pigs. I can't see her as a Florence Nightingale, and she'll have a shock coming when she has to empty their smelly bedpans!' Claire had said, almost gleeful at the thought of the prissy Pam Wyatt dealing with incontinent patients.

As the unwelcome thoughts were spinning around in her head, Kerry was aware of a severe shudder of nerves running through her. However noble and brave she might feel at the thought of caring for Tom, no matter what his injuries proved to be, it might be very different when the time came. But she would face that when it happened, and not before.

She heard familiar heavy footsteps on the Polbys' stairs,

and her eyes watered uncontrollably when her Aunt Lil came into the room. But she wouldn't weep, not now. Not when Mrs Trevellyan needed her to be strong. She would keep her weeping until she was alone in her room.

'Well, this is a right old carry-on, isn't it?' she heard Aunt Lil say.

It was strange how the tritest words came out at such times, just as if the world hadn't come crashing down on someone's hopes and dreams.

But the initial shock had lessened now, and Tom's mother was telling Lil more calmly what details she knew, and Lil was nodding and murmuring sympathetically and keeping a weather eye on Kerry at the same time, as she very well knew. Older women like these two seemed to have their own special ways of communicating with each other in times of trouble.

'At least he'll be coming home,' Kerry managed to say in an effort to sound positive. 'That's good news, isn't it?'

'Of course it is, my dear,' Lil said. 'And I'm sure the village will put out the welcome mat for him when that day comes.'

Better than a memorial hassock, Kerry couldn't help thinking. She turned her face away from Mrs Trevellyan, wondering if a similar thought had entered her mind. If it hadn't yet, it surely would. The memorial hassock was finally finished, beautiful and fresh in all its vibrant colours, and the service in Michael's memory was due to be arranged very soon. Inconsequential thoughts still kept flitting in and out of Kerry's head, keeping at bay for minuscule moments the fact that her darling Tom had been wounded.

After a discreet amount of time, Mrs Polby appeared in

181

her own sitting room to ask if there was anything else the trio of ladies required.

'No, thank you, Mrs Polby,' Tom's mother said with a great effort. 'I'm grateful for your hospitality but I should be getting home now. Mr Trevellyan has gone to see the doctor to see if he has any idea about what will happen to Tom next, so I'm anxious to see him.'

'And Kerry and I will come with you,' Aunt Lil said resolutely.

'Don't come back to work today, Kerry,' her employer said, though it was doubtful whether Kerry even heard her, or cared.

There were sympathetic glances towards them all the way back to Tom's house. The village grapevine had worked swiftly, Kerry thought, without rancour. So much the better. It saved painful explanations. She hadn't seen anything of Claire, though. Perhaps library customers hadn't conveyed the news to her yet. Her thoughts were still coming in staccato bursts, and she tried to pull herself together. She had been briefly elated at the thought that Tom was coming home, despite his injuries.

But after all the anxiety of recent weeks, of hearing about Michael, sharing Claire's relief about Glenn, then learning about Chuck, and Marvin . . . now she felt as if the world was crashing down on her again. And if she could fall apart so easily, how much worse must it have been for Claire and her family when they got the news about Michael?

Tom's dad was already in the house, an older, greyer version of Tom, with the same twinkly eyes, except that they were anything but twinkly now. His wife went to him at once, and he put his arms around her and held her tight for a private moment, leaving Kerry and Lil momentarily shut out.

'Sit down, all of you,' he said. 'I've seen Doctor Graham, and found out what little he could tell me. Not knowing the extent of Tom's injuries, he can't possibly say anything for certain, of course. But what he suspects is more or less what we've been told. They will have tried to extract as much of the shrapnel as possible before sending him by hospital ship to England. He'll most likely have to stay a few days in a hospital close by after landing, probably at Dover, and when he's well enough to travel, they should transfer him to a Cornish military-based hospital, hopefully near Truro.'

'Near enough for us to see him,' breathed Tom's mother.

Kerry found her hands were clenched tightly together. Mrs Trevellyan sounded suddenly relieved, as if the doctor's reassuring words had put everything right. But it wasn't all right, and what did Doctor Graham really know? It all sounded so hazardous. Even though she knew this must be happening for thousands of wounded men, this was none of those nameless soldiers. This was Tom, her Tom, and she couldn't bear it.

'I think I'll go home now,' she said unsteadily. The only way she could get any contact with Tom was to write to him, and she wanted to do so as quickly as possible, even though there was no knowing if he would ever get the letter. She just needed to feel she was with him in spirit.

'You'll let us know if you get any more news?' she heard Aunt Lil say quietly, and then she was being ushered out of the house she knew so well and into the open air. She took deep breaths, feeling as though she had been running a long long way. Outside, the sun was shining, birds were singing their hearts out, and the scent of late summer roses was heady on the air. It was all so heartbreakingly normal, a perfect Cornish summer, as if men weren't shooting each other to bits just the other side of the Channel.

'Do you want to stop at the church to say a prayer for Tom's recovery?' Lil said, her voice as gentle as if Kerry was an invalid.

'No, I don't,' she replied, suddenly angry.

What help had God been in keeping Tom safe, when she had asked him a thousand times to do so? Nor did she want to visit the church right now, where Michael Roddy's beautiful memorial hassock was currently on display at the front of the church for all to admire and remember him by.

'I'll do it for both of us, then,' Lil said, not taking offence. 'You'll probably want to be alone for a while.'

She let go of Kerry's arm that she had been holding tightly and walked off in the direction of the church, leaving Kerry with tears stabbing her eyes at her thoughtlessness. She *did* understand. Of course she did. Hadn't Lil been through this herself, so many years ago? She walked blindly on home, glad to close the door behind her and be alone with her thoughts and the silent prayers that came into her head anyway, no matter how much she wanted to reject them.

For the last week, Tom Trevellyan hadn't been aware of anything much, other than the stinging pains in his shoulder and his leg, and every damn where else on the left side of his body. The only time it eased was when the bastard medic stung him again every few hours with the needle the size of a horse hypo that shot the pain relief into him. It should have sent him into welcome oblivion, and he supposed that it would have, if it hadn't been for the bloody hallucinations that started as soon as the evil stuff took effect. He wasn't into ghoulies and ghosties, and things that loomed up like monsters into his face, and he wanted to scream out with the horror of it, but because it was a nightmare no sounds came out. If they did, he didn't hear them.

He'd seen enough blood and gore and horror since being in this godforsaken place, and he could do without these devil images rampaging through his subconscious. At least it temporarily shut out the constant noise of gunfire and explosions that rattled windows and shook the foundations of the field hospital he was told he was in. The only other thing he knew was that it was somewhere near the coast of northern France. It could have been Timbuktu for all he knew or cared.

The times when, thankfully, he did come out of the hallucinatory state, he desperately wanted to move his bloody arm without it sending excruciating pains through him. Half the time he never even bothered to try. In any case, he was supposed to rest it. If he had to suffer the indignity of having medics coping with his every bloody personal need, at least they were male medics, and soldiers like himself. They had probably seen more private bits than he'd had hot dinners, he thought grimly. What a way to pass your days.

'How much longer is this going to last?' he croaked in desperation when he saw the medic with the horse hypo heading his way again.

The man was infuriatingly cheerful.

'Not much longer, mate. You're doing really well and the wounds are healing nicely. They're sending an ambulance for you tomorrow and then you'll be on a hospital ship heading back to England. You'll need plenty of "recup", but you'll mend.'

For a moment Tom thought he must be hallucinating again. He hadn't really heard those words about heading back to England, had he? If he could have grabbed the medic with his bad arm, and the bloody hypo wasn't already pumping the lethal stuff into his other one, he'd have screamed at him for playing a cruel joke on him.

The news had quickly spread around the village that Tom Trevellyan had been wounded but would eventually be repatriated. Claire was white-faced when she rushed round to Kerry's house after work.

'I've only just heard! Why didn't you tell me?'

Kerry looked at her wearily. She had spent the afternoon trying to write to Tom and hardly knowing what to say. Every word seemed so feeble compared with what he must be going through. In the end she had abandoned it. By now she had a splitting headache and sore eyes. She had alternately wept and berated herself for being so damn spineless, and finally apologised to Aunt Lil for seeming to turn her back on God, which she knew had offended her aunt greatly.

'Sorry,' she said to Claire now. 'I was too busy being with his mum and dad, and then feeling sorry for myself. I didn't feel like talking to anybody, but I'm glad you're here.'

'So tell me all. I keep getting garbled reports from people who don't know much, but the stories are getting more elaborate by the minute.'

Kerry could imagine. The Cornish delighted in being great storytellers, whether it was myth or ancient legend to regale some unsuspecting visitor with, but when something happened to one of their own, the imagination was in danger of running riot too.

She told Claire as concisely as she could what little she knew. Her reaction was the same as Kerry's had been at first.

'So he'll be coming home! That's something to be thankful for, isn't it? He'll probably get an honourable discharge and you'll have him home for good.'

Kerry looked at her in horror.

'He'll *hate* that! You know how proud he was when he joined up, and he went away to fight, not to be sent home like a naughty schoolboy after a scrape! He'll feel as if he's been thrown onto the scrap heap.'

'My God, Kerry, you've got some weird ideas, haven't you? He'll come home with a medal for doing his bit. Be grateful for that,' she said bitterly.

Kerry knew she was thinking about Michael at that moment, who wouldn't be coming home at all. And her friend was right. Her ideas weren't only weird, they were twisted.

'Sorry,' she muttered again, wondering if she was going to be saying sorry to people for evermore. All the same, she knew Tom. She knew him as well as she knew herself. She knew the heart and soul of him. He wouldn't take to being discharged kindly, no matter what the reason for it.

'So how bad do you think he is?' Claire said, more evenly.

'I don't know. Shrapnel wounds could mean anything, couldn't they?' she said, making an effort to respond.

'Depends where they are, I suppose.'

'Mrs Trevellyan was told it was his shoulder and his leg. There were possibly more, but those were the worst wounds.'

Claire gave a half smile. 'Well, at least it wasn't his head or his heart, was it? He'll still have his brainbox and his other bits intact. Imagine how much worse it might have been if it had gone you know where!'

In no mood for frivolity, Kerry stared at her blankly.

Claire lowered her voice, knowing that Aunt Lil was somewhere around.

'His wedding tackle, you ninny!'

Minutes later, downstairs, deciding that food was the best comfort for fortifying the body if not the mind, Lil heard the most extraordinary sound of the two girls in Kerry's bedroom laughing hysterically. She felt a surge of relief. Laughter was always the best release there was, whatever the circumstances. Kerry might not be ready yet to thank God for Tom's safe deliverance, however maimed he was, but Lil sent up another silent prayer on her behalf.

The army ambulance jolted every bit of Tom's body as it travelled over the rough terrain. He had to keep gritting his teeth to stop from crying out. Whatever good the operations to remove the shrapnel had done, and what he called the brutal aftercare, it was probably going to the

188

dogs now. He'd be nothing but a wreck by the time he got to the hospital ship, let alone to England.

'Hang on, mate,' he heard one of the other occupants of the ambulance say in a strong northern accent. 'Won't be long till we're away from this effing country now and back in Blighty. Though if the bloody Jerries haven't done for us by now, the bloody seasickness will.'

He gave a guttural laugh at his own joke.

'I don't get seasick. I'm a ferryman.'

But Tom felt sick even as he said it. What use was a ferryman with a gammy arm and leg? It took strength to do the job he had always loved, and it was one more thing to rage against what fate and the enemy had done to him.

And then he took a good look at the soldier who'd spoken, seeing the one leg he had left and the tight bandage covering one eye, and the other two patients lying prone and still and needing constant medical attention on the short journey to the hospital ship. The sight of them filled him with shame. At least he'd been told his wounds would mend, however long it took. His companion was in a worse way than himself, and from the look of the other two, it wasn't likely they'd be doing anything soon, if ever.

'Where the hell are we?' he said hoarsely.

'Dunno,' the man said. 'Somewhere south of Calais, I think. They'll be taking us to Dover to be assessed in a hospital there, before they decide if we can go nearer home. That means Yorkshire for me. Where's home for you, mate?'

'Cornwall.' The image of it swept through his mind with such an unmanly force of nostalgia it almost took his breath away.

'Jeez, you've got as far to go in one direction as I have in t'other.' He gave another guttural laugh as if everything was funny.

Tom wondered what kind of medication he was on, and wished he could be given some of the same.

'You got a lass waiting for you?'

For a moment Tom couldn't speak, but in any case the soldier rambled on.

'My old woman's going to get a surprise when she sees me coming home as a peg leg! Good thing they only took off the lower part and left me with the working bits upstairs that matter, eh? I can still get one leg over, if not two!'

He was cackling at his own joke now, but it quickly turned into a coughing fit that left him gasping out the last words. It was all so slurred that for a minute Tom didn't twig what he was saying, and then, well used to army humour, even though this was a damn sight milder than most, he laughed with the man. It seemed the only thing to do. Laugh or cry.

'Come on, soldier,' came the medic's voice, leaning over the man. 'Time for another dose of mother's ruin for you.'

'You call this gin?' he answered weakly, as the hypo was plunged into his arm. 'More like cricket's piss if you ask me.'

The medic grinned at Tom. 'That'll keep him quiet until we get him to the coast and on to the ship. Another half-hour and we'll be there, so get some rest.'

'Will he be all right?' Tom asked, as if it mattered.

The medic shrugged. 'Course he will. His type are as tough as the devil.'

Tom doubted if they'd been saying the same about him. He was more lucid than he'd been a few days ago, and he cringed every time he thought about the times he'd begged for that damned horse hypo, and then cursed it to high heaven as it started to take effect and the hallucinations began. The only comfort was that he knew he wasn't the only one. He'd heard more grown men cry at that field hospital than he ever wanted to hear in the whole of his life. He tried not to think about it. Tried to make his mind a blank.

He wished he could see where they were going. Like the others he was strapped in for safety and the windows were blacked out and too high to see through. But at last he felt the ambulance slowing down, and knew they must have reached their destination. His talkative companion was now snoring loudly, and would probably know nothing more for a couple of hours yet, maybe not until they reached England.

His heart gave a sudden almighty lurch. It was really happening. He was going home to England. To Cornwall. To Kerry, his sweetheart, who he loved more than life. His throat was thick with emotion, and he was thankful that the three other patients couldn't see how pathetic he was. But he knew damn well they would feel the same, if they could.

As the vehicle came to a stop, the doors opened and the medics jumped out. Daylight streamed into the vehicle, and Tom's eyes filled with horror.

They had driven straight onto a pontoon bridge jutting out into the sea, where presumably the hospital ship was waiting. At either side of the bridge was what resembled a vision of hell. No artist could have painted it to a more dramatic effect.

The remains of what had once been popular holiday locations on the Normandy coast beaches were now strewn with the detritus of battle. There was so much military activity still going on that weeks after D-Day a grey pall still seemed to hang in the air above the tangled barbed wire; there were huge holes in the sand and dunes where mines had blown up, and scattered bits of weapons, munitions and vehicles. Tom's imagination filled in the rest . . . the stain of blood and tattered uniforms that would mar this once wholesome area for ever.

'Christ Almighty,' he whispered, wondering how anybody had ever got out alive from this place.

'You just thank Christ that you weren't in the middle of it, soldier, and let's get you out of here,' one of the medics said briskly.

Then there was no more time or opportunity to gaze around him, because many hands were now taking charge of the four casualties in the ambulance and transporting them on stretchers to the waiting hospital ship. Tom was the only one of the four awake to see it, and he wished to God he was not. In any case, his pain was returning, stabbing and burning, and once he was on board and made comfortable, for once he wasn't complaining about the effect of the horse hypo. No sleeping nightmares could be worse than the one he had just witnessed.

He had only crossed the English Channel once before, and that was in a fever of excitement and eagerness to fight the Hun, like the rest of his unit travelling with him. God knew where they all were now. Once he had been hit, he had known little else until he awoke in the field hospital en route to the coast, where they had the facilities to operate and remove as much shrapnel from his body as possible.

But when he came round after the last hefty dose of painkiller he knew he was at sea. He could feel the familiar throb of the engines beneath him, the movement of the waves, and the screech of seabirds following the ship's wake. It was hardly the same as the chug-chug of the motor in the ferry boat he used to ply regularly with goods and people between the outlying villages and Falmouth, but it was bloody wonderful to smell sea air again. It was good to be alive.

The thought entered his head for the first time in days or weeks, or however long it had been. It was rare enough to startle him. He turned his head to find the Yorkshireman grinning at him from across the makeshift ward.

'You bin shouting a bit there, matey. Bin having bad dreams, have you? Or dreaming abut that lass of yours? Perry or summat?' He chuckled before the effort started him coughing again.

'Kerry,' Tom corrected.

'The old get-up-and-go ain't dead yet, then. She must be a cracker if you was still dreaming about her after all the stuff they pump into you.'

'She is.' Without warning, Tom found himself smiling. It was such an odd sensation to feel his mouth curving upwards and to feel the image of Kerry seeping into his brain as if she was right there beside him. Filling his brain and his arms and his heart. Filling him.

It was so real, so beautiful, that for a wild second he

panicked. Was the image so real because he was actually dead, or dying?

But no, the Yorkshireman was still rabbiting on about something or other, and he could still feel the sting in his shoulder if he tried moving it, so he wasn't dead and he wasn't dying. And he had no intention of doing either, he told himself, with his first positive thought for days.

CHAPTER ELEVEN

The seasons had moved on in the south-east of England. In the more mellow county of Cornwall, summer always lingered on for a good while longer than in the rest of the country. The old men of the county always said it was an overcoat warmer in Cornwall than in the south-east, and two overcoats warmer than the north. As the hospital ship prepared to deposit its latest casualties at Dover before returning to France for more, Tom Trevellyan shivered in the chill of a September morning, and wished that something magical could whisk him straight home without any more fuss.

The Yorkshireman, whom everyone simply called Yorky now, repeatedly scoffed at him, calling him a soft southerner, and that he should go 'oop north' to the Dales where life was tough, and you had to be a hardy bugger where he came from, if you wanted to survive the snows of winter.

'Enough to freeze yer bollocks off and then some, if you really want to know,' was his graphic description, said with a lewd chuckle.

'I don't, thanks,' Tom replied with a grin, well used to him by now. They had been together all the while, and acquired a kind of enforced camaraderie, but there had been no more sign of the other two prone soldiers in the ambulance with them, and neither of them had felt inclined to enquire. It was often better not to know.

'I'm sending a wire to my missus as soon as I can get some nice little nursey to do it for me,' Yorky went on. 'It'll prob'ly give her a heart attack to know I'll be called Hopalong Cassidy from now on, but I reckon she won't mind that. She'll have been missing a bit of the old 'ow's yer father, so I reckon she'll still be glad to see me,' he added with a wink.

'Course she will, if we ever get away from here,' Tom said in frustration, ignoring everything else as the disembarkation seemed to be taking an endless time to get started.

'Let's hope to Christ we do it soon, then.' Yorky was unusually grim. 'They'd best move us out of the holding hospital soon as well. We don't want to have come through all this, only to be blown to bits by one of Hitler's effing buzz bombs.'

They had learnt more about them on the ship bringing them home, and Tom selfishly thanked God that they weren't aimed at the far south-west of the country. Hitler would be sure to want to target the Home Counties with his evil new weapons, not a tapering extremity of land from where the next stop on the horizon was America.

Another wave of nostalgia hit him, and he wondered if he was truly going as soft as Yorky said all southerners were. But what the hell if he was? If a man couldn't be loyal to his birthplace and long to be back there and be with everything and everyone he held dear, he wasn't much of a man anyway.

At last things seemed to be moving, and they were finally being transported into a Red Cross ambulance and whisked away to what the all-knowing Yorky had called the holding hospital. Tom had no idea where it was, but once they arrived, the contrast to what he had seen in France couldn't have been more marked or more blessedly welcome. The building looked out on green fields and trees, and the nurses wore crisp white uniforms and had gentle hands and warm smiles, in contrast to the burly medics he had known recently.

God knew he was forever grateful to them, of course, despite everything they had put him through. Without them he wouldn't have survived . . . but these were gentler nurses, who smelt good whenever they leant over him and attended to his every need once he was in a more comfortable bed on the ward, straightening pillows and bringing steaming cups of tea and biscuits to the new inmates.

'I could live with this, couldn't you, mate?' he heard Yorky say, winking broadly before he was trundled away to have his wounds checked as soon as possible on arrival.

Oh yes, thought Tom. He could live with this, for a while. It was wonderful to be in England again, but now that he was actually here the fever inside him longed for Cornish soil, and most of all to be with Kerry again.

It was a while, though, before his nerves settled down

properly. Until the tea had restored him a little he hadn't realised how knotted up they had been, as if crossing the Channel had all been a tantalising dream, and at any minute now the Jerry planes would swoop down on the ship and blow it to kingdom come. It was a pale shadow of a dream compared with the nightmare hallucinations he had been having recently, but it was nerve-racking all the same.

But it wasn't a dream, and he was definitely here, lying on clean sheets, and providing he could ignore some of the moans and groans coming from other beds, it was the calmest atmosphere he had known in a long time. He looked around to take in his surroundings properly and saw a shape hovering at the end of his bed, adjusting his notes. It was all so civilised, and a world away from the makeshift conditions of the field hospital.

'Nurse,' he managed to say when his throat would let him speak. 'Can you bring me a pencil and some paper?'

'Writing your memoirs, are you, soldier?' she said with a smile.

'No. A letter to my girl.'

And God, it felt so good to say it, knowing that it didn't have to cross the uncertainties of field post offices and the English Channel before it reached her. It could be there tomorrow or the next day, depending on how long he took to write it and to get it posted. In the end, not realising how stiff his good arm and his fingers had become with all the hefty injections and saline drips, he had to get the nurse to write it for him.

Three days later, Kerry didn't recognise the writing on the envelope, only that it had an English postmark, and not one of those stamped so anonymously by the army. She opened it apprehensively, nervous of what it might contain.

'*My darling Kerry,*' she read.

> '*I'm having to get Nurse Cathy to write this for me, as my good arm isn't quite up to it yet from all the injections I've had. But I'm as well as can be expected, and back in England in a hospital near Cambridge, or so they tell me. I don't know how long I'll be here, but I hope they'll send me back to Cornwall soon. Please let my parents know. I'm too tired for any more right now, except to send you all my love, as always, and hope we'll be together again very soon.*
>
> '*Your loving Tom*'

She felt choked by the time she came to the end of it, full of mixed emotions. It was just wonderful, so wonderful, that he was in England at last, wherever Cambridge was. On the other side of the country, and too far away for her to visit, that was for sure. The government was always sending out advertisements that screamed: '*Is your journey really necessary?*' Well, in her opinion, it definitely would be, but she knew Aunt Lil would forbid her to travel to where there was danger of the terrible doodlebugs.

But Tom was home at last, even if he had had to get this Nurse Cathy to write the letter for him, which necessarily made it more formal than she would have liked. Kerry could imagine him dictating the important messages, and keeping his deepest feelings under control, because a third person had had to become part of their private world.

Intruding on it. A female nurse. Nurse Cathy.

Without warning, a burst of jealousy rushed through her at that moment. What was this Nurse Cathy like? Was she young and slim and beautiful, the way you saw them in the flicks? Did she have soft skin and golden hair, and spend her days caring for her male patients and attending to their most intimate needs? To *Tom's* needs?

She tried to push the unworthy thoughts away, knowing that whatever indignities were being done to him now, it was ultimately going to bring him home to her. She tried, but without much success. Without realising it, she had constructed an instant image of the unknown Nurse Cathy in her head, and it wasn't one that she wanted to see.

She was ashamed of her resentment, but she just couldn't help it. She was also glad that Aunt Lil was out when the letter arrived, not seeing right through her and being outraged with her. She had to get her more sensible thoughts around it, and fast. And she had to do as Tom asked. To let his parents know. It was her duty to do that.

It was her immediate job. She put the letter back in the envelope and went out of the cottage with it in her pocket. And since the first person she bumped into was Claire, it was impossible not to show it to her. She didn't say a word as she handed it over. Claire read it quickly and looked straight into Kerry's eyes, and as if she was as canny as Aunt Lil, she saw all there was to see.

'So this Nurse Cathy had to write it for him, and you don't like it.'

'Would you? If it was Glenn? Or . . . or if it had been Michael?'

Kerry knew that was the wrong thing to say as soon as

she'd said it. Wouldn't any one of the Roddy family have welcomed a letter written by a hundred nurses on Michael's behalf, if it told them the news that he was still alive and not at the bottom of the sea?

'I'm not going to answer that,' Claire said. 'Just be glad he's coming home, and go and let his parents know. At least his first letter back home was to you and not to them.'

That was something else. Would the Trevellyans resent that? But surely not. Kerry thought she knew them well enough for that. They would be generous enough to know that Tom had been thinking of them as well as his girl.

'Thanks for that, Claire. See you later? We're supposed to be going to the flicks in Falmouth tomorrow afternoon, aren't we? Is it still on?'

'Is there any reason why it shouldn't be?'

They parted on good terms. However scratchy they often were with one another, it meant nothing compared with the strong friendship they shared. Nothing could ever touch that, Kerry thought, automatically crossing her fingers for luck as she thought it.

Mrs Trevellyan opened her door with a ready smile, always glad to see Kerry, and asked her in at once. For a moment the words she had to say stuck in her throat, and she forced them out.

'I've had a letter from Tom. Well, not from him, exactly. He got a nurse to write it for him, and I'm to pass on the news to you.'

As she said it, she knew it was coming out all wrong. She was supposedly articulate, but right now she seemed to have forgotten all the tactful words she might have used.

Thankfully, Tom's mother never seemed to notice as Kerry handed over the letter and waited for her reaction.

'Well, this is much better news, isn't it?' she said at last. 'The one thing his father and I were waiting for was to hear that he was back in England. We can cope with anything now.'

'You didn't mind that he had to get a nurse to write the letter for him, then?' Or that he wrote to me first?'

She listened to herself, and wondered what in heaven's name was wrong with her, making things worse, as if she was deliberately wanting Mrs Trevellyan to say something unpleasant to her. But that wasn't in her nature, and the older woman gave a soft laugh.

'If I was a young man with a lovely girl waiting at home for me, I doubt that I'd have written to my parents first, either, Kerry love. Has that been bothering you?'

'A bit, I suppose,' Kerry murmured. 'And wondering about Nurse Cathy.'

'Oh dear, it's a touch of the old green eyes, is it?' Tom's mother actually laughed. 'My love, let me tell you that most of these military nurses are dragons. They have to be for heaving some of these large chaps around. And as for Tom's eyes roaming, I can't see that in a million years. It's called trust, Kerry. After all, the local girls had plenty of chances when those handsome GIs were around, didn't they? But for those who were committed elsewhere, they didn't stand a chance, did they?'

Kerry felt a chill run through her at that moment. Was Mrs Trevellyan implying in a roundabout way that she knew something about Marvin Mcleod? But she couldn't, since there was nothing to know. She was sure Aunt Lil wouldn't have been so indiscreet as to mention him at the Friendship Club. But it only took a whisper here and a sly comment there, and gossip spread like wildfire in a village, whether true or false. If she didn't want to look guilty, however blameless she was, she knew she had to diffuse the situation quickly.

She smiled back as naturally as she could. 'It's a good thing Claire wasn't committed, as you call it, then. She's head over heels in love with her GI, but don't tell her I told you so.'

'Of course not. It's our secret, dear.'

Kerry suddenly felt as though the small house was stifling her. She had always got on very well with Tom's parents, who she had known all her life, and she was probably being totally paranoid in thinking that everything Mrs Trevellyan said to her had a hidden meaning behind it now. But it couldn't, she repeated to herself. There was nothing to know about herself and Marvin Mcleod except friendship. And it was a friendship that was no longer possible, since he had never been heard of since the D-Day landings, she thought with a tightness in her throat as she walked quickly away from the cottage.

She wondered how Marvin's family had felt when they got the awful news that he was missing, presumed dead. *Presumed dead* sounded so awful – and so unfinished. It was far better to know for certain than to have this hanging over you for evermore. How had Shirl felt, when she was told? Was she out of her mind with guilt over sending him the Dear John letter when he was so far away from home? She should be, Kerry thought angrily. It was a horrible thing to do.

But she had done what she had to do now, and shown Tom's letter to his mother. And at least she could write back to him. She didn't have to have a Nurse Cathy writing it for her, or reading it to him, either. She could say what was in her heart, and presumably his own inability to hold a pencil steady was only temporary. She felt cheered at the thought.

Saturday was half-day closing in Columbine. The weather was still good, so Kerry and Claire cycled to Falmouth to go to the pictures. The sea was like a millpond, and it was almost easy to forget for a while that there was still a war raging across the Channel and in other parts of the world. The Pathé News, awaited eagerly at every cinema now, announced that the Allies were winning on all fronts, having pushed the Germans back through Belgium and crossed into Holland. In London the recent child evacuations, begun again lately because of the V1 rockets, were suspended again for the time being.

'Good job too,' Claire whispered. 'Imagine having to send our Molly and Toby away to strangers for Lord knows how long.'

Better than having them killed by German bombs, Kerry thought, but refrained from saying so.

'I can't stand that man's voice,' Claire went on, as the overenthusiastic announcer continued. 'He makes it all sound like a game, as if we're all idiots and don't know the half of what's going on.'

She was shushed by those behind her, but Kerry knew exactly how she felt at the way some of the announcer's comments seemed to be spoken to children. It would be a cause for rejoicing when the war ended, at least for most, but not for those who had lost someone close to them, like Michael Roddy.

His memorial service had now been arranged for the coming Sunday. It wouldn't have been dignified to leave it much longer, and Kerry was guiltily glad that Tom wouldn't be home before then. It would be too painful for him. He would almost certainly feel a kind of guilt too, that he had survived and Michael hadn't, even though it was quite unfounded. But she knew the way Tom's mind worked.

She was glad when the Pathé News came to an end and they watched the antics of a short cartoon film before the main feature, a frothy, glamorous, typically Hollywood offering that was guaranteed to lift the spirits. It naturally had Claire bubbling with excitement when they came out into the early evening daylight again.

'I suppose you're thinking that life in America with Glenn is going to be just like that,' Kerry said.

'It might be!' Nothing was about to dim Claire's glow now.

'It *won't* be! For a start Glenn's home isn't always warm and sunny, with everybody singing all day long as Hollywood has us believe. Connecticut is in the north and has snow in the winter.'

'Well, you've been doing your homework, haven't you! Why are you so grouchy all of a sudden? I thought you'd be happy that Tom's coming home.'

'Of course I am,' Kerry snapped. 'I just don't want you to get a false impression of what life could be like in America, and you shouldn't see it all through rose-coloured glasses, Claire. You know I only want the best for you.'

Claire's voice softened. 'I know. And I also know that Glenn's the best for me. So shall we drop it now and go and get some chips to eat on the sea wall before we ride home?'

It was the best idea yet. Just the thought of chips wrapped in newspaper, doused in tangy vinegar and salt, was enough to make both their mouths water.

'How long are they keeping me here?' Tom asked the staff nurse impatiently a few days later. 'My shoulder's not feeling too bad now.'

It was only partly true. Providing he didn't move it too suddenly, or try to lift his arm higher than was comfortable, it was all right. Even if he knew it was never going to be completely all right again, he didn't want to stay here for ever. The pleasant surroundings he'd seen when he first arrived, that were so welcome after the carnage in France, only made him long for his own home surroundings more now.

'You'll be here for another week, Private Trevellyan,' the nurse said crisply. 'There's no hurrying war wounds, and each man's body has its own timetable of recovery, and you'll be all the sorrier if we send you home half mended.'

She had a strange turn of phrase, Tom thought, scowling, as she swished on her way. They didn't tell you much. Doctors came and went, muttering between themselves, trying to make him do exercises that gave him a job to stop crying out, but he was determined not to do so, in case it hindered his return home. Nurse Cathy, the nurse who had written his first letter to Kerry for him, seemed to have disappeared now, and when he casually enquired after her, simply to relieve the boredom of his day, he was told she was now working in another section of the hospital.

'Fancied her summat rotten, did you, Tom old son?' leered the occupant of the bed opposite him, an especially objectionable soldier with a strong cockney accent. He was older than most patients on the ward, and he ridiculed Tom's slower Cornish tones, and fouled the ward each night by his loud farting that he swore was leading up to farting 'God Save the King', which offended the other inmates even more.

'No, I didn't fancy her,' Tom snapped. 'She's old enough to be my mother.'

The man hooted. 'When did that stop anybody? You can always put a bag over the tart's head if you don't want to look at her, and it's any old port in a storm, ain't it, if you know what I mean!'

Tom knew exactly what he meant, and chose to ignore him. He'd already heard some very graphic descriptions of how the cockney had had his way with a couple of obliging French tarts before he got in the way of a bullet that nearly ripped out his guts. But the man wouldn't give up.

'Who's this girl you've got waiting for you out in the sticks, then? Does she spread 'em for you?' He made a rude gesture with his arm that had the other occupants of the ward alternately grinning and turning away.

Tom wished he'd give up. He wasn't a prude, and he'd learnt plenty since joining the army, but Kerry was special to him, and he wasn't going to give this lout the satisfaction of knowing anything about her.

'Give it a rest, Cockers,' one of the other patients called

out, tiring of his constant sniping. 'We all know how you like to spend your time when you're not killing the Jerries, but it's beginning to get on our tits.'

'Didn't know you had any,' came the snarling retort, 'but I always thought there was more than a touch of the ladyboy in you, Harvey. Like to have it both ways, do yer?'

Tom closed his eyes, glad for the moment that the cockney had turned his attention elsewhere. Despite his longing to get home, he was unutterably tired these days. He'd always been strong and healthy, yet it took so little to exhaust him now, and he supposed a lot of that was due to the jabs they were still sticking him with daily. He must look like his mum's pincushions by now, he thought with a pang, and his backside was going to be permanently chequered.

Half an hour later, while the other two were still going at it hammer and tongs, a doctor he hadn't seen before came into the ward with the staff nurse and straight to his bed. Ignoring the fact that Tom was there at all, he picked up the chart at the end of the bed and studied it, muttering to the staff nurse all the while, then finally gave Tom a tight smile.

'So how do you fancy a train ride the day after tomorrow, Private? Do you think you're up to it?'

If he could have leapt out of bed with joy at that moment, Tom would have done so. As it was, he could only mumble his thanks, and say he'd never been more up to it, as pathetically grateful as if the medic was his greatest friend and had just given him the biggest birthday present in the world.

'You lucky bugger,' the cockney practically bawled when the doctor had gone away again. 'I always said you bloody poncey farm boys had blue eyes.'

'I'm a ferryman, not a farm boy,' Tom yelled. 'I work all hours with my dad on our boat. It's bloody hard work, and there's nothing poncey about that!'

'Posh boy, then,' the man sneered, not giving up.

It wasn't worth retaliating. Let him think what he liked. Tom simply smiled benignly at the idiot, which only annoyed him more. But he didn't matter. His heart was soaring. What the hell did it matter what this lout thought of him, or called him? Two more days and he'd never have to see or smell him again. He wondered briefly where Yorky was now, and if he'd have the chance to say goodbye. That hardly mattered either. They were all ships that passed in the night in this bloody war, and the only constant that kept them going was the thought of the ones who were waiting for them at home.

Two days later, having received all his papers and travel warrant, he was transported to the special train reserved for wounded servicemen, and breathed an almighty sigh of relief as it steamed and snorted out of the station, belching smoke on its way to Truro. He could hardly believe it was really happening. By the end of the day he would be in his own home county, if not quite home in Columbine. He had had a letter from his mother, and another one from Kerry, and he knew how much they were looking forward to his return.

'You do realise you'll be sent to another hospital for a week or two, don't you, Private Trevellyan?' the staff nurse had warned him. 'You'll need to be assessed and a decision made as to whether or not you'll be returning to your unit or invalided out.'

It was the one thing he had determinedly blanked out of his mind. He wasn't a bloody invalid, and he didn't intend to be treated like one. The fact that his leg dragged a bit, and he didn't have the same movement in his shoulder as before, didn't mean he intended being treated like an old man. He was quite confident that within a few weeks' convalescence, he'd be back fighting the Jerries again. He admitted he wasn't quite ready for it yet, but it was what he'd joined up for, not to be put out to grass because of a few bits of shrapnel.

Much later, he had to admit that during the long hours of sitting in the train and being jostled by every blessed movement on the rails, the pain in his shoulder was becoming excruciating. The medic on board gave him a shot of painkiller, and he freely accepted that he had bloody well needed it. Maybe it would take more than the few weeks' convalescence he expected after all.

Kerry was jittery with excitement as she got ready to go to Truro with Tom's parents in his dad's old jalopy the following weekend. She had truly begun to think this day would never come, but she was actually going to be with Tom again after all these months, if only for the hour that visitors were allowed.

'It's a shame you can't go on your own without his parents there, spoiling your billing and cooing,' Claire had said with a grin.

'We don't do billing and cooing, idiot,' Kerry had laughed. 'And I'd never manage to get there on my own.

Tom's dad knows the way to Truro, and it's some distance away from there to the special hospital.'

'Are you nervous?'

Claire was more perceptive than Kerry expected.

'Very,' she said abruptly. 'I don't know why I should be, but so much has happened since he went away, and I don't know how he'll be now.'

'He'll still be Tom, won't he?'

'Of course he will, and I'm still me, and I'm just being silly.'

She tried to squash any feelings of apprehension, but she was still jumpy, despite her excitement at seeing Tom again. Perhaps Claire was right, and it was because his parents would be there as well, and it would be difficult to feel as natural with him as she wanted to be. But she put on the brightest face she could as the old car pulled up outside the cottage for her, and waved goodbye to Aunt Lil as she climbed in the back.

'This is a special day for all of us, Kerry,' Mrs Trevellyan said with a shaky smile, 'and one that some folks never thought they'd see again. We're the lucky ones, aren't we?'

'Now then, Mother, we don't want none of that talk, and no piping your eye, neither,' her husband scolded her. 'The boy don't want to see waterworks after what he's come through.'

He had a colourful way of talking, but it somehow reassured Kerry, because it was obvious that Tom's mother was nervous too. She patted the paper bag beside her, carrying two precious oranges out of the box that had just been delivered to the shop, and which Mrs Polby insisted that she should take for Tom.

Everyone was rejoicing in the fact that he was nearly home, and as Kerry breathed in the sweet succulent scent of the fruit, tangy and fresh and full of summer, she hoped that their arrival from distant shores on this very day was an omen for better days to come.

CHAPTER TWELVE

The hospital was situated in large grounds and there seemed to be a lot of patients strolling about or sitting on benches in the shade of the many trees. It was partly a convalescent home for those in need of recuperation, as well as a hospital for war wounded. Mr Trevellyan had parked the car around the back of the hospital, where there was a balcony around the part of the building facing the sun, and they could see that there were some patients lying down on what looked like movable trolley beds. Most of them were heavily bandaged, some being tended by nurses, and Kerry averted her eyes, feeling as though it was an intrusion to look at them. She was becoming increasingly nervous now, not knowing what to expect when she saw Tom.

Then she heard a familiar voice calling her name, and her heart stopped. She squinted into the sun for a minute, hardly able to believe it was Tom's voice.

'There's our Tom,' she heard his mother cry, almost breaking into an undignified sprint as the young man called out to them again from where he sat beneath a shady tree a few yards away.

But Kerry was quicker. She had passed both Tom's parents by the time he stood up. She hardly noticed that he was leaning heavily on a stick as she flung herself into his arms. She hardly noticed or cared about anything but the fact that he was here and that he was kissing her with all the pent-up passion of these months apart.

'God, how I've missed you, Kerry,' he breathed, before they were half stumbling back to sit down on the bench, still entwined. To blazes with dignity, Kerry thought dizzily. This was what they had been waiting for all this time.

But Tom's parents were upon them now, and there was no more time for private moments. His mother seemed to have lost all sense of where she was, because she was kneeling on the grass beside him now, weeping and calling him her poor boy, despite her husband's warning to keep calm, and he was constantly clearing his throat in lieu of tears.

'Come on, Mum, I'm not so bad,' Tom protested uneasily, clearly getting embarrassed at such a dramatic show of emotion. 'Look around you, and you'll see chaps far worse off than I am. I've learnt that since being here. At least I've got one good leg and one good arm, and they'll both heal in time. Maybe not quite as good as new, but good enough to help on the boat, eh, Dad?' he said with a cheery grin at his father.

'I don't care about all these other chaps, and may the Lord forgive me for saying so, but I do care about you,

214

my poor boy,' his mother said again, unable to control herself.

Kerry looked at Tom in desperation. This wasn't the way she had imagined it in her dreams. But neither had she imagined Tom's parents taking over this precious visit either. She had imagined these first sweet moments being for the two of them alone. She would rather have cycled all the way, just to be here alone with him. It wasn't that far, and they had all cycled much farther distances in days past. It was something to remember for next time.

It was Tom's father who finally broke his wife's monopoly, tugging at her arm, and encouraging her to get to her feet.

'Let's go and see if we can get a cup of tea somewhere, Mother, and leave these two alone for five minutes. You'll be parched by now, and there's sure to be a canteen of sorts, and Tom and Kerry will have plenty to talk about.'

Kerry flashed him a look of thanks, and Mrs Trevellyan went reluctantly away, saying they wouldn't be gone for long.

'Thank God for that,' Tom said. 'I thought she was going to cling on to me for ever. And much as I love my mother, there's only one person I want clinging to me right now.'

She snuggled up against him, her head on his shoulder, guiltily aware that there had been moments when she had wondered if this day would ever come. But it was no time to be thinking dark thoughts now.

'You look beautiful, by the way,' he said softly, 'and you're wearing my favourite blue dress. I knew you would.'

'Did you?' Kerry said.

215

'Of course,' he said with a laugh that sounded exactly like the old Tom. 'I know everything about you, don't I?'

Funny. She had always thought the same thing about him. But they didn't know everything about each other, not anymore. There had been too many months between. Too big a gap in their lives. How on earth did other couples regain those lost months or years . . . ?

'Kerry?' he said, when she didn't answer.

She gave a shaky laugh.

'It's crazy, isn't it? We've got so much to talk about, and right now I can't think of a single thing to say, except how wonderful it is to see you.'

'Too much water under the bridge, and too many changes,' he said, more seriously. 'But we do have things to say, apart from the obvious of how much I've missed you and longed to see you again. So how is Michael's family?'

The question gave her a jolt, and she answered carefully.

'Surprisingly well, considering. They have each other, and I know that's a great comfort to Mrs Roddy. The ladies at the Friendship Club have made a beautiful memorial hassock for the church too. There was a memorial service for him, and practically the whole village turned out for it. The hassock was displayed in a place of honour before it was put in the Roddys' pew.'

'Well, that's all right, then, isn't it?' Tom was suddenly harsh. 'They've all done their bit and everyone's getting on with their own lives.'

'What else is there to do, Tom?' Kerry said in a small voice. 'We can't ever go back to the way things were before, can we?'

He looked at her then, his eyes more intense than before, as if he wanted to see right inside her soul.

'Does that include you and me, Kerry? Can we ever go back to the way things were before, even if I've got a gammy leg and a wonky arm for however long it takes for them to get halfway back to normal?'

'Of course we can, and now you're being plain daft!' she said passionately. 'Do you think those things matter to me? You're still my Tom, and I still love you and I always will. You know that, and you shouldn't need to question it.'

She couldn't believe they were practically arguing, when she had so looked forward to them being together again. But perhaps it was inevitable. Perhaps it was necessary. In any case, he was grinning at her now, and as they saw his parents bearing down on them again with a tray of hospital tea, or what the inmates called *crickets' piss*, he muttered, his lips brushed her cheek again.

'And I love you too. Take no notice of me. It's just frustration at having to stay here doing damn fool exercises that are supposed to be strengthening my muscles, when I'd much rather be at home.'

'How long do they think it will be?'

'No more than a couple of weeks with any luck, and try to come on your own next time,' he managed to whisper, before his parents arrived.

She'd move heaven and earth to be sure that she did, she thought later, when they were back in the car and driving home to Columbine. Her last sight of Tom was of him standing up and leaning against the tree for support as he waved them goodbye, smiling the way he always did, and looking every bit as handsome as he had always looked. Of course they would get back to the way they had been before, she thought confidently. It would take more than a few bits of shrapnel to drive them apart.

She had been surprised at Mrs Trevellyan's reaction, though. She had always thought her a strong-minded woman, and to see her weeping like that had been embarrassing and sad. You wouldn't think so now, thought Kerry, as she chatted on and on in the car about how they must throw a welcome party for Tom as soon as he came home, and they would start saving up their food coupons immediately.

'I'm not sure he'd want that,' Kerry murmured from the back seat, knowing damn well that he'd hate all the fuss.

Mrs Trevellyan swivelled around in her seat to frown at Kerry.

'Well, dear, I think I'm the best judge of what I think is best for my son, and if I say he deserves a party, a party is what he'll get.'

'All right, Mother,' her husband said placatingly. 'Kerry was only passing an opinion.'

'It's not all right. He's been in France in the thick of it, even though he may not have been on those wretched beaches that the Allies stormed on D-Day. I daresay all those Americans will get a medal for it and a big fanfare, but our Tom's done his bit for Mr Churchill like all our boys, and he deserves a party.'

Kerry didn't like the way she brought a mention of the Americans into the conversation. She wondered again if Mrs Trevellyan had heard any rumours . . . and if she had, it was so unfair, and so wrong.

'Tom deserves a medal too,' she said defensively, 'and I'm sure he'll get one. We're all proud of him.'

After a moment or two she saw the woman's shoulders slump.

'Oh, Kerry love, don't take any notice of me. I don't know what I'm saying, and I certainly don't want to be mean to you. I'm just so thankful that Tom's safely home. I don't know what I expected before I saw him, and it was such a relief to see him standing up and looking just like my old Tom.'

She was weeping again, and Kerry found herself patting her back and feeling like an idiot for doing so. But she forgave her, of course she did. She was Tom's mother, and she would forgive her anything. Well, anything except unwarranted suspicion, she thought.

'It was a relief to me too,' she said steadily. 'But I never doubted it. All those years of working on the ferry made him strong, didn't it?'

'And he'll be working there again, God willing,' his father said. 'He'll need to build up his muscles before that happens, of course.'

'Oh well, you would be thinking about that, but there's no need to worry about having him working before he's even got home, Father,' his wife said tartly. 'He'll want to get acclimatised to being at home with his family and friends before any of that happens.'

He'll just want to get home first, Kerry thought, but this time she held her tongue. Tom loved the river and the ferry that plied between here and Falmouth Bay. He loved the water and the sea, and it had rather surprised her that he hadn't joined the navy instead of the army. But she also knew in her heart that he would want to get back on the front line again as soon as he was allowed. The last thing he would want was to be discharged as medically unfit. Nobody had mentioned it on the visit, she remembered. The hour had gone so quickly, and they had all skirted around the possibility, with three of them hoping it would happen, if it meant him coming home for good, and one of them certainly hoping it did not.

When they parted company, Kerry went indoors feeling as if she had travelled a hundred miles. Only now did she realise how difficult it had been with Tom's parents, trying to walk a virtual tightrope on their feelings for the immediate future, while ultimately they all wanted the same thing – for Tom to be restored to full health.

'So how did it go?' Claire Roddy asked her after church the next morning.

'He didn't actually look too bad, if you managed to ignore the stick he had to use when he walked, and the awkwardness in his left arm,' Kerry admitted. 'The worst thing of all was seeing how Mrs Trevellyan overreacted. I have never been so embarrassed as to see a middle-aged woman kneeling on the grass with her arms around his knees.'

'You're having me on, aren't you?' Claire practically squeaked.

'Shut up, they're not that far behind us. I'm not having you on at all. I felt sorry for the other poor devils on the balcony having to witness it, who looked far worse off than Tom. At least he was one of the walking wounded, not lying stretched out all day and having to rely on nurses for everything.'

'That reminds me, and you're not going to like this. Pam Wyatt's mother said that Pam might be working as an orderly at Tom's hospital quite soon, and that it would be nice for him to see a friendly face.'

Kerry glared at her, furious at the thought, and Claire held up her hands in mock defence.

'I'm only telling you what Mrs Wyatt told my mum, that's all. Maybe Tom will be home before it happens, anyway.'

'And maybe he won't. If he has his way, I know he'll want to go back to France. He'll want to finish the war off all by himself,' she added bitterly.

'Well, cheer up. Even if they do send him back, he'll be sure to have some home leave first. They wouldn't send him straight from hospital to France!'

Kerry relaxed. Of course he would get some leave first. And who knew how he might feel after a week or two at home in familiar surroundings, maybe having a try-out on his dad's boat and getting the feel of it all again?

And having the time to be together. A wave of shivering excitement swept over her. Maybe in the not-very-distant future, they would be spending time in their old haunts, holding hands in the cinema, walking on the moors, sitting by the river, making plans, making love . . .

She turned away from Claire, knowing her face must be scarlet at the wanton thoughts that were in her mind right then. And the one that came next . . . how long would it be before Tom was mobile enough and agile enough to do any of those things?

But she could see that there was something else on Claire's mind, and that she was bursting to tell her something.

'I've had another letter from Glenn, and there's news. I didn't want to say anything until I knew how it had gone with Tom yesterday,' Claire said, barely able to hold in the excitement.

Molly came skipping up behind her at that moment.

'I know what it is,' she chanted. 'It's about Kerry's Marvin!'

Kerry stared at the golden-haired child, wondering how such an angel could put such a sudden mixture of hope and fear in her heart. He wasn't 'her Marvin', and never had been, and the last thing she wanted was for anyone to think that he was.

'Don't be daft, Molly. Marvin's girlfriend lives in America and she's called Shirl,' she found herself saying, and wishing she didn't feel the need to defend herself in this way to a child.

'Scoot, Molly,' Claire said impatiently. 'I want to talk to Kerry.'

'Why can't I listen?' she pouted. 'I know all about it, anyway!'

'Well, somebody had better tell me, before I die of impatience,' Kerry snapped. 'I think your mother's looking for you, Molly.'

'No, she's not.'

'Yes, she is!'

The two girls said it together, and the child went off, sulking.

'Come on, let's go down by the river before she follows us, and I'll spill the beans,' Claire said.

Kerry's heart was pounding by the time they reached the bench by the river. The same one where, ages ago now, it seemed, she had sat and chatted to Marvin, and he had shown her the photo of his girl, the lovely Miss ex-Montana, called Shirl. But instead of sitting on the bench now, they stretched out full-length on the short sweet grass on the riverbank.

'Marvin's been found alive,' Claire said abruptly.

'*What? Honestly?*' Kerry said, completely overwhelmed after a moment of breath holding when she didn't know what she would hear.

So such miracles did happen. You heard about them from time to time, but they were so rare, and you never really believed in them. Until now.

Claire dragged out Glenn's letter from her pocket.

'I'll read out the relevant part,' she said with a grin. 'The rest is private.'

Kerry listened intently, hardly able to take it all in. But it seemed that when the Americans had landed on Omaha Beach on D-Day, a shell had exploded right next to Marvin, throwing him off his feet and sending him senseless and deaf. He was totally disorientated when he came round. Dust and smoke were choking him, and there was gunfire all around, and from what they could piece together later, he apparently crawled the wrong way from his unit, finally hiding in the dunes until it was safe to come out under cover of darkness many hours later.

By then, the troops had moved on, and still dazed and sick by the continuing sound of fighting, he must have wandered about for miles until he found himself in an area where a French family took him in and cared for him. He couldn't remember a thing, not even his name, but his dog tags were able to tell them who he was. But until he was well

223

enough to move on, they insisted he stayed put. Eventually, one of the Resistance people managed to contact his unit to let them know he was alive and safe, and he was at last able to get back to them for medical treatment. According to Glenn's account, he was going to be all right, apart from a small loss of hearing.

'Thank God,' Kerry breathed. 'It is something of a miracle, isn't it? And after all he's been through, his girl is surely going to take him back. His luck has to be on the turn now.'

'Well, if she doesn't, he can always come back to you,' Claire said with a grin, folding up the letter and tucking it away.

'No, he can't. I was only ever a sounding board, and you well know it. My heart only ever belonged to one man.'

But it was such good news, and the best anyone had heard for a long time – apart from Tom, of course. The Allies were making great strides against the Germans now, pushing them back in all directions, but it was the little personal stories, the triumph of one man against all the odds, that was the miracle that brought tears to the eyes and a gladness to the heart.

'I think I'll go home and tell Aunt Lil,' Kerry said before her thoughts got too mushy and sentimental. 'And when you write back to Glenn, you'll be sure to tell him how pleased I am about Marvin, won't you?'

'I sure will,' Claire said, already practising her new lingo for when she became the promised GI bride.

Still laying flat in the warm sunshine, Claire mused that it was a pity Kerry and Tom were as close as clams. It wasn't a serious thought, but it would have been an extra bonus if both of them could have been GI brides, even though the GIs in question lived hundreds of miles apart. Claire couldn't imagine the size of such a huge country, where the majority of people had never even seen the sea, so she easily dismissed such minor problems, and stayed there dreaming for a few minutes longer, until her little sister tickled her under the chin with a blade of grass and made her sit up pronto.

'Mum says you're to come home for dinner,' Molly screamed as Claire screeched at her, then scrambled up and began to race after her.

Neither Claire nor Kerry knew how long she had been hovering about, or how much she had heard. In any case, the good news was so amazing and so momentous that they would never have given a second thought to how devastating a child's eavesdropping could become.

'I'm really pleased to hear it,' Aunt Lil said when Kerry told her as they shared their own Sunday dinner. 'Good things do happen in wartime, even when all seems to be lost. And now that Tom's well out of it, let's hope he's home for good very soon.'

It was funny how she managed to turn the conversation from Marvin to Tom in an instant, Kerry thought. Funny, and significant.

'You know that Claire is hoping to be a GI bride when it's all over, don't you, Aunt Lil?' she said.

Her aunt looked at her sharply. 'I think her parents might have something to say about that. You can't know a person well enough after a few weeks to think about marriage, and especially when it entails going to a foreign country.'

'The Americans aren't foreign. They're our Allies.'

'That doesn't mean they think or live the same way we do, even if they do speak a kind of English,' Aunt Lil sniffed. 'Besides, we spoke it first, and look what they've done to it with their sloppy talk!'

Kerry burst out laughing. 'I don't suppose the natives thought too much of our *posh* way of talking when we first set foot over there and tried to cultivate them to our ways, either. And they were there before we were! Besides, Glenn's mother has written to Claire's parents and told them all about the family and the place where they live. If it all goes according to Claire's plans, I wouldn't be at all surprised if one day they all went to America on a visit.'

She didn't actually know any such thing, and it was no more than a bit of wild surmising that entered her head at that moment, but Aunt Lil knew when she was beaten, and said she didn't want to hear any more talk about Americans, and if Kerry was going to let her dinner get cold, there were plenty more starving Chinese who would be glad of it.

But nothing was going to dampen Kerry's spirits. Tom was safely back on Cornish soil and Marvin Mcleod was pronounced safe and well. What could be better than that? And next Saturday, she was going to cycle over to the hospital and get there before his parents, so that she at least had a bit of time with him on her own.

They didn't like it, of course, thinking she was snubbing them for not wanting to go in the car with them.

'I really need the exercise, Mrs Trevellyan,' she told Tom's mother. 'I feel so stuffy from being in the shop all week, and you know how Tom and I used to cycle for miles, so it won't be any hardship for me.'

'Well, if you're sure,' his mother said dubiously.

'Quite sure.'

And she was going to get there a good half-hour before they did. The visiting hour was supposed to be between three and four pm, but when they had arrived the previous week, it was obvious that plenty of visitors had got there before the allotted time. Hopefully, the hospital was fairly lax about the visitors for the walking wounded. How could anyone stop you seeing the patient you came to see, if he was sitting or strolling in the grounds? It wasn't a prison camp!

She got there soon after two-thirty pm and walked quickly to where she had seen Tom the previous week, expecting him to be sitting on the same bench by the same tree. He wasn't there, and she stood for a moment, puzzled, and not quite knowing what to do next. But she was here, and she wasn't going to waste this extra time, so she went inside the hospital and up to the reception desk where a nurse asked her business.

'I'm here to see Private Tom Trevellyan,' Kerry said, suddenly nervous. 'I know I'm a bit early, but I expected him to be outside in the grounds, so can you tell me where I can find him?'

The nurse consulted some notes. 'Are you a relative?' she said.

Kerry's heart leapt uneasily. This was what they said when there was some problem and they wouldn't let anyone see a patient except those nearest to them. Well, she was as near to Tom as anyone would ever be.

'I'm his fiancée,' she stammered, knowing it was as good as true. Did that count for a relative? Or was the nurse going to be difficult and deny her the right to see him?

'Wait here a minute,' the woman said. She walked off to consult with someone her senior while Kerry waited with her hands getting ever more clammy inside her cotton gloves.

It seemed an age before she came back. 'The doctor says you can see him now, but you musn't tire him. I'll take you along to the ward.'

'But what's wrong with him?' Kerry croaked. 'He looked so well last week. Please, you must tell me before I see him!'

The nurse was briskly efficient. 'He had to have a further operation yesterday. Some shards of shrapnel had moved in his legs and he developed considerable pain, and needed to have the shards removed at once before they travelled again. He'll be all right, but he's confined to bed for the next few days.'

Kerry followed her mutely through the maze of corridors that made up the hospital. She had no idea where she was going, nor how she would find her way back out. But none of that mattered. She had been so thrilled at being here early and seeing Tom on her own, and to be faced with this was an enormous shock.

She was finally shown into a ward where there were a dozen beds, and Tom was lying on the bed nearest the door. There was a sort of cage covering his leg beneath the bedclothes, presumably to protect it. Kerry dimly remembered hearing that the worst patients were always placed nearest the door, so that nurses and doctors could see to them instantly if their condition got any worse.

He seemed to be asleep, but he opened his eyes at once as she approached, as if some sixth sense told him she was there. He smiled weakly.

'I was just dreaming about you, sweetheart, and here you are,' he said, his voice moderately normal.

And God help her, she did exactly as his mother had done last week, and burst into tears. She sat down heavily on the chair beside the bed and fumbled for a hanky, while his hand reached out to hold hers.

'It's not as bad as it looks, Kerry. They had to fish out the last few bits of shrapnel, and I always knew this might happen, but now it's over and done with. There wasn't time or opportunity to let anybody know, and it was better that people didn't worry in advance. Especially Mum, if you know what I mean.'

'I do know, but just look at me! I'm like a drooping daffodil, aren't I? I'm no better than she was last week!'

'Don't be daft. Where is she, by the way? How did you manage to get in here on your own without Mum and Dad?'

'I rode my bike,' she said numbly.

After seeing him look so well before, it was an awful shock to see him like this. This was how she had steeled herself to find him last week. When she hadn't, she had assumed that everything was going to be fine from now on, and he would soon be home. Now, it didn't look that way at all.

'Is it all out now?' she went on huskily, knowing she had to say something.

'As far as they can tell. They don't anticipate any more,

229

so you can get that sad look off your face and come closer. Pull the curtain round so the other chaps don't see me kissing my girl.'

Kerry smiled for the first time since coming inside the hospital. It was all going to be all right, and this was just a minor setback that Tom seemed to have expected, even if she hadn't.

But the next ten minutes were completely satisfactory, even if the position was less than comfortable, but they could cope with that. It didn't last long in any case. Far too soon, the curtain was swished back by the nurse, and Tom's parents were being ushered into the ward.

'Now, before you say anything, Mum, I'm all right,' Tom said firmly, seeing his mother's eyes. 'And here's the good news. They're going to send me home in two weeks' time, once this last little lot has completely healed, so you'll soon be getting fed up with seeing me.'

His gaze went to Kerry then. He hadn't even told her the bit about him coming home. They had been too busy with other things. But he knew she wouldn't care that she hadn't heard it first.

What he didn't tell any of them yet was that because of muscle damage in his shoulder and the injuries to his leg, there was now little doubt that he would never be going back to the army, and that a medical discharge was almost inevitable. He didn't want to tell them until he knew for sure, hoping against hope that it wasn't true. He knew they'd all be glad. But he wasn't. He definitely bloody well wasn't.

CHAPTER THIRTEEN

Kerry was thankful she was on her own for the bike ride home. She couldn't have stood listening to Tom's mother being alternately tearful about the shock of seeing him in bed after another operation, and planning ahead to the proposed party for when he came home to convalesce. Although both Kerry and Tom's father had suggested they keep any notion of a party quiet for now, they could never rely on his mother not to be over-excited. Kerry knew that, according to Mrs Trevellyan, no matter what the doctors and nurses at the hospital did for her boy, nothing could compare with good home cooking and the tender loving care of his family.

She could almost hear Mrs Trevellyan saying the words in her indignant manner, and along with them came the certainty in Kerry's mind that when he did come home, she would also be shutting Kerry out. Maybe not intentionally,

231

but his mother would be the one looking after him. Tom would be labelled a hero – which of course he was – and pampered as if no other homecoming hero existed in the world.

Realising that her eyes were becoming blurred, her hands were shaking, and that she was wobbling all over the road on her bike, Kerry slowed down and slid off the machine.

It was *good news*, for pity's sake. Tom was all right, and he was getting out of the hospital very soon. He was actually coming *home*! What was there to be miserable about? She didn't understand her own crazy feelings but she didn't feel like going straight home until she had sorted them out, that was for sure. She would be quizzed by Aunt Lil, and if she voiced her feelings about Tom's mother, she would be seen as petty and selfish. Claire would understand. But right now, she didn't even want to talk to Claire. She wanted to be alone, until the little green devil inside her had cooled down.

She got on her bike again and struck off down one of the many winding lanes and tracks leading off the main road. The sun was still warm on her back, even though they were nearing the end of September now, and summer, even a glorious Cornish summer, would soon be at an end. It was her birthday in October, and by the sound of it, Tom would be home for it, she thought, with a sudden leap of excitement.

It was an unexpected bonus that she hadn't considered until that moment, and the thought was enough to cheer her up as she pedalled on until she got out of breath. She finally flopped down on a grass verge to take stock of her tumbling emotions in the sheer serenity of her surroundings.

Over the fence there were cows grazing, and somewhere in the distance she could hear the comforting noise of a tractor engine.

Bees still hovered in the fragrant hedgerows in the last throes of summer, and she felt her throat go thick, remembering Molly Roddy's sweet trusting certainty that Michael's bee was akin to being her guardian angel. Why else had she unerringly made the childish drawing of the bee that Jed had faithfully incorporated in the memorial hassock?

Kerry gave a final huge swallow and told herself she was being ridiculous to be lingering here, when she could be consulting with Tom's parents over the party they were going to throw for him. Maybe if she suggested tactfully that it could also be a birthday party for her, then Tom wouldn't be so against all the fuss, she thought cannily. It was worth a suggestion, and hopefully it wouldn't put Mrs Trevellyan's mother hen instincts out too much.

By the time she got home, she was much calmer, and found Aunt Lil to be in an almost kittenish mood herself.

'What do you think the silly old girl has done now?' she said brightly, the minute Kerry got inside the door.

'Well, since I don't know who the silly old girl is, I've got no idea. But do you want to know my news first?'

'Go on, then.'

'Tom has had to have another operation to remove some more shrapnel, but once it's healed, he'll be home on leave in a couple of weeks. Isn't that absolutely blooming marvellous?'

Of course it was! So how she came to be in Aunt Lil's arms and blubbing like a baby all over her, she had no idea.

One minute she was bursting out the news, and the next she was being patted on the back and told to sit down and have a drink of water.

'This is so daft!' she gasped out. 'I'm thrilled about it, of course I am, so I don't know why I'm reacting like this.'

'It's because you didn't expect it, and you're bowled over by it, that's why,' the all-knowing Aunt Lil said. 'So do you want to hear my news?'

Kerry stared at her, wondering how she could practically dismiss what had just happened so easily. And then being grateful that she could.

'What news is that, then?' she said huskily. 'Something about a silly old girl, wasn't it? Is that somebody at the Friendship Club? If so, it's not like you to call her names, Aunt Lil!'

'No, *no*. Who's the giddiest old girl you can think of? It's your Aunt Maud, of course! The merry widow!'

'Well, she's not a widow anymore, is she? Or has she bumped off poor old Bert already?' Kerry said with a grin.

'You can read her letter later, but I'll tell you the gist of it. She says that they're going into business and renting a little shop to sell second-hand clothes. People can bring their unwanted clothes to the shop and say how much they want for them, and Maud and Bert will do the selling and take a commission for their trouble.'

'Crikey! You've got to admire their get-up-and-go, haven't you?'

Aunt Lil sniffed. 'You might think so, but what do either of them know about shopkeeping? Bert worked at the docks before he retired, and Maud – well, Lord knows what bits and pieces she got up to in the past. She did a bit of sewing for people at one time, and that's about all I know. And it's probably all I prefer to know!'

'Well, I think it's a great idea. We don't know how long clothes rationing is going on, and if people want to recycle their old clothes and let somebody else have the wear out of them, what's wrong with that?'

'I can think of a lot wrong with it,' Aunt Lil said darkly. 'You don't know where the things came from, for a start, or who would have worn them. They might be smelly!'

Kerry started to laugh. 'Aunt Lil, you're such a snob.'

After a moment, Lil smiled. 'Yes, I suppose I am, and proud of it! Now, what do you want for your tea? You must be hungry, after all that bike riding.'

'I am, but first of all, I'm going round to see Tom's parents. I left the hospital without seeing them, so I'd better find out how they are.'

Aunt Lil clearly approved. 'You're a good girl, Kerry.'

She didn't know the half of it, Kerry thought grimly.

The Trevellyans were back home by the time Kerry got to their house. She knocked at the door and was welcomed inside. Tom's mother was beside herself with excitement, and had obviously recovered from seeing him less than mobile more quickly than Kerry had.

'Come in, Kerry love,' she said enthusiastically. 'I'm just making some tea for Father and me, so you'll have a cup, and a piece of my sponge cake, won't you?'

Kerry was obviously getting the red-carpet treatment for the moment, she thought, a mite cynically. But she couldn't begrudge Tom's mother her happiness, or that she could seemingly completely overlook the fact that Tom might never be as agile as he had once been. It wouldn't matter to her, and it wouldn't matter to Kerry, she thought, with a sudden lift to her heart.

'As a matter of fact, I wanted to ask you about something, Mrs Trevellyan,' she said carefully. 'It will be your decision, of course, but it was just an idea that came to me. If you don't like the sound of it, we can just forget it.'

And a little bit of flattery never did anyone any harm either . . .

'What was it you wanted to ask me about, Kerry?' Mrs Trevellyan went on comfortably, when they were sitting down with tea and sponge cake. By then, Tom's dad had taken his drink out to the garden at the back of the house to dig a few spuds for later.

Now that the moment was here, Kerry wasn't quite sure how the other woman was going to take it, and she took a great gulp of scalding tea that got her spluttering and coughing before she was able to do anything more.

'Well, whatever it is, you'd better spit it out before you expire, girl!'

'I'm sorry about that. It's about the party for Tom when he gets home.'

'And you want to be involved. Well, of course you do, dear. I never expected anything else. We both want him to enjoy it, don't we, and to make him feel at home as quickly as possible?'

If Kerry was unnerved by such a show of generosity, she tried not to show it. She plunged on before she lost her nerve altogether.

'It's just that it's my birthday on October the eighth, as you know, and it looks as if that's when Tom will be home,

236

so I wondered if we could make it a sort of joint party, in case he thinks it might be too much fuss. It's only an idea, mind, and of course it's up to you in the end.'

When Tom's mother said nothing for a few moments, she was sure she'd gone too far. 'It was only an idea,' she repeated lamely.

To her relief the other woman finally nodded slowly.

'It's a good one too, Kerry. I'm afraid I got carried away by it all myself, but I know Tom won't want to feel he's on display, so we'll think about doing exactly what you say, providing your auntie won't think we're treading on her toes by having the party here.'

The words said one thing. The look she gave Kerry said another. There was no way she was letting Tom's party take place in another woman's house!

'Oh, I'm sure she won't,' Kerry said hastily. 'She'll probably want to help by making my cake, and offering anything else you need, but you're such a good organiser, Mrs Trevellyan, and I know it will all be wonderful.'

'That's all arranged, then. If he's only going to be convalescing at home for a couple of weeks, we must make the most of it, mustn't we?'

'Do you think that's what it will be? Just a couple of weeks?'

'His father thinks he'll get his discharge, and I have to say I'd feel much happier about that. But I don't think Tom would be happy about it, so we'll just have to wait and see.'

So that was one hurdle over. Now all Kerry had to do was inform Aunt Lil of the prospective party arrangements and hope she wouldn't take offence. It would be Kerry's eighteenth birthday, after all, which was a milestone in any girl's life.

But when she got home again, Lil was still chuckling over the thought of her cousin Maud and slimy Bert setting themselves up as sellers of second-hand clothes, and wondering if she should send them some of her cast-offs for a start.

'I daresay Mr Churchill would be proud of them,' Kerry said. 'But I've got something else for you to think about now.'

And after all, there was nothing to worry about. Lil was perfectly happy for Tom's mother to get all the glory of the party, providing the birthday cake for Kerry had her own special mark on it.

'I'm going to write to Tom and tell him what's being planned. It's not supposed to be a surprise, and far better that it's not, or he'd be up in arms about all the fuss. I can tell him it's partly for my birthday and that will soften it.'

'You're becoming quite a devious little planner, aren't you, Kerry!'

'Only when I have to be,' she said with a grin. 'It won't hurt to remind Tom about my birthday, either, will it?' she added cheekily.

Claire was alarmed when she heard that Tom had had to have another operation to remove the shards of shrapnel. They had been for a bike ride, and were lazing on the grass before going home.

'It sounds horrible. How many more of the things do you suppose are lurking about inside him?'

'None, I hope,' Kerry said. 'That's what he's been told,

anyway, and he'll get leave as soon as it's all healed, so he'll be home for my birthday. His mother's planning a party for him, to include my birthday, so you're invited.'

'At Mrs Trevellyan's house?' Claire said, pulling a face. 'That means I'll have to be on my best behaviour and make sure I don't drop crumbs everywhere, doesn't it?'

Kerry laughed. 'She's not that bad.'

'Yes she is! At least, compared with our house. She should have a crowd of infants like we have. And then she'd see how hard it is to keep a place tidy.'

'I wish she did, then she wouldn't fuss over Tom so much.'

'It's because he's her one ewe lamb, that's why.'

'I'm Aunt Lil's one ewe lamb, but she doesn't keep me wrapped up in cotton wool all the time.'

'But you're not her daughter, are you? It's different.'

That was true. She no longer had Claire's advantage of having a mother who had to spread her love around between her brood. And she certainly wouldn't want one like Tom's, who would suffocate her with affection! Her brief bristle of annoyance at Claire's words faded, knowing she probably had the best of it with Aunt Lil if she ever stopped to consider it properly.

'Sorry, kid,' Claire said uncomfortably. 'I didn't mean to upset you.'

'You haven't. I was just thinking, that's all. So you'll come to the party once it's arranged, won't you? I'll need you there as a kind of buffer.'

'Thanks for the compliment! But of course I'll come. I'd have been mortally offended if you hadn't asked me.'

'My birthday's on a Sunday, mind, so I hope nobody's

going to make a song and dance because we're enjoying ourselves.'

'As long as we've been to church in the morning, I don't see why they should. Some will, of course, but they're not going to be invited, are they?'

As she prattled on, Kerry was already planning the day. They wouldn't want many people to overwhelm Tom, just the families and a few friends. He'd never been keen on parties, but the excuse of having a joint one to celebrate her birthday had been an inspiration, so he could hardly object to it either.

'Your Molly can come too,' Kerry added generously before they parted company. 'She'll only raise the roof if she's not asked, and Tom always made a fuss of her when he was round at your place.'

Neither of them said anything for a moment, each remembering the times that Tom had been round at the Roddys' house when he and Michael had been such great friends and practically lived in one another's pockets.

'I'll see you tomorrow, then,' Claire said quickly, and then she was gone.

Cycling home, Kerry wondered how long the feeling of walking on eggshells lasted. It was all too easy to say the wrong thing to bring the painful memories rushing back. But what was the use of hiding them? They weren't going to go away.

She paused on her bike to watch the builders putting the final touches to Mrs Holliday's house after the bomb damage from their last big air raids at the end of May. It was a long while ago now since that fateful night when Swanvale had been so devastated and the Americans had come out of virtual seclusion to lend a hand. Mrs Holliday had taken fright over what had happened to her house, insisting that she was in no hurry to return to it. But the house had been all but rebuilt for some time now, and at last it looked as though it was pretty well habitable again.

'Is Mrs Holliday coming back soon?' she asked Pam Wyatt's father, in charge of the building work.

'Looks like it, love,' he replied, easing his back for a minute or two. 'We've had our instructions to get it finished, so you'd better start looking out your dancing shoes.'

'I don't think so,' Kerry said with a laugh. 'But I'm sure that as soon as she gets home she'll be getting her troupe organised again. How's Pam getting on, by the way?' she felt obliged to ask.

'Fair to middlin', I daresay,' he said. 'Though to listen to her you'd think she was already a blessed matron and curing the whole hospital single-handed.'

'Where is she now?'

Be casual, Kerry told herself. *Don't make it sound as if you're desperate to know . . .*

'Up near Launceston. I'll tell her you asked after her.'

'Thanks,' Kerry said, giving him a beaming smile that had nothing to do with her good nature in asking after his daughter, but solely with the knowledge that Pam wasn't anywhere near Tom's hospital after all, dispensing her little drops of poison. She smiled at her own thoughts. Poison was the last thing a nurse should be dispensing!

'Well, you're in a good mood,' Aunt Lil remarked when she went indoors humming a tune.

'Why shouldn't I be? Tom's coming home. We're having

241

a party, and Pam Wyatt's working in a hospital near Launceston. All's right with my world,' she added for good effect.

'I'm glad to hear it,' Lil said dryly. 'So will you be going to visit him with his parents next Saturday?'

'I don't think so. I'll ride my bike again. It gives us all time to chat to him on our own. I'm sure his parents will appreciate that.'

And if Aunt Lil believed that, she was a monkey's uncle, Kerry thought irreverently.

'By the way, have you heard anything about when Mrs Holliday's coming back? Her house is almost ready, and I can imagine she'll be itching to get her troupe together for a Christmas show,' Kerry went on.

'They were saying at the Friendship Club that she'd be coming home in a week's time,' Aunt Lil informed her.

Kerry resisted a smile. What they didn't know at that Friendship Club wasn't worth knowing.

The curtains were drawn around Tom Trevellyan's bed where he had been instructed he had to stay until he was told anything different. His recent wounds were healing rapidly now, and he was impatient to be up and about again for his daily exercise, instead of being stuck here in bed. But until the doctors turned up, he had to do as he was told, like a ruddy schoolkid.

And when they arrived, in their lordly manner . . . He admitted to a tug of fear whenever he thought about it. The strain of not knowing whether or not he would be able to return to his unit in due course was almost as bad as actually learning about his future. He hated the not knowing. Like anybody else, he looked forward to when this bally war was over and he could go home and lead a normal life again. But he hadn't joined the army to be slung out just when things were hotting up and the Jerries were finally on the retreat.

There was movement around the end of his bed now, and then several white-coated doctors carrying clipboards entered his space, along with the staff nurse. From the looks on their faces, things didn't look too promising, and he steeled himself for what was to come.

'Now then, Private Trevellyan,' the head man said with false heartiness.

Although there was only a week between hospital visits, Kerry had hoped he would be writing to her. She had written to him, knowing the letter would get there in good time now, and she was slightly disappointed when he hadn't returned the pleasure without the awful censorship that had so inhibited their previous letters.

His parents had been perfectly agreeable to her going on her own, and getting there first. They knew he'd be home on leave soon and living under their roof again, so they could afford to be generous, Kerry thought. And this time, she saw him straight away, sitting in the grounds under the same tree as before. Unconsciously, the words of a song swept into her head . . .

Don't sit under the apple tree with anyone else but me . . .

She waved out as soon as she saw him, the laughter bubbling up inside her for the sheer joy of being with him.

'You look a lot better than the last time I saw you,'

she said cheerfully, making sure to sit down beside him on his right side, and lifting her face for his kiss. It was surprisingly secluded here, and in any case other patients with their own visitors took no notice of a pair of lovers holding one another tight.

'So when are they sending you home, and for how long?' she asked eagerly, after a very satisfactory kiss.

Her sixth sense detected the small chill between them, then. She was sure it wasn't directed at her; it was something within himself that stopped him answering for a few seconds. But it was long enough.

'What have they told you, Tom?' she almost whispered.

He turned his face away from her, but she couldn't mistake the bitterness in his voice.

'They're sending me home next week. For how long? For good, that's how long. I'm to be pensioned off, like a ruddy old man. They've had enough of me, and I'm now unfit for duty, like a bit of old rubbish. Never mind that I can still walk and still hold a gun – probably. Apparently, I'm not mobile enough for their precious army.'

Kerry didn't know what to say. She knew it was his worst nightmare. But, for God's sake, hadn't he had worst nightmares than this? Hadn't other servicemen got off far worse than he had? What about those who had lost limbs, or had half their heads blown off? And what about Michael Roddy, who had never had the chance to look forward to a life after the war? How *dare* he feel so sorry for himself?

She jumped up from the bench before she could stop herself, her eyes blazing. Never mind if she was about to say all the wrong things. She couldn't bear to listen to him being so dejected, and so *pathetic*. This wasn't the Tom she had always known, and she didn't like the one she was seeing now.

'You know what, Tom? I'm ashamed of you! You should look around you and realise how lucky you are. Some of these men here are never going to go home, and here you are, whining about something most of them would give their eye teeth to see. I can't stand to look at you, and I'm going inside to get some tea for us both while you stew in your own juice.'

Kerry was trembling by the time she finished, and he was looking at her with astonishment, but she meant every word, and she marched off across the grass to the canteen inside the building that was for the use of patients and visitors alike. Her eyes stung with tears, not knowing if she had done irreparable damage to their relationship. If she had, perhaps it was better now, rather than later. But she was seeing a side to Tom that she had never seen before, and she didn't like what she saw.

She sat down for a few minutes to steady her nerves before buying the two cups of tea, and as she looked out of the window her heart sank to see that Tom's parents had already arrived, and were sitting beside him now. Miserably, she wondered what tale he was telling them about how she had flounced off when he was at his lowest.

She turned around and ordered two more cups of tea and asked for them all to be put on a tray to take outside. Might as well do the dutiful thing, she thought, almost in desperation.

To her amazement, when she neared the small family group again, she found them all sharing a joke. Clearly,

Tom's parents had been able to do what she could not, and bring back the smile to his face.

'I've brought us all some tea,' she practically stuttered, remembering how she had left Tom.

'Good,' he said, smiling at her as if nothing had happened. 'Mum's brought some of her little cakes too, so we can have a picnic.'

Kerry put the tray on the grass, and sat beside it to hand round the cups of tea. Even if there had been enough room on the bench for them all, it wasn't much fun to be sitting in a row. She caught Tom looking at her, and they both mouthed the word 'sorry' at the same time, and both laughed at the end of it.

'You both look very shifty, so what were you plotting before we got here?' his mother said, in a very good humour now that she would have heard Tom's news.

'Nothing,' they said spontaneously.

'Have you told him about the party, Kerry?'

'What party's that, then?' Tom said, even though he already knew from Kerry's letter. He hadn't mentioned it since, though, and she hoped that whatever he might think about it, he was not going to upset the apple cart after she had told him a few home truths in her outburst.

'A welcome home party, of course, so don't go spoiling it, Tom, by saying you don't want one,' his mother said tartly. We're having it on October the eighth, to coincide with Kerry's birthday, so her auntie will be making a special cake.'

The three of them waited to hear his reaction, and Kerry still found herself holding her breath. He was more unpredictable than of old, and it was understandable, she

246

supposed, but if he threw this back in his mother's face after all, she would hate him for it.

'I suppose I'll just have to enjoy it, then, won't I?' he said blandly.

His father chuckled. 'Well done, son. We can always go off in the boat for a spell when all the partying's over and done with, so it's best to give the womenfolk a little of what they want, right?'

'Right,' said Tom solemnly.

He was looking intently at Kerry as he spoke, while his mother busied herself with getting out the bag of cakes she had baked for him. She felt her face go hot. What did she want? She wanted him back, strong and whole and her special boy. She wanted him to show her that he loved her and wanted her with all his heart, the way she wanted him.

As if he could read every one of her thoughts then, his mouth curved into a slow seductive smile, and she knew he wanted exactly what she did.

She finally came away from the hospital feeling somewhat more relieved than when she arrived. She had thought her passionate reaction would only make Tom angrier and ready to lash out at her, but it hadn't done so. After she had stalked off, he had obviously had time to think about what she had said, and she was wildly relieved that they seemed to be back on an even keel again. She couldn't have borne it if she had gone home knowing he was furious with her.

He was even all right about the party, which was something! So far, neither she nor his mother had thought seriously about who was going to be invited. All she knew was that it should be kept small, although a party with just

247

Tom's family, herself and Aunt Lil, and Claire had seemed ridiculously small, and hardly worthy of being called a party at all, and of course, she wanted Claire to be there on her eighteenth.

It could be a bit insensitive to invite all the Roddy family, but how would they feel at being left out? They had all been such friends in the past, and the sensible thing to do would be to consult the Trevellyan parents and Claire about it before doing anything else.

CHAPTER FOURTEEN

'I think they may like to be invited,' Claire said dubiously. 'But perhaps I'd better ask Mum what she thinks first. Anyway, would Mrs Trevellyan want all of us traipsing through her house? Have you thought about that?'

'No, I haven't. Oh Lord, it's all getting a bit complicated, isn't it?'

'Yes. If Michael hadn't been so awkward and got himself drowned, we wouldn't have this problem, would we?'

The minute she said it, Claire was aghast and tearful. The words had just come from nowhere, a shock to both of them.

'I can't believe I just said that! Now I feel terrible!'

Kerry didn't know how to answer, and then Claire gave a tremulous smile.

'Perhaps it's a healthy sign that I'm no longer creeping

around trying to watch every word I say about Michael. What do you think?'

She looked at Kerry in desperation, wanting her to agree.

'I daresay you're right. Just don't let your mum hear you say it, that's all. So forget it, Claire. Anyway, if Michael had been here to hear it, I'm sure he'd be laughing now.'

'He would, wouldn't he? He could always see the funny side of things.'

'So to get back to what we were talking about. Perhaps I should also see what Mrs Trevellyan thinks about the party first, and then you could suggest it to your mum. Let's leave it for the moment. One thing I am sure about, though. As soon as Tom gets home, he'll want to come round and see her.'

Tom was thinking the same thing as he finally prepared to leave the hospital that afternoon. It gave him a peculiar feeling now, to think he would no longer be bound by army rules and regulations, nor hospital ones. His papers had come through, and he was officially discharged. They didn't waste much time, he had thought bitterly. But perhaps it was better so. What was the point of dithering, when the outcome was inevitable? The irony of it was, he didn't even feel so bad now, other than a natural bit of apprehension at going home, where everybody would be showing him sympathy. He definitely wouldn't appreciate that.

Sure, his leg was a bit stiff, and his shoulder didn't have the same movement as before, but he wasn't a ruddy cripple and he had no intention of being one or acting like one. He fully intended carrying on with the strengthening exercises he already did every day, and if the army didn't want him, then he wouldn't want them, he thought, in a final surge of bravado.

His parents arrived to fetch him in the car, and after a lengthy number of goodbyes to the staff and patients he had got to know, he admitted that he was feeling exhausted, and it was only the painkillers that were keeping him going.

'I thought Kerry might have come with you,' he said tiredly, when they were on the road at last.

'It's Friday afternoon, son, and she's at work,' his father reminded him, 'but your mother's invited her to come round and have tea with us the minute the shop closes.'

Of course. Life went on. Shops opened and closed. Gardens were dug for victory. Meals were cooked with dried eggs and whatever else the ingenious housewives could concoct out of nothing. Victory was just around the corner and the Hun were on the run, and all that morale-building propaganda guff.

'Are you all right, Tom?' his mother asked when he was silent.

'I'm fine. Just taking stock of everything around me,' he said with an effort. 'You don't appreciate how green the countryside is until you've been living in dust and grime and on army rations.'

'Well, all that's behind you now, and you'll find no dust and grime in our house,' Mrs Trevellyan said briskly, just as he might have expected.

'Have you seen anything of the Roddys lately?' he asked next.

251

'They come to church every Sunday as usual, and Mrs Roddy seems to be coping well enough as far as anybody can tell. I can't say anything for Michael's father, of course, but they have the younger children, and they're a great comfort to them, I'm sure.'

Tom nodded, hardly knowing why he'd asked. Nor did he think that having a dozen other children would make up for the loss of one, but he didn't comment on that. But he supposed that the family would at least have got used to Michael's death by now, if you ever did get used to such a family tragedy.

He didn't know what he was going to say to them all, but he wasn't going to baulk at going round to see them as soon as possible, either. They would expect it. There had been a time when he was there all the time, except for the times when Michael was at his own house. Growing up in a close-knit village like Columbine made for special childhood friendships that lasted a lifetime.

His jaw clenched as the last thought entered his head. Michael's lifetime had been so short. Barely twenty years, the same as his own. It made you realise the sense in making the most of what you had while it lasted.

'Claire would have been a great help to them as well, especially with the little 'uns,' Tom went on, just for something to say. 'She'd have been clucking around them like a mother hen.'

To his surprise, his mother sniffed audibly, and he grinned faintly, well aware of her disapproval of some of the scatty young girls in the village. But that didn't apply to Claire, surely!

'What's she done to annoy you, Mum?' he said.

'Leave it, Mother,' his father warned her, alerting Tom's senses at once. But they knew it was useless to protest when her mind was set on something.

'From what I hear, she's practically got herself engaged to one of those GI fellows who were stationed here until D-Day, and she's hardly known him for five minutes. I don't know what her mother will have to say if she wants to go off to America after the war and become one of those GI brides.'

Her tone said it was worse than going to the devil.

'How do you get to hear all this stuff?' Tom said in amusement, indulging her. But he should have known.

'Friendship Club, of course,' his father put in, chuckling. 'What those old biddies don't talk about there ain't worth knowing, picking over everybody else's dirty laundry, I don't doubt.'

'Thank you, Father,' his wife said freezingly. 'Mrs Roddy's started coming to Friendship Club again, so that's a good sign, isn't it? And I'll thank you not to refer to me and the other ladies as old biddies.'

Tom saw his father wink at him through the driving mirror, and settled back in his seat, smiling to himself after their little spat. Perhaps the resumption of familiar normal life wasn't going to be so bad after all.

It was interesting and unexpected to hear about Claire and her GI, though. He wondered why Kerry had never said anything about it to him in her letters, or when she had visited him at the hospital. Since the girls had always been as thick as thieves, he would have expected it to be one of her priorities to pass on such momentous news.

* * *

Kerry was in a fever of expectation all day Friday, finding it hard to concentrate on anything. People were always asking after Tom, and it was wonderful to be able to say he was coming home that day. She was also careful to say he was on convalescent leave. Anything else should be left for him to tell people himself.

Mrs Polby finally told her to go home in the middle of the afternoon and get herself prettied up for having tea with her 'beau', as she called it. She had an old-fashioned turn of phrase that often made Kerry and Claire laugh, but Kerry was too excited to be laughing now.

'Thanks, Mrs Polby,' she almost gasped, and raced out of the shop, nearly colliding with Claire, who was just coming in to buy some writing paper.

'Is he home, then?' she said at once.

'Not yet, as far as I know. I'm just going to get changed and tidy my hair.'

Claire laughed. 'I don't think he's going to care what you're wearing or if your hair was looking like a haystack, which it isn't, by the way.'

'Thanks. Can't stop, Claire.'

Nor did she want to stop and chat. Tom should be home very soon, and she didn't want to lurk around outside his house like an idiot waiting for him to return, but since she couldn't concentrate on anything else, that was probably just what she was going to do.

When she got home, the cottage was empty, and she fumbled through her wardrobe, deciding which dress to wear for this special occasion. But she had always known there was no real choice. It had to be the blue one. Tom's favourite. She brushed her hair until it shone, put a dab of lipstick on her mouth and took a deep breath as she surveyed her reflection critically in her dressing table mirror, as ridiculously nervous as if she was meeting him for the first time.

'Oh well, it's the best I can do,' she muttered, and clattered down the stairs to find that Aunt Lil had just come home from one of her many meetings.

'Well, you look a real picture,' Lil said after a moment. 'I think I saw the Trevellyans' car as I came through the village.'

By then she was talking to herself, as Kerry was flying out of the door and through the narrow streets until the saw the old jalopy parked outside Tom's house. He was home. Well, unless anything had gone terribly wrong, and they had kept him in the hospital a bit longer . . .

Try as she might, she couldn't get the little knot of fear out of her head. Until she actually saw him inside his own front room, she wouldn't believe it.

She didn't have to wait that long. He had obviously been watching for her, and as she reached the front door it was flung open and she was in his arms. How long they held one another, she couldn't have said, until his mother's voice broke through her senses.

'Come on now, you two, there's plenty of time for all that, and you don't want to be giving the neighbours a peep show!'

They broke apart, but only slightly, and Tom grinned down at her before murmuring in her ear.

'She's right. We've got plenty of time for *all that* from now on.'

But his cheek nuzzled hers for a moment more, and she

was thrilled by the understated passion in his voice. What had she been so scared about? Tom was here at last, and despite his injuries she was sure he was going to adapt to being home as quickly as he had adapted to army life.

It was a slightly awkward couple of hours all the same. Tom's mother was overprotective, fussing over his every move, and his father seemed to be forever trying to calm her down a little. Finally, Tom could take no more of it.

'I think Kerry and I should get out of your hair for a while, Mum,' he said at last. 'I know you'll be wanting to put all my stuff away to your liking in my room, and I'll only be in the way. We won't be gone long.'

Kerry wondered how his mother was going to take this. She guessed that she dearly wanted to protest, or suggest that she came with them . . . but in the end, prompted by a few murmured words from her husband, she gave in.

'Just don't tire yourself, Tom. You're only just out of the hospital, remember,' she couldn't resist saying.

'I know, and I've had plenty of time to adjust while I was there, and you know I'm supposed to exercise. I'm not an invalid, Mum, and I don't intend to act like one,' he said.

'Don't forget your stick, then,' Mrs Trevellyan added.

He grabbed it, but from his attitude, Kerry knew very well it was likely to be flung into the garden until they came back from their walk. He almost exploded as they got outside the house.

'I knew it would be like this. She'll try to smother me with kindness!'

'You can't blame her, Tom, but I'm sure she'll settle down in a few days when she gets used to having you around again. And by the way, telling her you knew she'd be wanting to put your stuff away to her liking was a master stroke. She'd never be able to resist tidying her little boy's bedroom the way she always used to,' she finished with a grin.

'Oh well, I do have some tricks up my sleeve,' he agreed. 'So where shall we go? Take a walk around the village, where we're bound to meet people who'll stop us all the way? Or down to the river, so I can take a look at our boat? Or go to see Michael's folk?'

Before he finished speaking, she knew what he wanted to do most. And if she had hoped for an hour or so alone with him, she knew those times could wait. There were things Tom had to do first.

'I think you should go and see Michael's parents,' she told him. 'And if you'd rather I didn't come with you, just say so, Tom.'

'Don't be daft,' he said roughly. 'I've waited too long to be with you, and I don't ever want to let you out of my sight again.'

He tucked her arm inside his. It was wonderful to be pressed so close to him and to feel the warmth of his body next to hers, even though she couldn't be sure if it was because he was wishing he'd brought the stick with him after all. But she wasn't going to ask him. She knew it was his pride that had made him discard it, and he was still more fragile than of old, in mind as well as body. Telling everyone that he was now home for good had been a painful thing for him to do. His mother had made no secret of her relief, but Kerry didn't want to puncture his pride, even though she rejoiced so much in the fact that he was never going away again.

'Maybe I'll ask Dad if I can borrow the car and we can

go for a drive sometime,' he went on. 'We could go to the pictures, or up on the moors – or anywhere you like, come to that. There's no way he's going to let me start work again yet, and if he tried, Mum would have something to say about it, so we might as well make the most of my freedom.'

Kerry knew him well enough to detect the note of bitterness in his voice, but she decided to ignore it.

'That sounds wonderful, Tom. We could be like tourists and explore the countryside. You've been to France, and I know that wasn't any picnic,' she added hurriedly, 'but do you realise we've seen hardly anything of our own county yet? We should get out the map and see where we want to go.'

'Well, all right, but I'll have to ask Dad about the car first. He may not be agreeable. And he might not want to spare the petrol.'

It was something he hadn't thought about until that moment. It just seemed that he had to weigh everything up twice as much as he used to. Spontaneity had to take second place to mundane things, like having enough petrol for the ruddy car, and when Kerry was working, and whether he had done his daily exercises. Things that would never have entered his head before. Nor had he needed to bother his head about such things while he had been fighting in France.

They all knew about rationing and suchlike, but the privations at home had seemed as if they belonged in another world, and the world he had so recently known had taken up all his focus and his energy. War changed everything. War changed people. He only had to remember some of the poor sods at the hospital he had just left to know that. The ones who would never go home.

'Just as long as your mother doesn't want to come with us,' he heard Kerry say uncertainly, when he was silent for a few minutes.

They had left the main part of the village behind them now. She wasn't sure she should have said it in such a dour voice, but to her astonishment Tom started laughing. She never really noticed how desperate it was, only that it was such an amazingly warm and refreshing sound that she was laughing too. The day had already faded into twilight, and Tom pulled her into his arms and was kissing her as though his life depended on it.

'Crikey, Tom,' she stuttered when they finally moved apart. 'What was that all about?'

'That was making up for lost time, at least a tiny part of it. Are you objecting?'

'Of course not!' she said, starting to laugh again. 'It's the first time we've managed to be away from your parents or anyone else, so why would I object?'

'That's why I want us to get away from the village when we can, so that I don't feel suffocated by all the attention I know I'm going to get.'

'Well, you are the conquering hero, don't forget.'

His mouth twisted. 'I'm hardly that. Just the wounded soldier, like thousands of others.'

'You're all heroes,' Kerry said stubbornly, 'and don't you forget it. So don't let's get downhearted again. Michael's family won't want to see you looking miserable.'

Or perhaps they would. How did she know? How did anyone know how to handle situations that had never occurred before? Nobody told you how to behave at times like these. Kerry couldn't begin to imagine how Mrs Roddy would feel when she saw Tom home, safe and reasonably well, when Michael was not. But there were no rules. You could only use inadequate words to convey what your heart felt and hope that it was enough.

Anyway, there was no more time for thinking because they were at the house now. She felt Tom's hand squeeze hers for a moment, and then he knocked on the door. The next minute it was opened, and Claire gave a little squeal of delight and almost pulled him inside, with Kerry following.

'Mum, look who's here!' Claire shouted.

'Hush, girl,' they heard her mother say, 'you'll have the young'uns out of their beds and downstairs again in a minute.'

And then she was at the door, and her face broke into such a welcoming smile that both Tom and Kerry knew there had been no need to be anxious. Within seconds, he was enveloped in her embrace, and if everyone's welcome was laced with tears, well, who could blame them?

'It's so good to see you,' Mrs Roddy said, wiping her eyes. 'Your mother told me you were coming home today, Tom, and I'd have been mortally offended if you hadn't made our house your first port of call once you'd settled in. So come and sit down, both of you, and take a glass of our elderflower champagne with us. We'd been saving it for when Michael came home, but we'll have it now to celebrate your safe return. Fetch the glasses, Claire.'

Tom found it hard to resist gasping at her composure, and the natural way she spoke about Michael, but it was only when Michael's father had poured the glasses of his home-brewed elderflower champagne and she handed it round that he noticed how her hands were shaking. Then he knew how much of an ordeal this was for her, just as it was for him.

Kerry was glad the two smaller Roddy children were in bed. Jed was now allowed to stay up later, and she was glad he was there, since he started asking Tom all kinds of things about the war. Not sure if this was a good idea at first, she realised that his eager questions were breaking the tension between them all.

'Have you got any bits of shrapnel that they cut out of you, Tom?'

'Jed, don't be so gruesome,' Claire grimaced.

'It's all right,' Tom said with a smile. 'I was as gruesome as you, Jed, and wanted to see what it looked like. It's all cleaned up now, don't worry,' he added, seeing the look of horror on the female faces. 'I've got a few pieces, and you can have one if you like.'

'Gosh, thanks, Tom,' Jed said in awe. 'I can take it to school and show it to everybody. They'll be mad jealous.'

'Yes, well that's enough talk about bits of shrapnel for now,' his father said. 'So what are you going to do now you're out of the army, Tom?'

Kerry saw his lips tighten a little. The village grapevine had obviously been working overtime again. But then he shrugged.

'As soon as I can I want to get back to work on the boat again. It probably needs another lick of paint by now. Dad's never been keen on painting, so I daresay that'll be my first job.'

'Once you're properly fit, you mean,' Kerry reminded him. 'You don't want to rush things, do you?'

She knew she shouldn't have said it by the glare he gave her. He didn't want to be reminded of the fact that he wasn't ready to resume life the way it had been before he went away, but there was no use hiding his head in the sand.

'Kerry's right, Tom,' Michael's mother said quietly. 'You've got plenty of time to get back to normal. I only wish—'

She stopped abruptly, but they all knew what she wished for. They knew she would be remembering the many times that Michael and Tom sat here, drinking tea or something stronger, laughing and joking, and spinning tales of derring-do for the kids to listen to, open-mouthed. And in a flash, Kerry found herself feeling thankful that Tom no longer wore his uniform, because that would really have poured salt in the open wound that this family still felt.

She cleared her throat, but since nobody seemed to know what to say next, she spoke quickly.

'Tom's parents are giving a small welcome home party for him on Saturday week, and as it's my birthday we're celebrating that at the same time. Claire's invited, of course, and the children too if they want to come – and I don't know if you and Mr Roddy would feel like joining us?'

She was leaping in, when it wasn't her place to do so. Claire probably hadn't even mentioned it to her parents yet, and the Trevellyans knew nothing of the extended invitations. Although it had been a genuine request, she was relieved when Mrs Roddy shook her head gently.

'It's a lovely thought, but it's too much for us, Kerry. I'm sure Claire and the other children will enjoy it, though.'

'And you can give me the piece of shrapnel then, Tom,' Jed said excitedly, 'or I could come round to your house and collect it.'

Tom laughed at his eagerness, but his heart tugged as he saw the echo of Michael in his shining eyes.

'I'll bring it round tomorrow morning,' he promised. 'I can have a few private words with your mum then, too.'

Of course, that was what he would want, especially now that they had broken the ice. It was necessary for both of them, thought Kerry.

'And how are you, Claire?' Tom said, turning to her. 'I've been hearing a few things about you.'

She went bright red as she glanced at Kerry.

'Well, you don't want to believe all you hear, but if you mean have I got a new boyfriend, then it's true.'

'He's a Yank,' Jed put in importantly, 'and when our Claire gets married and goes to live in America, we're all going there for a visit.'

'Now you hold on with your nonsense, young fellow,' his father said sternly. 'Claire hasn't known Glenn for very long, and there'll be no talk of marrying anybody until this war's over. Then we'll see what happens.'

'He's her pen pal now,' Jed went on stubbornly. 'He went to France on D-Day, so you might have seen him there, Tom.'

'Not very likely, kid,' Tom said with a grin. 'I was otherwise engaged at the time, and out of the thousands of troops who landed on the beaches, I doubt that I'd have picked out one Yank called Glenn.'

Jed lost interest, and Kerry breathed a sigh of relief, not wanting the talk to centre on the GIs who were stationed here while Tom – and Michael – were away fighting the Jerries. Claire was the lucky one to have found love with Glenn. But there was also Marvin, who had been no more than a genuine guy she had befriended – but who knew what Tom might make of it in his present state? She was quite sure he was more vulnerable than he tried to make out, still furious at being discarded from the army, as he interpreted it, and not yet ready or able to be back in spirit to where he belonged.

'I think we should go soon,' he said to Mrs Roddy. 'I wanted to see you as soon as possible, but I told Mum I wouldn't be too long, and you know how she fusses.'

'She has every right to fuss over you while she can, Tom, so indulge her a little, won't you?'

'I'll try, and I'll see you again tomorrow morning,' he promised.

They left soon afterwards, and Tom gave out a long drawn-out breath.

'I needed to go there, but it was more difficult than I imagined, and we didn't even talk about Michael, did we?'

'I think you'll feel more able to do that when you see his mother again tomorrow. This first meeting was bound to feel a bit strained, but you did well.'

'Thank you, teacher.'

'I wasn't criticising.'

'I know, so don't let's talk about it. I want to go and see the boat.'

His thoughts seemed to switch from one thing to another like quicksilver, as if he simply blocked off the things he didn't want to talk about, or to hear.

'It's dark now,' Kerry remonstrated, 'so you're not going to see much.'

'Go home if you don't want to come, then. I need to see it, that's all.'

Kerry hugged his arm, feeling the tension in it. 'Of course I'm coming with you. Don't shut me out, Tom.'

Why had she said that? But then, why did it feel as if he was doing exactly that? Shutting her out of his feelings, his memories, his terrible experiences? Even Jed had got more out of him than she knew. He had never mentioned bringing home any bits of shrapnel the surgeons had evidently given him. Was this the sort of trophy all wounded heroes kept? It was ghoulish and pathetic and defiant, all at the same time.

'I'm sorry,' he said, his voice rough. 'I don't know what I'm saying sometimes. Of course I want you with me, and I don't mean to shut you out. How could I?'

Well, he could, and he did, but she let it pass.

'We won't see much on the river at this time of night,' she said instead, 'and as the tide's out, most of the boats will be beached or stuck in the mud as usual at low tide.'

'Sounds normal, then,' he said, sounding calmer. 'I just want to see it for myself, just as I need to acclimatise myself with everything about the village again. There were plenty of times when I thought I might never see it again.'

Kerry didn't dare comment. She had the feeling that, from now on, she would be hearing dribs and drabs of his experiences, rather than full-blown accounts. Some things were too sensitive for that, and he had always tried to minimise what was happening while he was in France, but she was intuitive enough to know that the experiences would have cut deep into his heart.

For the first time ever, she understood what it meant to be a conscientious objector – those men known derisively as 'conchies' – who were often vilified for refusing to enlist and go to war, either on religious or moral grounds. Going to war meant killing people. It was necessary. But Tom had never liked to kill anything in his life, and she had often teased him for carefully lifting a butterfly out of harm's way, or refusing to kill a wasp or a bee, saying they had a right to enjoy the countryside as much as he did. She had loved him for that, and she loved him now.

As they started walking along the towpath she realised how his footsteps had slowed, his left leg dragging a little. He should have brought his stick after all, but she wouldn't mention that, either. She was already becoming wise to his moods, and she suspected there were going to be many more of them.

'Maybe that's far enough after all,' Tom said suddenly. 'It's better to take a look at the boat in daylight to see the state of it, anyway. I can come down here any time now, and I've got a feeling young Jed will want to come with me.'

'I'm sure he will,' Kerry said evenly. All boys together and all that.

Yes, she thought, Jed Roddy might well become his little shadow. And not so little at that, either. He was growing so tall now. Just as long as the two little ones didn't trail along too, as if Tom was some kind of Pied Piper . . .

'So let's go home,' he went on, his arm going around her waist and pulling her closer. And no matter how tricky things might be from now on, thought Kerry, she had never heard sweeter words.

CHAPTER FIFTEEN

She couldn't expect him to walk her home, and in the blackout it could have been tricky for Tom not to stumble without his stick for support, but she daren't make it seem as though she was mothering him.

'You'd think that with all the rest I've had, I'd be bursting with energy, wouldn't you?' he said when they were nearing his own house.

'I don't know. What I do know is that Aunt Lil didn't think I'd be out this long, so shall I see you tomorrow, Tom? I'm working in the morning, so I'll come round in the afternoon if you like.'

It was a haphazard way of letting him know she was going to go on home by herself. He didn't say anything at first, and then he spoke slowly.

'You don't know how good that sounds, sweetheart. Saying that you'll see me tomorrow, I mean. But I'll want to say hello to your auntie, so I'll come round to your house. I may have persuaded Dad to let me have the car by then, so stand by – if I can still remember how to drive it!'

But there was a definite note of taking charge in his voice now, which was a relief. Kerry leant up and kissed him, and then told him teasingly to remember to pick up his stick before he went indoors, or his mother would be after him.

'I will if I can find it again,' he said with a short laugh. 'If not, it can stay where it is. I don't need props.'

He kissed her again and then he waited until she was gone before limping up the path to his front door, more fatigued than he had ever expected to be, but determined not to show his mother just how much. You didn't learn discipline in the army not to know how to use it when it was needed. But the painkillers the army doctors had provided him with were going to be high on the agenda a little later, or he knew he'd never sleep that night.

As it was, lying in his own bed, which should be so familiar and comforting to him after so long, seemed completely alien now. In France he had slept on camp beds, on palliasses, on makeshift straw mattresses, on dusty floors. He had slept lying at full stretch, sitting down or standing up, on rough blankets, and in narrow hospital beds that were as hard as iron. But in this most welcome of beds, with a soft mattress and sweet clean sheets he could only move restlessly, trying to find comfort for a body that suddenly ached all over and gave him no peace.

As the night wore on, he began to feel panic wash over him. Why was he feeling this way? What was wrong? He had reluctantly accepted that he was out of the army for good, but he was on the mend now, as far as he would ever be, and the hospital doctors had told him so. He knew it would still take time, but his impatience and his own will to survive had made him scoff privately at the doctors' words. Once he was home again, everything would be fine. He would show them. He would show them all!

But he wasn't thinking like that now. What if they hadn't removed every bit of shrapnel after all? Fear was throbbing through his body now. They had had to perform a second operation that hadn't been expected. What if there was more of the stuff inside him, tiny invaders with a life of their own, moving insidiously around his body ready to strike at his heart without warning?

What if a sliver of metal pierced a tendon, a vein, a major artery, so that he slowly bled to death? What if . . . *what if* . . . ?

He wasn't aware that he had been shouting out, or that he had even been in the throes of nightmare dreams. He was only aware of a man's hand grasping his, and a man's voice soothing him and telling him everything was all right, and he was home and in his own bed. He didn't know the man. Was it a doctor? And who was the woman hovering behind him? One of the vampire nurses, ready with a hypodermic needle full of the nectar that would stab him into blessed unconsciousness?

'Hold on, son, and your mother will fetch you some water and some clean pyjamas. You've had a bad dream,' his father said steadily.

Clean pyjamas? Why would he need those? He knew he was sweating all over, but he had put on clean pyjamas when he came to bed.

Then he felt the hot wetness in the bedclothes and shame swept over him, realising he had peed himself.

'Oh God, I'm sorry,' he croaked.

'Don't be sorry, and don't be a bloody fool,' his father said, using a word Tom rarely heard him say. 'Do you think we can't deal with this? Let me help you out of bed while we sort you out, son. It's a privilege to be able to do these things for you.'

Tom's eyes stung. It shouldn't be a bloody privilege for a middle-aged man to be doing these things for a grown-up son. It should be the other way around, the son helping the father when he reached old age. But his dad wasn't old, and he wasn't a child, and he didn't want his father – or his mother – to see him like this. Especially not his mother. *Oh God.*

'I don't want Mum to have to do any of this, Dad,' he whispered, starting to struggle out of bed himself.

'Don't worry about that. I'll see to it, son. When your mother's brought you some water and a wash bowl, and the clean pyjamas and sheets, I'll insist that the rest is men's work,' he promised. 'It's no different from what the army medics did, and it'll be no hardship now.'

Tom didn't know how his mother would resist raised eyebrows at such an unlikely comment that all this was men's work, nor did he know how she would react to being out of full control, fussing and fretting over him. There were clear defining lines between what was men's work and women's work. But somehow his father had persuaded his mother to leave him to it, and between them it was the two Trevellyan men who did what had to be done, until Tom was finally back in his own bed, exhausted by all the activity, and wondering what the hell was happening to him.

'I didn't expect any of this,' he said huskily to his father. 'I thought I was over the worst of it.'

'You are, son, but you're not over the memories yet, and they'll take some time to fade, if they ever do completely. Any old soldier will tell you that, if they tell you anything at all of their experiences. People say that time is a great healer, and it's true, as you'll discover for yourself. You've got your future ahead of you now, and a lovely young girl to share it with.'

'I know, and I don't need reminding that I'm one of the lucky ones,' Tom muttered, still restless, still haunted by the memories of the nightmare.

'Let me give you a bit of advice, Tom,' his father said. 'It's a little trick I learnt years ago. When you go to bed, no matter how active your mind is, try to think of something pleasant, so that it's the last thing in your head before you finally drop off. It might be a funny story you've heard that made you smile, or the places you used to go with Kerry, or even something from your schooldays.'

'Like running wild with Michael,' Tom said without thinking, his handsome mouth twisting. 'I'm not sure that will give me a good night's sleep.'

'You'd be surprised. The mind has a clever way of concentrating on the things you want it to. Schooldays with Michael might help in other ways too.'

Tom didn't want to delve any further into his father's philosophy, and in any case his mother was back upstairs with a cup of cocoa for him, even though he saw by his bedside clock that it was past two in the morning now, and she must be tired as well. They both must be, since they usually retired early, and couldn't have expected such an upset on his first night home.

It was strange that he had worked alongside his father all these years since leaving school and even before that, and he had never known him to be so masterful, so sensitive to his needs, so everything a son would want in a father.

'Thanks, Mum, and I'm really sorry,' he began awkwardly, but she put up her hand to stop him.

'That's not a word I want to hear again, my dear. You drink this cocoa now. It will calm you as much as any doctor's pills, and then get your head down again. Things always look brighter in the morning.'

She turned to leave the room, practically under orders, Tom thought, and his father paused to give Tom a wink as he followed her.

'I love you both,' he told his parents in a choked voice, hardly knowing if he had ever said such a thing before in his life.

And then he was alone, and he did as he was told. He drank his cocoa and got his head down, to think of pleasant things, of Kerry, his sweetheart, and the glorious fact that he was going to see her tomorrow, and the next day, and every other day for the rest of their lives.

'So how was Tom?' Aunt Lil asked Kerry the minute she got home on Friday evening. 'I daresay he found it a bit stifling to be in that house again, with his mother being her usual protective self.'

'You couldn't really expect anything else, could you? I think he was quite glad to get out of there after tea, though, so we went round to Claire's house. Tom wanted to see Mrs Roddy as soon as possible, but nobody mentioned Michael much, and he's going to see her again tomorrow morning.'

'I'm sure he'll want to talk to her privately about Michael,' Lil said understandingly.

'I hope he gets the chance, then. The kids were in bed except Jed, and they'll be all over him. You know what a fuss Molly always made of him.'

When she paused, Lil sensed that she had something else to say.

' *And?*' she prompted.

'It was something Jed said, and it bothered me. He asked if Tom had brought home any bits of shrapnel he'd had cut out of him.'

Lil laughed. 'The little ghoul! But boys love all those horror things. What did Tom say to that? It didn't upset him, did it?'

'That's the funny thing. He said he'd got several pieces and he'd give Jed a piece of it, which Jed was going to take to school to show all his friends as a kind of war trophy.'

'There you are. That's what I mean. Boys and their horror trophies!'

Kerry shook her head. 'That's not what *I* mean. Tom had never told me any of that. It just came out when Jed asked him about it.'

'So you're jealous that you had to hear it in front of little Jed Roddy and his family, are you?'

This was coming out all wrong. It wasn't what Kerry had meant at all. At least, she didn't think so. It was just something she hadn't known, and she thought Tom would have told her about it first. It was completely illogical, but it was the way she felt.

'Kerry, love, I'm sure there are very many things that have happened to Tom in the last six months or so that you may never get to hear about. And plenty of other things that you will only hear in Tom's own good time. For goodness' sake, he's only been home a few hours, and I don't suppose the first thing he wanted to tell you was about a few bits of shrapnel he's kept in a jar or wherever they are.'

'Oh, I know you're right, Aunt Lil, and I'm just being silly.'

Lil went on relentlessly. 'Yes, you are. You've both had different experiences in the time you've been apart, and you have to adjust to being together again. How do you think couples cope when they've been apart for years? You all emerge as different people, and you've got to learn to know one another all over again. Providing the roots are strong, even the weakest plant will survive, and then nothing else matters. Just ask Mr Middleton!'

'I didn't know you were in cahoots with the wireless gardening expert,' Kerry said, chuckling for the first time since coming home.

'I'm not, but what he says makes sense in other areas as well as planting a few potatoes in the back garden. And now I'm going to my bed, and I suggest you do the same. Oh, by the way, we've had a new idea at the Friendship Club.'

Kerry groaned. When did they not have new ideas at the Friendship Club? Some of them came to fruition, and some did not.

'Go on,' she said with a grin.

'It was Maud's letter that started me thinking. You know, about her and Bert renting a little shop and selling off second-hand clothes.'

'You're not thinking of renting a shop, are you, Aunt Lil?'

Lil was impatient with her amusement. 'Of course not. Since we're still subject to these meagre clothing coupons, and likely to be for some time to come, we ladies at the Friendship Club are considering having a small table once a month where we can donate good-quality clothes we no longer want. We shall invite people from the village to help themselves to anything suitable in return for leaving one of their own garments in exchange. We won't make a profit, and it will all be done with the emphasis on good quality, and cleanliness, naturally.'

'So it won't be much different from what Maud and Bert are doing, really,' Kerry said, hardly able to contain her laughter. 'I thought you disapproved of all that, because you didn't know where the stuff would be coming from or who had worn it before.'

'This will be quite different,' Lil said stiffly. 'We will check everything before it's placed on the table for exchanging.'

'How can you do that with people bringing clothes in on the day? Won't they need checking too? Have you got an X-ray machine to check for bugs and so on, or are you just going to sniff them?' she added mischievously.

'Now you're being really silly, but we obviously haven't thought things through yet, and it's only an idea. It may come to nothing. And now I shall say goodnight, Kerry. You may lock up, and I'll see you in the morning.'

Oh dear. She had probably offended her aunt now, but

Kerry had a shrewd feeling that when the ladies at the Friendship Club reconsidered what they were proposing, the idea might well be abandoned. Maud's shop was a much better idea, even if Aunt Lil was loath to admit it, Kerry thought with a chuckle, and she had to give her and Bert full marks for enterprise.

But she couldn't spare too much thought to any of it as she followed her aunt's instructions and then went up to bed herself. She lay inside the bedcovers with her eyes wide open, her mind buzzing with excitement, and far too excited to think of sleep. Tom was home, and home to stay. It was the only important thing in her life right now. She had no doubt they would have a few ruffled feathers to overcome, but they could deal with those. Being together again surmounted everything else.

And where would they go tomorrow afternoon? If he was really allowed to borrow his dad's car, anywhere was possible. Was he able to ride his bike, if not? They used to cycle for miles around the immediate countryside, usually ending up in some secluded spot on the moors where no one mattered in the world but themselves. The delicious thoughts spun round and round in her head until she finally dropped off to sleep with a smile curving her mouth.

Tom wasn't up too early the next morning. Despite having had very little sleep, and hugely embarrassed by the memory of what had happened in the early hours, he hardly knew how to face his parents over the breakfast table. They were both early risers, and he might have known that by now his mother would be all efficiency,

278

and his father was twiddling with the wireless, trying to get a good reception. He turned it off as soon as Tom appeared.

'You don't need to do that on my account, Dad,' he said. 'I know the war's not going to stop because of what happened to me.'

'Needs a new accumulator, son, and I don't want to waste the bit we've got left,' his father said calmly.

'Sit down and have some toast and scrape, Tom,' his mother said. 'There's some of my rhubarb-and-ginger jam to go with it.'

'I'm not really hungry, Mum, so I'll just have a slice, thanks.'

'You need to build yourself up, my dear, and there's no sense in starving yourself. I could do you a boiled egg instead, if you like.'

'Leave it, Mother,' his father said. 'The boy knows what he needs. And he'll eat when he's hungry.'

Tom flashed him a grateful look. The *boy* just wanted to get out of here as soon as he could, and to get some good Cornish air into his lungs. It might still be too early to land on the Roddys' doorstep, but he could take a stroll and reacquaint himself with some of his old haunts.

He cleared his throat. There was something that needed to be said first.

'Look, about last night . . .'

His mother gave him his slice of toast with its scrape of margarine, together with the pot of home-made jam, and put one hand on his shoulder. He barely managed not to wince, even though the pain was more expected than actual. Then she poured a large cup of tea from the big, brown, earthenware teapot and put it in front of him. She spoke determinedly.

'Last night was last night, and this is another day, my dear. It's always best not to dwell on what's past. I'm sure you've thought that many times.'

He wished he could have thought so last night, when the nightmare was so real he thought he was living through his private hell all over again.

'Your mother's right, as always, Tom. You've got to leave it behind you, and look to the future.'

He supposed they meant to imply that what had happened in his shameful and unmanly hours last night didn't matter, but it bloody well mattered like hell to him. He prayed to God it never happened again, but there were no guarantees. You couldn't control dreams or nightmares, any more than you could stop the fear galloping through him that sent control of normal bodily functions going haywire. He concentrated on breakfast, forcing himself to eat the thick piece of toast, even though it threatened to gag him and was only helped down by the scalding tea, laced with the saccharin that left a bitter taste in his mouth.

As soon as he decently could, he left the house. He couldn't bear to see his parents' considerate faces a minute longer, knowing what he had put them through last night. He remembered he was going to ask his dad about borrowing the car, but that could wait until later. He remembered he had promised Jed Roddy a piece of shrapnel, and he slipped it into his coat pocket, wrapped in a piece of old newspaper. He remembered Kerry, and for the first time that day, his heart lifted. He was also horrified to think that she hadn't even come into his mind until that moment. He had been too concerned with his own problems, still too introverted because of pain and the minutiae of hospital life, as so many patients he knew had been. He hadn't thought he was one of them, but he knew how quickly a well-adjusted person could turn into a self-pitying hypochondriac.

He concentrated on the serenity of the day as he walked down to the river, the water fresh and gleaming in the morning sunlight. For early October, the weather was still balmy, with only a few murky clouds hovering in the distance. He would have walked farther on upriver, to where their boat was always moored, but the urgency to see Michael's mother and get their painful talk over with was becoming too strong.

As he knocked on their door, it was flung open, and he was almost knocked over by an assault of flailing arms and screeching voices.

'It's Tom!' Molly screamed. 'Mum, it's Tom!'

Toby was only slightly less vocal as he hopped up and down. 'Our Jed says you're bringing him a bit of shrapnel. Have you got some for me too?'

Tom laughed at their excitement. As it was Saturday with no school, they were still in their pyjamas and bare feet, and it was so much like the old times when he'd come calling for Michael and teased them. He'd always been like an extra big brother that the younger ones had taken to their hearts and adored.

'I've only got one piece to spare,' he said, 'but I'm sure Jed will let you see it and hold it as much as you like. You'll have to be careful, though, because it's sharp. Now, can I come in, or do I have to stand on the doorstep all day?'

Over their heads, Mrs Roddy smiled at him. The

atmosphere was not as tense as last night, and for that Tom was thankful. Jed came crashing down the stairs at that moment, eager to see his trophy, and Tom unwrapped it carefully, spreading out the old newspaper until the piece of metal was revealed.

'Is that all? It's not very big, is it?' Toby said, disappointed.

'What did you expect, a dagger?' Tom said with a grin. 'It was big enough, I promise you.'

'Was that thing inside you, Tom?' Molly asked, having clearly heard from her brothers what it was all about – and in gory detail, Tom had no doubt.

'Yes, it was, and I'm glad it's out,' he replied briefly.

Their mother took charge.

'I want to have a little talk with Tom, so you three can go and get yourselves properly dressed, and you can talk to him later.'

She shooed them upstairs and Tom followed her into the sitting room. He was glad Michael's father was out, so he could simply say what he had come to say while he still had the courage. He sat beside her on the sofa. He meant to be dignified, but as the words began to spill out, his voice trembled uncontrollably.

'I could tell you how sorry I am about Michael, but I'm not going to. That's what other well-meaning people say, but I'm not other people, am I? I'm his best friend, his brother, and I miss him like hell. Even coming here and seeing all of you without him is tearing me apart.'

He went on and on, not knowing what he said or how impassioned he became. He was aware of Mrs Roddy's arms around him, and he felt himself heaving against her.

God, this was awful, shaming, but he couldn't stop it. He couldn't stop weeping for his best friend, his brother . . .

'I'm so sorry,' he finally gasped as he broke away, wretched with embarrassment. 'You've already been through so much, and I'm not helping.'

'Yes you are, my love. It helps me a great deal to know how much you cared for Michael, the same as we all did, and still do. In fact, I can't tell you how good it was to see you walk through the door last night, making this family almost complete again.'

She was so strong, stronger than he was. She could still smile through the shine of her tears. She was unbelievable. Tom swallowed the threat of choking bile in his throat.

'Thank you,' he almost whispered.

There were still so many things to be said, but he gradually became calmer as Michael's mother told him about the terrible day they had received the news, the effect it had had on all of them, especially his mother, and how they knew they all had to pull together for the sake of each other. She would want Michael to be proud of them for that, she added with a catch in her throat. She told him about the memorial hassock that the caring ladies at the Friendship Club had made, based on the drawings of the Roddy children.

'You'll see it when you go to church, Tom,' she went on, her eyes daring him to say he couldn't face the village congregation just yet. If she could do it, then so could he. 'Will you be there tomorrow morning?'

'Mum will expect it, so of course I will, providing the vicar's sermon doesn't go on too long, and that I can sit still long enough.'

It was the only reference he made to his own disability. Compared to what this family had suffered, it didn't seem like so much after all. It was bearable because he still had the rest of his life to live.

The hammering on the sitting room door reminded them that the children weren't going to be kept out for much longer. Mrs Roddy smiled.

'Go and talk to your adoring public,' she said lightly.

He pressed her hand for a moment and then opened the door to see Molly's eager face.

'Our Jed and Toby have gone out to show the shrapnel to some of Jed's friends, so I've got you all to myself, Tom,' she shrieked, unable to talk quietly.

He gave a mock groan. 'Heaven help me, then.'

'Heaven's where the angels live, and our Michael's an angel now,' she said, important with Sunday school knowledge.

His heart lurched at the simple words. It must be wonderful to be five years old and have such faith . . . even if much of that faith was whittled away as you grew older. And yet hadn't there been a thousand times when he'd begged God to get him through his own ordeal?

'Why don't you two go and sit in the garden and I'll bring you out some lemonade?' her mother said, seeing the look on his face.

'Come on then, pest,' he said, trying to sound more teasing. 'Come and tell me what you've been doing while I've been away.'

It was an open invitation, and she chattered on endlessly as they sat on the garden bench drinking her mother's lemonade.

'I'm going to be a bridesmaid one day,' she said suddenly.

'Is that right? I thought you were going to be a bride and marry me! Or have you gone off me now?'

She screamed with laughter. 'No, silly. But I shall be a bridesmaid when Claire marries her Yank, only Daddy says I should call him a Yankee Doodle,'cos it sounds nicer, and Daddy says there's a song about a Yankee Doodle.'

She prattled on with Tom smiling and indulging her, and hardly needing to put in the odd comment now and then. It felt so good to be back here now, and it really was almost like old times, except that it could never be like that. But for now it was enough. It had to be enough.

'Kerry had a Yankee Doodle as well.'

For a moment, Tom felt his heart stop and then race erratically again. He wasn't sure he had even heard those words, since Molly hadn't stopped her endless flow of chatter, rushing on from one topic to the next. She was now trying to decide what colour frock she was going to wear when she became a bridesmaid at Claire's wedding.

'What about Kerry, Molly?' he finally forced himself to say.

She stopped in mid flow, turning her large brown eyes towards him.

Don't say it, something inside him begged. *Don't say those words again, shattering everything I believed in and yearned to come home to.*

But he had to know, and Molly gave him her beatific smile, not realising in her innocence that she was about to break his heart.

'Kerry had a Yankee Doodle. Marvin was his name. We

285

only saw Glenn, though. Glenn brought us things, and gave me cuddles. I like Glenn, and when he marries our Claire, he'll be my new brother, won't he?'

Tom was no longer listening. His heart was pounding so fast it felt as if it was about to burst. He got up from the bench clumsily, feeling the sharp sting in his leg as he moved too quickly, but it was nothing compared with the kind of pain that was washing over him now.

'I've got to go, Molly. Maybe I'll see you at church tomorrow. I don't know yet. Go indoors now and say goodbye to your mum for me, OK?'

He almost staggered away from her, knowing that if he hadn't given her the instruction she would have followed him the way she always did, holding on to every minute spent with her idol.

He didn't know where he was going. He only knew he had to be alone, to digest the news he least wanted to hear, and had never in his wildest nightmares expected to hear. The childish words made it all the more difficult to believe. And yet how could they not be true?

Kerry, his Kerry, had a Yankee Doodle . . .

CHAPTER SIXTEEN

Kerry was in a fever of excitement by the time she finished work at the shop on Saturday morning. She rushed home to have a quick snack with Aunt Lil, though she couldn't possibly think of anything so mundane as eating, then had a wash and change of clothes, and tried to curb her impatience as she waited for Tom to arrive. It gave her a thrill just to think the words. And how grand it would be if he turned up in his father's car, as he had suggested, and they could take a drive to another town or to the seaside, just like proper tourists. Or like a proper nearly engaged couple, out for a Saturday afternoon drive, she thought, with renewed excitement. She thought he would be just as eager, but as the time went on and he didn't arrive, small seeds of doubt crept in.

'You'll wear that curtain out if you keep peering behind it like a nosy parker,' Aunt Lil remarked. 'He won't get here any quicker, no matter how much you keep fretting over it.'

'But where is he? I hope nothing's wrong, Aunt Lil. I can't help worrying, and if he doesn't get here soon, I'm going round to his house.'

There was nothing Lil could say to stop her, either. She gave it ten more minutes, and then she made up her mind.

'Right, I'm off, and if we happen to miss each other and he turns up in the meantime you can say . . . oh, I don't know – say anything!'

She didn't wait for an answer. Something wasn't right. She didn't know what it was, but anxiety was gnawing at her now. No matter what difficulties Tom might have at home with his mother fussing over him, or however awkward the meeting with Michael's mother had been that morning, she was sure he would want to be with her as soon as possible. So why wasn't he?

She reached the house. The car wasn't outside as usual, which could mean that Tom was on his way, or that Mr Trevellyan was using it. When no one answered the front door, she went round to the back. There was washing on the line, even though it wasn't the usual Monday washday, and Kerry barely registered that there were pyjamas and sheets drying in the breeze. Mrs Trevellyan was chatting to a neighbour over the fence.

'Is Tom here?' Kerry said quickly. 'I was expecting him to call for me this afternoon, but he hasn't turned up yet.'

Mrs Trevellyan looked none too pleased at the interruption.

'He went out this morning, and I haven't seen him since. He was going to see Michael Roddy's mother, and then come home for a while before going to see you, so I've no idea where he's got to now.'

The neighbour put in her twopenn'orth.

'With so many folk to see and wanting to stop him and talk to him about his war experiences, especially some of your old school friends, Kerry, I daresay he's just got caught up somewhere, and lost count of the time.'

'Not the entire day, I wouldn't think,' she muttered.

Besides, she should count for more than other folk and old school friends, she thought jealously.

'When you find him, you might tell him that he shouldn't have forgotten his stick,' his mother said more severely.

'All right,' Kerry said, turning to get away from the gossipy pair, and having no intention of doing any such thing. There were far more important things for her and Tom to talk about than fussing over a stupid stick.

She couldn't deny the growing feeling of anxiety. He was going to the Roddys, so perhaps he had truly lost count of time and stayed there reminiscing with Michael's mother for longer than he intended. *But not until the middle of the afternoon.* Unless Michael's mother had been overcome by a fresh attack of grief after seeing Tom, and he had felt compelled to stay with her.

There was only one way to find out. She had to go there. Claire would be home by now and she would be sure to get the truth out of her.

The house seemed unusually quiet when she knocked on the Roddys' front door. One or other of the kids was always about, shouting, laughing, or playing with a ball or a top in the garden. Mrs Roddy opened the door and smiled at Kerry in some surprise.

'I thought you'd be with Tom this afternoon,' she said at once.

Kerry stared at her. 'I should be, but he didn't call for me, and he's not at home, so I thought he might be still here,' Kerry stuttered.

'Sorry, love, but he left at about midday.'

'Is Claire here, then?' She felt as though she was clutching at straws, behaving like an idiot, the mother hen she despised, the lovelorn idiot . . .

'No, she's not. Mr Roddy's taken the children to a funfair in Falmouth, and Claire's gone with them to help keep them in order.'

Kerry felt totally frustrated. It seemed as though everyone she wanted to see had simply vanished off the face of the earth. But that wasn't possible. Short of a Jerry bomb making a direct hit, or lightning striking, it just didn't happen.

'Thanks, Mrs Roddy,' she almost gasped.

She walked down to the river bank, her thoughts in a turmoil. He had come home. He was so tantalisingly near, and yet he had vanished.

A loud flutter of seabirds overhead startled her. The tide was in, and the river was full. Her heart suddenly clenched. Surely Tom wouldn't have been so foolish as to take the boat out on his own? He wasn't fit, and he wasn't ready. But when he needed time to think, for whatever reason, where else would he go, but to the one place he loved the most?

She began to walk quickly along the towpath to the upper part of the river where she knew the boat was always tied up. It would be afloat now, and it would be easy for anyone feeling hopeless and dejected to simply untie it, lie down and let it drift where it would. Her heart was thumping wildly. Thoughts like that could lead a person to madness, and Tom wasn't hopeless or dejected, or suicidal . . .

She felt a surge of relief as she rounded a bend in the river to see that the boat was still tied up alongside the bank. And then she saw him. He was sitting inside the boat, and he was hunched up, his arms around his knees, his head hanging low. It wasn't the pose of a man who had come out of the war relatively unscathed and was looking forward to a homecoming celebration.

Kerry ran the last few steps, wanting him to hear her, wanting to rid him of the air of defeat that seemed to hover over him.

'Tom, I've been looking everywhere for you,' she called out. 'Did you forget you were going to come round for me this afternoon?'

She was right up to the boat then, and he turned and looked at her, and she almost recoiled from the look on his face. It wasn't what she expected. It certainly wasn't love. It was anything but love.

'Did you forget *me*?' he said.

'What? I don't know what you mean.'

The tide was allowing the boat to drift outwards into the river, as much as the mooring rope would permit.

'Look, you know I don't like boats much, and I'll probably fall in the river if I try to clamber into it when it's bobbing about, so please come out of there, Tom.'

'I said, *did you forget me*?'

She was bewildered by his mood, but she was getting increasingly piqued too. She hadn't done anything to

291

deserve this. She had done nothing but love him and wait for him and long for them to be together again, and now he might as well have been a thousand miles away from her from the coldness in his voice.

'I'm not going to say anything else to you until you come off that boat,' she said angrily, and she sat down on the grass with her arms firmly folded.

After a few minutes he got up stiffly, holding on to the seats and the side of the boat, so he could manoeuvre himself to the side nearest to the stern. He pulled on the mooring rope until he was able to climb out, and Kerry sat there with her heart in her mouth, knowing how difficult it must be for him, and not daring, nor wanting, to offer him any help.

He didn't sit down beside her, and she was forced to squint up at him. The thought that he looked like a colossus standing over her didn't help her sudden feeling of apprehension.

'Who's Marvin?' he said flatly.

Kerry's nerves were so on edge now, she couldn't speak for a moment, let alone think properly.

'*What?*'

'You're not deaf, are you?'

She scrambled to her feet. She didn't know how this had happened, and she was perfectly sure Claire wouldn't have said anything about Marvin, but it was very clear that Tom had somehow got to hear his name, and possibly a lot more than that.

Her thoughts were in a whirl, trying to think of anything, or anyone, who could possibly have mentioned Marvin's name to him. Had he run into Pam Wyatt that morning since leaving Michael's house? Kerry had no idea when she came home from her nursing job. It would be just like her to drop in little bits of poison that were totally untrue.

She clutched his arm, feeling how rigid it was. How hostile he looked.

'Tom, can we find a bench somewhere?'

'I'm quite capable of standing up.'

'Well, I'm not,' she snapped. Truly, she felt as though her legs were going to give way beneath her at any minute. And this wasn't the way it was meant to be. This glorious homecoming that she had longed for so much.

The day had started out so well. Even the weather was still holding out, although the air was muggy and very heavy, and the murky sky had dark clouds scudding across it now. She shivered, thinking it just added to the tension of the moment. Everything looked better in the sunlight, but it was sadly missing now.

Without warning, the heavens opened, and a downpour threatened to soak them in minutes. Kerry's summer frock began to cling to her, and her hair hung down in rats' tails. She could have wept, because she had wanted to look her best for Tom, but none of it seemed to matter anymore.

'We'd better find some shelter. There's an old barn of sorts in the field over there,' he said roughly, seeing her shiver.

He grabbed her hand, and even though he wasn't in any fit state to run, he somehow managed, and between them they fell gasping inside the old tumbledown barn. It was little more than a feed shed for cattle, but there was straw

293

on the ground, and it was dry inside. They sank down close together, catching their breath. Then Tom gripped her hands, not letting up for a second.

'So who's Marvin?' he repeated.

Kerry ran her tongue over her lips. They tasted cold with rain, and she knew that the next few moments were going to be very important.

'Tell me where you heard his name first,' she said shakily.

He gave a short laugh. 'Why? Did you think you were going to keep it a secret for ever?'

She sat up quickly, furious with him for the unspoken condemnation in his voice. He knew nothing, but he assumed everything.

'I won't tell you anything unless you tell me who gave you his name,' she said, just as stubborn as he. 'Was it Pam Wyatt? It's just the kind of thing she would do, to try to get in your good books.'

'I haven't seen Pam Wyatt in months, and why the hell should I be interested in anything she had to say to me?'

'Well, because she always fancied you, for a start.'

'It wasn't Pam Wyatt.'

Kerry had the strangest feeling that, having begun this conversation, he was almost as keen as she was to keep the truth of it at bay. Once it was out in the open, it had to be faced, but it was too late now. It was like a roller coaster. Once started, it couldn't be stopped until it had run its course.

'For pity's sake, Tom, are you going to tell me or not?'

'It was Molly.'

She stared at him, unbelieving.

'Molly Roddy?' she said, starting to laugh. 'What the hell does a five-year-old know about anything, except what she makes up in her head?'

She was shivering again, vaguely remembering the gist of one of the many conversations she had had with Claire. Surely Molly hadn't been eavesdropping? And if she had been, and passed on any of it to Tom in her innocent way, how distorted had the facts become?

'Are you going to deny that you know this bloke called Marvin?'

Tom was suddenly her accuser, not giving her the benefit of the doubt. In his mind, the crime had already been done, and she was guilty, m'lud. Ready to be hung, drawn and quartered.

'No, I don't deny it,' she snapped. 'It would be pretty silly if I did, wouldn't it? Compounding the crime. Isn't that the correct term for it?'

Tom leant back against the straw, needing to ease the stress on his leg and shoulder now. The effort of slumping in the boat for however long it had been, and then rushing to get out of the rain, had blotted out any need for caution. But even though he was aware of the wounds throbbing like the devil right now, the last thing he was going to do was admit it.

'So how well did you know him? I see now why you never mentioned anything at all about the Yanks stationed here, even though Mum did in her letters. I would have thought you'd be all too keen to tell me about Claire and this Glenn that I've heard about now, but I suppose it would have meant me asking too many questions.'

Despite her fury at his lack of trust, and his believing

295

unreservedly in the word of a five-year-old, Kerry felt a weird sense of calm come over her. She had done nothing wrong, and no matter how much he accused her, she knew that.

'So what else did Molly tell you?'

'Nothing. She didn't have to.'

'What did she actually say, then? If I'm being accused of something, I have the right to know what it is, don't I?'

'She said, "Kerry's got a Yankee Doodle as well."'

Kerry's laugh was almost hysterical. 'A Yankee *Doodle*?'

'Oh, you can laugh about it, but apparently her dad told her to call them that as it was nicer than calling them Yanks.' He glared at her. 'So did you have a Yankee Doodle, Kerry?'

'I thought you knew me better than that, and I'm hurt that you don't.'

'Then tell me it isn't true. Tell me about this Marvin. He obviously exists,' he said, in growing desperation, and wishing to God he had some of the medics' magic painkillers with him.

'Of course he exists – just. He's a GI, and he was one of the group who came to the concert we gave to welcome them here,' she said evenly. 'And before you ask, I danced with him, and I liked him, and that was all. Except . . .'

'Go on.'

'Well, you couldn't ignore them while they were here. Before D-Day when they simply disappeared into the night, they were everywhere in the village, and local people generally liked them. Claire certainly did, and when she met Glenn it was love at first sight for both of them.'

'I don't want to hear about Claire. I want to hear about you.'

Kerry didn't speak for a few minutes. Inside the barn it was hot and musty, and their thin clothes were drying out fast on the dry straw. She swallowed hard, remembering those few times she had spent with Marvin Mcleod, and how his life had somehow become entangled with hers. But in a way that she desperately needed Tom to understand.

'If I tell you everything, will you promise to listen and not to judge me, then?' she said, wondering how she could ever have to say such things to Tom, who she had known all her life, and was the only love she had ever wanted.

'I'm listening,' he said.

'We talked a few times. I told him all about you, and he showed me the photo of the girl he intended to marry. Her name was Shirl, and she was beautiful, like a film star, really. In fact she'd won a beauty competition. Miss Montana,' she added with a tremulous smile.

Tom didn't say anything, but he clearly hadn't expected to hear anything quite like this. Kerry went on relentlessly now.

'Then one night when Claire saw Glenn, he told her that Marvin had received a Dear John letter from Shirl. Do you know what that is?'

'All the blokes know what that is,' Tom said grimly.

'Well, it hit Marvin really hard, and he went AWOL for three days before going back to his unit.'

'Christ Almighty!'

Kerry ignored the expletive. 'Apparently his superior officers were very understanding, and through Claire I got a brief note from Marvin later to say he was going to try to win Shirl back. I'll show it to you if you like. Then D-Day came and the Yanks were gone.'

'So that was the last you heard of him?' Tom said finally.

Kerry looked down at the piece of her skirt she had been twisting together without realising it. Outside the rain had stopped, and she was starting to feel stifled in the cloying atmosphere.

'You must know all about D-Day, Tom. My God, you were almost in the thick of it yourself – but not quite, of course.'

'No. I was too busy getting bits of shrapnel cut out of me at the time,' he said, full of self-pitying sarcasm. 'Sorry, go on.'

'It was agony for Claire, waiting for news of Glenn, but at last she got a letter, and he was safe. But it contained such sad news as well. One of his best buddies had been killed as soon as they landed, blown to bits by a mine, and Marvin Mcleod was missing, believed dead.'

She was suddenly crying, but not for the reason Tom might think. She had grabbed hold of his hands now, gripping them tightly, begging him mutely to understand.

'You can't imagine how I felt at that moment. It was somehow that as long as Marvin was safe, then you were safe too. I don't know why I felt like that, but hearing that he was missing, presumed dead, just terrified me, Tom. It was like a nightmare. I was so fearful for you, and when I knew you'd been wounded, it was such a relief. Oh, I don't mean that I wanted you to be hurt, but at least you weren't *dead*!'

He was holding her now, and she leant her head against

him. She wanted this distance between them to end, to be the same as before, yet knowing that it could never again be exactly like that. They could never go back to being the same two childhood sweethearts they had always been. War had changed all that.

'No, I'm not dead, Kerry,' he said huskily.

'And nor is Marvin!' She jerked away from him, needing to tell him the rest before he thought she was holding out on him. 'That was the incredible thing. Aunt Lil says you should never give up hope, and that sometimes miracles happen, and people are eventually found safe and well.'

'So are you telling me that's what happened to him?' Tom said disbelievingly.

'Why? Did you hope that was the end of it?' She was the accuser now, wondering if he could be so callous as to wish the other man dead. Wondering if she had ever really known him at all.

'Of course I bloody didn't. It's just so unlikely, that's all.'

'Well, according to Glenn, they eventually discovered that Marvin had been completely deafened and shell-shocked in the midst of the horrific beach landings, and had wandered away from his unit, dazed and disorientated. They assumed he'd had it, and it was a long while later that they learnt he had been picked up by a French family and hidden from the Germans, and gradually his hearing and his senses came back. He eventually found his way back to his unit. He's lost some of his hearing for good, though, but he's alive and that's all that matters.'

When he didn't say anything, she looked at him sharply.

'So what happens now, Tom? Are you going to accuse me of waiting to see if he comes back to Cornwall in the hope of being a GI bride like Claire intends to be? Do you think I'm so shallow?'

'I never thought that.'

'So what are you thinking now, then?'

He was quiet for such long minutes that she wondered if this could truly be the end between them – except that his eyes had at last lost their hard accusing look, and his face had visibly relaxed. His voice was finally slow and halting.

'I'm thinking that I never really appreciated what people at home were going through. It might be a very different war from mine, but it was a different sort of hell as well. I'm thinking that you were always the best, the bravest girl in the world. And I'm thinking that if my bloody leg and everything else would allow it, I'd like nothing more than to make love to you, here and now, and to hell with everything else.'

Kerry's breath was coming heavily now, as heavily as Tom's, and she leant forward to kiss his lips, both salty with tears and rain, and she whispered against his mouth.

'We'll never know unless we put it to the test, will we?' she said, inviting him, wanting him, needing him so much, and loving him with all her heart.

Nothing else mattered . . . and somewhere inside her there was a vague sense of his need to prove that he was still a man, despite what the war had done to him. She lay back on the bed of straw, feeling the familiar touch of his fingers on her skin, ruffling up the hem of her skirt. Then she was helping him, removing what was necessary, and feeling the weight of him covering her, and entering her, and sending her senses spiralling into a kind of delirium.

Sharing one another's bodies and being as close as any two people could possibly be was something she had dreamt of ever since that magical first time, and had sometimes feared that it could never happen again. And although this time it was slower and not so prolonged, there was still the same sense of belonging that nothing else in the world could ever convey.

When it was over, he continued to whisper incoherent endearments into her ear, but when he finally leant his head on her shoulder his voice was muffled and contrite.

'I should never have doubted you, darling. I never knew I was capable of jealousy until that little wretch Molly put all kinds of thoughts into my head.'

'You mustn't blame her,' Kerry whispered, still holding him close. 'She's only a child, Tom, and she didn't think she was doing anything wrong.'

'You were always the forgiving one, weren't you?' he said with a wry smile.

'Why not, when there's nothing to forgive?' she said steadily.

He got the message, and ran one finger around her soft lips.

'Well, now that we've sorted it all out, and my girl is back where she ought to be, I think we should head for home. You need to change your wet clothes, and I need some of what the doctor ordered.'

She was concerned for a moment. There had been nothing but love in his face in the last heady minutes, but now she could see the strain in it, and she recognised the guarded way he said he needed some of what the doctor ordered. A woman would have just said she needed to take some pills. But he was a man and he had his pride.

'Well, at least our crumpled clothes can be put down to being caught in the rain, and thankfully it's stopped, so let's go, Tom,' Kerry said as crisply as she could.

She linked her arm in his, and snuggled up to his side, as clingy as a sweetheart had every right to be. In reality, it was to be sure he had her support for the walk home without actually reminding him of the fact that he needed it.

They walked back to the towpath across the sweetly smelling damp grass. The sun was shining again, and they were drying out quickly now. They didn't talk very much, but it was a warm and comfortable silence. And after all, Kerry was relieved that all the information about Marvin was out in the open, and since she never expected to see or hear from him ever again, they could put all the nonsense behind them. She could easily forgive Molly for her childish indiscretion, because there was truly nothing to forgive. It was best forgotten.

They reached the village after a long slow walk home, and Kerry was sure it was also a painful one for Tom. He caught his breath now and then, but wisely, she didn't press him to ask what was wrong.

'I think we should part company for now, Tom,' she said instead, when his house came in sight. 'We both need to get changed, and I'll have to wash my hair, so if you like, I'll come round to your house after tea for an hour.'

'Or I could come to yours. I still haven't said hello to your auntie yet.'

Kerry improvised quickly. 'I think she's going out this evening, but you'll see her at church tomorrow.'

'I haven't decided whether I'll be there yet, with half the village staring at me,' he said morosely. 'But yes, come round tonight, sweetheart. And . . . thanks.'

'Don't mention it,' she said with a laugh. Though what he was thanking her for, she didn't quite know. Not for letting him make love to her, that was for sure, when she had wanted it as much as he had. For putting his mind at rest over Marvin Mcleod, presumably, and if the little devil inside her told her that he should never have doubted her anyway, she ignored it.

Uncaring whether or not there were any curtains twitching now, he pulled her into his arms and kissed her in full view of whoever wanted to look.

'You can't imagine how many times I've dreamt of doing that,' he said.

'What? Shocking the neighbours?' Kerry said.

He laughed, and it was a good sound, a practically normal sound.

'Something like that. I'll see you later, then.'

She waited until he had gone inside his house, not missing how carefully he was walking now, as if every step was an effort, and then she walked quickly home, her eyes smarting with suppressed tension. It had been such a different afternoon from the one she had expected, even though it had ended up so ecstatically, lying in Tom's arms and knowing that he still loved her as deeply as she loved him.

Aunt Lil was out, and Kerry closed the door behind her and leant against it for a few moments with her eyes closed, because the happiness couldn't quite blot out the ugliness of what had happened before. Her brain hurt with all they had gone through in those few hours. She knew she must get out of her messed-up clothes and wash the rain out of her hair to make her feel human again. She must find the note from Marvin that she had promised to show Tom. It was necessary.

But before all that, the enormity of the afternoon swept over her with the force of a whirlwind as her legs seemed to fold up beneath her and she sank to the floor and burst into tears.

CHAPTER SEVENTEEN

'What on earth's happened and where have you been? You look terrible,' Mrs Trevellyan exclaimed the minute she saw her son. 'I was worried when you didn't come home this morning when I expected you, and then Kerry came looking for you this afternoon because you didn't turn up at her house. You're only just out of the hospital and you've been doing too much too soon, just as I knew you would, and I'm sending for the doctor.'

'For God's sake, Mum, don't go ranting on, and I don't want any bloody doctor. I've seen enough of them in the past few weeks. I've got some pills to take and I'll be as right as rain after a lie-down, so leave me alone.'

'You most certainly don't look as right as rain, and I'll ask you not to use bad language in this house. It might be all right in your army barracks among your soldier friends, but it's not all right here,' she said, affronted.

'Will you leave it, Mum!' Tom shouted, in a way he had never shouted at her before, and she stood open-mouthed as he blundered his way upstairs to his bedroom and slammed the door behind him.

He had fumbled for the bottle of pills and stuffed several of them in his mouth, swallowing them down without water, before he heard the bang of the front door below. So his mother was in a huff now, and he knew he'd have to apologise to her. But that was for later. Right now, all he wanted was for the bloody pills to take effect so that he could sink into blessed oblivion for a couple of hours.

'It's a pity we don't live well away from the coast,' Lil Penfold remarked to her niece as she was planning their Saturday fry-up with fried spuds and the couple of sausages she'd managed to get from the butcher.

'Is it?' Kerry said listlessly, not bothering to try following her aunt's train of thought.

Lil looked at her sharply. 'I don't know what's happened in the last few hours, but for a girl whose young man has just come home from the war, I would have expected to see a permanent smile on your face. Are you going to tell me what's gone wrong, or do I have to guess?'

'Neither,' Kerry said shortly. 'So why is it a pity we don't live well away from the coast?'

Lil sighed, knowing when she was being fobbed off.

'The government has relaxed the strict blackout regulations for non-coastal areas, so upcountry towns can have moderate street lighting again, as you would very well know if you'd been taking any notice of the news recently.'

'I've had more important things to think about,' Kerry muttered. Who cared about street lighting in other parts of the country, if they couldn't have it here?

'It's also been decided that trains and buses can have limited lighting, so that people can read in them again. Aye, and there's the rub,' Lil went on dramatically.

When she paused for effect, Kerry forced herself to take in what she had been saying, knowing that something else was expected.

'Have you been reading bits of Shakespeare or something at your Friendship Club?'

'So you recognised it. You're not acting quite the dummy, then.'

Lil was unusually sharp, and pushing aside her own unease over Tom's health, Kerry realised that she was definitely put out about something.

'I'm sorry. Tell me what's wrong.'

'You first,' Lil said.

Kerry bit her lip. The last part of her afternoon with Tom had been intimate and beautiful, and everything she had ever wanted. But she still couldn't rid her mind of what had gone before, and it kept coming back to haunt her. But Lil was waiting, and deserved to know more.

'Tom wasn't at home when I went there, and I eventually found him in his boat, just sitting there hunched up. I persuaded him to get out of it, and then it began to pour with rain and we dashed for shelter in an old hut. I could see he was upset . . . well, in an awful state, really, and I thought it was because of talking about Michael with Mrs Roddy, but it wasn't that.'

'Go on.'

'He suddenly asked me about Marvin Mcleod.'

Lil drew in her breath and nodded slowly, and the look in her eyes said she had known all along that this was going to happen. But not so soon.

Kerry's voice became choked. 'I was horrified that he didn't trust me, Aunt Lil. We had an awful row, but I knew I'd done nothing wrong, and there was nothing to tell.'

'Kerry, in a small village like this, it was inevitable that someone was going to say something. The Americans had practically become part of village life. People liked them, and people will always gossip. It may be vindictive or quite innocent, but it's human nature, my love.'

'It wasn't people gossiping. It was Molly. Molly Roddy,' she said abruptly. 'She was telling Tom about Claire and Glenn, and then she said . . . she said, "Kerry's got a Yankee Doodle as well."'

'*What?*'

The wretched tears wouldn't stop now. Today had begun so wonderfully, with every hope that she and Tom would be spending the afternoon together, possibly driving out to the country in his dad's car, and renewing all the love they had ever shared. Well, they had finally done that, but the memory of all that had gone before it was like a horrible black cloud over everything, and she couldn't forget it.

'I know Molly didn't know what she was saying,' she wept, 'but she must have heard Claire and me talking, and she just blurted it out to Tom.'

'That poor boy,' Lil said softly.

Kerry glared at her through tear-stricken eyes.

'*That poor boy?* What about me, having to defend

myself for something that never happened? What about that *poor boy* believing the word of a five-year-old and accusing me as if I was a criminal?'

'But you knew you were innocent of all charges, didn't you?' Lil said mildly. 'His mind must have been in turmoil, but you could afford to be reasonable and tell him the truth. Which I hope that you did.'

'Of course I did. I told him about the few times we had talked, and about Marvin's girlfriend, and the Dear John letter, and the AWOL, and then how he was reported missing, believed dead after D-Day, and then what had happened after he was found to be alive. I also told him about the note Marvin sent me, and that I was going to show it to him. I didn't know what else I could do if he still didn't believe me,' she said shrilly.

'And did he?'

Kerry lowered her eyes. There was a limit to how much she was prepared to tell her aunt, or anybody. Some things were private.

'I think so. Well, yes, I know he did, eventually.'

'So if I were you, I'd stop fretting about what's done.'

Kerry took a deep breath, knowing she was right. What did she have to be fretting over now? In the end, the afternoon couldn't have ended up any sweeter than it did between her and Tom.

She dragged her thoughts back to what Lil had been saying earlier.

'So what's all this about "aye, there's the rub", then? I know there's something you're dying to tell me.'

'It's your Aunt Maud. She's wasted money on sending a telegram, even though she must know that most folk are in danger of having a heart attack when they see the telegram boy coming up the path.'

From her tone of voice, Kerry knew nothing bad could have happened to Maud or Bert. So it had to be something else.

'So what's she done now?' she asked with the glimmer of a smile.

'It's not what she's done, but what she's going to do. She knew it was your birthday next Sunday, and she says that she and Bert are coming down by train to share it with you. They've already arranged to be put up for the weekend at Gillagy's Farm. I ask you! Just when I thought we'd seen the back of them!'

Kerry was more concerned with the prospect of the pair of them muscling in on her birthday than anything else.

'But they can't!' she blurted out. 'We've arranged to share it with Tom's homecoming at his house, and his mother would never agree to having Maud and Bert there as well.'

She could just imagine how awful it would be. The house-proud Mrs Trevellyan, and the brash rough-and-ready Maud and the spivvy Bert. She hoped she wasn't turning into a snob as well, but the thought of it was just, well, *awful*.

'I'm not sure what we can do, other than changing our plans and having your party here and maybe suggesting tactfully to the Trevellyans that it would be much nicer for Tom to have a separate homecoming do,' Aunt Lil went on.

'Best of luck for doing it, then.'

'Oh no, my girl, that will be your doing! I'm not sure that

310

Mrs Trevellyan was all that keen on the idea of the combined party, anyway. She'll have wanted to do everything herself for her one ewe lamb.'

'Don't call him that, Aunt Lil. It makes him sound like a mummy's boy.'

'I know he's anything but that, my love, but it might be how his mother sees him, especially now. She'll want to wrap him up in cotton wool if I know Mrs Trevellyan. But wouldn't you rather have all the Roddy children here anyway? They can be as noisy as they like and I won't turn a hair.'

That much was true, and it did seem like the best solution, even though it had seemed such a lovely thing for her and Tom to have a joint party. It had sounded almost like an engagement party . . .

'I'm going round to Tom's this evening,' Kerry said hurriedly before she got carried away with what-might-have-beens. 'I'll tell them all then, and blame it entirely on Aunt Maud. Since Mrs Trevellyan's met her, I'm sure she'll be relieved not to be seeing her and Bert in her pristine palace.'

She surprised herself by feeling a mite resentful and defensive on Maud's behalf right then, but she was family, after all, and it was the best solution all round. Aunt Lil was right. The Roddy children could be as noisy and messy as they liked, and it would all be good fun. And of course, Tom would be invited too. It would be mostly a family party, and that was how she would present it tactfully to the Trevellyans.

When she arrived there an hour or so later she saw two cars parked outside the house. One was Tom's dad's, and the other one . . . Kerry's heart jumped at once. Doctor Graham wasn't known for making house calls on a Saturday evening unless it was absolutely necessary, so it must be something serious.

It couldn't be Tom, Kerry thought feverishly, since he'd been perfectly all right when they parted, so it must be one of his parents.

She knocked on the door and opened it without waiting to be invited. The doctor was talking to the Trevellyans, his face solemn, and Tom was nowhere to be seen.

'What's happened?' she stuttered.

'Come and sit down, Kerry,' Tom's father said quickly, since his mother seemed incapable of saying anything at that moment.

Doctor Graham held up his hand, taking charge. 'If I may, Mr Trevellyan. Kerry, I understand you were with Tom this afternoon? Did he seem quite well when you left him?'

'Yes, of course, but will you please tell me what's happened?'

He glanced at Mrs Trevellyan, and she nodded for him to go on.

'Tom seemed in a distressed state and was in obvious pain, so Mrs Trevellyan wisely decided to send for me. When she took him up a cup of tea a little while later he was unconscious and making growling noises.'

'*Oh, no!*' Kerry whispered.

'Unfortunately I was unable to get here any earlier,' the doctor went on, as if to remind them that he had a normal life too, 'but it looked as though Tom had taken too many painkillers. The contents of the bottle were scattered on the floor. I managed to rouse him sufficiently to give him an emetic, and he will recover completely. A couple of days' rest and he'll be able to resume his exercises again and start to get back to everyday life.'

His voice was becoming brisker, and from the clothes he was wearing he obviously had somewhere else to go, and Kerry found herself thinking wildly that at least Tom hadn't thrown up all over the doctor's smart suit.

'You're sure?' she said huskily, even though you never questioned a doctor's words. She didn't know why that was. They weren't *God*, but everyone treated them as though they were.

'Quite sure, and now I'll be on my way. I've adjusted his medication and I don't think you'll have any more trouble,' he commented to Tom's father, almost as an aside.

What the hell did he mean by that? Was he implying that Tom had taken too many pills on purpose? He wouldn't have done that. He had no reason for it. The memory of how much torment he had obviously been in at finding out about Marvin Mcleod had surely been overcome by now. For pity's sake, she had put his mind at rest, and they had made the tenderest love and then walked home with their arms entwined. He couldn't have still been brooding about it, not enough to want to kill himself . . .

She was hardly aware of Mrs Trevellyan showing the doctor out as the hateful thought surged into her head. But Tom wouldn't. He wasn't spineless. He hadn't come through his own war to be unable to face a personal battle that didn't even exist.

'He will be all right, Kerry,' Tom's father was saying gently. 'He was probably trying to do too much too soon.

313

Even seeing Michael's family must have been an ordeal for him, but you know what he's like. Everything has to be done at once, but after what he's been through, it's all going to take time. He had a bad nightmare last night, so on top of that, it's just taken too much out of him.'

'So can I see him?' she said numbly, most of the talk washing over her.

His mother came back into the room. 'I can't stop you, Kerry, and Tom wouldn't thank me if I tried. I don't know what you got up to this afternoon, but please don't tire him.'

She sounded odd and she was tight-lipped. She was clearly shocked by what had happened, but surely she wasn't blaming *her* for this. As for what they *got up to* . . . the snide words were enough to send the hot colour rushing to her face. But she didn't know, and she couldn't know, and she was never going to know!

'Of course I won't tire him. As for what we got up to, well, it was ages before I found him. He was just sitting in the boat, thinking, and I assumed it was his chat with Michael's mother that upset him,' she improvised. 'I persuaded him to get out of the boat, and then it began to rain and we had to shelter in a shed. We had to run for it, which wouldn't have done his leg any good.'

Why did she feel as though she had to keep defending herself? But that was often how she felt with Tom's mother, who naturally didn't think any girl in the world was good enough for her son, not even Kerry, who she had known since she was an infant.

'Well, as I said, don't tire him,' Mrs Trevellyan said at last when Kerry simply stared her out.

Kerry didn't wait for any more. She sprinted up the stairs and into Tom's bedroom. The door was open, and he had obviously heard a lot of what had gone on downstairs. He looked pale, as was to be expected after being given an emetic to make him throw up. But he gave her the ghost of a smile.

'Don't let the buggers get you down, kid,' he said huskily. 'Come and sit on the bed. I can't talk too loudly, because my throat's sore.'

She rushed across the room, her eyes watery.

'It gave me such a fright when I saw the doctor's car outside,' she said, just as croaky.

'You didn't think I'd snuffed it, did you? I might be a bit of a wreck, but I'm not ready for the knacker's yard just yet.'

He looked at her sharply, his feeble attempt at a joke falling flat. 'And in case you think I'd taken too many pills deliberately, forget it. I've got everything to live for, haven't I?'

'I never thought that for a minute,' she lied.

'Not too sure about the party next week, though.'

He leant back on his pillow, as if saying as little as he had was enough to exhaust him, but it gave Kerry the lead for what she had to say.

'Well, we won't be having it here after all, though I haven't told your mother yet. My Aunt Maud and her new husband are coming down from Bristol for my birthday. I told you about them in my letters, Tom. They're going to stay at Gillagy's Farm for the weekend, and I think your mum will be very glad not to have them around here.'

'So what's the plan?' he said, sounding more tired by the minute. 'I'm sure you've got one by now.'

'We'll postpone your celebration for now, and it'll just be a birthday tea at my house next week. You'll be invited, of course, and the Roddy kids, and that's all, apart from the aunts and Bert. Do you think your mum will object?'

'I doubt it,' he said with a grin, remembering all she had told him about the flamboyant Aunt Maud and her spiv of a husband.

'I'll go and tell her, then,' Kerry said, aware that he wanted to rest more than talk. 'I'll see you tomorrow, Tom.'

She leant over and kissed him, trying hard to hold back the tears. She hated seeing him like this, so vulnerable, and clearly a long way back from full health yet. He was just out of hospital, for pity's sake, but Tom-like he had already thought he was ready to conquer the world.

'I love you,' she heard him mumble, already drifting back to sleep.

'I love you too,' she whispered, and then she turned and fled.

After she had explained everything to Mrs Trevellyan and seen the relief in her eyes that she wouldn't have to share a table with Maud and Bert, Kerry was far too jittery to think of going straight home again.

It was getting dusk, and now that the rain clouds had faded away, the sky was full of a soft gentle twilight. It was impossible to think that earlier in the day there had been that sudden squall of rain. And if there hadn't been . . . would they have gone scurrying away to find shelter in a straw-filled shed . . . and would that turbulent afternoon have ended in their gloriously making love? It was strange how fate intervened at the least expected times. Fate, or inevitability.

Without any definite thought of where she was going, she found her footsteps nearing the Roddy house, and knocked on the door. The younger kids would be in bed by now, but it was Claire she wanted to see. Claire, who would understand, and be happy and sad for her, as the moments dictated.

'I thought you'd be out with Tom tonight,' Claire greeted her, and then she saw her face. 'What's wrong?'

'I want to talk to you.'

'We'll go up to my bedroom. Mum's busy as usual, and Dad and Jed are playing draughts.'

Once upstairs, Claire closed the bedroom door firmly, and they sat down on her bed. 'So what's up?'

It all came out in a rush. Kerry felt as though she had lived through a lifetime of emotions since last night, and she spared Claire nothing, except the vital part that was too private to share.

'You mean our Molly let it slip about Marvin? Oh God, Kerry, I'm so sorry!' She was aghast at the realisation.

'Don't blame her, and don't say anything about it to her,' Kerry urged. 'She didn't understand, and if I'd only mentioned something about the Yanks to Tom myself, it wouldn't have seemed as if I was keeping secrets, even if I wasn't!'

'But he believed you, didn't he? Bloody hell, Kerry, you two have been like Siamese twins since junior school. How could he think you'd look twice at anybody else?'

'He believed me in the end, but it took a bit of persuading, and I can't deny that it hurt. We made it up, and we were fine when I left him, but now this has happened. But there's something else I want to talk to you about.'

She didn't want to dwell any longer on the fact that Tom had been so ready to believe Molly, and mistrusted her. It was in the past, and it was going to stay there. She went on quickly to tell her of the altered arrangements for her birthday tea, and that Claire and the kids were invited.

Claire grinned. 'I can just imagine Mrs T's horror at the thought of entertaining Maud and Bert, to say nothing of our lot clambering over everything. It's a much better idea, anyway, and Tom's OK with it, is he?'

'I think so. He was never too keen on a party to celebrate his homecoming in the first place. It was all his mother's idea. All he wants is to get back to normal without any fuss.' She looked down at the floor. 'Though I'm starting to wonder what's normal and what isn't.'

'Well, you didn't expect him to come home and be exactly the same as he was before, did you?'

'If I'm honest, I suppose I did,' Kerry said slowly. 'Stupid, wasn't it?'

She was angry with herself for even admitting it. It was naive to think that anybody could go to war and come back exactly the same. They had memories that other people couldn't imagine. Memories nobody else could share. Memories to give them nightmares.

For no reason at all, she had a sudden image of the pyjamas and sheets on the Trevellyans' washing line that morning. She hadn't even thought about them before, but they had to have been Tom's, so the nightmare must have been terrible for him to need fresh linen in the middle of the night. She didn't want to start imagining anything more than that, but she was guilty at the thought that she had been less than understanding all this time.

'I'd better go now,' she said, scrambling off Claire's bed, not wanting any more probing about Tom, however kindly meant. 'Oh, and I nearly forgot. Aunt Lil says the party will have to be on the Saturday now, so that Maud and Bert can go back on Sunday. You can tell the kids about it if you like.'

'Of course I will, and I know they'll want to make you a present.'

'I don't want any fuss,' Kerry began, and then stopped, realising she sounded just like Tom.

Why wouldn't she want any fuss when it was her eighteenth birthday, for pity's sake? What girl wouldn't want to celebrate?

As her emotions changed direction again, she felt herself bristling. She wasn't going to walk on tiptoe around Tom for ever, no matter what anybody thought. He'd hate that, and so would she. She was his lover, not his nurse. His lover . . .

'It'll all come right in the end, you'll see. See you at church tomorrow, then,' Claire said cheerfully, sliding off the bed and heading towards the door.

'Probably,' Kerry said.

Why had she said such a daft word? Of course she would be at church tomorrow. Aunt Lil would see no reason why she shouldn't be there. She always said that only flood, famine and fever would keep her away. That, and death, she always added, with what was meant to be a joke.

Kerry was sure that Tom wouldn't be there, but she wouldn't mind betting that his mother would be. His father had never been a churchgoing man, and would hold the fort at home, but his mother would want to spread the news that her boy was home and 'as well as could be expected', in the time-honoured hospital phrase. She would get the sympathy and the glory . . .

By the time she reached home, Kerry was feeling more cynical by the minute. It was just as she had told Claire. Foolishly, she *had* expected everything to be back to normal the instant Tom came home, and she could see now how totally unrealistic that had been.

Unwittingly, her thoughts flew to Marvin Mcleod. His perception of normality had changed too. How was he coping after what he had been through? Would he be invalided out of the army as well, if his loss of hearing was too bad for him to remain as a serviceman? And would his Shirl, the one-time Miss Montana, welcome him back with open arms?

She didn't want to think of him at all, she thought in a panic. She had given him all the sympathy over Shirl that she could spare at the time, but it was their problem, not hers. And having seen Tom's reaction to her even knowing Marvin, she didn't want him in her thoughts for another minute.

She banged the door behind her when she went indoors, making Lil jump, almost dropping a few stitches in her knitting.

'Careful, miss, or we'll have that door off its hinges

before long. What's the matter now? Did you see Tom? I didn't expect you back so soon.'

Kerry stared at her. She had been gone less than a couple of hours, and in that time, her whole world seemed to have shifted again. Tom had been ill and his mother had called the doctor, and the party arrangements had been changed, and Claire didn't seem to understand what she was going through anymore. Or was that all in her imagination too?

She spilt it all out to Lil in a matter of seconds, feeling slightly hysterical that something so important could be said in so few words. But that was how it was. Things happened. You spoke about them. Or not. You moved on.

And, oh God, all this homespun philosophy was making her head ache. She didn't want to be wise and clever. She wanted to be young and frivolous and flirty, and to run wild with Tom through the woods and over the moors, the way they had done as children and in the first heady days when they had discovered that childhood friendship had turned into love.

'It was bound to happen,' Lil said in answer to her garbled words. 'It's a natural reaction to being home and wanting to do everything at once. Tom was always an impetuous young man, but he'll settle down in a day or two.'

Kerry blinked. She had been so lost in her own dreaming then that her aunt's words took her by surprise.

'I suppose so,' she muttered.

'And deep down, he's still the same person he always was, Kerry. Life changes us all, but thankfully our hearts and souls remain the same. It's one of God's mysteries that we're blessed with.'

Kerry didn't want to hear about any of God's mysteries

right now. Nor for Lil to get on to one of her Bible stories that she held such store by. She tried to think of something else to say.

'Anyway, Mrs Trevellyan was all right about the change of plans for my birthday,' she remembered, knowing that this would divert the conversation. 'The minute I mentioned that Maud and Bert were coming for a visit I could see her face go pale.'

It hadn't, but it was enough to bring a smile to Lil's face.

'I'm not surprised. Those two are enough to try the patience of a saint,' she said dryly. 'But they're family, and a cross that we have to bear.'

'I've seen Claire and invited all the Roddy children as well. That was definitely all right, wasn't it?'

'I told you it was. And Tom, of course.'

'And Tom, of course.'

That went without saying. In fact, it was odd to think that if he hadn't been wounded all that time ago, and had finally been able to come home, he might never have been here for her birthday at all. It was a weird sort of silver lining, she supposed, but these days you had to take what you could get.

She kept that thought in mind when she went to bed that night. Somewhere in the distance she could hear the rattle of a train as it hurtled along the track in the darkness. There might be a war on, but people still moved about from place to place, whether it was bringing families together for birthday teas, or carrying wounded soldiers to hospitals, or home to their loved ones. Life went on. People grew older, and no amount of war could prevent that.

She thought about her party, and was suddenly enormously glad that Maud and Bert were going to make the long train trip to be there. How odd was that! But the kids would be intrigued by Maud, and she would gush all over them, and tell them tall stories to make Lil frown, and Bert would probably show them some party tricks, if he had any. Kerry guessed that he did.

And Tom wouldn't have to be the centre of attention, which she knew he wouldn't want. Tom would be her very special guest, but he wouldn't feel he was being paraded for all to see and comment on, and asked about his time in France that he wouldn't want to mention.

If all this sudden insight was being wise and mature, then she was glad of it. The panicky earlier feeling that being normal was never going to happen to them again was beginning to fade into the ether, where it belonged. Tom had come through his war, and maybe she had come through a kind of minor war of her own, however feeble compared with his.

She wasn't going to win medals for it, nor have her name inscribed on the stone memorial in the centre of the village for all to see, but she felt as though she had fought an inner battle with herself, and won. It was crazy, and not something she would want to share with anyone. But that was the best thing about thoughts. They were private and personal, and belonged only to her.

CHAPTER EIGHTEEN

Kerry still felt as though she was living in some kind of a dream during the next week. She saw Tom every day after work, and by Wednesday he was outside the shop waiting for her at the end of the afternoon, well recovered by then. People constantly asked how he was, and if he was glad to be home, and he gave them his well-rehearsed answers, but Kerry could see that it was beginning to get on his nerves. There were still black moods to contend with.

'I don't really know what they expect me to say,' he said with a frown on Thursday afternoon when they were on their way back to Kerry's house for tea. 'If I say I'm glad to be out of it, they'll think I'm being disloyal to my mates who are still over there, and if I don't, they'll start being sorry for me which I can't stand. I can't win, can I?'

Kerry wouldn't rise to the bait. It was all too easy for

him to snap at her when she was only trying to help. 'They probably don't know what to say, Tom, but in a little while everybody will be used to seeing you around, and that'll be the end of it. By the way, I hear you went into Falmouth with your dad this morning to take a look around,' she said, to stop him looking so gloomy.

'Now, how do you know that? It was only decided last night.'

'It's a village,' she said with a grin. 'Everybody knows everything about everybody else around here, or had you forgotten?'

She immediately wished she hadn't said that, remembering what little Molly Roddy had told Tom in all innocence. Thankfully, his face relaxed, and she breathed more easily.

'You're not supposed to know anything about it, nor what we went shopping for,' he said mysteriously.

'It's my birthday present, then. That's it, isn't it?'

She was instantly excited. Not so long ago, this couldn't have been happening, and she'd have had to be content with a letter or a card from France, or a present he'd asked his mother to buy for her. Whatever it turned out to be, it would have been bought by proxy, but now it would be doubly precious to know that Tom had been able to buy it himself. She hugged his arm.

'Are you going to tell me what it is?'

'Certainly not. It wouldn't be a surprise then, would it?'

But his teasing was so like the old Tom that she rejoiced inside and sent up a little silent prayer of thanks, if it wasn't too skittish to be doing so, when there was so much more to be thankful for in this war that was slowly but inexorably going the Allies' way now.

Something was nagging away at her, though, and it was something that had to be done. Whether or not he had forgotten it, she hadn't. She was reluctant to break the cheerful mood they were in now, but after tea, she was determined to show him the note Marvin Mcleod had sent her, as the final bit of confirmation that she had been a friend in need, and no more.

Aunt Lil would be going out. These days she was more often out than in, either at the Friendship Club, or her knitting circle, or another of the village meetings she attended regularly, having a finger in so many pies. But it meant that she and Tom would have the house to themselves.

She wasn't going to think ahead, though. Long ago, they had made a pact that they would try to curb their passion as much as possible, until the time came when they could be married and start their lives together. It had been easy to do when he had been away, but now that he was home, she wondered how difficult it was going to be. Since the time they had sheltered in the hut out of the rain, and the doctor's visit, there had been neither opportunity nor inclination to do anything more than be together in an almost platonic fashion. But how much longer that was going to last, Kerry had no idea.

There was something else, too. However glorious the closeness at the time, making love could result in a baby out of wedlock . . . Her heart fluttered uneasily every time she thought of how scandalous it would be, for themselves, for Aunt Lil, for his strait-laced mother . . . but it hadn't happened, and it was something they dare not risk. They should discuss it, though, however delicate. But she had always been able to talk to Tom about anything, so they should surely be able to talk about the most intimate thing of all.

'You've gone off in a trance,' Tom said, with a grin, 'and I'm still not telling you, no matter how impatient you are.'

Kerry started, so wrapped up in her own thoughts that she had forgotten that he had been teasing her about her birthday present. She laughed, glad he didn't really know where her thoughts had been going, and feeling her face go hot.

'I'll have to be good, then,' she promised.

'But not too good,' he said, brushing her lips with his, and then moving away hastily as Aunt Lil bustled back into the room, wearing her hat and coat and carrying her knitting bag and her little torch.

'Now then, you two, I'll be back in an hour or so, so you can listen to the wireless or some gramophone records, providing you don't play them too loud for the neighbours' sake. Tom won't want to stay too long, so Kerry, you can also make a list of the food you want for your birthday tea, providing the rations will stretch to it with Maud and Bert being here as well.'

'Yes, ma'am,' Kerry said, trying hard not to laugh as it was so obvious she intended them to keep busy while they were alone.

Lil gave her a hard look and then a half smile that said she wasn't so long in the tooth that she had forgotten what it was like to be in love.

'So shall we obey orders and put some records on,

sweetheart?' Tom said a little while later when they had snuggled up together on the sofa in a very satisfactory cuddle.

'You sort them out while I fetch something I want to show you, Tom.'

It had to be done, and she wasn't going to baulk from doing it, but she felt decidedly nervous when she went up to her bedroom and found Marvin's little note. Was it a mistake to bring back the suspicions in his head that she so wanted to allay? Wouldn't it be better to let sleeping dogs lie? But what if it still festered somewhere in the back of his mind, and he remembered this note that she had conveniently forgotten to show him, or even destroyed? What if he doubted that the note even existed?

Her hands were shaking as she reread it again. It was perfectly innocuous. It was the note from a friend to a friend, and nothing more. He *had* to read it.

She heard the strains of 'Don't Sit Under the Apple Tree' floating upstairs from the gramophone. Was this significant, and was Tom trying to tell her something? Her heart was beating too fast, and she was probably overreacting as usual . . .

'Remember this? It was always one of your favourites, wasn't it?' he said with a smile as she came into the room. 'Which version do you like best? Glenn Miller or the Andrews Sisters?'

'Don't mind,' she said huskily.

'Well, we're stuck with the Andrews Sisters tonight. You sang it at Mrs Holliday's concert last Christmas just for me, didn't you?' he went on.

'Of course I did. Didn't I always sing just for you?'

Kerry sat down beside him again, glad that he remembered, and for a moment she leant her head on his shoulder as the emotive words drifted into the room.

'Don't go walking down Lovers' Lane, with anyone else but me . . .'

She wished it had been the Glenn Miller instrumental version, although she would still have the words running around in her head. Marvin's note was still in her pocket, and she was so very tempted to let it stay there, and not to break into this sweet and dreamy mood.

'So what have you got to show me?' he prompted.

There was no help for it now. He had remembered, and short of making up some stupid lie, she knew she had to get it over with. She took a deep breath.

'Do you remember I promised to show you the note that Marvin Mcleod sent me just before he left on D-Day?'

Immediately she had said it, she knew she had been less than tactful. Why mention D-Day at all, when at that time Tom had been fighting his personal and painful battle with his shrapnel wounds? Why bring Marvin's name into it – but how the hell could she have done otherwise?

But there was no doubt that the atmosphere in the room seemed to have gone a couple of degrees colder. As if to emphasise the change in mood, the music on the gramophone had come to an end, and the scratchy noise of the needle on the sterile part of the record seemed to scream through Kerry's head.

'I'll turn it off a minute,' she said nervously.

'I'll do it,' Tom said, getting up awkwardly from the low sofa to lift the needle from the record and switch off the machine. He turned back to her and she could see the guarded look in his eyes now as he sat down again. The small distance between them seemed ominous to Kerry, but her nervousness was replaced with a sudden anger.

How dare he doubt her after everything she had told him? She had been completely honest with him, and for all she knew he might have been chatting now and then with a French girl. They did that sometimes. They called it 'fraternising'. It wasn't all one-sided – and if he had, would she have minded?

The small burst of anger subsided, because she knew damn well she would have minded! She drew out the envelope from her pocket.

'When you read this, I hope you'll understand, Tom,' she said. 'I've told you everything honestly.'

'I'm not sure I want to read it,' he said stubbornly.

'Then I'll read it to you,' she snapped in a sudden rage. This evening wasn't going at all as it was supposed to, but she wasn't going to let him get away with this.

She opened the envelope and her eyes blurred at Marvin's brief, dignified words, knowing all that he had gone through after D-Day. Then Tom held out his hand, and she handed him the note silently. He scanned it and then he slowly read it aloud.

'Since we'll be moving out real soon now, I want to thank you for your friendship, Kerry. It means a lot to us guys. I also want to let you know that I'm going to move heaven and earth to try to get Shirl back. I don't believe it's all over for us, and I think she's just got cold feet. Wish me luck. Marvin.'

Tom didn't say anything more for a few seconds and then he finally spoke.

'And that's it?'

'Well, apart from the dozens of love letters upstairs that I'm keeping hidden from you, from all the other GIs I met,' Kerry said sarcastically.

He grabbed her hands now, needing to stop them from shaking.

'I'm *sorry*. I didn't mean anything by that. If you want to know, I'm ashamed of myself for taking any notice of what Molly Roddy said. She's just a kid, and I should have laughed it off instead of letting it fester inside me.'

'But you didn't,' Kerry said bitterly. 'You preferred to believe it.'

'I didn't bloody prefer it! It put me through hell, if you must know.'

'And now?' Her voice was still brittle with hurt.

'Oh God, Kerry, now all I want is for us to be the way we always were. We always kidded one another that we'd grow old together, but there were times when I wondered if that was ever going to happen. My feelings were so mixed when I knew I was being chucked out of the army like an old sock, but I knew you would always be there. And then when Molly said what she did, it nearly sent me off my rocker. I wasn't seeing sense. All I could see was that after everything, I could be losing you.'

'Don't be stupid. You're never going to lose me,' Kerry whispered.

She was startled by how emotional he had become. Boys could be emotional too . . . and perhaps she had never really understood how he felt.

'Anyway,' she said, trying to lighten the mood, 'for all I know, you might have had pretty nurses looking after you day and night in your various hospitals. Do I have anything to be jealous about?'

He had relaxed his grip on her hands, but he still caressed them loosely.

'Hardly. They were usually male medics, and hefty ones at that, and those that were female were mostly old battleaxes.'

'Pam Wyatt's hardly a battleaxe.'

'What is it with you and Pam Wyatt! From what I remember of her, she was never going to make Miss World. Or the ex-Miss Montana, or whatever you called this Shirl!'

They looked at one another. He had said the words so naturally, clearly remembering all that she had told him about Marvin's girl. To Kerry, it had sounded almost heartbreakingly normal, and she bit her lips to stop them trembling. She leant into him, her cheek close to his.

'I'm definitely growing old with you. But not just yet!' she said with a strangled laugh.

When Lil came back from her knitting circle, it was to find them with their heads close together, writing out a list of items for the birthday party. On the gramophone, Bing Crosby and the Andrews Sisters were belting out 'Don't Fence Me In', and Kerry hid a smile, knowing it would be a bit modern for Aunt Lil's taste, but not too evocative, either.

'You've been busy, then,' she remarked.

'It wasn't too difficult, knowing what the Roddy kids

like,' Kerry said with a grin. 'Jelly and blancmange and fish paste sandwiches, and anything else we can scrape up. Oh, and some lemonade and a birthday cake, I hope.'

It wasn't exactly a long list, but between them they had laughingly made many crazy suggestions as if there hadn't been a war on, and food was in plentiful supply – and had scratched out many more items to make sure Aunt Lil thought they had been busy with the list and hadn't been canoodling all this time. If she only knew, thought Kerry . . .

'I'd better go,' Tom said at last. 'I've been sitting for too long, anyway. I'll see you tomorrow, Kerry.'

'Goodnight, then, Tom,' Lil said. 'Mind how you go in the blackout.'

She retired to the kitchen to put the kettle on for their last cup of cocoa, leaving them discreetly alone as Kerry went outside the house to say goodnight properly. She felt as though they had come a very long way in the last couple of hours, but at last the air was completely clear between them, and she knew he would never doubt her again.

'I do love you,' he said, as they clung together for a last kiss, 'and I always will.'

'That goes for me too. You know that, don't you, Tom? There's never been anyone else, nor ever will be.'

She watched him go until the darkness swallowed him up, and then she went back indoors. Lil had turned off the gramophone, and was frowning over the note Kerry had left on the sofa.

'You showed him, then,' she said. 'Was it the right thing to do?'

'It was never more right, Aunt Lil. No more secrets between us.'

Lil nodded. 'Good,' she said briskly. 'That's how it should be. So now we have Maud and Bert descending on us tomorrow. They'll want to meet Tom, of course, so I hope you've warned him about them.'

'If I haven't said enough about them, his mother surely will!'

She laughed, but although Lil was still groaning about her cousin and whom she still thought of as her 'fancy man' coming down again for a visit, Kerry was becoming quite glad. They were characters, and the world needed colourful characters like them, if only for the more pious and upright citizens of the world to have someone to be smug about.

As might have been expected, the station taxi turned up with the pair of them in tow early on Friday evening. They seemed to have an enormous amount of luggage for just a weekend stay, but that was Maud, Kerry thought with a smile. She'd heard her say before that why would anyone want to travel light if you could carry everything but the virtual kitchen sink! Even if it was poor Bert who had to do most of the carrying. But Maud swept in to the house ahead of him, reeking of cheap scent, and with all the aplomb of a Hollywood film star.

'So how are my favourite backwater cousins?' she bellowed, with a comment that was hardly likely to endear her to Lil.

But to give her credit, Lil's welcoming smile didn't falter. Probably because she knew they would be off to the Gillagys' farm pretty soon.

335

'We're fine, and you two look blooming,' Lil said evenly.

Maud looked critically at Kerry. 'Well, you certainly do as well, dearie, now that your young man's home from the war. He must be doing something to put the roses in your cheeks!' she added with a sly wink that made Kerry squirm.

Hopefully, she would get all the snide innuendoes over before Tom arrived, and certainly before she got anywhere near Tom's mother! Maud would almost certainly have to make a queenly trek around the village and her old haunts before she and Bert went back to Bristol.

'So how are you getting to the farm with all that luggage?' she said, in what she hoped wasn't too pointed a fashion.

'We've asked the taxi to come back for us in an hour to take us there,' Bert said, 'but Maud wanted to get reacquainted with you both first.'

Lil sniffed, clearly thinking that money seemed to be no object to this pair of charmers.

'Business must be doing all right, then,' she said.

'First class,' Maud beamed. 'In fact, we've brought one or two pieces for you and Kerry, old girl, so we'll be leaving the box with them here before we leave. There's a bit of ham, too, that our friendly butcher let us have for the party tomorrow. No point in having friends in high places if you can't do a bit of bartering now and then, is it?' She winked again. 'So how about a cup of Rosie Lee, girls? Bert's been saying he's so parched he thinks his throat's been cut.'

There was no stopping her, but at least her heart was in the right place, Kerry thought generously. And she was itching to know what the bits and pieces were in the box

336

they were leaving for them. After an exhaustive hour when Maud seemed to have talked non-stop, the taxi arrived for them, and she and Lil wilted. A short while later Tom knocked at the door.

'Talk about timing it right! You've missed the visitors,' Kerry said.

'Oh well, there's always tomorrow. Anyway, I've got news.'

Kerry's heart plummeted. He looked more animated than before and she should be glad. But with the crazy thoughts of a madwoman . . . surely the army hadn't gone back on its word and decided they wanted him back after all?

'For one thing, I've cycled over here tonight without any trouble, and the doc's pleased with the way I've persevered with my exercises. He says the best thing I can do now is to get back to working on the boat with Dad, providing he does all the heavy stuff at first. I can start in two weeks' time.'

'Oh Tom, you can't. It's too soon!'

'What, are you the expert now?' he said, disappointed at her reaction. 'I thought I only had one mother, not two.'

'It's wonderful news, Tom,' Aunt Lil said quickly. 'There's nothing like the incentive to get back to normal to make it come all the quicker.'

Kerry was annoyed at her own reaction, and tried to cover it.

'Well, of course it's wonderful, and you can test your strength by getting all the string and tape off this box that Maud's brought down for us.'

It wouldn't test a ten-year-old, but it was the best she could think of, and he had it all undone in a minute. They had no idea what they would find inside, but there were several blouses and skirts and other odds and ends, plus a little woollen coat that was Molly Roddy's size rather than either of the Penfolds.

'Are these the proceeds of their new shop?' Tom said with a grin.

'I suppose so, and we're obviously their first charity case.'

Some of the blouses were really nice and they were all very clean. And if Aunt Lil was turning up her nose at the idea of charity, Kerry certainly wasn't. It was ages since she had been able to buy anything that was half decent, and she wasn't going to say no to any of it.

'I'm going to try some of it on,' she announced. 'I'll give you both a fashion parade.'

She dashed upstairs with several of the blouses. Minutes later she appeared wearing her own skirt and a nearly new sky-blue blouse with a floppy bow at the neck and puffed sleeves.

'It's very nice,' Lil conceded. She was forced to say the same about the other things, and avoided sounding too enthusiastic by saying she would give everything a good wash before they were worn in public.

'Now then, I'm going to be busy tonight, making your birthday cake, so you can both make yourself scarce.'

'Now that you're mobile again, we could always cycle over to Gillagy's Farm for you to meet Maud and Bert and get it over with, Tom,' Kerry said, and he agreed at once.

'If this is the only way I can get you on my own, it'll have to do,' he said, once they were outside. 'It's like old times, isn't it, except that I could do with a brighter headlight to see where the hell I'm going.'

'And alert the Jerries?'

'What Jerries? When was the last air raid here, Kerry?'

'End of May. It was a terrible night, but it all seems a long time ago now.'

She resisted telling him how much the Americans had helped that night, and how things might have turned out very differently without them. It was five months ago, and so much had happened since then. The best of all was that she was cycling along the lanes with her sweetheart, and apart from the enforced darkness and the patchy moonlight, it was easy to imagine that there was no war, only the peace of the Cornish countryside that they had always known.

As they neared the farm, somewhere in the night they heard a cow cough. The sound was so human-like that she gave a little squeal, and her bike wobbled over a gritty patch in the lane. She almost ran into him, but it was enough to start them both laughing and slide off their bikes to walk the last few hundred yards.

'Don't expect me to carry you back,' Tom joked. 'I may be getting fitter, but not that fit! I'm saving myself for when I carry you over the threshold.'

She wasn't sure she had heard him right, but of course she had. It was just so unexpected after the trauma of the past weeks.

'You still think I'm going to marry you, then?' she asked.

'Well, aren't you?' he said, with all the arrogance of the caveman.

* * *

339

The Gillagys were clearly completely bemused at the way Maud was regaling them about their new shop and how their business was a roaring success, and when they heard the knock on the farmhouse door, they both shouted 'come in!' to whoever was bringing them a welcome interruption.

Kerry and Tom were greeted with glasses of Farmer Gillagy's home-made cider, which probably wasn't such a great idea as they had to cycle back, but being very thirsty by now, they didn't argue. Kerry was so exalted by what Tom had said that she didn't even worry that Maud was blatantly quizzing him about his time in the army, and his injuries, and what was going to happen next. She thought he'd be uptight about it all, but he seemed to find it hilarious, especially as the more ingenuous Gillagys sat there, open-mouthed, as Maud expertly winkled every last bit of information she wanted out of him. Everything he was willing to tell her, at least. Finally, Kerry managed to get a word in edgeways, and said they had better go.

'We'll see you tomorrow, then, dearie,' Maud said gaily. 'Don't fall in any ditches on the way back, and don't do anything I wouldn't do!'

She gave her that scrunched-up wink again that was obviously supposed to be meaningful, but which only gave her the expression of a gargoyle and spread some of the heavy eye make-up over her cheek.

Tom almost exploded with laughter once they got outside and rescued their bikes from the side of the barn. 'Bloody hell, she's a card all right! How did your Aunt Lil ever come to be related to her?'

'Lord knows, but thankfully you can choose your friends,

even if you can't choose your relatives,' she answered with a chuckle.

They cycled back to the village comparatively quickly, still laughing at some of Maud's more outrageous remarks. No matter how much she loved Aunt Lil, Kerry had to admit that there was a lot to be said for the lighter side of life, and Maud was certainly a good example of that. At the door of the cottage, Tom kissed her goodnight and told her he'd see her the following afternoon.

'Come early before the rest of them,' Kerry said.

'You mean you can't wait to see what I've bought you,' he teased.

'Oh, have you bought me something?' she said, wide-eyed.

He caught her around the waist and his kiss was more passionate now, and she felt the old familiar thrill at being held tightly in his arms.

'You'll just have to wait and see, my impatient little witch.'

Then he was gone, and Kerry went indoors with the smile still on her face to see Aunt Lil putting the finishing touches to the birthday cake. Restricted by food coupons, and the lack of dried fruit to make a richer cake, it had to be a sponge cake filled with Lil's home-made jam, but she had unearthed an old cake frill and a few candles from earlier days, and although eighteen of them would have overpowered the cake, it would be enough of a show for the Roddy kids to cheer when she blew them out.

'It's lovely, Aunt Lil.'

'Good. So were Maud and Bert in good voice?' she said.

Kerry laughed. 'Very, I'd say. I don't think the Gillagys knew what had hit them. Bringing all that stuff for us was thoughtful, though. She means well, doesn't she?'

'Oh ah. She means well.'

And that was it. Kerry knew there was never going to be any love lost between the two of them. Lil tolerated her because she was family, and that was all, and wisely, Kerry didn't say anything more. But she was beginning to like her more. She was lively and outgoing, and there was nothing wrong with that. But this was no time to ponder on any friction there may or may not be between her aunts. Tomorrow she was going to celebrate her birthday, and she would be sharing it with all the people she loved best. Especially her one and only, and what better birthday present could there be than having Tom home?

She helped her aunt clear away the cooking materials, had a last cup of cocoa with her, and went to bed, feeling more content than she had in a long time. She was almost eighteen, the age when many girls got married, she thought dreamily. And although she didn't anticipate herself and Tom tying the knot for some time to come yet, they had made a promise to one another long ago that theirs would be a for ever kind of love. They had promised themselves to one another, and they were promises to keep.

CHAPTER NINETEEN

Even though Kerry's birthday wasn't until Sunday, everyone was now going to honour it on the Saturday. You couldn't have a party without birthday cards, though, and as well as an early card from Aunt Lil there was also a small flat package beside Kerry's breakfast the following morning.

'What's this?' she asked excitedly.

'This is something I've been saving for your special day. It should be for your twenty-first, but call it a little nest egg with all my love for the future.'

Inside the wrapping was a savings book with an amount of money deposited in it that made Kerry gasp.

'Oh, Aunt Lil!'

'Now, don't go all weepy on your "nearly birthday". It's no more than I'd give to my own daughter if I had one, and since you're the nearest thing to a daughter I've ever had, I want you to have it.'

'But where . . . ? And how . . . ?'

'No questions now. As I said, I've been saving all these years, and what would I want with money when I already have everything I need?'

Kerry flung her arms around her, trying not to cry. It said so much about the lack of a real family in Lil's life, and in hers too. But she knew her aunt well enough not to go all sentimental over her.

'Thank you,' she said simply. 'For everything.'

'Yes, well I hope that includes your "almost birthday" breakfast egg before it gets cold,' came the brisk reply. 'There'll be another one tomorrow.'

A birthday egg and fried bread too . . . it threatened to choke her, but you couldn't waste food these days, so she ate every scrap, and then rushed to the door as the postman delivered some cards. These wouldn't have been delivered on a Sunday, either, so celebrating her birthday a day early made sense.

When she had opened cards from the Roddy family, Tom's parents, the Polbys and old school friends, it was time to go to work, knowing she would get more later. From Maud and Bert . . . a special one from Claire . . . from Tom . . .

'So here's the birthday girl,' Mrs Polby greeted her. 'Don't suppose you feel any older, do you, Kerry love?'

'Not until tomorrow,' she grinned. 'But thank you for the card. You should have saved the stamp!'

'Ah, but there's nothing to beat the postman delivering it, is there? And a treat to have something cheerful to open these days, rather than a telegram.'

Kerry didn't want to think about that. She just wanted

344

the time to pass quickly, so that she could go home and prepare for her party. Claire looked in halfway through the morning to say that the kids were driving everybody mad at home, looking at the clock every five minutes until it was party time.

'They've made you a picture,' she told Kerry. 'Try to look pleased when you see it,' she added with a grin.

'Of course I will, and what are you looking so pleased about as well? A letter from Glenn, I suppose?'

'What else? I'll tell you later,' she said hastily, as several customers came into the shop. Whatever it was, it was obvious she was bursting to say more, but she blew Kerry a kiss and went out, leaving her wondering.

But there was no time to wonder on anything as they got busy, and at last the morning ended, and she could go home. She wouldn't be seeing Tom until the afternoon, as he had become meticulous in doing his prescribed exercises every morning, in order to get fit as soon as possible, especially with the added incentive now of getting back to work soon.

She hoped he would be the first to arrive at the house, but Maud and Bert were already there, and from the look on Aunt Lil's face, they had already been gabbling her head off for quite a while.

'Here she is at last,' Maud said gaily. 'You'd think they'd have let you have the day off to get ready for a party even if it's not strictly your birthday yet, but anyway, me and Bert have brought you a present, and as we won't be seeing you tomorrow, you can open it now.'

Kerry opened the wrapping. Inside was a beautiful silk scarf that looked as if it had cost a lot of money, but the look in Lil's eyes told her it had probably come out of stock at their shop. It didn't matter. The delicate muted tones of blue and turquoise were perfect, and nothing like as garish as Maud's own taste.

'Bert chose it,' Maud went on. 'I fancied something brighter and more colourful, but he thought this would suit you.'

Kerry almost laughed as it echoed her own thoughts, but all thanks to Bert, and she flashed him a grateful look.

'I love it, and thank you both,' she said.

Then she saw Tom coming up the path, and everything else went out of her head. She didn't want to open his present in front of everyone else, and she went outside before he could reach the front door.

He kissed her in full view of whoever might be watching, and she dragged him around the side of the house with a laugh, saying they didn't want to give Aunt Maud a field day.

'The old trout's here, then,' he said with a mock groan. 'She beat me to it. I hoped I'd be the first.'

'Never mind her. You're the only one I want to see.'

'I was going to keep this until tomorrow, but I guess everybody else will be giving you presents, and I know how impatient you get, so you'd better have this now,' he said, drawing a small package out of his pocket to give to her.

Inside was a small heart-shaped locket on a silver chain, and Kerry drew in her breath. It said so much. It said everything. It gave her his heart.

'It's beautiful, Tom, and I love it. I love *you*,' she said. 'Put it on for me, will you?'

She felt his fingers, warm against her skin, as he fastened

the locket at the back of her neck. His touch caressed her, sending shivers through her as she felt the coolness of the locket at her throat, and she suddenly yearned for so much more than just seeing him every day, miraculous and wonderful though that was. She wanted him close to her night and day, for always, building their lives together the way they had always dreamt.

'You've got a strange, faraway look in your eyes,' Tom said.

She teased him. 'Have I? Perhaps I was looking into the future.'

He laughed, knowing these private moments were coming to an end as they heard the excited chatter of the Roddy children coming down the road.

'You can tell me sometime what you see, as long as I'm included in it.'

Before she could say anything more, Molly Roddy had rushed up to the house, and catching sight of them, had thrown herself against him.

'For heaven's sake, Molly, be careful,' Claire called out anxiously.

'It's all right,' Tom told her. 'I won't break.'

'My mum says you're having two birthdays, but we've only got one present for you, and we're going to sing "Happy Birthday" to you when you blow out your candles,' Molly shrieked.

'We'd better go indoors, then,' Kerry said, seeing how she could hardly contain her impatience, and Toby wasn't much better. Jed was as dignified as ever, just waiting for his chance to chat with Tom.

She loved them all, and with a sudden flash of intuition,

or foresight, or whatever the psychics might call it, she thought how wonderful it would be if someday in the future, she and Tom had a little family like this.

But she was being bundled inside the house now, and Aunt Maud was gushing over the kids as they pressed the large flat envelope into Kerry's hands. She opened it and tried hard to keep a straight face, as it had obviously been created with all the care of little hands, plus a few extra bits of attention from Jed, she guessed. It was a drawing of two girls, who were obviously meant to be her and Claire on the stage, and wearing the dance costumes that Mrs Holliday provided.

'It's lovely,' Kerry said.

'It was all my idea,' Molly crowed, leaping up and down in excitement. 'Jed helped us a bit, but me and Toby did the colouring with our crayons.'

'I shall stick it on my bedroom wall,' Kerry told them solemnly, 'then I'll be able to see it every morning when I wake up.'

Claire had bought her a book of quotes that Kerry had seen in a bookshop a while ago, and nobody missed seeing the silver locket around her neck.

'So that's what Tom and his dad went into Falmouth to buy the other day,' Claire said. 'It's gorgeous, Kerry.'

'What were you so eager to tell me?' she said, under cover of the general noise going on as Lil and Maud prepared the table for tea, and Bert was in his element entertaining the kids with tales of his youth.

'Later,' Claire said, as Tom hovered near.

What was it that couldn't be said when Tom was around? Her heart jolted for a moment. It surely couldn't be anything to do with Marvin Mcleod. He was out of her life, and had hardly been in it for very long, but Claire was looking so mysterious now that she didn't dare to ask.

'Time for tea,' Lil announced. 'Everybody sit at the table, and you little ones will have to squeeze up to make room.'

There weren't enough chairs for them all, but the sofa had been pulled near, and piled high with pillows and cushions so the kids could see over the edge of the table. It was quickly turning into a noisy, boisterous, family party, and Kerry loved every minute of it. As the 'nearly birthday' girl, she sat at the head of the table and they all sang 'Happy Birthday' as she blew out the candles.

'You've got to make a wish,' Molly and Toby shrieked together.

She closed her eyes and wished for the thing that was dearest to her heart. When she opened her eyes again, she looked straight into Tom's, and knew they were wishing for the same thing.

'What did you wish for, Kerry?' Molly shouted.

'She musn't tell you that,' Jed scolded her. 'If she tells you what she wished for, it won't come true.'

Oh, but it would . . .

'That's right. It's a secret,' Kerry said with a laugh.

'I bet I can guess,' Aunt Maud put in with one of her sly winks.

'Keep it to yourself, then,' Lil said, unexpectedly sharp. 'We stick to the old traditions here, as you very well know, Maud. There's no telling, and no guessing. Secrets are meant to be private.'

'Well, all right, old girl, I was only teasing, and I can keep a secret with the best of them, as you know,' Maud said, mildly affronted. 'Here, Bert, why don't you show the kids some of your card tricks after tea? I bet young Jed would like to learn a few to show his mates at school.'

The small tension passed, and when the meal was finished, Bert did as he was told and began to entertain the kids while the women cleared the plates and dishes from the table. But it soon became clear that Molly had eaten far too much and was starting to look paler than usual. Coupled with her excited jumping up and down, it wasn't doing her stomach a lot of good, and it finally erupted all over one of Lil's best cushions.

'Oh, Mrs Penfold, I'm so sorry,' Claire gasped.

'Don't worry, my dear. These things happen,' Lil said stoically, lifting the entire cushion by two corners and holding it well away from her as she carried it outside into the back garden. 'I'll deal with that later. Let's just get the little mite cleaned up.'

Kerry had already fetched a facecloth and towel and was preparing to wipe Molly's ashen face.

'Are you sure you've finished?' she asked, as Molly clutched her chest. 'If not, you'd better come outside.'

Molly shook her head mournfully, but it was probably doubtful that there was much more inside her to come up. Tom had brought her a glass of water and held her head as she took a few sips, while Maud and Bert stood around looking momentarily helpless, unused to dealing with children of their own. Toby was giggling at his sister's distress as only small boys could, and Jed was trying to hush him up for being so rude.

'I'd better take her home,' Claire said at last. 'Sorry to end your party like this, Kerry.'

'I'm sorry for her,' Kerry said. 'But the boys can stay a bit longer if they like. I'm sure Bert's got more to show them yet.'

They clamoured to be allowed to stay, and Kerry reluctantly showed Claire and Molly out, and although Molly was protesting feebly, she'd probably be glad to be at home and tucked up in bed for an hour or so. There was nothing like your own bed when you were feeling poorly.

'Well, come on, this is still a party, isn't it?' Maud exclaimed. 'How about putting some records on the gramophone to liven things up, Kerry?'

'I should think we've had enough liveliness for now,' Lil said, coming in from outside, after managing to scrub the worst of it from the cushion, and hoping it would dry out eventually. 'We don't want any more little accidents.'

'I won't be sick,' Jed said importantly, 'and Toby's all right, aren't you, Toby?' He nudged him in the ribs to make him say yes.

'Come on, then. What records have you got?' Maud persisted. 'You could sing for us, Kerry!'

'No, I couldn't.'

'Oh, why not? I've never heard you sing before.'

'Because it's my day, and I don't have to do anything I don't want to do,' she said in mock defiance.

'Attagirl,' Tom breathed in her ear.

She smiled at him, wondering if he'd been thinking the same as she had before the excitement of the party had descended into chaos. Was this how it was with a small family? And would theirs be anything like this? A small family of girls or boys or a delightful mixture of both, like the Roddy children. She felt herself blush, her thoughts

351

winging much farther ahead than she had intended.

'Oh, all right, Kerry, but we can still have some music,' Maud went on. 'I suppose you think you have to act properly now you're a grown-up. You'll be thinking of getting married next, I daresay. What will you do then, Lil, when your chick leaves the nest?'

'I won't be getting married for ages,' Kerry said quickly, seeing how the remark had made Aunt Lil draw in her breath. Maud's tongue ran away with her far too often, putting ideas into people's heads that shouldn't be there.

'She's got to be asked first,' Bert joked, and to Kerry's horror everyone turned to look at her and Tom. It was as though time stopped for a few awkward moments, and then Tom gave an easy laugh.

'If you're trying to get anything out of me and Kerry on that score, you'll have to wait a long time. Whatever we know, we're not telling!'

For one horrified moment, Kerry found herself thanking her lucky stars that Molly Roddy had thrown up all over Lil's best cushion, and hadn't been here to pipe up with the words: *Perhaps Kerry will marry her Yankee Doodle . . .*

Her head seemed to spin for a few seconds, and she had a nightmare vision of it actually happening, knowing that everything she had told Tom about Marvin would have been wiped out in a moment and would have come to nothing. But then she looked around, and nobody seemed aware of anything out of the ordinary. Tom was still smiling at her, and Maud had given up on her teasing and was sorting out records to put on the gramophone, and Bert was shuffling the deck of cards he seemed to carry around with him everywhere, to entertain the boys.

It was only Kerry who seemed to be in the grip of something that was telling her that this wasn't over yet, and however much she tried to push away the shadow, it was as though there still had to be a reckoning. Everybody said that the past eventually came back to haunt you, and she had the strongest feeling that her past, however innocent, hadn't done with her yet.

It was only much later, with the party long over, when Maud and Bert had gone back to the Gillagys' farm, and Tom had gone home with the Roddy boys under his wing, that she lay in bed and thought about the day. She was relaxed and happy now. In many ways it had been a lovely day, a perfect day, with everyone she loved around her, and once they were alone, Tom had reminded her in no uncertain fashion that there was only one person who was going to marry her . . .

Tom had brought her a small advance gift from his parents, and there had been the lovely birthday cards from families and friends. The only thing to spoil it was that poor Molly had thrown up after leaping about too energetically and eating too much, so that Claire had had to take her home.

The moment she thought about Claire, Kerry's senses were alerted. Claire had something important to tell her, but there had been no chance after she had taken Molly home. She thought she might have come back to the house later, but she hadn't done so, and it would have to wait until tomorrow after church. She had had a letter from Glenn, Kerry remembered, so no doubt it was more impassioned words of undying love.

She smiled in the darkness, thinking how lovely it was that they both had a boy who loved them, and wishing that they were going to spend the rest of their lives here in Columbine. But Claire wouldn't be doing that . . . not unless Glenn decided that he wanted to say here in Cornwall after all, so that even being a GI bride didn't mean Claire had to leave her family to travel halfway around the world with him when the time came. Maybe that was what Claire was going to tell her, Kerry thought hopefully, as she drifted off to sleep.

By now, she thought that Tom was more or less ready to face the world, but if she expected him to show up with his mother at church the next morning, she was mistaken, and after the proper birthday wishes were exchanged, Mrs Trevellyan spoke in some annoyance.

'He and his father have gone off to inspect the boat,' she told Kerry after the service, with a sniff that was worthy of Aunt Lil. 'I know the ferry is their livelihood, but I sometimes think it's as much a case of boys with their toys as anything else.'

'I'm sure you're right, but I'm just glad that Tom feels able to get his hand in again,' Kerry said non-committally.

'Well, we're all glad about that, and I understand your party was a happy occasion yesterday, Kerry, apart from Molly Roddy's mishap. It didn't cause too much damage, I hope.'

'Not at all. It was only a cushion and it was soon cleaned,' she said brightly, knowing that the house-proud Mrs Trevellyan would have been far more horrified than Aunt Lil at having her precious home spoilt. But they were only belongings and belongings could be mended. Unlike people.

'Has Maud gone back to Bristol now?' Tom's mother said next.

'As far as we know. She and Bert were going back this morning, so that was the last we saw of them yesterday.'

'I saw them briefly,' Tom's mother said, openly disapproving.

'Tom hasn't been to see Michael's hassock yet, has he?' Kerry said suddenly, wanting to get her off the subject of her flamboyant Aunt Maud.

It still surprised her that he never mentioned the hassock the ladies had worked so hard on, but perhaps he couldn't bring himself to do so.

'Not yet. He'll do it in his own good time. We know that his injuries are well on the mend, Kerry, but it takes time for a person to recover inside his head from all he has gone through. Added to that, the shock of hearing about Michael's death, and coming back here to face it, was something else he had to deal with. He's flatly refused to have a party for himself now, by the way.'

Kerry hadn't heard her speak quite so openly before, and she felt a tug of compassion for her. 'I'm sure he knows what's best,' she said awkwardly.

Out of the corner of her eye she saw Claire coming towards her, and she said goodbye to Tom's mother quickly. They had been talking for long enough, in her opinion, and she turned to her friend gratefully.

'Thanks for rescuing me.'

'Don't mention it. And happy birthday.'

Kerry pulled a face. 'I feel as if that all happened

yesterday, and today is just an anticlimax. Tom's coming to tea, and that's it – not that I'm objecting to that, of course!' she added hastily. 'So what did you have to tell me?'

Claire looked at her warily, and Kerry felt a stab of apprehension. Something wasn't right, and as yet she had no idea what it was. Surely Glenn hadn't decided he didn't want a GI bride after all . . . but it couldn't be that, or Claire would never have seemed so happy yesterday. It had to be something else.

She linked her arm in Claire's and began to move away from the church and the congregation still milling outside, and walked determinedly towards the river where they had always shared their secrets. There was a distinct chill in the day now, and the smell of autumn was definitely in the air, as it should be.

'What's happened? It can't be bad news, or you couldn't have kept it to yourself this long.'

'No, it's not bad news. It's the best. Glenn's getting leave.'

'Well, why didn't you tell me that yesterday?'

Claire had that uncertain look on her face again. 'It's not going to be until the end of the month, so I've still got a few weeks to wait. But that's not all of it. Half of his section is getting the leave too, and of course, they can hardly go all the way home to America and then back again, so they're coming here to their old base.'

'What do you mean – half of his section?'

But she knew immediately. What Claire was obviously trying to avoid telling her was that Marvin Mcleod would be getting leave as well. He would be coming back to Columbine. He would expect to see her, and he would meet

Tom. That was why Claire hadn't mentioned it yesterday.

'Oh God, I don't know what to say. I'm thrilled for you, Claire, of course I am, but, well, you know what I'm thinking now. You do mean that Marvin's getting leave as well, don't you?'

'That's what Glenn says.' She looked annoyed now. 'Don't tell me you begrudge him that, after all he's been through. Glenn says he's been in the thick of it quite a few times, but I don't know any details, only that he's had some injuries. He deserves some leave as much as anyone, Kerry.'

'Of course I don't begrudge it,' Kerry muttered. 'I know I'm being selfish, but I really never wanted to see him again, and I never thought I'd have to.'

'Yes, you are being selfish,' Claire said bluntly, in a definite huff now. 'If you want my honest opinion, you don't know when you're well off, Kerry. Our Michael's never coming home again, and you've got Tom back, more or less in one piece. Glenn and Marvin and the rest of them who went over there on D-Day have been stuck there ever since. You should thank God for what you've got.'

'I do! Every day!'

And a damn fine birthday this was turning out to be . . .

'I don't know how I'm going to tell Tom, that's all,' she went on.

'Just tell him Glenn's coming on leave with some of his buddies. That's all he needs to know, isn't it? I'm sure *he'll* be pleased for me.'

'Oh Claire, you know I'm pleased for you too. I just thought all that bad business between us was over and done with. The last thing I wanted to do was to have to mention Marvin's name again, and now I don't see how I can avoid it. Once Tom knows some of the Yanks are coming back, he'll ask if Marvin will be among them, and it will stir things up all over again.'

'He should have more faith in you, then,' Claire retorted.

It must have been fate allowing her to have the best day yesterday, before this bombshell. Kerry didn't know which was worse – to have her birthday ruined by having all this hanging over her now, or spoiling things for Claire, which she knew very well she was doing by the hurt look on her face.

'I'd better go home,' she said, not knowing what to say to put things right between them. 'When Tom comes round this afternoon, I'm going to tell him straight away. It's better than letting it fester. And I do think it's wonderful news for you, Claire, really I do.'

She turned and walked away quickly, knowing that if she said anything more, she was only going to make things worse between them. But how could Claire possibly understand the shock of that moment when Tom had hurled Molly's innocent words at her?

Kerry's got a Yankee Doodle as well . . .

Yes, he should have had more faith in her, but how could she have expected otherwise when it had sounded so positive, even from a child? She groaned. In her head at that moment she could hear the vicar intoning the words from one of the psalms in one of his lengthy sermons:

Out of the mouths of babes . . .

She thought Tom had been completely understanding

when she showed him Marvin's note. To anybody with any sense, it was obvious from the words that Marvin wanted his girl back. He wanted his Shirl, his beautiful ex-Miss Montana. But now, uneasy thoughts were creeping into Kerry's head. What if someone with a suspicious mind read more in the note than was actually intended? She didn't need to try too hard to remember the exact words, since she had gone over them a hundred times.

Since we'll be moving out real soon now, I want to thank you for your friendship, Kerry. It means a lot to us guys. I also want to let you know that I'm going to move heaven and earth to try to get Shirl back. I don't believe it's all over for us, and I think she's just got cold feet. Wish me luck. Marvin.

She tried to imagine it through Tom's eyes. Did it imply that her friendship had been more than a passing thing? How long had that friendship lasted? How many intimate moments had there been, and secrets shared? Was Marvin saying that since he knew she already had a boyfriend he was going to try to get his own girl back as a kind of consolation prize? She had never thought that for a minute, since it simply wasn't the way it had happened.

But however well Tom was feeling now, she knew that deep down he was still vulnerable and touchy at being thrown out of the army before he was ready, and hearing what he had from Molly had shaken his fragile confidence. So how would he feel when these handsome GIs came back to the village in their smart uniforms, welcomed by the local people who had been so impressed by their good manners and charm, and by the way they had all pitched in on the awful night when Swanvale had burnt?

They would be welcomed as heroes, and deservedly so. There might even be a small reception for them. The Friendship Club would probably want to arrange it once they got wind of it. Hands across the ocean and all that . . . And long before she reached home, Kerry's nerves were in such a state that she was beginning to feel, after all, that this was the worst birthday she had ever known.

Lil was preparing their dinner when she banged into the house. Her sharp words about door hinges faded when she saw the look on Kerry's face.

'Don't tell me you and Claire have fallen out again. I saw you go off with her after church. You two are like a couple of squabbling cats sometimes.'

Kerry burst out with it without thinking.

'She's had some news. Her Glenn is getting a week's leave at the end of the month, and coming back to Columbine. In fact, half of his section is getting the leave, and they'll be spending it at their old base. It's great news for her, isn't it, Aunt Lil?'

Her eyes brimmed with tears. For the life of her she couldn't say the words as to why it wasn't such good news for herself, since it was shaming to be so ungenerous to a friend. But she didn't need to explain anything. Lil turned off the gas under the saucepan of potatoes, and came to put her arms around her niece.

'It'll be all right, love,' she said gently. 'You and Tom are like the Rock of Gibraltar. You've got good foundations, and when the foundations are solid, everything else is strong too. Always remember that.'

Kerry hid her head against her aunt's shoulder for a moment. Lil was like a wise old owl. But Kerry knew that she and Tom hadn't attained the wisdom of age yet. They were both young and hot-headed, and who knew how much this was going to tip him over the edge, or if their love was going to survive it?

CHAPTER TWELVE

CHAPTER TWENTY

Tom came to the house in the middle of the afternoon, self-consciously carrying a bunch of flowers.

'You've got to have something on your birthday or it won't seem like a birthday at all,' he said with a smile.

She buried her face in the rose-red Michaelmas daisies for a moment, wondering if they were a subconscious nod to Michael Roddy.

'I'll put them in water, and then why don't we go for a walk?' she said quickly, since she didn't want to say anything in front of Aunt Lil.

He didn't need second sight to sense there was something on her mind.

'So what's happened now? Maud and Bert haven't decided to stay on for a week, have they?' he joked, once they had left the house and headed away from the village towards the open farmland. As if by unspoken consent, neither of them felt inclined to go towards the river.

'No,' Kerry said. 'Though Aunt Lil reckons they're going to keep on turning up like bad pennies. At least they liven the place up, don't they?'

It might have been easier all round if Maud and Bert *had* stayed for longer, she thought, almost to her own surprise. At least they would have been a buffer between her and however Tom was going to take the news about the GIs. But he had to know, and she had to be the one to tell him.

They were strolling along the hedgerows in the fields now. Cows were grazing in the distance, and there were still a few bees buzzing about in a late homage to summer, reminding Kerry instantly of Michael again. She dashed the weak threat of tears from her eyes. This was no time to get mopey.

'It's a shame we don't have a basket with us,' she said suddenly. 'There are still blackberries about and it's not October the eleventh yet.'

'What's the date got to do with it?' Tom said, humouring her.

'Oh, it's one of Aunt Lil's old superstitions. I bet your mum will know all about it, though she would probably condemn it as being anti-Christian.'

'So are you going to tell me or not?'

'Well, it's said that if you pick blackberries after October the eleventh the devil gets into them.'

'Oh yes,' Tom said with a grin. 'And you believe that, do you?'

'I don't, but Aunt Lil does. It's a really old saying because apparently that's when the devil was kicked out of heaven and he landed on a blackberry bush. He was so angry that every year he spoils the blackberries on that date. He either spits on them or pees on them, so they don't taste very nice.'

Tom was laughing at her now, clearly thinking she was mad if she believed such rot. 'I don't suppose they would.'

'Well, whatever you think,' she said defensively, 'Aunt Lil won't cook them after the eleventh, or even have them in the house.'

'Good job we haven't got anything to put them in, then,' Tom said dryly.

'Oh, we'd be all right today,' she began, and then realised he was teasing. 'I have to live with her, Tom, so I have to respect what she thinks.'

'And what do you think?' he said, standing still and forcing her to do the same. 'I'm sure we haven't come out here to talk about blackberries, so what else is on your mind?'

Absent-mindedly, she had reached for a bramble and picked one of the overripe succulent blackberries from a branch and put it in her mouth, letting it linger there for a moment and ignoring the way the juice stained her fingers dark red. Like blood.

She looked at him. 'Claire's heard from Glenn. He's getting some leave in a couple of weeks and he's coming here, so she's all excited, of course.'

'The Yanks were always freer with their leaves than us,' Tom said shortly. 'Rest and relaxation it's called – R & R – and never mind that there's a war on.'

'It's not only Glenn,' Kerry went on in a rush. 'Apparently half his section will be here too, according to Claire, staying at their old base for a week.'

He didn't say a word, and she wondered if the sudden sour taste in her mouth after swallowing the blackberry was because the devil had come early to taunt her, and she tried to ignore such pagan thoughts.

'You know what I'm saying, don't you, Tom? Marvin Mcleod will be among them,' she said, jittery now.

'I heard you. I'm not deaf.'

'Marvin is, though. Partly, anyway. I told you that. Glenn told Claire he's been wounded a few times since D-Day as well, but that's all I know.'

'Well, if he's had surgery as many as nine times, he'll be sent back home. They're like cats. Nine lives is all you're allowed in their army.'

She couldn't follow his mood. She didn't know whether his words were true, or if they only applied to the Yanks, or if he was just being sarcastic. In any case, having to undergo nine surgeries, or even one, sounded horrendous. Not that she knew if that applied to Marvin.

She couldn't even be sure if Tom was being sarky because he himself had had to be demobbed after being struck by a few bits of shrapnel. But everybody knew that shrapnel wounds could be devastating. They could pierce the heart or tear the face off a man in an instant. She shivered, knowing how relatively lucky Tom had been, and resenting his bitterness not for the first time.

'I think many people in the village will be glad to see them here again, anyway,' she said defiantly. 'And it'll be good for you to meet Marvin, Tom.'

'Why would I want to meet him?'

'So that you can get this ridiculous jealousy out of your head once and for all,' she snapped, in a rage with him now.

She strode ahead of him, wondering how this day could be turning out so badly. It was her birthday, for goodness' sake, knowing it was one she would want to forget.

He caught up with her as they neared the Gillagys' farm, and her heart sank as she saw Mrs Gillagy in the yard. The last thing she wanted was to have to stop and chat with her, but the farmer's wife had already seen them.

'Kerry, how nice to see you, my love, and Tom too. Come inside and have a cup of something with Farmer and me.'

They had no choice if they didn't want to appear rude. Tom said nothing as she accepted the offer as cheerfully as she could.

'It was good to see your auntie and her new husband,' Mrs Gillagy said with a chuckle. 'She's a card, isn't she? And talks the hind leg off a donkey.'

She didn't do so bad herself, thought Kerry, but she was glad of the respite, and Tom was obliged to answer Farmer Gillagy's questions about his time in France, while not saying anything very much, and had to listen to his own reminiscences of earlier times.

By the time they left, Kerry hoped that his mood had improved. He said very little as they went back to her house. Finally, she could stand it no more.

'Look, if you don't want to have tea with Aunt Lil and me, you only have to say so. She'll put it down to your gross bad manners, of course, but I'm sure you won't give a damn about that.'

'Of course I'm having tea with you. It's still your birthday, isn't it?'

'You could have fooled me,' Kerry muttered.

If only Claire hadn't told her about the GIs' leave. If

only it could have waited a few more days. But life was full of 'if onlys' and what good would that have done? The Yanks would still be coming, and Tom would still have to meet Marvin. You'd think there were more important things going on in the middle of a war, she thought bitterly. But when it came to it, personal relationships were still the most important of all when matters of the heart were involved.

'I'm sorry, Kerry,' he said abruptly, 'but I can't help the way I feel.'

'Neither can I,' she said. 'So shall we call a truce?'

This was awful. It was breaking her heart. It was a situation she had never expected to happen. It was obvious that Glenn would come back for Claire, but she had thought it would be when the war ended, and not before. Or was that being selfish? Claire would want to see Glenn as much as she could, and she couldn't squash her friend's happiness over the coming visit. And since Tom was still stiff with anger over something he couldn't control, she swallowed her pride, and put her arm around him.

'You know I've only ever loved you, Tom, and I always will. If that's not enough for you, I don't know what is.'

After a moment when she wondered if she was even getting through to him, he put his arms around her and kissed her, uncaring of who might be about, and she felt a surge of hope.

'It's more than enough, and more than I deserve.'

When she saw Claire again, she confided in her as always. By then, the news of the forthcoming American visit had travelled around the village, and it was clear that they were going to be treated like conquering heroes. Claire had had another letter from Glenn, and was able to tell Kerry a bit more about what had happened to Marvin.

'He didn't want to say too much, but I think it must have been really bad, because this will be Marvin's last leave. They're sending him home, Kerry, and he'll go straight from here back to America to be repatriated, along with one of the other guys in their section who was also badly wounded.'

'It sounds pretty awful, then,' Kerry said, upset to realise that perhaps Tom's scoffing had been right after all.

Nine times injured meant the final journey home – if it really *was* that many. Common sense said it didn't need to be if they were really serious. How could any man cope with so many injuries? And, since she had no idea what kind of injuries they were, how would Marvin cope? Or Shirl? No matter how she tried to resist it, Kerry felt as though she was entangled in their lives now, and she dearly wanted to know that the outcome was a happy one.

Just as she had had the strange feeling that whatever happened to Marvin, it somehow reflected what happened to Tom, and vice versa, she desperately wanted Marvin and Shirl to have their happy ending, and then their own would be assured. However illogical it might be, it was somehow indelibly imprinted in her mind.

'You've got that faraway look on your face again,' Claire said. 'Are you still worried over Tom's reaction when he meets Marvin?'

'No, I'm not,' she said. 'I'm more worried over mine.'

'Why?'

She shrugged. Some things were too deep to explain,

even to Claire, and she didn't want to be thought a madwoman.

'I just want to believe that Shirl came to her senses in the end, and also that he's more or less all in one piece, if you know what I mean.'

Claire grinned. 'Like no shrapnel below the belt, you mean!'

'Something like that.'

Mrs Holliday was in full flow once she heard that a small group of the Americans were coming back to Columbine for a week. With the agreement of the Friendship Club, she was busily gathering up the younger members of her dance troupe to arrange a small concert during the celebrations at the village hall to welcome them back. Claire had declined to be part of it, and Kerry had vehemently done the same. There was no way she would be singing onstage with both Marvin Mcleod and Tom in the audience. How ghastly would that be?

He had seemed to accept the situation now, but a week later his mother came into the shop, full of disapproval over something, as she so often was.

'I don't know if you can say anything to him, Kerry, but it's simply ridiculous,' she began.

'Tell me what he's done now,' she said, trying not to sigh.

'He's gone back to work with his father. He's not supposed to do so for another week yet. He says he's perfectly capable, and of course, he thinks he knows better than any doctor. You must talk to him.'

'Well, I can try,' Kerry said, knowing that there was no

way she was going to dissuade him. She didn't even want to. She knew intuitively that this was his way of saying he wasn't down and out yet. He was still a man, doing a man's job, and she wasn't even surprised at his decision.

When she saw him that night, she knew his mother would have said she had spoken to her, and that he was prepared for a fight.

'Let's have it, then,' he said.

'All I'm saying is – what took you so long?' she said mildly.

He laughed, and it was the best sound she had heard in ages.

'I don't know, but it's given me a new lease of life,' he said. 'I didn't know how much I'd missed being on the river.'

'I always said you should have joined the navy,' Kerry said.

'What, and get torpedoed? I'll stick with what I've got, thanks.'

Their banter was so much like the old days that she chalked up a silent tick in her mind. She had to admit he was looking much better, more healthy and self-confident, and working on the ferry with his dad was turning out to be the best therapy. There was only one more hurdle to overcome, and soon.

Naturally, Claire could neither think nor talk of anything else. She had begged to have a few days off from work while Glenn was on leave, so that she could spend as much time with him as possible. All the Roddy children were excited about seeing Glenn again – their nearly new brother, Molly told anyone who would listen, making him sound like a second-hand commodity – and it had done much to lift the spirits of that sad household.

Days before the visit was due, the reception in the village hall had been fully planned, and Mrs Holliday's dance troupe were now well rehearsed. The day of arrival was a Tuesday, when the GIs would be transported by army truck to their base with full facilities available. Jeeps were put at their disposal and from then on they were free to spend their leave as they wished, and Glenn's first port of call was to see Claire.

'I had a job to get him to myself for five minutes,' she told Kerry much later. 'The kids were all over him, and even Mum and Dad looked pleased to see him, so it was a lovely day for us, and we had such a lot to talk about.'

She had to ask. 'Has he said anything about Marvin?'

Claire shook her head. 'Not much. They never do say much about their experiences, do they? Dad wanted to know more about D-Day, but he seemed to clam up on it, even though it's months ago now. But Marvin's coming to the reception tomorrow night, so you'll see for yourself then.'

Maybe it would be better to see him again in the middle of a crowd. Better as far as Tom was concerned, anyway, because of course, he would be there too. Most of the village would turn out to greet the returning GIs, and he couldn't very well refuse, even if he wanted to.She admitted she was jittery, though partly because she still had no idea how badly Marvin had been hurt, and it wasn't something she could discuss with Tom.

'So everything's all right between you and Glenn, I take it?'

'It's more than all right. I haven't changed my mind about him, Kerry, and he feels the same about me. We've already been making plans. In fact, we've been doing it through our letters for some time now, and we know exactly what we're going to do. Once the war's over, he's going to come and stay here for a few months, so that my parents see that we're really serious about each other. Then we want to get married in the village church before we sail to America.'

'You'll really be leaving, then?' Kerry said, with a definite pang.

'I have to. I want to be with Glenn, and that's where his home is.'

'But yours is here.'

When Claire's lips became mutinous, Kerry knew that it wouldn't matter what anybody said, and she gave up trying. They would only end up getting twitchy and upset, and she couldn't spoil this for her and Glenn.

A few hours before the official reception was due to begin, there was a knock at Kerry's door. Aunt Lil had already gone to help get the hall ready with the rest of the Friendship Club. Assuming it would be Tom, Kerry opened the door with a smile on her face, and then it froze.

'Can you spare a few minutes for an old crock, honey?' said Marvin Mcleod. 'I wanted to see you asap, so my buddies have dropped me off.'

She opened the door wider, and he stepped inside awkwardly. He moved very stiffly, his back slightly bent, and she couldn't miss the hearing aid in his ear, nor the livid scar down the whole of one cheek. The fresh lines etched on his face indicated that he had gone through considerable pain at some time.

'Marvin, it's really good to see you,' Kerry said, hardly knowing what to say. 'Would you like a drink or something? Tom will be here in a minute and we can go to the hall together.'

She stopped, not knowing how mobile he was, and too embarrassed to ask. She also needed to mention Tom, to let him know this wasn't going to be any sort of tête-à-tête. To her relief he smiled as he came inside and sat down.

'Don't worry, kid, I can still walk, if a bit slower than before, and I don't need anything to drink. I'm looking forward to meeting this guy of yours, though. I hear he got a packet as well.'

She had never felt so awkward in her life. They were strangers, and yet not strangers. They knew so much about one another and she dearly wanted to ask about Shirl. But after a period of months it wasn't something she could just blurt out, especially if the answer wasn't going to be a good one.

When Tom arrived, he gave a less than charitable look at the back of the stranger sitting in one of Lil Penfold's best chairs. He couldn't mistake the American uniform, and Kerry prayed that it wouldn't make him feel inadequate because he was wearing civvies. Then Marvin stood up and turned to greet him, and Kerry saw his expression change as the American held out one hand with two fingers missing. How the hell had she missed noticing that! But his hands had been clenched for more or less the whole time until now, she registered. She mumbled an introduction, though it was hardly necessary.

'I've heard a lot about yours, Tom,' he said enigmatically. 'Tough break.'

He was actually sympathising with Tom, when he looked a hundred times worse, thought Kerry. She could have wept for him, and she prayed that Tom wasn't going to be difficult or think he was being patronising.

'You too,' he said. He looked at Kerry. 'But I was one of the lucky ones.'

Marvin didn't miss the look that said so much. He gave a slight smile, and then he looked at Kerry too.

'We've got something else in common, then. I've got somebody waiting for me back home in Montana, so I'm not too sorry to be getting out.'

'You do mean Shirl, I hope?' Kerry couldn't help asking.

'There was never anybody else for me,' he replied. 'We got over our problems a long time ago now, and we plan to get married just as soon as possible. Once I get on that ship for home, I'm not letting her slip through my fingers a second time, not even the ones I've got left.'

Kerry admired his pluck for making a joke of it, and she was mightily relieved that his Shirl was waiting for him after all. He deserved it.

'We'd better go, I suppose,' Tom said in the small silence. 'I take it you're coming to the show with us, mate?'

'If it's all right with you.'

'Of course it is.'

Kerry was starting to feel slightly light-headed as the two of them seemed to be discovering a bond with one another. She guessed it came from shared experiences, even though neither of them said anything specific. They didn't need to, and it was almost telepathic.

When they reached the village hall, she found that it

was the same everywhere; the dozen American GIs had integrated into the various family groups almost as though they were in the midst of long-lost relatives. It was a sort of miracle, Kerry thought, and being able to introduce Marvin to her Aunt Lil so naturally was another minor miracle. But best of all was the way he and Tom were getting along, and nor did she miss the way his GI buddies kept a watchful eye out for him, as well as for the one who had lost an arm and looked very lucky to have made it this far. Those who had once mocked the Yanks for being 'overpaid, oversexed and over here' had no idea of the generous, big-hearted young men they really were.

'I can see that you young people have a lot to talk about, Marvin, so you'll come to tea on Sunday, as well as Tom, won't you?' she heard Aunt Lil say next.

'That would be great, thank you, and me and my buddies will be at church on Sunday morning too,' he replied, sending his approval rating even higher.

Kerry added a few words without thinking. 'You must take a look at the beautiful hassock that Aunt Lil and the ladies from the Friendship Club made for Claire's brother, Marvin.'

It was only then that she remembered that Tom hadn't even seen it yet. He had refused to set foot inside the church since he had come home, much to his mother's annoyance. It was as though he hadn't been able to bear seeing the hassock created especially for Michael Roddy, his best friend. It would be too permanent a reminder that Michael was dead. Even the memorial service for him had still to be arranged, when the Roddys felt able to do so. Were they, perhaps, waiting for Tom to come to terms with it too?

After a long moment she heard him speak in an odd sort of voice. 'I haven't seen it myself yet, and I'll take a look in the church with you on Saturday afternoon if you like,' he said. 'I can drive over to the base and collect you, unless any of your mates are coming into the village.'

'Say, that would be terrific, Tom. I want to see this ferry of yours too.'

As they continued talking, Kerry listened to them in something like amazement. It was as if they had known one another for years, instead of barely an hour. It was crazy to think for one moment that she was being shut out, but if she was, it was such a glorious feeling to realise that the two men she had felt closest to, in such very different ways, were behaving practically like brothers. The way Tom and Michael used to do, she thought, with a catch in her throat.

It was weird that it had taken Marvin to make Tom relax in a way he hadn't done since coming home. It might have made her jealous, if she hadn't been so thankful. It was as if through Tom meeting Marvin, she had somehow been given back her sweetheart. And if she didn't rid herself of these surreal feelings, she was going to go completely potty.

There was no time for any more soul-searching as the proceedings got underway, and the evening was an undoubted success. There was the minimum of speech making, just enough to make the visitors feel welcome in what was now being called their second home. Mrs Holliday's dance troupe got huge applause, and much later, when it was all over and the GIs had gone back to their base in their jeeps, Aunt Lil remained at the hall to help the ladies clear up and to hold their usual powwow on how the evening had gone.

Tom walked Kerry back to her house in the soft darkness. He was unusually quiet at first, but it was a companionable quiet, and his arm was around her waist, her head leaning against his shoulder.

'I've been a fool, haven't I?' he said at last, when they were both safely inside the house.

'Of course you haven't,' she said carefully.

He gave a wry smile. 'You're not a very good liar, sweetheart, and that's something else I should have remembered. Molly Roddy's chatter about you having a Yankee Doodle was just her being her usual excitable self, wasn't it?'

'I don't blame you, Tom. You had a lot to deal with, and how could you know what was happening here, when you were so far away?'

'But I should have known it wasn't how it seemed when she said those words. I should have known *you*, darling. And now that I've met the guy, I really like him, so I can see why you did as well.'

'And you really intend to go to the church with him on Saturday to see Michael's hassock?' Kerry said, holding her breath. It might not seem much to most people, but she knew that to Tom it would be an enormous milestone.

'Yes I do. I think Michael would have approved. If he'd been here, we would have been comparing notes on our war by now, laughing over the good times, and commiserating over the bad. It's difficult to talk about it all to people who haven't gone through it themselves, even those we love the most. They wouldn't understand.'

'But Marvin would,' she said, following his thoughts.

She sat close to him on the sofa, thinking that somehow they all seemed to have come a very long way tonight. It was weird and wonderful, and not something to question. The war wasn't over yet, but all the omens were good. There was talk of the Home Guard being stood down shortly, and that was definitely a good sign. Little by little, things were getting back to normal, at least on the Home Front. It had to come to an end soon, and then everybody's life could begin again.

Once peace was declared, Claire would have Glenn home in Cornwall for a few months, and then they would be married. Kerry had no doubt of that. She would go to America, and Kerry would lose her best friend. That would definitely be a day for tears, but life had to go on. Marvin was about to go back to Montana and pick up the threads of his life with Shirl. And as for her and Tom . . . someday they would reach their own happy ending, she was sure of it. As if he read her mind, his arms went more tightly around her and he folded her into him. His kiss was warm on her lips, and she responded with a fervour.

'Seeing that you're definitely going to marry me, Miss Penfold,' he said, almost arrogantly, 'I've been thinking lately that Christmas would be a good time for us to announce our engagement, but I'd much prefer it to be sooner, like right now. We've kept the village in suspense for long enough, so what do you think?'

'What I think is that I'd probably burst if I had to wait much longer,' Kerry said, with something that was halfway between a laugh and a sob.

They would be able to tell their American friends their

news as well, which might give them a boost when happy news was often in short supply. Apart from Marvin, and the other very sick man in the group who was going to be repatriated, the rest of the GIs still had to go back to France to serve out their time. So if this small boost was what Tom subconsciously had in mind, then that was fine with Kerry too, and would seem to bring everything to a perfect conclusion.

Aunt Lil came home from the village hall some while later, to find two young people in a very close embrace on her sofa, oblivious to anything else but themselves. With a satisfactory smile on her face, and even before removing her hat, she went discreetly to the kitchen to find the bottle of sherry she had been keeping for important occasions. With no need of any Cornish intuition, she was pretty certain that this was one of them.